ARM AND HAMMER

JONATHAN K. WADE

Published by Gambit Publishing 2022, a literary subsidiary of

MBR Agency LLC, Culver City, California.

ISBN 978-0-9943380-6-8

www.jkw.press

www.mbragency.com

3908 Ince Boulevard, Culver City,

California 90232 United States

"An epic rollercoaster rendition of this infamous scandal so compelling it
beggars belief."
— TONY HARRIS

"PULP FICTION meets SCARFACE. Spectacular."
— MALIK JACKSON

"Drugs, sex, political corruption, and the CIA gone bad. Brilliant."
— SEBASTIAN ALLEN

"Beneath cool 80's motifs and pops of butt-clenching action, the seemingly
archetypal characters ultimately reveal surprising depth to their conflicted, and
finally realized, humanity."
— STEPHANIE L. LORENZO

"If it were a movie, it'd be a cocaine-infused cocktail of equal parts Tarantino
and Affleck with a splashing of Scorsese."
— ROGER A. CARSON

"Too controversial, too political, too grandiose given the historical calamity it
portrays, and that's what makes it utterly outstanding."
— FIONA WEBB

CONTENTS

Por mis amores, Sasha y Leo

1981

I

CARLOS CABEZAS

Glowing embers ignite the tip of her menthol cigarette as freshly painted red lips wrap around the end and suck. With the white stick hanging loosely from her mouth, the air hostess fixes her thick wavy brown hair with a few passes of hairspray. As smoke wafts lazily over her face, she tucks a tight button shirt into the waistline of a blue pleated skirt and pushes up her bullet bra to refresh the fullness of her breasts. Then, feeding her arms through her fitted blazer, she adjusts the shiny winged name tag (Sofia) and gives her mirrored reflection a long-lashed wink before slamming the narrow locker closed.

'Ladies and gentlemen,' a pilot crackles on the cabin speaker, 'we have begun our descent into Los Angeles International where the ground temperature is currently a cool fifty-one before reaching a top of seventy-five for a sunny and clear day. We should have you at the gate a few minutes ahead of schedule arriving at approximately six-thirty-five-am. Remember folks, Costa Rica is one hour ahead of the West Coast so be sure to wind your watches back. The air hostesses will soon prepare the cabin for landing, and on behalf of Captain Miller, co-captain Suarez, and myself, we want to thank you for flying with Pan America today and wish you a pleasant stay. Gracias, buenos dias.'

'Have you decided, Lucile?' the red lips say.

'Have I decided what?' a petite blonde replies sitting on a jumpseat massaging her feet, preparing them to be squeezed back into a pair of heeled pumps.

'Whether you're going to fly up to Frisco for the weekend?' Sofia says taking another long drag of her cigarette.

'Look, I don't know.'

Rolling her eyes, 'Come on, San Fran is where it's at, baby. Plus, the Nicaraguans are connected now.'

'Yeah, but there are too many fag boys with big hair and skinny legs in Frisco.'

Laughing, 'No one is asking you to fuck them, Luci. Besides, I heard Julio has his eye on you.'

'Julio? Carlos's pal?'

'Mmm hmm.'

'But he's so criminal,' Lucile says making a face.

'Baby,' Sofia says taking another drag, 'anyone who's anyone is a criminal these days.'

'Stewardess?' a gentleman says leaning his head into the aisle. 'Excuse me, stewardess,' he calls again.

Annoyed by his interruption, 'What?' Sofia asks sharply.

'Can I get a water, please?'

Exhaling smoke and frowning, 'Sir, can't you see I'm preparing the cabin for landing,' she says before whipping the curtain closed.

Lucile has her blue skirt hiked up between her legs as she adjusts the elastic of her sheer stockings.

'Oh, *¡Jolin!* You gotta be kidding me!' she says noticing a pull on the back of her leg. 'This is the second one this week.'

Sofia laughs.

'It's not funny. Do you know how expensive these are?' Lucile says pouting.

Taking the cigarette from her mouth and giving her friend a dry look, 'Do you remember how much money you're making from these flights now?'

Pulling off the stocking and throwing it into her open locker, 'That's not the point.'

Smirking, Sofia bends down so that she is eye-to-eye with her, 'No, that's where you're wrong, Luci. Money. Solves. Everything.' Then, raising an eyebrow she lifts Lucile's chin and kisses her softly, giving her lips a light coating of *Color Sensation Velvet 695.*

Standing and straightening her skirt, 'Now, smack your lips, *chica*,' Sofia tells her warmly, 'because we need to look sexy for security.'

Morning sunshine sparkles off of the white fuselage of the *Pan America* aircraft as the Blue Meatball coasts through a cloudless Los Angeles sky en route for a safe and routine landing. On board are one-hundred and sixty-three passengers, three pilots, six air hostesses, and twenty-four kilos of pure Colombian cocaine. *You can't beat the experience.*

The *fasten seatbelts* sign blinks on, the passenger's ears pop, and the flaps engage, slowing the airspeed of the plane with a shudder. Descending through the smog haze, the *Pan Am* plane sways towards the runway before the sudden squeak and smoke of tires skidding the runway jerks the craft to touchdown and applause.

With faces freshly powdered and lips layered in lipstick, the leggy Latino hostesses are last out of the gate striding in toe, while rays of orange sunlight beam across their matching outfits. With high-heels click-clacking they march six-abreast as though filming a commercial for the airline, or *Maybelline*. Their name badges read Sofia, Lucile, Isabella, Luna, Paula, and Romina—goddesses of the air, patron saints of joyous voyage from foreign lands, and now saviors from the flaccid functioning of everyday banality to the altitudinal highs of benzo-induced ecstasy. *Say hello to Pan Am.*

'Hello, Sofia, baby.'

'*Hola*, Jimmy. *Buenos dias?*' she says kissing the security guard's soft white cheek and leaving a wonderful red outline of her lips.

'How are you, baby?' he says jumping up from his swivel chair and leaning an elbow on the x-ray machine.

Feigning a yawn, 'Oh, so tired, *papi*. These night flights kill me. I think they're making me look old,' she says miserably.

'What?' Jimmy says dramatically. 'You're kidding, right? Look at you. I mean, look at you,' he says undressing her with his eyes.

Swallowing, she gives him a reluctant smile.

Security checks for flight crew are abysmal. A fandangle metal detector that's rarely switched on and an x-ray machine whose operator just wants to get into the hostesses' panties. Not that this matters. The goddesses load their carry-on bags of personal effects onto a conveyor one by one as the marvels of technology outline the content of their belongings. Meanwhile, slung across their shoulders are their small *Pan Am* standard-issue tan leather tote bags. Casually unzipped and open for all to see, each tote reveals a pair of white leather gloves and a cropped pillbox hat sitting atop a neatly folded spare button shirt, navy scarf, or torn pair of stockings. Nestled below such effects, however, and much to the astonishment of airport security should they ever bother to look, are four cling-wrapped one-kilo bags of white powder. That's two-hundred and forty-thousand dollars of uncut Colombian cocaine walking right past Jimmy Stanson, Redondo Beach High dropout class of '76 and now assistant manager for airport security, graveyard shift.

'You're always so sweet, Jimmy. Thank you.' The girls are all through except for Sofia who fakes another yawn to stop him from asking her out, again. 'I'll see you soon,' she says blowing him a kiss.

And that, ladies and gentlemen, is the safest, quickest way to bring cocaine into the country. FAA chaperoned and hand-delivered.

Stepping out into the crisp LA spring air, the women make their way across the busy pickup lanes and into the airport staff-parking garage. Sofia spots Carlos leaning against a pearl-white Cadillac Deville and smiles.

Wearing a black turtleneck beneath a dark green cotton suit almost glowing despite the darkness of the garage, Carlos Cabezas maintains an enviable panache no matter the time of day. A former lawyer, accountant, *and* Air Force pilot for the bloodthirsty Nicaraguan National Guard, this tall drink of rum on the rocks brings sophistication and order to the otherwise sketchy and prone-to-mishap world of drug trafficking.

Flicking his cigarette onto the ground and smothering it with the toe of his black snakeskin wingtip, he adjusts his package, licks his teeth, and opens his arms, '*Hola, mi amor.* Aren't you a sight for sore eyes,' he says before working his tongue into Sofia's mouth.

'Ladies, *buenos dias*,' he says using his thumb to wipe a red smear from his lip.

'*Hola*, Carlos,' the women reply like a group of Girl Scouts out selling cookies.

'Everything run okay? Everything smooth in San Jose?' he asks.

Sofia replies, 'Of course, *papi*. *No problema*. The Peruvian is always square, you know that.'

'*Bueno, bueno.*'

'Hey, Carlos,' Romina begins, 'the Peruvian, he's ace and all but we've been doing this for four months now and we still don't know his name?'

'You see,' Luna buts in, 'Romina has the hots for him,' she says teasingly.

Carlos smirks, 'Well, unfortunately, that's just how it's going to stay, my dear.'

'But how come is what I'm saying?' Romina pouts.

'Because the less you know the better. And if you don't even know something as simple as a man's name then what, if anything should go wrong, can you tell the authorities if that is how little you know? *Claro?*'

Romina shrugs, 'I suppose.'

Carlos gives them a wink before walking to the trunk and popping it open. Inside are empty plastic *Safeway* shopping bags, which the women promptly unload their cling-wrapped dope into.

Tapping on the passenger side window, 'Julio, wake up,' Carlos says.

Preferably asleep in his own bed but now awoken and disgruntled in a car seat, 'Huh? *Que pasa*, man?' he says hoarsely through a half-open window.

'The money,' Carlos says clicking his fingers at his young cousin.

A well-liked and generous—if not frivolous—man, Julio Zavala is blessed with model good looks and a short fuse, making him an ideal drug trafficker. Persuasive and charismatic, people are often eager to please him, yet he's partial to shooting kneecaps over the smallest of discrepancies.

Opening the glove compartment, he grabs a brown paper bag and passes it through the window before rolling onto his side and attempting to sleep once again.

Returning his attention to the stewardesses, Carlos begins handing each of them a four-thousand-dollar wad of cash.

'Okay. Ladies, once again, thank you for your tireless work and your exceptional dependency with such delicate matters. Your efforts are appreciated to no end.'

'*Gracias*, Carlos,' the women intone before walking away.

Staying behind and wrapping her arms around Carlos's waist, 'So, *papi*, am I going to see you later?' Sofia asks.

'Of course, my love. When is your flight to Frisco?'

'In an hour.'

'*Bueno*. After we finish the deliveries, I'm flying straight back. Julio is driving the money. I have an important meeting with Norwin tonight.'

'What about your important meeting with me?' she says teasingly.

Playing along, 'Oh, that meeting is this afternoon at the apartment, as soon as I get off the plane,' Carlos says gently pulling her shirt open and glancing down at her breasts, 'because I've missed these *tetas tanto*.'

Tracing a finger across her collarbone and down the crevasse between her bosoms, 'Well, *papi*, these *tetas* have missed you too,' she says playfully. '*Te he extrañado*.'

They kiss passionately before Carlos turns Sofia around and smacks her bum lightly, 'Get going. *Hasta luego, mami*.'

Winking a goodbye Sofia saunters off.

Carlos gets back in the car, 'Okay. You ready, Julio?'

Rubbing his eyes, '*Si, hermano. Vámonos*.'

Rolling north up Lincoln Boulevard beneath a bright morning sky of almost white, warm air rushes through the open windows, while Carlos and Julio, the Cadillac, and twenty-four kilos of cocaine stashed in baking soda boxes begin making their weekly rounds.

Stopping first at a little roadside taco joint in Santa Monica, they handover two kilos of coca to a fat middle-aged Cuban named Paco in exchange for a couple of bean burritos before heading into Palisades, a plush mansion-filled neighborhood full of white bankers and lawyers and dentists. Meeting Riccardo in the car park of one of those law firms, the legal aid will have his college tuition paid off within the year now that he sells an ounce a week to his six-figure-earning type-A co-workers who now routinely visit Las Vegas for prostitute and gambling-fueled weekends. With the sun a little higher and the sky a little bluer, the Nicaraguans head east along Wilshire Boulevard. Pulling into *Mario's Pizzeria* on the corner of Broxton and Weyburn in Westwood Village, Julio rather conspicuously swaps brown paper bags under a corner table with a UCLA student who happens to major in business economics. With a deep understanding of supply and demand—and considering there are over thirty-thousand enrolled students—the Bruin pitches cocaine as a wonder study drug, selling grams to academics, math club members, kids in the school band, you name it. Even teachers are scoring off of him. After three slices of the best *Sicilian* this side of the Atlantic, the Nicaraguans jump back in the Cadillac and cruise along Miracle Mile stopping in at *Sal's Launderette & Dry Cleaners, Mr. Kim's* grocery store in Korea Town, and *Diamonds & Loans*, a second-hand jeweler in Westlake for drops ranging in modest one and two-kilo amounts. At *Angelo's Barbershop* on Olive and 5th Street in Downtown, the Stucci brothers are the only bona fide drug dealers Carlos and Julio have connected with so far. Despite buying, selling, and gambling on just about anything, Tony and Frank are only buying four kilos a month, but that's as good as it gets for a pair of Italians on the wrong coast of America. After a strange conversation about pastrami and horseracing, the two Nicaraguans thunder north along the I-5 for their last LA drop, a twenty-minute drive out towards the Valley.

'Watch your speed, *primo*. We don't want to get pulled over,' Carlos says gently with the wind ruffling his thick brown hair.

'Yeah, because a couple of Nicaraguans driving a Cadillac would probably mean a damn strip search,' Julio says cynically.

Surprised by his tone, 'What's that supposed to mean?'

'It means, we're fucking *payasos* here in LA. Jokers,' his cousin says pursing his lips.

Raising his eyebrows, 'Where did this come from?' Then, putting his hand out of the window, 'It's a beautiful day, the sun is shining, and we're delivering the coca. What's your *problema*?'

'How much coca, is my *problema*. Look at us, man. Driving around like fucking taxi drivers barely making any fucking money. In Nicaragua we had everything. Nice houses, cars, women, you name it. What have I got here? A shitty apartment and a trunk full of coca that I gotta drive from LA to San Francisco every other week,' he says with a sigh that's more blowing off steam.

'I understand, *primo*,' Carlos says, realizing his cousin's frustration. 'We are new here, and so is the coca. It won't be long until they know what it can do for them, how rich it can make them.'

'Yeah, and how long is that? I'm tired of this shit, man. My ass hurts from all this driving.'

Looking out of the window, 'I know,' Carlos says a little more seriously, all too aware of the struggle of uprooting his entire life. He doesn't need to be reminded of what they lost or the effort now to rebuild, especially by his hot-tempered cousin who has always had work and money handed to him. Now, Carlos must start over, and although selling drugs is something he had never done before the revolution, trafficking coca in Central America is looked upon as a rather respectable profession.

It's all a matter of perspective anyway, Carlos thinks, from how much money you make or how you earn it. Some people are always going to think you have too much—or not enough—and that's not to mention the only real difference between what is an acceptable living and what's not is purely how visible the process is. They tell kids to stay away from drugs but *Coca-Cola* kills more people than dope does.

Passing Burbank Studios, Julio pulls into *Bob's Big Boy* on Riverside Drive; the seventy-foot tall pink and white neon sign a hypnotic halo even in the daytime. Welcoming them is the blue-eyed, cow-licked, red-and-white chequered chubby Boy hoisting high his double-deck melted cheese hamburger for all to see. If you listen carefully, you can almost hear him whisper, *It's your Big Boy*.

Pulling into a full parking lot, they think they see Bob Hope sitting in his car hoeing into a west coast slider. Following the moss-green and black terrazzo walkway beneath cream canopies snapping quietly in a breathless breeze, Carlos and Julio enter the wooden clapboard and brick veneer restaurant; the heart and soul of American diner culture and hallmark institution that says, yes, if you build it, they *will* come.

Inhaling deeply, 'Ah, you can smell the American spirit, no?' Carlos says enthusiastically.

Frowning, 'Smells like grease, fat, and fake cheese,' Julio says over his shoulder. 'Soon these *Americanos* won't know what real food is. They'll forget that to get the juicy burger you have to kill the cow.'

Giving him a disapproving look, they stride alongside a wide band of windows before sliding into a red-leather corner booth to their awaiting buyers: a trio of young up-and-coming studio execs fully aware that it's not what you know but whom you know in Hollywood, and bringing cases full of blow to the right parties coincidentally introduces you to the right people.

'Gentlemen,' Carlos greets taking a seat.

Barely pulling the cup of coffee from his mouth in time, 'Carlos,' Ted says excitedly, 'help us out with this idea for a film we're working on.'

'Don't worry, it's an action movie,' Mike reassures.

Raising his eyebrows at Julio, Carlos gestures for them to continue.

'Yeah,' Buzz says pushing aside a plate with a half-eaten burger on it, 'you guys are from—where is it—Honduras? That's a pretty beat-up place, isn't it?'

Julio gives Carlos a dry look before correcting him, *'Somos de la coño de tu madre,'* he says smirking.

Confused, 'What's that?' asks Ted.

Clearing his throat, 'He said, we are from Nicaragua,' Carlos says gently.

'Oh, right, right. Nicaragua,' Buzz concedes.

'So, we have this guy—' Mike starts before Buzz cuts him off.

'And he's a real badass ex-marine.'

'Commando,' Ted mumbles sipping his coffee.

'That's right,' Mike continues. 'He's come back from Vietnam—and I know that's not Nicaragua, but war-torn is war-torn—and he's just drifting along, doesn't have a place to call home, that kind of thing.'

'And while passing through a small town, the local Sheriff doesn't take a liking to him.'

'Tells him to leave.'

'But he doesn't.'

'You see, this guy's been through the wringer, his whole life is in tatters.'

'What life, more like it?'

'That's it isn't it? He's got nothing left.'

'But that doesn't mean he's going to take shit from some Sheriff and his deputies.'

'So, he stays. One man against a bunch of hillbilly cops.'

'A real-life David versus Goliath.'

Like a three-headed hydra in matching suits spitting storyboard ideas like word vomit, each man finishes the other's sentence with Nostradamus-like seamlessness.

Are they high right now, Carlos wonders before asking, 'Then what happens?'

'Well, a battle ensues.'

'And one by one, this Commando takes them out.'

'All of them.'

'Using tactics he learned in the jungles of Vietnam.'

'What do you guys think?'

Shrugging, 'Sounds fun, I guess,' Carlos offers.

'You're not convinced,' Ted says disappointedly.

Giving an uncertain look, Carlos doesn't know what to say.

'They're not convinced,' Buzz capitulates.

Shaking his head, 'They're not convinced.'

'Well, what do you guys watch back home?' asks Ted.

Julio chuckles.

Smiling, 'What's so funny?' Buzz wonders.

'We don't watch your movies back home.'

'Really?' Mike says surprised.

'Why not?'

'Because all we get is John fucking Wayne and Clint fucking Eastwood.'

There is a collective pause from the Hollywood hydra.

'Big *Americanos* swinging their dicks around,' Julio says scornfully.

Shifting uncomfortably, the executives aren't certain if he is joking or not; and with no interruption, the young Nicaraguan continues.

'It's cute though, you, Hollywood, these handsome *gringos* who come and save the day. You make movies with fake bad guys and fake guns and fake blood. But where we come from it isn't fake, you know. Not the guns, not the blood, not the killing. You like to pretend in this country, make everything look how you want it to look; nice and shiny and all beneath a pretty star-spangled banner. But you forget about the places that are ugly, where the fields are soaked in blood and the cities get their buildings blown up. That's where I come from, man. That's why I don't watch your fucking movies.'

After a tense few moments, Carlos smiles broadly, 'What do you guys think? Incredible, no? What an actor,' he says grabbing Julio by the back of the neck and squeezing. 'If you guys are ever looking for the next Jose Ferrer, here's your man.'

Looking at one another, 'Damn, Julio, that was pretty good.'

'You should come to a script reading sometime.'

Julio gives a wry smile.

'Yeah, if you ever feel like giving up that other business of yours,' Buzz says with a wink.

Frowning, 'Maybe if you guys had bigger *cojones* I wouldn't need to change business.'

'*Cohonies?*'

'Balls,' Julio says plainly.

'I-I don't get it?' Buzz says confused.

'Come on, man, this is Hollywood. Two kilos of coca is nothing for you guys. You sure you don't want to start getting another key or two?' Julio suggests keenly.

Laughing, 'What do we look like, drug dealers?'

Putting down his coffee, 'Oh, speaking of,' Ted says tapping the top of a black briefcase resting between his legs. Then, sliding it over with his foot, 'This one is for you, Mr. Cabezas.'

Exchanging it with the briefcase he brought in, 'And this one is for you,' Carlos says kindly. Then, checking his watch, 'Well, gentlemen, it is a pleasure as always but I'm afraid we must be going. I have a plane to catch.'

'Don't let us hold you up,' Ted says.

'Time is money after all,' Mike adds.

Standing from the booth, 'Indeed, it is.'

'Hey, thanks for your help, by the way, Julio,' Buzz offers.

'Yeah, that whole speech was some really powerful stuff,' agrees Ted.

'Yeah, well, the problem with movies is it makes everyone believe in heroes,' Julio reflects.

Leaving the executives with those rather strange departing words, the Nicaraguans leave the diner two kilos lighter in coca, but eighty-thousand dollars heavier in cash.

Getting back in the Cadillac, Carlos reproaches Julio.

'You want us to lose business? What's wrong with you?'

'What? I'm tired of this shit, man,' Julio complains. 'I didn't come to this country to be a fucking errand boy. We are bringing in the best coca in the world and not only are we not making big money but we have to deal with *putas* like that. I feel like I'm trying to sell cattle to a chicken farmer.'

'Calm down, *primo*. They're not the ones who are going to make us money. No, the real money will come from you know who.'

Turning the ignition, 'Well, let's go see them then,' Julio says coolly before screeching out of the parking lot.

Driving down the 110 they head towards Inglewood for their one and only connect into the black neighborhoods; brothers Henry and Diego Corrales. Casual if not lazy Nicaraguans whose father was employed high up in the Somoza administration during its final years, most of their family moved to Miami but Henry and Diego headed for California and opened a restaurant called *Fiesta Bar & Grill*. Not coincidentally, they both have always had a thing for black pussy and now they live knee-deep in it.

Despite residing in the nice little suburb of Morningside Park, it's still in Inglewood, and any neighborhood south of the 10 is immediately considered part of South Central. A working-class neighborhood of mostly educated black folk, Morningside is dotted with middle-class, two-parent homes with yards and swimming pools and kids riding bikes in the street, but stray just a few blocks over you'll find Crenshaw, Compton, Watts, Imperial Courts, and Willowbrook. Neighborhoods with proud community members like the Bloods, the Crips, Athens Park Boys, the Brims, Hoover Criminals, Rollin' 60s, the Bishops, and the list goes on. Street gangs at war with each other for the last decade, fighting over property, turf, drugs, power, and street credential.

This is why Henry and Diego Corrales are so important to Carlos and Julio. Their current distribution networks are all modest, reliable, and for the most part fine upstanding professionals. And this is precisely the problem. Sure, they have the Stucci brothers buying a key a week but they're a couple of Italians on the wrong coast of America. Carlos, Julio, their boss Norwin and the rest of the recently exiled Nicaraguans have lives to rebuild, businesses to start again, and money to send to their families who've fled the newly established Sandinista Socialist government. Twenty kilos of cocaine a week isn't enough, not by a long shot, and not with that many mouths to feed.

At the corner of 8th Avenue and 82nd Street sits a charming powder-pink two-bedroom house with a terracotta-tiled roof with a backdrop of palm trees and power lines. Freshly cut verges and lush green hedges adorn the sidewalks, while a park and playground sit innocently at the end of the street.

Henry pushes open the screen door and greets Carlos and Julio on the porch, '*Hola, muchachos. Como estas?*'

'*Bien, bien,*' says Carlos.

'My, my, what a day,' Henry says squinting against the sunlight. 'Come in, come in.'

Inside, cream carpets match the curtains with pastel mint sofas, a Michigan Oak laminate dining table with chrome-legged walnut vinyl chairs on rollers, a smiling cat clock, brushed-steel record player, and a huge art deco painting of a pair of flamingos hanging from a cladded feature wall of sandstone brick; it's middle-class America right out of the catalog.

Standing by a teak liquor cabinet, Diego is filling little faux-crystal shot glasses with white rum.

'*Hola, amigos,*' he says cheerfully bringing the drinks over and placing them on the glass coffee table next to Carlos's briefcase full of coca.

Sipping the rum, 'How's the restaurant going, *muchachos?*' Carlos asks.

'It's okay,' Henry says casually.

'But not great,' Diego adds with a sigh. 'The blacks want fried chicken and greens with collars, the whites want Tex Mex, and nobody wants Nicaraguan food.'

'No one wants Nicaraguan food?'

Diego inclines his head disappointedly.

'Have you got *Rosquillas* on the menu?'

'Fried doughnuts? Of course.'

'What about pork tamales and *pinto*?'

'Would we be Nicaraguans if we didn't?'

Smiling sympathetically, 'Don't worry about it, they'll come around.'

'And what about the coca?' Julio asks abruptly.

Slamming his rum back, 'Oh, that is no *problema*,' Henry says with a shrug. 'The customers keep buying so they must be happy.'

'Why wouldn't they be happy? It's pure fucking powder,' Julio says bitterly.

Carlos chides him with a gesture.

'What?' Julio rebukes.

Frowning, 'Is there a problem?' Diego asks.

'Yeah, why aren't you guys moving more of this shit?' Julio gestures to the coca on the table.

'What are we supposed to do, man?' Henry says defensively. 'We're doing what we can.'

'Yeah, Julio,' Diego adds, 'It's not easy, *amigo*. It's not like we can put a sign out the front saying, friendly Nicaraguans selling A-grade cocaine. We have to wait until our buyers introduce us to someone new or Henry builds a friendship he can trust from diners at *Fiesta*.'

'Yeah,' Henry defends, 'you gotta remember all around here for blocks in every direction is gang territory. We move what we can to people we know won't come and shoot us in the night or burn the restaurant down. We got a life here, man.'

'And what about the lives back home, eh? The businesses we lost, our homes, our livelihoods,' Julio fires back.

'Hey, you gotta chill out, man. You've only been in Cali for a few months, it takes time to adjust.'

Julio waves a dismissive hand.

'Maybe you need to take a trip to Fort Lauderdale or Pompano Beach, see some friends, take a load off. You guys left Managua late, you know, waited till things fell apart. You should have come over earlier.'

Lured back in, 'We stayed because we tried to protect what we had,' Julio responds.

'Hey, some of us didn't have it quite as good as others, man.'

'Okay, that's enough,' Carlos calmly intervenes. 'You're right, Henry, we stayed too long. But we stayed because President Carter was meant to protect us. He said the Sandinista would never take power but they did. Then he said he'd keep the National Guard together but he couldn't do that either. So, we had to leave everything behind, more than those who left before us.'

Shaking his head, 'Now, Reagan gets on the television with open arms and says all Nicaraguans are welcome. Fucking bullshit,' Julio spits.

The men are all quiet.

Hunching over and rubbing his forehead, 'It's okay,' Carlos says tactfully. 'Keep going, keep making friends with the African-Americans. Eventually, the market will open up to us.'

After shaking hands and kissing each other on the cheek before leaving, Julio jumps in the driver's side and they head towards LAX.

'You've got to stop being so hard on Henry,' Carlos begins.

'The man has no *cojones*. Look at where we are; the heart of the blacks and he can't move more than a kilo a fortnight.'

'It'll be okay. These *Americanos* don't know what cocaine is yet, it still hasn't hit them. This is going to be the start of something big and we are in the driver's seat, *mi hermano. Tener paciencia.*'

'I know, I know,' Julio says squeezing the steering wheel and planting his foot on the pedal.

* * *

Shards of light pass through the drawn Venetian blinds and cascade across the bed. Beneath a tangle of white satin sheets their bronzed naked bodies breathe heavily. Rolling over Sofia grabs two cigarettes, lighting the first one and handing it to Carlos and then lighting her own. The ceiling fan's slow gentle spin pulls and pushes the smoke around the apartment bedroom.

'God, I missed your cock, *papi*.'

Carlos chuckles.

Turning on her side and running her fingers through his sweaty chest hair, 'How's business?'

'Okay. Could be better.'

'Why is Julio always so *frustrado?*' Sofia wonders.

Smirking, 'Because he always wants to make more than he can. He has no patience.'

'Is he going to get you in trouble?'

'I hope not.'

'Then why do you work with him?'

'He's my cousin.'

'I know that. But that's family, this is business.'

'He's okay. He knows how to get things done. But the network is small here so we have to do a lot of things together. It's harder than you think, selling coca.'

'Is it?'

'Everybody wants to make money but not everybody knows how.'

'Oh.'

Nodding and staring into the smoky air, 'It takes time to find the right people, to know them, to trust them. And they need to know how to handle a lot of money. People like that are difficult to find.' Carlos takes a long drag of the cigarette before continuing, 'That's why Julio is so hot. We're struggling to make ends meet here, while other Nicaraguans in Miami are already making big business. But California is untapped.'

'Is that why Norwin's here in Frisco? To tap it?'

'No. Norwin's here because the Sandinistas are in power. I'm sure he'd rather be at his beach mansion in San Juan.' Looking at her sideways, 'You asking a lot of questions, *mami*. You sure you're not with the DEA?'

'Would the DEA suck your cock so good?' she says tracing her finger around his dark nipple.

Thinking for a moment, 'No. Probably not.'

Picking up his watch from the bedside and checking the time, 'I need to go, baby. I'll call you later, okay.'

Showered and wearing a grey suit Carlos arrives at *Cesar's Auto Shop* on the corner of Van Ness and 26th street. This is Mission District's southeast corner, a cultural nexus of Nicaraguans, Salvadorians, Guatemalans, and you name it South Americans who've all mostly fled civil wars and political instability.

Despite the heavy traffic, Carlos catches a whiff of Latin food lingering in the air and as the setting sun bathes building tops in an orange glow he has a sudden pang of longing to be back in Managua—the lazy humid day making his chest and brow perpetually bead with sweat as tall palms rustle in a warm afternoon breeze, while cubes of ice crack, melting in a tumbler of *Diplomatico Reserva* rum against the faint sounds of car horns and scooters in the distance floating softly to his balcony overlooking the glistening lake and dark mountains beyond.

'*Casa,*' he says quietly. '*Un dia.*'

Inside the garage, Charlie and Romero are under the hood of a burgundy Ford Cortina. He greets them before heading to the apartment upstairs. From the stairwell, he can hear Gloria yelling, but this is nothing new.

Three knocks, then two. Gloria shuts up. Footsteps walk over to the door and he knows it'll be Peña looking at him through the peephole. He hears his name said from the other side and Gloria goes back to yelling.

Opening the door is Roberto Peña, a slick Nicaraguan with sharp eyes and a cool demeanor who says far less than he knows.

'*Hola*, Peña.'

Roberto doesn't reply, instead leads Carlos toward the living area. The apartment is wide and open, with rooms not separated by walls but by furnishings (except for the bedrooms at the back). Busy packing a small suitcase with clothes folded and laid out on the dining table, Norwin doesn't acknowledge Carlos's arrival. His wife, third or fourth—no one can remember—is pacing and yelling and speaking so fast and incoherently that Norwin isn't bothering to answer her.

Carlos makes himself comfortable on a soft mustard corduroy sofa.

'Hey, Carlos,' a man in a white suit calls out from the kitchen, 'you hungry?' he asks.

Frying small wedges of corn on the cob topped with grated cheese and a sprinkling of paprika, Sebastian Gonzalez is Peña's nephew though their personalities couldn't be further apart.

'No, gracias, Seb,' Carlos says warmly.

Ignoring Gloria's relentless shouting, 'You sure, man? They're gonna be *delicioso.*'

Carlos smirks and shakes his head.

'*Que pasa?*' Peña asks half sitting on the window ledge and lighting a cigarette, his gaze cast to the street below.

'*No mucho,*' Carlos replies. 'Just finished making the rounds in LA. Now I'm here.'

'How goes LA?' he says without looking over.

'Slow.'

Peña nods. After a moment, 'And Julio?'

'Driving back as we speak.'

'With the monies?'

'*Si*, with the monies.'

Now looking at Carlos and taking a long drag, '*Bueno,*' he says coolly, smoke drifting across his face.

A sudden loud slap makes both men look up. Clutching the side of her face Gloria is silent. Norwin, a short scrawny man of almost comical stature with neat thinning black hair, a bulbous nose, and a thick broom of a mustache is not the most imposing man, but often they are the one you need to watch out for. It is not a rage that dwells inside him nor a meanness or cruelty; he lacks a moral compass, sure, lots of men do, but there is a darkness in him, a shadow born to those who have lost some or all of their soul to an indiscriminate and unrelenting world of chaos and death, who know that life can end as quickly as it comes, no matter whose name is attached to it. He is a man that can seemingly be pushed and pushed, only he does not break, he does not even bend, all you are doing is slowly entering his darkness until in the most unexpected moment you find yourself suddenly dead because he had enough of your complaints or demands.

Whimpering and hurrying off into the bedroom goes poor Gloria, wife to a drug lord and a devil who wears ill-fitting shirts and counts the pennies in the ashtray. Mumbling and cursing he continues packing his things until he suddenly recalls that someone had arrived.

Turning around, 'Ah, Carlos, my boy,' Norwin says with a fat smile obscured by a smoldering cigar. Taking a seat on a brown leather armchair, 'Tell me, how goes LA?'

Raising his eyebrows, 'Twelve kilos delivered and paid for, Julio is driving back now and will take two more keys to Alfredo in Richmond, and two to Pedro from the strip club in Oakland, leaving us with six on hand.'

Taking the cigar from his mouth and smirking, 'But?'

Sighing, 'That's it. No new buyers, no new markets. Just like last month,' Carlos says flatly.

'It's okay, Carlos. LA isn't Miami. And the Latin connect is small here in Frisco. In Florida, we have friends everywhere, family everywhere. Don't think I don't know this.'

Carlos can't hide his disappointment.

Laughing, 'Look at this boy, Peña. Look at him,' Norwin says affectionately.

Squinting, Peña drags on his cigarette without expression.

'So much pride, so much purpose,' Norwin continues. '*No te preocupes*. The coca floods into Miami on planes and yachts and ships hauling seafood. In California it trickles in in the purses of sexy stewardesses,' he says chuckling. 'But all that is about to change. I am flying to LA tonight to meet a Nicaraguan, and in the morning, we are catching a flight to Tegucigalpa.'

'Honduras? What's there?' Carlos asks.

'Not what, who. A secret meeting is being held with many high-ranking officers and political figures.'

'What are they doing?'

'They think they're going to take back Nicaragua,' Norwin says with a smirk.

'So, what do they want with you?'

Wedging the wet cigar into the corner of his mouth, 'Money, Carlos.'

Confused, 'In what way?'

'That's what I'm going to find out,' Norwin says fixing his bushy mustache.

'And who's this man in LA?'

Blowing a long draft of smoke, 'A man sent over by none other than Aristides Sanchez, that's all I know.'

II

THE COLONEL

He can hear the phone ringing from outside his office; the office he's just been appointed to and has yet to step foot in. He grabs the shiny brass handle and turns, while the ringing pierces through the unlit room smelling of fresh paint, turpentine, and leather. Quickly reaching across the desk he picks up the receiver fearing he may miss the call, while simultaneously apprehensive about who might be on the other end.

'This is Colonel North.'

'Good morning, Colonel. I suppose a congratulations are in order.'

'Who is this?'

'Ted.'

'Ted who?'

'The only Ted worth knowing.'

Silence. And then the penny drops. Oliver North can almost hear the man smile on the other end.

'Is this a secure line?'

'Would I be calling you if it wasn't?'

He raises his eyebrows and exhales, not realizing he was holding his breath.

'Go on, take a seat. This is your office now and that chair will see a lot of hours with your ass in it.'

Frowning, the Colonel scans the dark room for security cameras and then quickly realizes how preposterous it would be if he were being watched now, already. But not impossible. He slowly sits, sinking audibly into the taut brown leather chair, the cherry oak frame creaking under his weight and the chrome wheels pressing into the rug.

'*There, isn't that nice?*'

North's back molars grind for a moment, 'To what do I owe the pleasure, Ted?'

'*As I said, to congratulate you on this esteemed and illustrious position that has been bestowed upon you.*'

'Well, thank you,' he says matter-of-factly.

'*Oh, come now, Ollie. There may be dirt on my shoes but I'm someone you never want to lose ties with.*'

'Is that so? Even now that you're no longer with the Agency.'

'*Tsk tsk. When you leave, you're never really gone. You should know that.*'

Of course, North knows the Blonde Ghost isn't out of the picture. Anyone with a high enough clearance only has to peer into the darkest shadows of US foreign policy, occupation, or interest to catch wind of his presence. And that's *since* his forced resignation as Deputy Director of Operations back in '79. No, the Blonde Ghost is a cold untouchable mist whose fog-like anonymity is juxtaposed with merciless participation in some of the US's most damning programs: Operation Mongoose, JMWAVE, and the varied plots to kill Castro; Cuban political sabotage and propaganda during the Missile Crisis years; Operation Fish Farm and the training of Cuban-exiles to become assassination-squads; penning *The Third Option*, a training manual for terrorists and guerrilla warfare in foreign lands; a consultant during the MK/ULTRA years experimenting with chemically-induced mind control attempting to produce psychologically programmed spies and assassins; supervising the overthrow and murder of President Allende of Chile and the installation of the right wing tyrant Augusto Pinochet, which saw the country spiral into two-decades of social misery, torture, and execution; the training of the Shah of Iran's secret police who routinely tortured and murdered the Shah's opponents; director of the infamous Phoenix Program overseeing the neutralization by interrogation, torture, and murder of forty-thousand Vietnamese civilians; Station Chief in Laos and Saigon where his Secret Team along with General Vang Pao monopolized the heroin trade in South East Asia selling it to international mafia figures like Roselli, Giancana, and Trafficante, or worse, smuggling the drug into the US in the gutted bodies of dead GIs, and yet, such feats have made him one of the most decorated agents in CIA history.

In more recent years the Ghost's Secret Team, a merry band of bad men ranging from anti-Castro ex-Cubans Rafael Quintero, Felix Rodriguez, and Luis Posada, to shadowy CIA agents Thomas Clines, Carl Jenkins, Edwin Wilson, and ex-Air Force Major General turned arms-dealers Richard Secord and Iranian-born export businessman Albert Hakim, and who knows how many others, alive or dead. Together since the '60s, this delightful group has been involved in drug trafficking, arms smuggling, money laundering, covert wars, assassinations, political sabotage, and popping up in places like Panama, Cuba (still), Chile, Czechoslovakia, Syria, Afghanistan, Libya, and who knows where else doing God knows what.

Sure, the Blonde Ghost's web of clandestine companies and networks was a bubble bound to burst eventually, but it didn't matter. He was right, no body that leaves the Agency is never really gone. And certainly not those so well connected. They open offshore bank accounts and set up corporations and subsidiaries around the world to conceal the ongoing engagements and transactions of their CIA-secured contracts. Like, *Lake Resources Inc* in Switzerland, or *Companie de Services Fiduciaria, CSF Investments*, and *Udall Research Corporation* in Central America, or *Orca Supply Company* in Florida and *Consultants International* in DC. All of them, then or now, have the Blonde Ghost's mark somewhere on them; a key to a deposit box with his fingerprint on it, a wire transfer with his signature, or maybe just his name as the password. He runs as deep and dark as the ocean, and just like it, countries and borders and international treaties mean nothing to him.

Why the Ghost's resignation then? EATSCO is why. *Egyptian-American Transport and Services Corporation*; just another one of those shell companies facilitating weapons smuggling and money laundering. EATSCO wasn't doing anything different than the other aforementioned corporations except getting busted defrauding the Pentagon of eight-million dollars. But it was its most important customer that really got it into hot water. Who? None other than the Libyan dictator, Moammar Gaddafi. EATSCO was Ed Wilson's primary company, and it was also the one that brought the Ghost down from his ethereal heights.

Edwin Wilson was with the Agency from '55 to '71 and then the Navy Office until '76. An old hand who'd been around the block enough times to know just about everybody, he had a long history of running numerous arms companies either owned by himself or the CIA. In the months after leaving the Navy he continued to run the CIA-fronted companies amassing a fortune in the tens of millions. The next few years were spent making even bigger profits in international arms smuggling while hosting dinner parties with the political and military elite on his 2,500-acre farm in northern Virginia. Eventually, Wilson recruited an ex-agent who wasn't keen on being an accessory to illegal activities of such geo-political magnitude.

Meanwhile, after Ford's shock re-election loss to the Democrat Carter, straight-lace Jimmy placed Stansfield Turner, an outsider, as head of the CIA. Turner wanted to clean up the Agency which was a wet blanket for corrupt agents sponging off of the black budget thinking they could get away with, well, murder.

So, Wilson's new recruit pulled the pin, information was leaked, Turner investigated, and both Clines and the Ghost were asked to leave the Agency because of their close relationship with Wilson and EATSCO. Although Wilson was indicted by the Justice Department he had already fled to Libya where his old buddy Gaddafi naturally refused to extradite him.

'Did you hear the latest with Edwin?'

'The DOJ sent some shady businessman to con him into flying to London. Got duped. Now he's in New York awaiting trial.'

'Ernest Keiser. Can't believe he did it. Ed's a smart man.'

'Who's this Keiser fellow?'

'Don't know. We—I mean, you—don't have a file on him. CIA thinks he's German-born. He says he's an American. Odd though, speaking with a Kraut accent.'

'Well, is his birth record legit?'

'Doesn't have one. Anyway, have you heard the latest?'

'Yeah, he's awaiting trial.'

'Tsk tsk. Ollie, you need to keep your ear closer to the ground.'

There go those molars again.

'Ed tried to recruit a fellow prisoner to kill the federal prosecutor. Offered the man's family a million cash. The prisoner snitched, they set Ed up with an undercover and he got taped hiring the agent to kill the prosecutor, six witnesses, and his ex-wife.'

'Jesus.'

'I suppose going from the top of the food chain to an eight-by-eight cell will do crazy things to a man's sensibilities.'

'When did this happen?'

'Three days ago.'

'Do you think he's going to spill the beans on EATSCO and all the others now?'

'No, he is not.'

'You sound certain of that?'

'Because I went and saw him.'

And if the Ghost is meeting you in person, then you best do what he's telling you.

'So, tell me, what have you got started for this little situation we have in Nicaragua? And pretend I don't know anything.'

Shaking his head, 'What makes you think I need your advice, Ted?'

'Because everything you're about to do I've already done.'

'And just what am I about to do?'

'You're about to get dirty, Ollie. Really dirty.'

Switching the receiver from one ear to the other, North pinches the bridge of his nose searching for some kind of salvation he knows isn't going to come.

'Okay, I'll go first. It's not just money the Contras need urgently but equipment. There's a weapons warehouse already up and running in Tegucigalpa called R & M Equipment. It's run by Ron Martin, he's ex-CIA, and his partner James

McCoy served with the US military attaché to the Somoza regime. They're good boys, you can trust them.

'Now, I know you and Richard Secord have already done a little treasure hunting with each other last year selling AWAC aircraft to the Saudis. And I know you've privately sold arms to Iran as a means to backchannel funds for the Contra effort. A wonderful idea. But you can't trust the Ayatollah as far as you can throw him, so in the interim may I suggest going through our friends in Israel.'

'The interim?'

'That's right. Now, as you know, Richard is a good friend of mine so I'm going to tell you what he's going to say during your meeting with him on Tuesday. He and Albert Hakim are in the process of setting up the Stanford Technology Trading Group International. Stanford Tech will act as the umbrella for a complex network of subsidiaries to facilitate the continued sale of arms to Iran and anyone else should this stint in Central America take longer than we anticipate. Both Richard and Albert are just waiting a little longer for the heat to die on their side of the FBI EATSCO investigation before the company goes operational.'

Sighing, 'And let me guess, you've got one hand on this umbrella?'

'Well, of course, I do. Not that anyone else will know of course. Richard will have full control of the company and knows exactly what he's doing. If we learned anything from Laos it's that however many layers you think you need to put between you and the deal, you need more. Stanford Tech, which we're calling the Enterprise, will be tighter than a pair of nun's undies.

'Moving on. Out of the NSA, you've got Clark and his deputy McFarlane, but neither have the backbone for this. They're both buddy-buddy with the President but keep Clark out of the loop as much as you can or he'll cause trouble. Bring McFarlane in but only throw him the bones he likes the smell of. Now, your CIA head of Latin America is Dewey Clarridge who loves nothing more than killing Cubans. He likes to play dirty. You'll get a lot done with him in the region. As for the Director, well, Bill Casey is a funny one. He's close with Noriega, far too close but for some goddamn reason, he likes the man. No doubt you'll meet the General soon enough but tread softly, Noriega's a can of worms waiting to pop. Now, Casey will be happy for you to do just about anything in Nicaragua but he won't want

his fingerprints on any of it. He'll give a helluva lot of okays but if shit hits the fan, he'll deny all of it. You listening, Ollie?'

'Yeah, I'm listening.'

'Good. You're going to need someone on the ground down there to look after the whole show for you. Someone experienced, someone you can trust, and someone willing to do very bad things.'

Frowning, 'Why do I have the feeling you already have that someone?'

'Dewey and I hand-picked him. His name is Felix Rodriguez. He's a CIA veteran and already in Costa Rica. There should be a file on him there on your desk.'

Clicking on the brass table lamp the light reveals a stack of manila folders, the top one embossed with CIA insignia and the name tag *Felix Rodriguez*.

'He's also one of my guys, so you can trust his loyalty to no end. He'll do what needs to be done. You'll also need a floater down there, someone not with the Agency. You'll want them to be everywhere and anywhere, a messenger, a voice for yours to liaise between parties who cannot or should not be communicating with each other. Start recruiting now. Obviously, you've been briefed on the CIA scripts regarding the FDN in Honduras?'

'Of course.'

'Then you also know the mobilization of revolutionary forces in the southern mountains has been sluggish, to say the least?'

'I'm aware.'

'And the Argentinians the Agency hired to assist in running those training camps have voiced concerns about the FDN's seed money already running dry.'

'I know.'

'Good. So, how do you plan on raising money for the Contra effort between yesterday and when Congress agrees to some paltry amount of financial support?'

'Well, the weapons to Iran. Richard said he was going to contact John Singlaub and use his connections with Taiwan and South Korea.'

'Cash flow from the Iran sales will be months away. As for John John, I've known him a long time and despite how much he loves America he won't do anything that isn't above board. Any deals he brokers will be by the book, which means you won't

see the funds well into next year. So, I ask you again, Ollie, what are you going to do for money now?'

'I-I—'

'I'll save you. You're already doing everything you can. But what you're not doing is getting dirty yet.'

His brow furrows, heavy and hard.

'Now, what has South America got that can raise funds faster than anything you or I or the President can?'

North's eyes dart across the table as his mind searches for an answer.

'Think outside that box of yours, Ollie.'

After a long silence, 'the white stuff?'

'Very good.'

'I won't do it, Ted.'

'Don't be stupid, Ollie. You don't have a choice. You need money, and lots of it. You need it sooner than whenever Congress will allow you to have it and you'll need five times more than whatever they approve. Privately selling arms to Iran, Syria, the Mujahideen, and whoever else you've got in the works is great but it won't happen soon enough and nor will it be enough.'

Pinching the bridge of his nose again, the Colonel doesn't respond.

'You don't have to touch it. You don't even have to see it. All you have to do is turn a blind eye. Do you know how many people made tens of millions out of Long Tieng? I don't, there were too many of us. It's a commodity, Ollie, a resource no different to oil or gold or guns and it's already coming into the US. All you have to do is let the right people down there know you're looking the other way but that you want your share.'

Silence.

'Look, if you don't open your own pipelines, you can't fund the Contra effort. It's as simple as that. The fledgling FDN will amount to nothing without your support and dare I say collusion. And then you'll have not one but two Communist nations in Central America, one with Russian nukes and the other signaling to the rest of the shithole region that the Yanks can't stop the red fever even when it's on our doorstep. And that'll be how your once decorated legacy will end; the failure to stop

Communism spreading right beneath our very feet, while we watch missiles sail through the sky over the Gulf killing millions of Americans.'

Sighing, 'You've gotta be kidding me,' North whispers to himself.

'Clocks ticking, Colonel.'

'What do I need to do?'

'At a boy. Nothing. They've already been told they can.'

'What? By who?' North says incensed.

'Felix.'

Fuming, 'Goddamn you, Ted. I was meant to be calling the shots on this campaign.'

'Oh, you will be, don't you worry about that.'

Shaking his head and squeezing the receiver so tightly his knuckles begin turning white.

'Rest assured, this is going to be your show. But I am here to help you, Ollie. We're all friends in this. Now, there's a pilot we've used in the past, his name is Seal, and he heads a team of Cessna cowboys who have a chequered history of running drugs out of South America. We're in the throes of setting him up with a nice little airfield in Mena, Arkansas. His cover is that he's to ferry guns to camps in Honduras and Costa Rica and then load up for the return trip.'

'Load up?'

'Don't make me say it. He'll deliver to the Nicaragua émigré where those profits will eventually return to the Contras.'

'Unbelievable, Ted.'

'But, as I said, all of this is in the works. Once you get into contact with Felix, you'll be overseeing its execution. Now, tell me what I don't know?'

After a long pause and a deep breath, 'The President will be signing off on a security directive hopefully by the end of the week, securing nineteen million for the Contra effort.'

'Nowhere near enough. How long until the funds clear?'

'Another week, at the most.'

'What else?'

'Despite the stalling of the main resistance army in southern Honduras, Enrique Bermudez has been successfully marshaling smaller insurgent forces in the north. We have already set up a small military base there to finance, train, and equip these groups.'

'I always liked Bermudez.'

'Eden Pastora popped up on the channels just before Thanks Giving.'

'Now, here's a firecracker. What did you hear?'

'Well, as you know, ever since he successfully led the siege on Somoza and the Nicaraguan Congress in '78, Sandinista-sympathizers think him a hero. He was there for the revolution, fought hard against the National Guard, held several high-ranking posts in the new Government but has recently defected.'

'Really?'

'Rumor is he felt the newly found power had corrupted and disillusioned the Sandinista's ideas.'

'Where is he now?'

'We don't know for sure but we think he's likely headed back to southern Nicaragua where he originally commanded the FSLN's southern front. He'll have friends down there, comrades, weapons, supplies.'

'You keep a close eye out for that one. Eden Pastora is a wildcard and doesn't know whose side he's on until he wakes up in the morning and checks which way his Johnson is leaning.'

'I'll keep that in mind. As for the FDN leadership, Aristides Sanchez is rallying the Union and what's left of the National Guard as we speak to bring together the most powerful and influential Nicaraguans under the one united banner. Adolfo Calero, as I'm sure you know from the CIA scripts, has relocated to Miami in an effort to raise private funds for the effort, while Popo Chamorro and Octavio Cesar have both been very active with their communication down the ranks. So, things are moving along, I suppose.'

'What about his brother?'

'Whose?'

'Adolfo Calero's.'

'I haven't been briefed.'

Silence.

'Is there anything I need to know about him?'

'His name is Mario. And if he isn't on your radar yet, he will be soon.'

'I see.'

'Well, Ollie, I have to go but before I do let me say one more thing. Always be forward-leaning. Leave no stone unturned. Move fast, don't wait for Congress to approve something because by the time they pass it, if they pass it, your opportunity to take the kill shot will be long gone. And with the world you're stepping into time is a luxury you don't have. Be a proud Republican, be a proud patriot. I'll be in touch. Godspeed.'

The receiver beeps, hollow and distant. Oliver slowly hangs it up. His ear is hot but his skin is cold and clammy. Rubbing his forehead, he realizes he had been sweating at some point. The Blonde Ghost, he thinks to himself, everywhere and nowhere.

III
ARISTIDES SANCHEZ

In a dimly lit banquet room of the gaudy art deco *Hotel Plaza Del Libertador*, the most powerful and influential of Nicaragua's exiles gather in cigar smoke secrecy to discuss the reclaiming of their country from the newly formed Sandinista Government led by former friend turn foe, President Daniel Ortega.

An ambitious undertaking seeing as the victory resulted at long last in the toppling of not only the Somoza leadership but the Somoza name, which had ruled the nation for over four decades after the first Somoza had murdered Augusto Sandino during peace talks. Bending the Constitution to his favor, concentrating power into his hands, and appointing relatives and cronies to top government positions, the Somoza family tree would go on to accumulate wealth through bribery, industrial monopolies, land grabbing, and the siphoning of foreign aid. That was until two years ago when the regime was overthrown by the *Sandinista National Liberation Front* led by none other than rebel guerrilla hero, Edén Pastora, whose forces captured two-thousand hostages at the National Palace and set in motion the final stages of revolutionary triumph.

Sitting at round tables draped in white linen, the who's who of Nicaragua's remaining elite—eager to plunge the devastated country into yet another revolution—listen intently to the emphatic speech by the man at the lectern.

Adjusting the microphone, 'It has been two years since our home was taken from us,' Aristides Sanchez begins, 'and two years since any of us, or our families, have seen the sun rise and set over our beautiful country. Anastasio Somoza was not a great leader. He, and his family before him, ruled Nicaragua with an iron fist. To some, he was a king, but to most, he was a tyrant and a thief. In the end, no one lives beyond the reach of their destiny, and for Tachito, he let our beloved country go up in flames and now he is ash.'

Performing a quick cross from forehead to shoulder, 'God has spoken.'

Clearing his throat, 'Carter closed the door on Somoza but in doing so he left us all in the dark. Look around, we are proud Nicaraguans from proud families with long histories that chapter great moments in our country's success. And yet we are now all marked as exiles, as political refugees banished from the very cities we helped build. Businesses, factories, farms, even lands and homes that have been in our families for generations are now owned by the Government, just like that,' he winces painfully. 'No. That is not right, that is not fair, that is not Nicaraguan.'

Taking a breath, 'We gather here not just as countrymen, not just as friends and allies, but as leaders of our respective associations that want nothing more than to see Nicaragua climb from those very ashes and be a proud unified nation once again. But this hope is an impossibility so long as the *Frente Sandinista de Liberación Nacional* and Daniel Ortega and the rest of those Communist thieves sit the seat of power in Managua,' Sanchez says slamming the lectern with a fist, while the people in attendance murmur in agreement.

'Tonight, we bear witness to the future of Nicaragua. The *Nicaraguan Democratic Union* has agreed to join with the National Guards, and on this day do we proclaim the formation of the *Fuerza Democrática Nicaragüense*.'

A cheer erupts and people bang the tables with their knuckles.

'The new *Presidente* of the United States, this Reagan, is a proud, proud man, like us, and has promised to aid the FDN in the reclaiming of our country. He understands our plight, he knows the Communist regimes, wherever they may be, must be fought at all costs. And unlike Carter, this Reagan and his administration are not afraid to spill Communist blood if that is what must be done. The Sandinistas force people to live a life they do not choose for themselves. They censor the news, they censor the media, they teach lies to our children in schools, and they take people's hard-earned monies and give it away. No, that is not how you build a future. Nicaragua is not Cuba, and we will not let our country be cut off from the rest of the world. We will not allow our well to be poisoned by Socialist and Marxist bastards!'

The attendees cheer raucously.

'It will take time but we will get there. That is why tonight is so important. It marks day zero of the biggest fight of our lives. And our fight is not on our doorstep but in our very own house, and we must take it back. This is the beginning, and there will be blood.'

Raising his glass of rum and yelling, 'We are the FDN and every true Nicaraguan is a soldier!'

Sitting at a small table at the back of the room, Norwin Meneses leans back in his chair chewing a smoldering cigar.

'So, this is it,' he says casually. 'These are the players set to take back the country, eh. Big fucking job when you can't set foot on the soil, no?'

Inclining his head slightly, Danilo Blandon is more concentrated on scribbling in his diary.

'What are you doing?' Norwin asks.

'Taking notes?'

'What for?'

'It's what I do. I'm a bookkeeper.'

Raising his eyebrows and wedging the wet cigar back into his mouth, 'Do you know any of these people?'

Looking up and pointing with his pen, 'That's Jose Cardenal and Mariano Mendoza from the Union. The little man in the military cap is Commander Enrique Bermudez. To his right is Edgar Chamorro, Alfonso Callejas, and Alexandro Zeledon.' Looking across the room, 'The woman is Lucia Salazar, widow to Jorge Salazar, God rest his soul.'

'The coffee grower.'

'Coffee Tycoon, *si*. And next to her is Adolfo Calero—'

'Oh, I know him,' Norwin says proudly. 'He's a big shot in Miami.'

'Him, Bermudez, and Aristides, they are the big shots,' Danilo says delicately.

Frowning, 'You sure know a lot of people, or is it just their names?'

Closing his diary, 'My family were landowners from the Matagalpa region. We did a lot of business with these people.'

'What kind of business?'

'Cattle, coffee, clothing,' Danilo says with a shrug. 'Not quite the coca business but a commodity is a commodity after all.'

'*Hola*, my dear friend,' Aristides Sanchez says suddenly appearing at the table. '*Cómo estás?*'

Taking the cigar from his mouth, Norwin stands and embraces him.

'*Bien, bien.*'

'Ah, *senor* Blandon,' Aristides says holding out his hand, 'I'm so pleased to see you here.'

Smiling, 'Of course.'

Putting his arm around Norwin's shoulder, 'Come with me, I must speak with you. *Senor Blandon, disculpe un momento, por favor.*'

Standing by a window mostly blocked by thick gold-leaf velvet curtains with Tegucigalpa's urban-encrusted valley dipping below, 'I have big plans for you in America,' Aristides says sipping his glass of rum.

'And him?' Norwin says looking towards the bookkeeper.

'Him too.'

Squinting, 'Can I trust this man?'

'*Si*, entirely. I have done business with his family for many years.'

'If you say so,' Norwin says unemotionally.

Leaning close, 'He will be able to turn things up in California for you. I'm certain.'

'I see.'

Glancing around the smoke-filled room, 'Some of the FDN directorates don't want to acknowledge how much the coca fills our coffers. They are old and stubborn and ignore what a valuable commodity it is. Nicaragua, Costa Rica, Honduras, they are all beautiful countries with green jungles, mountains and valleys, crystal clear water and white sandy beaches. Yet, we do not have the same resources to make ourselves rich as other countries do. We have few. But if one of them happens to be coca, so be it.'

Taking the cigar from his mouth, 'Every country has its commodity, but money is the one that speaks all the languages,' Norwin says thoughtfully.

'Exactly, that is why I am happy, more than happy, to use it. The end justifies the means. That is why *senor* Blandon is here. He knows how to procure goods, establish supply chains and distribute.'

Chuckling, 'I've been doing that ever since I stepped foot in America.'

'I know, but this is different now. We have to fund a civil war, my friend. You sneak the coca in any way you can. Danilo will make this an international business for you. The *Americanos* have given us seed money until they can establish sanctioned funding for our cause. But until then, coca is what is going to feed, clothe, and arm our soldiers. This is why you need—*we* need Danilo, *comprenday?*'

Looking pensively, 'Who in the US is helping us?'

'The CIA, of course. One of their agents has already contacted us from Costa Rica. His name is Max Gomez and he says he will be securing an outfit in El Salvador for us to use.'

'An outfit?'

'A private airbase. Then, our man in the White House is Oliver something, North, I think. A Colonel. But he is with the NSC.'

'NSC?' Norwin inquires.

'National Security Council. It's like the President's private team of advisors for national security and foreign policy, but it's part of the, what do they call it, Executive Office.'

'Which means what?'

'Which means not only do they not require Congress's approval but they don't even have to tell them what they're doing. If the President feels something needs to happen and maybe it's better that Congress or the public shouldn't know about it, it gets the go-ahead. No questions asked.'

Norwin smirks.

'It's beautiful, isn't it?' Aristides chuckles. 'America, the great democracy, so righteous, so moral, and always fighting the good fight. If only the people knew how stained the President's hands are in blood. I shouldn't laugh. These are not laughing times. I like the sound of this Ronald Reagan. He means business, and is happy for the dirty work to get done.'

Nodding, 'So, what's this Gomez fellow doing for us?'

Swirling his drink, 'He's our direct link to North. Says the Colonel is the one who will pull the strings for us from the capital and this Gomez man is the go-between.'

'When will we hear from this North?'

'Soon, I hope.'

'Gomez also says Reagan is working on Congress to pass a directive to give us proper funding. Regardless, we need money now, and lots of it, Norwin. This moment is critical. To have everyone together like this, in agreement under the one roof.' After a moment, 'Look, I know you are not a political man but I cannot let this opportunity slip through my fingers,' Aristides implores.

Norwin thinks for a moment, 'That's right. I am not a political man. My father was, and so were my brothers, God rest their souls. I am a businessman. Ari, I understand what you are asking and I understand why you are asking it. We have lost our country and it will require great patriots to get it back.' Taking a gulp of his rum, 'I love Nicaragua but I am not a great patriot. You are asking my business to support your war,' looking at him before wrapping his lips around his cigar, 'and of course, I will.'

A wide smile parts Aristide Sanchez's lips, 'Good. That makes me very happy.'

'So, this Gomez and this North know that we will move the coca? And they are okay with that?'

Sipping his drink, 'Not in so many words. They would prefer us to rely on their own funds rather than with coca. But this Gomez says the people in the Whitehouse, the important ones, are willing to turn a blind eye if that's what will bring the Contras together.'

'Contras?'

'Si, counterrevolutionaries they are calling the fighters.'

'Okay, so what do you want me to do in the meantime?'

'Go back to San Francisco and get ready to move as much coca as you can because the floodgates are about to be opened.'

Wedging the cigar into the corner of his mouth, 'What assurances do I have?'

'Assurances, none. The CIA and NSC can't have their fingerprints on any of this. But as I said, they are happy to look the other way.'

Norwin nods.

'This Reagan, by any means necessary,' he says nodding enthusiastically.

'Okay, what protection am I going to get?'

'Gomez has promised CIA intervention over FBI, DEA, and US Customs. Naturally, you still need to be discreet, but should anything go wrong, any seizures and such, I have a list of names and numbers your people are to use that should get them out of trouble.'

Raising his eyebrows, 'Just like that?'

'*Si*, just like that,' Aristides says smiling. 'When the CIA man organizes this airbase in El Salvador, I'll be in touch.'

'*Muy bien.*'

Holding up his glass of rum, '*Para Nicaragua,*' Aristides toasts.

'*Para Nicaragua,*' Norwin says, glass clinking.

1982

IV
CARLOS CABEZAS

Beneath a mid-morning sky of heavy clouds threatening to rain, Carlos has the heater on high, rebelling against the bleakness of a West Coast winter as he descends into East Bayview near San Francisco's south basin. Running for blocks on end are warehouses and storage yards with rusty and discolored galvanized-iron roofing, blanketing the horizon like meadows of mid-century industrial boom.

Turning down a series of drab-looking streets before parking in front of a commercial warehouse for a linen cleaning business that services several motels in the South San Francisco, Daly City, and anything this side of the 280 Freeway areas. Huge washing drums and steaming ovens billow plumes of warm vapor into the warehouse before escaping up ventilation stacks, while sirens of varying octaves, flashing amber lights, great silver machines *humming* on spin-cycle, and a chorus of various Latin dialects fill the air as Carlos makes his way through what would be an immigration officer's wet dream.

With a charcoal suit and olive-green scarf setting him apart from white aprons and yellow rubber boots of employee distinction, Carlos strides to the rear of the warehouse. Entering a small windowed office where a wooden desk sags beneath stacks of yellow invoices and an inconspicuous door appearing to lead to a closet or perhaps restroom, in fact, leads to the adjoining warehouse of whose branding and business dealings appear indeterminate from the outside.

Through a warren of dully lit corridors, Carlos enters the main storage area, which, even through the darkness, he knows is mostly empty except for a dozen drums on wooden pallets and a forklift parked insensibly somewhere. Above, windows aglow, mumbled voices float from an upstairs office.

'Carlos,' Norwin greets before peering back over Danilo Blandon's shoulder intently, 'I've been waiting for you.'

Leaning over Danilo and dropping occasional ash on his collar from a fat, half-smoked cigar, Norwin scrutinizes each pencil stroke the bookkeeper is making. Large ledgers sprawl across the table covering piles of cargo receipts from the docks, Class E airspace registration papers from a variety of private airstrips, utility bills and rental forms from a variety of leased properties, and other documents pertaining to the recently ramped-up coca business.

Although he has several warehouses around the Bay area, each holding various amounts of cash or coca or both, the Bayview warehouse is where Norwin keeps all of the accounts. Office, yes, but also bachelor pad for the string of mistresses Norwin has on the ready. Behind the L-shaped table and beige filing cabinets, soft brown-leather chesterfield sofas lie at the far end next to a billiard table and a big screen television sitting in the middle of two six-feet long liquor cabinets. There's also a *Murphy* pull-down bed fastened to the wall for when the discomfort of going home to Gloria is too excruciating.

Hanging his coat and scarf on a wooden stand, Carlos takes a seat across from the two men, sitting quietly cross-legged, while black cast-iron radiators gurgle quietly above the focused scratches of lead on paper and the intermittent puffs exhuming from Norwin's mouth.

'Okay,' Danilo says pushing back on the chair, his plump face flushed from furiously calculating numbers and his armpit revealing a sweat patch as he fixes his thin mustache with thumb and forefinger. 'Last year you moved nine-hundred kilos, give or take. That's less than twenty kilos a week and with no other major competitors we should be doing double that.'

'Triple,' Norwin blurts barely able to get the cigar out of his mouth.

Raising his eyebrows, 'Miami is doing a hundred kilos a week,' Danilo states plainly. 'New Orleans fifty. But California is a gold mine, only—'

'With no fucking gold,' Norwin finishes, looking broodingly through the windows into the dark warehouse below.

Danilo clears his throat, 'But we're close. Distribution has already gone up thirty percent in the last three months. The restaurants, the nightclubs, the car yards and carwashes are working. From Richmond to Oakland, and all the way down to Silicon Valley, San Fran is doing okay.'

'LA,' Norwin says distantly. 'Seven and a half million people in the County area. Double the entire population of Nicaragua, in one city.' Then, turning to Carlos, 'Back home they called me *El Rey del Drogas*.' Tapping his chest, 'The king of drugs. In this country I am a nobody,' he says with a shrug. 'More people know who Griselda Blanco is, the crazy bitch. And in New York, those two Frank negroes are more respected.'

'It is a good thing, to go unnoticed,' Carlos offers. 'Look at Blanco, she had to flee the country. And even she couldn't crack LA.'

'That's right, she failed,' Norwin says frowning. 'We've been in California for over a year now and *still*, nothing happens in LA.'

Carlos starts but Norwin cuts him off, 'It's okay. I'm not blaming you. But we're in a position to own this fucking place. To completely control the market here, and we're not. I am losing my patience with LA, that's why Danilo is moving back next month.'

Carlos is unable to hide his surprise.

'Don't feel threatened. You are my eyes and ears flying back and forth overseeing the network, and that won't change. Which reminds me,' he says taking a folded bit of paper from his shirt pocket, 'have you been to San Pedro Sula before?'

'*Si*, once. Why?'

'Aristides has asked for you to make contact with some of the FDN in Honduras. Here are the details.'

Carlos reads the note before putting it away, 'So, things are finally moving forward with them?'

'Who knows? We are still waiting to hear about this secret airbase of theirs,' Danilo says.

'Whether we'll use it or not is another matter?' Norwin states.

'Why wouldn't we?' Carlos asks curiously.

'I'm not in the business of putting all of my chickens in the one henhouse, Carlos. Especially, when a CIA fox is hiding in there.'

'I thought you agreed to support the FDN?'

'I did and I am. But the longer I can hold off using their pipelines the longer it is before they can dip their filthy hands in my pockets.'

Clearing his throat, 'But the coca supply has increased, and there's also the protection our channels are getting now—'

'Not that we'll know until something goes wrong,' Norwin interrupts.

'And for that, we are providing regular donations to the Nicaraguan émigré in Miami,' Danilo offers. 'But there is no reason to sell ourselves out entirely if nothing becomes of this Contra revolution. Aristides Sanchez is a hopeful man—'

'Desperate,' Norwin mumbles sucking on his cigar.

'He promises that things are still being moved into place, in Honduras and Costa Rica. That we still very much have US backing. Perhaps that is why he has arranged for you to meet the FDN in Honduras; maybe things are moving forward finally and they need to communicate with us in person.'

'That's right,' Norwin jumps in. 'There is a lot of chatter now. Word is spreading that the US Government is going to start letting a lot of coca slip through. That's why we have to strike! Get in before others do.' Then, wedging the cigar back in his mouth, 'Carlos?'

'*Si?*'

'Keep our FDN friends happy down there, you hear me?' Norwin says seriously. 'There will be a lot of people willing to participate in the freeing of Nicaragua now, as well as making a name for themselves, staking a claim in this business.'

'Of course.'

'Good, good. Important people are depending on us. Nicaragua is depending on us.'

***

Two days later the Nicaraguan exiles fly into Tegucigalpa before immediately boarding a thirty-seater *Islena Airlines* regional plane headed for a dirt landing strip otherwise known as Tela Airport. The flight is loud, bumpy, and the faint odor of gasoline coupled with the co-pilot chain-smoking makes Julio do the cross half a dozen times. The view out of the window, however, is breathtaking; an unobstructed stretch of glistening green rainforest and dark valleys, dappled here and there by shadows of low-lying clouds in an otherwise bright blue sky. At least if they crash and die, Carlos thinks, it will be somewhere beautiful.

Thirty nerve-racking minutes later they touchdown on a dirt runway with dust sweeping up from the still-turning propellers and one hundred percent humidity welcoming their arrival to the northwest corner of Honduras. With only carry-on luggage, they jump in a cab and descend into San Pedro Sula, a quaint city of Spanish Colonial architecture, urban insolvency, and skyrocketing unemployment. The city serves most effectively as a transport hub as a tangle of highways connects Guatemala, Belize, and El Salvador to several portside towns with direct access to the Caribbean Sea. A perfect location for fringes of the FDN leadership to base themselves and their activities.

Pulling up at the corner of *Bulevar Morazan* and *Avenida Norte* to a genteel six-story semi-Colonial- semi-art deco hotel offering views of the city to the east and the oppressive Merendon Mountains to the west, Carlos and Julio climb out of the cab, while the effort to retrieve their bags from the trunk initiates ceaseless perspiration.

'So, this is it, huh? What a shithole,' Julio admires.

'You didn't know?'

'I never been to Sula before. Where are all the nice houses I heard about?'

Carlos smirks, 'You're thinking of Cortes, along the beach. Still a part of San Pedro. But this is downtown,' gesturing towards the honking traffic, graffiti, street-sellers, concrete buildings, and a CBD lacking any kind of flare or décor.

Inside, a foyer of polished brass and vintage-style furnishing, thick burgundy carpets, and vested bellhops cling to the establishment's former glory. After checking into separate rooms, showering, and donning clothes of light linen, they meet at the bar and share a glass of rum.

'So, where are we meeting these FDN?'

'Across the river. Campisa is where the rich live. Those who bother to stay here.'

'And who are we meeting again?' Julio asks sipping his drink.

'The Sanchez brothers, Troilo and Ferdinand. That's all I know.'

'Should I know them?'

'You know of their cousin, Aristides.'

Julio whistles. 'So, what the fuck are they doing in this place?'

'Sula is smack bang in the middle of Central America. Highways connect east to west, ports on the north and south, and not only is the Honduran government completely corrupt but President Paz Garcia is real friendly with the CIA. Has been for years. What better place?'

Carlos checks his watch and bottoms up his drink, '*Vamonos.*'

Ruffling the fronds of nearby palm trees, a warm breeze blows as dusk descends on the streets of Sula, and despite the sun's departure over the horizon the temperature has yet to drop, or so too the humidity. Streetlights blink on and cheap restaurants and bars glow in dull neon giving downtown a kind of eerie and vacant carnival feeling.

Out of nowhere, a black Ford Bronco suddenly pulls up onto the curb.

Winding down the window, '*Eres Carlos y Julio?*' the fat goateed driver with black wrap-around sunglasses asks.

'*Si.*'

'Hop in, *muchachos.*'

The driver takes them north through the city, across the rivers, and up into the ritzy gated community of Campisa where large Spanish-style estates nestle at the base of a small mountain overlooking the hazy city to the south.

Pulling up to a large iron gate, the driver nods to a guard who radios their arrival before letting them in.

'It seems the FDN isn't doing so badly,' Julio remarks as the car crunches along a gravel driveway towards a glowing mansion of pastel yellow and terracotta roofs.

'*Hola, caballeros. Buena noches,*' a well-dressed man greets them.

'*Buena noches,*' Carlos says shaking hands.

'*Mi nombre es, Horacio Pereira.* Thank you for making the trip, gentlemen.'

'Of course.'

'Please, come in.'

Leading Carlos and Julio through the plush mansion adorned with conquistador statues, heavy oil paintings of the Spanish Inquisition, and past a white marble fountain of water-spitting cherubs, Horacio opens the door to a dining room thick with smoke.

'*Buenos noches, senores,*' a man in a cream silk shirt says from the head of the table with a cigar smoldering between his fingers. 'I am Troilo Sanchez, and welcome to San Pedro.'

'*Gracias,*' Carlos and Julio respond in unison.

Seated around the large oak table are several men, none of whom Carlos has met or seen before.

Gesturing to two empty chairs, 'Please, take a seat and allow me to introduce you to my guests,' Troilio says warmly. Standing and walking around the table, 'This is my brother, Ferdinand,' he says placing a hand on the man's shoulder before moving along. 'Business partners Jaun Matta and Frank Moss. Luis Hernandez here owns a seafood shipping company operating out of Costa Rica that is very supportive of the Contras. Across from you is Popo Chamorro from Miami. And you have already met Horacio Pereira.'

Pouring two large glasses of rum from a liquor cabinet and handing them to Carlos and Julio, 'Now, we are all compatriots here so, please allow me to be frank, *senores*, then we can relax.'

'By all means,' Carlos says smoothly sipping his drink.

'*Muy bien,*' Troilo says taking a gulp of rum. 'Aristides Sanchez has asked you here under the guise of maintaining channels of communication between the FDN and Norwin Meneses. Now, the number one objective of the FDN at present is to raise money. That's it. Without it, we cannot do anything. If we are to successfully mobilize a counterrevolutionary force to take back our country, we must have the means to do so. This is food, clothing, weapons, cars and trucks, wages for soldiers, medical supplies, and as you can imagine the list goes on.'

Taking a breath, 'I know you are probably thinking, hasn't Aristides already spoken directly to Norwin? Hasn't he already secured his contribution to the cause? Yes, he has. But Norwin is not a patriot, he is a drug lord. It has been six months since they spoke the night the FDN was formed and in that time, Aristides has become apprehensive in regards to Norwin's efforts. Popo here receiving but paltry donations every other week,' Troilo says disappointedly.

'You, however, *senor* Cabezas, are formally of the National Guard, and with that Aristides knows where your loyalty lies. We understand, of course, that you move coca for Norwin and we do not wish to get in the way of that. However, *senor* Meneses only cares about making money, he is a businessman after all and so are we, Carlos,' Troilo says with a chuckle. 'But what use is being in business if we cannot be in Nicaragua? It is our job to see the FDN succeed, and that success is a victory for all Nicaraguans near and far.'

Furrowing his brow, 'What are you asking, exactly?' Carlos inquires.

'We would like you to divert a small portion of Norwin's coca to FDN associates in Miami,' Troilo says plainly.

Julio shifts in his chair.

'Look,' Troilo continues, 'Norwin is still a very valued Nicaraguan, but we simply need more than he is giving. With all the money being made out of the US, the FDN feels it should be receiving greater support, such is the pertinence of our cause. The amount of powder coming out of Bolivia and Peru by the Medellin and Cali cartels is staggering. It is no longer a question of if it can be moved, but simply, by who. Road, boat, or plane, it's already coming.' Shaking his head and smiling wryly, 'All around us people are making millions of dollars every month, and all we want is a small political contribution so that we may reclaim our country. Is that so much to ask?'

Rubbing his chin thinking, 'How exactly do you expect me to divert coca belonging to Norwin?'

Swirling his drink, 'The amount of coca that he purchases each month from the Cali Cartel is approximate is it not?'

'Correct.'

'And you are his overseer, yes? You meet the shipments in Costa Rica and confirm the final value before sending it on its way.'

Raising his eyebrows, 'That is true.'

Shrugging, 'So what, a few kilos don't make it onto Norwin's ships and planes, and instead finds its way into the hands of our friends in Miami, what's the harm?'

Frowning, 'The harm is that I am stealing from Norwin Meneses,' Carlos says with a disbelieving chuckle.

Making a fist, 'And giving it to Nicaragua,' Troilo says emphatically.

Sighing, 'Let's say I agree to this arrangement, what quantities are we talking and where would I be delivering to?' Carlos inquires.

'At this early stage, we would be happy to secure twenty kilos a week. Delivery will be to trusted Nicaraguan émigrés in Miami, namely Popo. That said, you would not be required to do anything beyond ensuring the coca gets redistributed when it arrives in Ilopango.'

'Ilopango?'

'That is the location of the CIA-secured airbase just outside of San Salvador.'

Giving Julio a quick look, 'And for what reason am I to tell Norwin for us coming here to Sula?' Carlos asks.

'Exactly that. Tell him that the airbase is a month or two away from operation. He will no longer need to send his coca over to the US on ships, instead, we'll have trusted pilots flying it directly into the US.'

'Like who?'

'Salvadoran and Honduran Air Force pilots on CIA payroll with covers that they are delivering humanitarian aid. They'll be able to fly in and out of Texas without going through customs or any other checks.'

With a dubious look on his face, Carlos places his drink on the table, 'You are talking over a hundred kilos a month, maybe double that if all this goes to plan. Do you really think it will be that easy?'

Smirking, 'The pilots are already flying back and forth unchecked, *senor* Cabezas. At the moment they are delivering weapons and supplies but the plan is for them to load up on coca for the return flight to the US. There, the powder will be sold and profits passed on to the CIA and FDN so we can purchase more equipment and supplies for our soldiers.'

Carlos gives a long, uncomfortable sigh.

'*Senor* Cabezas, I apologize for propositioning you so forthrightly, but as I said we are all compatriots here and this is a matter of life and death is it not? This is why Aristides requested Norwin's support in the first place. The money made from the coca is crucial to the revolution and the amount of powder limitless, so long as it is for the FDN. And yet, Norwin appears reluctant to help, so now you understand our frustration. With the CIA's involvement the coca will land on your doorstep; for that, is it too much to ask for a healthy cut?'

Rubbing his forehead, 'I don't know what—' Carlos begins.

Waving a disregarding hand and smiling, 'Carlos, you do not need to give me an answer here and now. Think about it for a couple of days, yes. But may I remind you that this request comes directly from Aristides Sanchez. And with that, so too is its importance and confidentiality. Do not underestimate how eager we are to secure financial support. Naturally, the FDN's struggle is a political one, and although it has intertwined itself with drug traffickers, it is solely because it must reach out for help wherever it can. The FDN accepts that its cause is greater than the means it takes to achieve it. The revolution will proceed but at what pace is up to those willing to help, *senor* Cabezas, and at the cost of how many lives?'

* * *

After two days in Honduras and three in Costa Rica, Carlos and Julio disembark their *Pan Am* flight at LAX before making their way to check in for their final leg home to San Francisco.

'Have you decided if you're going to do it or not?' Julio asks walking through the terminal.

Raising his eyebrows, 'You said it yourself; we live like errand boys here compared to what we had back home.'

'So, that's a yes then?'

'I don't know. If Norwin was more giving, the Sanchez brothers wouldn't have even had to ask me.'

'But he isn't. He's tighter than a nun's *coño*.'

Carlos laughs.

'Look, *hermano*,' Julio continues, 'it's dicey to play such a game with Norwin, but Troilo is right; twenty kilos isn't too much, not with things starting to pick up now and definitely not much if we can start flying the coca straight in.'

'So, you think I should?'

Smiling cheekily, 'Hey man, I don't get paid enough to make that decision. That's why Norwin pays you the big bucks.'

Carlos chuckles before considering his options, 'I'm going to suggest to Norwin that we start sending coca through Ilopango despite his reluctance. I'll explain that the speed this coca arrives will be worth the cut the FDN receives, this way I can get coca going directly to the Sanchez brothers. Then, assuming this whole Contra-CIA revolution takes off and the supply of coca goes through the roof, Norwin should be happy to show greater financial support seeing as he will be making a huge amount of money from the situation, and when that happens I'll no longer have to skim anything for FDN. Norwin wins, and so too the Sanchez Brothers.'

Raising his eyebrows, 'See, big bucks,' Julio says warmly.

Arriving at the check-in desk, a pretty brunette in a tight navy uniform greets them.

'Hello,' she says with a smile, 'how can I help you, gentlemen?'

'Carlos Cabezas and Julio Zavala,' Carlos says. 'We have a flight to San Francisco at six-thirty.'

'Certainly, let me bring that up for you—oh, Mr. Cabezas,' she says stopping.

'Yes?' Carlos asks.

Handing him a pink slip of paper, 'There's a telegram for you.'

His face awash with concern, Carlos reads it quickly.

'What's it say, *hermano?*' Julio asks.

'We have to go see Henry,' Carlos says seriously.

'What? Now?'

'*Sí.*'

'What about our flight to Frisco?'

'We'll catch a later one. The message says it's urgent.'

Making a face, 'That *pendejo* wouldn't know what urgent was if it bit him on the ass.'

Jumping in a cab, Carlos and Julio head for *Fiesta Bar & Grill* in west Inglewood on the corner of Manchester Boulevard and La Brea Avenue; fortunately, only a fifteen-minute drive from the airport. With the sun setting under a patchy sky, the air cool and crisp, Carlos offers the driver a fifty-dollar tip if he can go faster.

Pulling up to the restaurant the car park is full and customers can be seen through the windows.

'Well, at least it hasn't been burnt down,' Julio remarks.

Ignoring the joke, Carlos can feel his pulse throbbing in his neck despite his efforts to remain calm. He knows it's most likely a consequence of the proposition by Troilo Sanchez weighing heavy on his mind; a seed of deceit planted and now unnecessary worry blooming at any opportunity.

Pushing through the entrance, the Nicaraguans are greeted with a clamor of plates smashing making Carlos instinctively reach for a gun in his waistband that isn't there.

Bursting from the kitchen, '*Aye, aye, aye!*' Henry shouts. 'Don't worry ladies and gentlemen, just a few broken plates. It's good luck!' he says jokingly to the startled customers, while a young waitress, flushed with embarrassment, begins collecting the broken glass.

'Hey, *muchachos*,' Henry says smiling until he sees Carlos's face, his eyes wide and unblinking.

'It's okay, Carlos, just some plates. What's the matter with you?'

Swallowing, 'You left a message to come see you,' Carlos states plainly.

'Urgently,' Julio adds.

'Yes, yes. Great news, *muchachos*. Great news,' Henry says ushering them towards a corner table at the back of the restaurant.

Taking a seat beneath vintage photos of Nicaraguan cattle raisers and a bone-dry bovine skull, Julio gives Carlos a dry look.

'Boy, have I got news for you,' Henry says enthusiastically. Then, clicking his fingers signaling to a waitress, 'Maria! Go get Diego, please. Oh, and three beers!'

'Well, go on,' Carlos says impatiently.

Licking his lips, 'Okay. So, there's this black guy,' Henry starts. 'Alan Fisher and his wife, they've been coming to the restaurant every week for the past couple of months. They love it. He's a real nice guy, his wife too, real sexy. Anyway, one night a couple of weeks ago he comes in on his own. We were quiet so I decided to sit with him at the bar and have a few drinks with him on the house, you know, because he comes here so often. We get to talking and he's asking all these questions about Nicaragua, the food, the women, the drugs. I tell him how it was before the revolution and how it is now. Then I talk a little about how drugs in South America ain't like drugs here in the US. You know, you can get an ounce of weed for like forty dollars and buy coca straight from the taxi driver, that kinda thing.'

Carlos and Julio exchange a worried look.

'Hey, hey, guys. Don't worry, I didn't say anything about the coca situation. Well, not yet.'

Arriving at the table with four beers in his hands, Diego's forehead is dotted with sweat, and his white apron is stained from cooking in the kitchen.

'*Hola, muchachos,*' he says putting the beers down and sliding next to Julio.

'*Buenas tardes, Diego,*' Carlos says.

Taking a quick sip, 'So, anyway,' Henry continues, 'it's a good conversation, we're having fun, telling jokes, and remember we're drinking the whole time. Before I know it, the restaurant is almost empty, the girls are starting to pack up for the night, you know. And by now we're a little drunk but he's a great guy, real chatty. Anyway, he's a teacher at one of the schools around here, I knew this already, but he starts telling me how he lives so comfortably because he sells the marijuana. Now, I know he's looking at me like I'm some immigrant, who am I gonna tell this shit to. So, I ask him how he does it, where he gets his gear from, this sort of thing. He says he fucking grows it himself. Are you kidding me? You gotta remember we're a bit drunk, you know. I ask him where the fuck he grows it, he's living in South Central. Oh man, this is the best part, listen to this. This guy, this upholstery teacher, he grows the weed in the back storerooms of the school. It's crazy, I know. He tells me only he has the keys to get in there, it's all set up right, and because he deals with glues and chemicals and shit, he's got all this ventilation back there. He doesn't have to worry about the power company asking questions, the water, nothing. It's incredible. He's been doing it for three years now. So, I think, well, if he can trust me to tell me this then I'll ask him if he wants to move some coca for me. I just pretended I had a little bit but it's real pure stuff straight from back home. He says, yeah sure, he'll give it a try. He says how everyone knows what coke is but there's no real market for it, only a few high rollers move it. Anyway, I give him an ounce and say no pressure. He comes back three days later because it's all gone. So, I give him a quarter of a pound. Then half a pound. A week later another half a pound. Then he knows I don't have this shit just lying around—and I wanna cover our asses—so, I ask him who he's getting to buy so much coca? Because if he's in with the Bloods or the Crips or something I don't wanna fuck up what we've got going here. He says to me because he's a teacher he knows a lot of school dropouts who are always hustling. Anyway, there's this one kid who's real street smart and he's the one moving most of the coca. But get this, he said the kid is cutting it with something, making it go double the distance but at a quarter of the price.'

Frowning, 'What's he cutting it with? This is pure Colombian, man,' Julio says horror-struck.

'No, don't you see, the people here are poor, they can't afford pure coca, man. That's the *problema*. That's always been the *problema*. Cocaine is out of their price range. But that's why this kid is making moves. He calls it—what did he say—ready rock. It looks like these little hard clumps of chalk, only a bit yellow.'

'Yellow?' Carlos questions.

'*Sí*. And get this, he sells it for only twenty dollars a hit.'

'Twenty dollars, are you crazy?' Julio fires. 'He'd have to make hundreds of sales a day!'

'That's the thing, *muchachos*, he is,' Henry says grinning.

Carlos looks to Diego for some kind of reassurance.

Sipping a beer, 'It's true, man. Henry saying it like it is. That mouth of his finally got us in with the black dealers,' Diego says with a wry smile.

After a moment, 'But why did you need to see us urgently?' Carlos asks.

'Because I'm already out of coca, *amigos*,' Henry says smiling. 'This kid moved a kilo in three fucking weeks.'

Carlos and Julio give each other an impressed look.

Laughing, 'This is it, this is what you've been waiting for,' Henry says slapping the table. 'Fuck dealing with the gangs, we'll probably wind up dead one day. But this black kid, he's a weaselly fucker, short and skinny with buckteeth, his hair is all dreadlocks like a dirty mop, but he's real sharp.'

'You've met him?' asks Carlos.

'*Si*, of course.'

'What's his name?'

'They call him, Freeway Ricky.'

V
FREEWAY RICKY

Bubbling delicately in a silver saucepan, a cloudy off-white goo slowly develops from a granular texture into a gravy-like liquid as heat dissolves baking powder and cocaine into a single, fully integrated substance. Being careful to melt but not boil the ingredients, he caresses the surface of the soup with a fork as steam gently rises, carrying with it a sting of hydrochloride salt vapor.

Squinting with focus, 'That's it,' Rick says softly. 'A little more. Keep stirring. Watch that heat and use the fork to stretch it. Stretch it, nigga, come on,' he tells his young apprentice. 'Okay, see how it's starting to gel up? That's what we want. Keep stirring. That gooey shit is what you want. All right, get it off the heat and get the ice cubes from the freezer.'

Junior, another young novice cook Rick has been training, cracks the ice cubes free from the tray and tosses them into the pot one at a time.

Watching the liquid closely, 'Let's go another couple cubes in there,' Rick says. 'Okay, that'll do.'

'Now what?' Junior asks.

'Now we let the pot cool right down. Give it an hour and it'll be nice and hard. Then we rinse off any shit that didn't take, any of that chalky baking powder shit, and what we got left is a nice hard biscuit.'

'Of crack?' Junior says eagerly.

'Of money, nigga,' Rick says with a laugh. 'Yeah crack. Break it all apart and you got ready rock ready to smoke. We just flipped two ounces of coke into four ounces of crack,' he says proudly.

'Just like that?'

'Just like that. Well, you gotta get the coke first. That's the hard part,' he says laughing. 'Okay, let's go again. You got a kilo still to get through. This time I'm gonna let you do it all from the start.'

After an hour of cooking and with Junior's cheffing skills coming along nicely, they're about halfway done. Half a dozen cheap silver *Costco* cooking pots sit along a Laminex benchtop cooling, all at various stages of transformation. The tiny kitchen of cracked white cabinetry and green chequered Lino flooring filled with a metallic odor wafting its way through the bare apartment. Standing over a large plastic tub Freeway Ricky breaks apart yellow Frisbee-sized discs into smaller chunks before weighing the pieces on a triple beam scale to precisely one ounce and zip-lock bagging them.

'What you say?' Rick says suddenly.

'Huh?'

'You say something, homie?'

'When?' Junior's face frowns with confusion.

'Just now.'

'Just now? I didn't say shit, nigga. I just been staring at this damn ice melting.'

Forcing his already bulgy eyes open with thumb and forefingers, Rick stares about the kitchen. Asleep in the living room Fat Clarence—all three-hundred pounds of him—seems to be testing the structural integrity of a cream *La-Z-Boy* with a Beretta M9 resting atop his enormous stomach rising and falling with each labored breath.

Rick pops his head through the doorway, 'Yo, Clarence. You say something, nigga?'

Startled, 'W-when?'

'Just now.'

'I don't think so, Rick.' Wiping dry spit from his mouth, 'Why you holding your face like that?' Clarence asks curiously.

Ignoring the question, Rick returns to the kitchen, and releasing his eyes he gives a series of blinks followed by a shudder, 'Shiiit. I think I'm contact high as a motha fucker.'

'Contact high, what's that?' Junior asks.

Rubbing his cheeks, 'It's when you get high from the fumes, while you cooking.' Then, checking his watch, 'Goddamn, is that the time! All right, I gotta jet but I'll be back later. Once you've finished cooking, break all this shit apart like I've been doing into exactly one-ounce baggies. When you've done that put it all into this ice cream container and put it in the freezer, okay.' Looking around the kitchen, 'Then tidy all this shit up. And open a window or something.'

Divvying up varying quantities of crack and putting them into empty fast-food bags—*KFC, M&M's, Wendy's, Burger King*—Rick storms back into the living room clapping his hands.

'Clarence, wake yo fat ass up. You a goddamn bodyguard.'

'I-I know, Ricky.'

'Y-you know. Then what the hell you doing sleeping?'

'I-I—'

'Don't answer that. I'm leaving. Don't open this door for nobody. Not the police. Not your sister. Not your dead mamma. The fridge is full of *KFC* and *7UP* so you don't need to go nowhere. I'll be back later and yo ass best be awake.'

Rick is out of the door before Clarence can answer. Outside he is met with a blinding overcast sky and a brisk morning breeze forcing him to zip up his orange and blue *Fila* tennis jacket. Parked in the driveway is a beat-up two-door Chevette riddled with rust and missing its hubcaps; in a former life it was a cherry red color but now neglect and sun bleaching has turned it a lovely shade of pink. Climbing in to the wail of a door on its last hinge, Rick throws the fast-food bags on the passenger seat and blows warmth into his hands. After a few goes turning the key the car finally starts, the radio crackling to Dolly Parton's *Working 9 to 5*, and hits the road.

From Willowbrook into Athens, beneath spaghetti junction, across Imperial Highway, through Magnolia Square, and then Vermont Vista, Rick drops off bags of freshly cooked crack to his drug houses. With his system down pat, each drop is done the same; Rick pulls into the driveway, presses the horn three times, and holds a fast-food bag out of the window like he's dropping off breakfast. Keithy on South Broadway is first, then Kenny's spot on 113th just behind *Wingstop*, followed by Shrimp, and lastly Johnny Mumbles on 81st Street, South Central's infamous buffet line of drugs.

This narrow suburban road is dappled with street dealers and hustlers—even at ten in the morning—selling anything from weed by the gram or ounce, PCP by the stick, Primos if you're feeling fancy, and now crack by the rock. Between Hoover Street and Vermont Avenue, 81st is a smorgasbord of junkies, chopped cars, Pitbulls, barbwire, Cadillacs and Fleetwoods with all the trimmings, homies wearing gold chains worth more than their mamma's houses, and mattresses and closets hiding tens of thousands of dollars at any given minute.

Why don't the cops raid these houses? Firstly, they'd need a warrant. To get a warrant you need to do surveillance and collect evidence, and there is no way a cop is getting away with surveying anything in the hood without the little birdies—kids getting paid twenty dollars a day to keep a lookout for cops—sounding off the alarm. Secondly, they'd need to know which houses to hit; the only problem is the drugs and the money are rarely kept in the same place. The only thing worse than raiding a house in South Central is raiding a house in South Central and not coming up with anything. Lastly, the cops would have to give a damn about poor black folk getting drugged out and staying poor black folk. And they don't.

Slowly cruising the street Rick rolls his window down nodding at homies he knows, while the ones who don't recognize him snigger at his rust bucket. Towards the end of the street, he pulls into a driveway and pushes on the horn. When no one comes out of the house Rick beeps again. Frustrated, he's ready to press one more time when Mumbles stumbles out of the front door all skin and bones beneath a loose tee shirt, hugging himself for warmth.

Squinting against the grey sky, 'Yo, Rick, you bring me a bacon and egg muffin?' he says excitedly seeing the white *Wendy's* bag hanging out of the window.

Rolling his eyes, 'No, I did not bring you a bacon and egg biscuit,' Rick says painfully.

'Oh. Some hash browns then?' Mumbles says a little disappointedly.

Stunned, 'What, I look like Santa Clause or something? I got your crack, nigga. Shit,' Rick says shaking the paper bag. 'Here. You got a half-pound already cut up. Oh, and we're dropping the price of an ounce by two hundred.'

Mumbles' eyes go big, 'Two-hundred dollars! Why in the hell you doing that, Rick? You know there ain't no reason for these people to go anywhere else.'

'Because I said so. And when I come back, I better not hear people paying three a piece instead of twenty-eight hundred, ya hear?'

'Yeah, I hear. What about eight-tracks and grams?' Mumbles asks skeptically.

'Nah, keep the street prices the same for those.'

'Okay,' he says with a shiver.

Squinting with concern, 'Lemme see your teeth?' Rick asks.

'Huh?'

'Lemme see your teeth?'

Sticking his fingers in his mouth, Mumbles pulls his cheeks apart.

'Hmm. Stick your tongue out.'

The teeth separate and a big pink tongue lolls out.

'Listen to me, Mumbles, you're meant to be selling this shit not smoking it.'

'I—I ain't, Rick. I swears.'

'Yeah, you swears,' Rick says dubiously. Then, poking his head out of the window, 'Why you standing barefoot on the pavement for? You gonna catch a cold.'

Mumbles gives him a blank look.

'Well, shit, get inside and put some clothes on. The hells wrong with you?' Rick says crunching the car into reverse and leaving Mumbles looking confused.

With all the morning drops made, Rick screeches into the palm-sparse sprawl of Magnolia Square and parks in the driveway of a cream house with no fence. Climbing the front steps, he grabs the morning paper off of the step, tucks it under his arm, and gives the door a bang.

'Yo, it's Ricky. Lemme in.'

A pair of eyes peek through the blind of a window before the door opens.

'Sup, Freeway,' Moses greets him wearing a white tank top, slippers, and an AK47 hanging from his shoulder.

The same metallic smell hangs in the air flushing Rick with another distilled wave of crack fumes.

'*Poo-wee*, I know what I'm smelling and I'm smelling what I like,' he says walking in.

Entering the kitchen to the heat and steam of a four-burner stove cooking four pots of crack, Rick's best friend, Ollie, is at the helm, fork in hand and joint in mouth, stirring the saucepans of white goop with Michelin Star dexterity. On the kitchen island mounds of fluffy white coke peak like snow-capped mountains, while orange cartons of baking powder, tubs filled with yellow ready rock, mixing bowls, zip-lock bags, spoons, and triple-beam scales litter the bench tops making the place look like a grade school science class.

'How you doing, Ollie?' Rick asks.

'Fly, baby. Real fly. Two keys down, one to go.'

'That's my boy.'

'How's Junior going at the new spot?' Ollie mumbles with lips wrapped around a joint.

'He coming along just nicely.'

'Cool.'

Peering into each of the pots, Rick is checking the quality of this new batch of crack.

Holding up a fork, 'I can't believe how much of this shit we cooking now,' Ollie says shaking his head.

'I know it,' Rick says, his gaze fixed on the bubbling yellow-white mixture. 'To think a few months ago we was working our asses off, struggling and hustling to get to fifty-grand and now we turning over fifty grand a week.'

'Fifty? What about when we sold that half-pound for Mr. Fisher and he said his supplier could only sell us a minimum of one kilo upfront,' laughing. 'Shit, they had no idea how broke-ass we were. How in the hell were two young punks gonna come up with forty-gees?'

'Yeah, thankfully Buddy was a cashed-up OG.'

'You mean, thankfully we used to steal cars for him.'

Laughing, 'Yeah, that too. If it wasn't for Buddy buying that first key for us and then hooking us up with Montel and Ramone so we could keep buying bulk, we wouldn't be where we are, that's for sure.'

'I know it.'

Passing Rick the joint for a puff, 'How long you think we gonna be able to do this shit for, Rick?' Ollie wonders. 'I mean, we making huge bucks and I don't want this to end any time soon.'

Raising his eyebrows, 'I dunno,' Rick says holding in a deep breath before finally exhaling. 'Them Nicaraguans saying this is only just getting started. Whatever we can move they can supply, no questions.'

Ollie smirks, 'You trust these cats, Henry and Diego?'

'More than I do the Bloods or the Crips. And maybe even more than Montel and Ramone. Them Nicaraguans ain't gangbangers, they businessmen. Their operation is tight, hell, it has to be if they bringing in this much coke.' After another long puff, 'I don't know how they getting it in but they are and that's all that matters to me. And I know that's all that matters to them too.'

'Word.'

'Hey, speaking of Montel and Ramone, what's going on with them?'

'Man, I don't know.' Looking over his shoulder to the mounds of coke piled on the counter, 'We've got maybe one or two kilos left, tops, and they still ain't gotten in contact with us about buying again. We'll have this all sold by the end of next week, easy.'

Shaking his head, 'The whole point of buying coke with them is to get a good price, but if we out-selling them then maybe it's time we stopped.'

'Hold the phone, homie,' Ollie says seriously. 'Montel and Ramone are made niggas. We can't just cut them off. They're the whole reason we've been able to buy dope from the Nicaraguans on the regular.'

'So, what? We just meant to stop expanding our business because they ain't moving as much as us?'

Ollie makes an uncomfortable face.

'I ain't saying we cut them off, but we are making more than enough now to get the coke by ourselves without having Montel and Ramone in on the transaction.'

'And all I'm saying is tread softly because them there niggas you don't wanna burn.'

'Yeah, and if they can't keep up, that's on them. Look at me, every few days I'm finding someone new to buy our crack. And I'm gonna keep going too.'

'Who you got now?'

'You remember Tommy and Haney from middle school?' Rick says.

'Yeah.'

'Well, they came through my mamma's house yesterday morning asking if I can teach them how to cook.'

'No shit, you gonna get them on board too?'

'Yeah, they good kids. Plus, Tommy is popular as hell since he almost got that baseball scholarship.'

Laughing, 'Damn, Rick, you gonna be starting a cooking school in no time.'

Chuckling, 'But right now I gotta go see some bird named Goldie.'

'Goldie,' Ollie says thinking, 'Friends with Tracy and Monique.'

'Yeah, that's who said I should go see her. Apparently, she's been selling heroin small-time but heard about crack and wants in.'

'She still over on 96th Street in Westmont?'

'That's the address I got.'

'That's a good spot. Her apartment backs onto the *M&M's* there, so people just look like they out waiting to get some soul food.' Then, taking the joint from his mouth, 'Hold up, there's barely a drug game in Westmont though,' Ollie adds curiously.

'That's right, there isn't but that's exactly why I wanna hook her up. Ain't you been listening, Ollie? I want people all over LA selling our dope. If we keep doing what we're doing we're only going to get what we've already got, which is why if Montel and Ramone wanna drag their feet they can, but this nigga's just getting started.'

'Damn, you hungry for this or what?'

'Hungry ain't even close to it.'

Smiling and shaking his head, 'Aiit, how much you taking Goldie?'

Standing over the kitchen island, Rick picks up two small zip-lock bags filled with clumps of yellow chalky rocks, 'I'm gonna take her a couple eight-tracks. These good to go?' he asks holding the dope up.

Nodding, 'Cooked fresh this morning.'

'Cool. And I'm gonna take a couple ounces of un-cut now to show Tommy and Haney how to cook later tonight.'

'Aiit.'

Sticking his hands in his jacket pockets, Rick pulls out three messy wads of crinkled bills held tight with rubber bands, 'Where's the stash at? I got another thirty-gees here to add to it.'

'In the living room. Moses is sitting on it.'

Peering one more time into the pots of bubbling goo, 'Well, you look like you're all set here.'

Crooking a smile with the joint hanging perilously from the corner of his mouth, 'I learned from the best,' Ollie says warmly.

'You need anything while I'm out?'

'Nah, we cool.'

In the living room, Moses is watching *Different Strokes*, while eating a bowl of Frosty Flakes—the bowl resting atop the AK47.

'Hey, Mo. Where the cash at?'

'Under there, man,' he says pointing a milky spoon at a green corduroy armchair.

Beneath a worn seat cushion is a brown grocery bag filled with ten-grand stacks of cash. Rick grabs it, tosses in the extra wads before putting it back and slamming the door on his way out.

VI
THE COLONEL

Under a cloud-laden sky threatening to rain, morning frost coats the dark and emerald-like White House lawn, while his freshly shaven cheeks fight the frigid air and his breath steams in long foggy drafts.

Checking his watch, 'Late,' he whispers to himself.

Standing as if at attention in a thick woolen coat and moleskin gloves, he rocks back on his heels and closes his eyes. A fountain trickling softly behind him entrances the Colonel's thoughts; his mind swirling with briefings and directives and scenarios, each outcome varying in consequence and significance. Strength, honor, and loyalty he reminds himself. And like Vietnam, he can feel the nation, the people, and the President calling on his leadership once again, requesting his unwavering devotion to the American flag and to do what he must for freedom and democracy.

Pulling him from his trance, the soft crunch of gravel underfoot approaches behind him.

'Ahoy, Colonel,' Reagan's National Security Advisor, Robert McFarlane says.

Shaking hands, 'Morning, sir.'

'You wouldn't know it was spring, not today. Christ, it's cold,' the stick-thin man with thin white-blonde hair says rubbing his hands together. 'Why the heck didn't I wear gloves? And why the heck are we meeting out here?' he says looking around frowning.

'Bill said there were too many eyes and ears at Langley for what we needed to discuss,' the Colonel offers.

'Of course, the Director of CIA would say that,' McFarlane says with a roll of his eyes. Then, blowing warmth into his fists, 'How are you finding your new position, Colonel? Straight into the frypan with this whole Nicaraguan revolution thing, isn't it?' he says smirking.

Giving a wry smile, 'I'm afraid we don't often get to pick our battles, not when you're trying to make the world a better place. They pick us,' North says thoughtfully. 'I won't lie, Nicaragua is a sticky situation, but it's no different to the Soviets or the Afghans or Cubans. Just another problem that needs solving.'

'Quite right, Colonel,' McFarlane says with a nod.

The western gate squeaking open makes both men turn to see CIA Director Casey climbing out of a black SUV. Pulling his black woolen coat tight around his body, the squat man marches along the gravel path as thick puffs of cigar smoke trail behind him like a veil.

Looking particularly grumpy already, his sagged colorless face appears whiter than usual and his cloudy eyes are lightly bloodshot.

'Bill,' McFarlane greets. 'It's only eight-thirty and you already look beat.'

'That's because I've been on the phones since three in the morning with the Beirut office,' Casey says gruffly.

'Trouble?'

'Not yet.'

'Anything the NSC needs to be briefed on?' North asks eagerly.

Puffing on his cigar and waving a dismissive hand, 'No, no, nothing the CIA can't handle. Merely, the ongoing repercussions with Iran because we never extradited our buddy, the Shah. Seems that pissed off a lot of people.'

'So, what's that to do with Beirut?' McFarlane asks.

'Hezbollah.'

'Again?' he says outraged.

'Don't be so surprised, Bud. They're an anti-American extremist faction and they're always going to be up to something.'

Frowning, 'And what's something?'

'Our agents are gathering intelligence that there may be more hostage situations on the horizon,' Casey says unimpressed. 'Looks like they're using the civil war in Lebanon as hostile means to build leverage for themselves.'

Worried, 'Does the President need to know?' McFarlane asks.

'No, not yet. But welcome to my world, Bud. Must be nice getting your eight hours every night.'

Ignoring the remark, 'See, I knew we should never have dealt with those damn terrorists. What happened to no negotiations, no concessions? Now that we've set a precedent with them, they think they can get away with it again. And that Khomeini, he's the one supporting Hezbollah I'd like to point out.'

'Thanks for the tip, but we didn't negotiate with Hezbollah, we negotiated with Khomeini, and there's an important difference there,' Casey says firmly. 'And maybe I should point out if the Ayatollah didn't cooperate with delaying the hostage release to make Carter look weak then Ron may never have gotten elected and you may never have landed this job.'

'I'll have to keep that in mind,' McFarlane says sourly.

'Besides, Khomeini accepting our weapons as payment set a precedent of its own too,' Casey says knowingly.

'I just don't trust Khomeini,' McFarlane complains.

'Well, no one does, Bud.'

Shaking his head and sighing, 'Negotiating with terrorists in the Middle East, Jesus Christ,' he says distantly.

Chewing on his cigar, 'So long as the ends justify the means.'

'Is that so? Trust the CIA to see it that way.'

'It's the only way to see it.'

'And where's the end then, Bill?'

'Couldn't tell you. It's an evil world out there, Bud, and we're doing God's work to make it a better place. That's all I need to know. And occasionally that means negotiating with religious fundamentalists and terrorist organizations, which we do far more often than anyone likes to think.'

'Christ, I don't want to know.'

'My point exactly,' Casey says with a smirk. 'That's why we need the White House to keep peddling the Soviet-El Salvador arms pipeline to the papers so we can push our presence further in Central America *and* get on top of this Nicaragua situation.'

'Oh, please, Bill. The Soviet-El Salvador thing is smoke and mirrors and has all but been exposed as Government disinformation already.'

Pursing his lips, 'Yes, but you're missing the point of it, Bud.'

'Which is?'

'First impressions are lasting impressions. It doesn't matter what the facts later come to show, people remember what they first see and hear, and that's up to us. Think about the presidential election debate.'

'What about it?'

'Eighty-million viewers. You can say what you damn well like and eighty million Americans will hear it. Who gives a hoot if reporters write an article a few days later saying Reagan lied or exaggerated, who's going to read it? Two-thousand people, twenty-thousand, two-hundred-thousand? Sure as hell ain't no eighty-million.'

Both McFarlane and North look a little taken aback by the Director's cold casualness with which truth can seemingly be bent at will, or discarded altogether.

'The American people need to hear what we want them to hear, and that isn't always the facts,' Casey continues. 'Now, if disinformation allows us to get more resources into the region, then we can force Nicaragua into a stalemate with its neighbors and put the clamps on this Sandinista uprising; or did you forget there's still a Cold War going on and the last thing we need is more Soviet influence with our Latin American friends?'

Pinching the bridge of his nose, McFarlane breathes a loud sigh.

Sticking his cigar back in his mouth, 'We need you fellas in the Administration to start pulling your weight with Congress. The CIA has been in recovery mode ever since Carter and Turner purged the Agency of all our good men. It's time we start getting ahead of the game again.'

Rubbing his forehead, 'Well, I hate to be the bearer of unfortunate news but it doesn't look like Congress is going to play a part in this Nicaraguan revolution,'

McFarlane says hesitantly. 'The nineteen million you received in January might be just about it.'

Whipping the cigar from his mouth, 'Excuse me?' Casey says.

Raising his eyebrows, 'Word on the floor is they're seeking to cap CIA funding for any purpose that involves the destabilizing of foreign governments.'

Incredulous, 'Are you fucking kidding me, Bud?'

'We can't have another Vietnam,' McFarlane says plainly. 'The American people don't want it.'

'The American people don't want it? What would they rather, Commies storming up the beaches of Florida for chrissake! You're the Deputy National Security Advisor, Bud, *advise* them we need funding to protect our damn country. I just told them in December that covert operations down there are in the interest of national security. Do they even listen to the CIA?'

'Oh, calm down, Bill. The Senators have to answer to the people in their districts and the people are dubious about meddling in another war that isn't ours.'

'Well, of course, the American people don't want that but in order for us to prevent Soviet and Communist threats we have to, by definition, destabilize the foreign governments that want to pursue such endeavors.' Then, looking angrily across the lawn, 'I'm going to have to source some PR firms to doll the public on this,' Casey says frustrated by yet another Congressional setback.

'You could always call Roger Stone,' McFarlane offers.

Frowning, 'That quack? He spins so much bullshit his head is likely to twist off.'

Recalling the phone conversation he had with the Blonde Ghost, North would strongly prefer selling weapons and circumventing the profits over the alternative.

'If nineteen million is all we're getting then our only option here is to continue selling weapons to Iran,' the Colonel says plainly.

McFarlane shifts uncomfortably.

'Don't give me that, Bud,' Casey says with renewed irritation. 'If you can't convince Congress to give us money to support the Contras then where else are we going to get it?'

'Well, Jesus, Bill. The United States is meant to have a weapons embargo with Iran *and* we're publicly supporting the Iraqi invasion.'

'And if we don't supply Iran with weapons to fight the Iraqi's then that opens them up to Soviet support, which needs to be avoided at all costs.'

'That's right,' North adds. 'Seeing as we're secretly sending Khomeini military aid anyway, we can continue to divert those proceeds to the Contras. It's win-win.'

Looking skeptical, 'If it comes to light that we're supplying Iran with weapons we're going to need more than good PR to get us out of that hole.'

'Don't worry, it won't,' the Colonel reassures. 'We're in the process of shifting the supply chain of weapons and transactions through the Israelis.'

'The Israelis? Who's overseeing?' McFarlane inquires.

'Major Richard Secord,' North reveals.

Frowning, 'Secord? Isn't he suspended pending FBI investigation with that whole Ed Wilson EATSCO debacle?'

'He's about to be cleared and reinstated,' North says. 'But between us, he's going to take early retirement and run things privately.'

'Oh, this is getting out of hand.'

'Focus, Bud,' Casey cuts in. 'Iran is still the biggest threat in the Persian Gulf, and as much as we may not like it, or Khomeini, it's in our interest to stay in good stead with the country. Besides, if we're not getting any funding for Nicaragua then we're going to have to source money from somewhere, and lots of it.'

McFarlane shakes his head and sighs.

'Can you at least make sure the President sees the importance of aiding Iran through safe backchannels and diverting profits to the Contras?' Casey stresses.

'That shouldn't be too difficult. The President has already said irrespective of what Congress stipulates, the Contras are to be kept together body and soul. He doesn't want a Communist uprising to happen on his watch any more than you gentlemen do.'

Looking unconvinced, 'Be that as it may, Carter has left a bunch of pacifists in Congress and we've got a shitstorm brewing in Central America if we're not careful. I can feel it,' Casey says bitterly.

Checking his watch, 'All right, I've got a meeting I need to get to. Ollie, we'll speak soon. Bill, a pleasure.'

'As always,' Casey mumbles through his chewed cigar.

Watching McFarlane hurry off, North and Casey stay behind to continue their conversation.

'How can the soon-to-be Advisor to the President be such a pissant?'

'Soon-to-be?' North asks.

'Clark's on his way out. Too much rancor in the inner circle. Anyway, have you found your floater yet because we can't have Felix doing what he's doing down there and then getting on the phones to us every week?'

'I have. Robert Owen from Dan Quayle's office,' North says.

'Ah, Rob. Great choice. A good kid, smart, loyal, and knows which side to be on.'

'Not too young you think concerning what he's going to be exposed to?'

Shaking his head, 'Oh, no, not at all. The kid looks strait-laced, and he is for the most part, but he was in Thailand at the back end of 'Nam and privy to some low-level CIA operations. I know Quayle well too. He and his staff, including Rob, played their part in making sure Carter didn't get re-elected. He'll be fine. Like I said, great choice.'

'Good. I'm meeting with him this afternoon to offer the position formally. For the time being, I'll leave him in Quayle's office but have him fly into Central America once a week or so on foreign policy and diplomacy business until a permanent relocation is made.'

'Very good. I trust your judgment on this, Ollie. If there isn't anything else—'

'Actually, sir, there is. I know we need to support the FDN, and I know we need to sell arms to Iran to do it, but do we need to be cooperating with drug smugglers?'

'I know,' Casey says understandingly. 'Look, the situation is what it is, Ollie. You heard Bud. Congress is going to screw us, hell, they're already screwing us. I'll agree it's not the best scenario getting into bed with goddamn traffickers so we can fund this pathetic excuse for a war but it's a lose-lose situation if we don't. Those wretched drug dealers are getting the stuff into the country as it is no matter how hard the DEA and Customs try and prevent it, so we may as well put the situation to good use and benefit from it.'

North crunches his molars.

'Don't make a mountain out of a molehill here. We've done worse in the past and I'm certain we'll do worse in the future. What's most pressing right now is financial support, without it the FDN is screwed.'

Chewing his lip, North breathes a long sigh.

Putting a hand on the Colonel's shoulder, 'Okay, Ollie, you want the all-clear. Here it is. Dial it up down there. Show em' who's boss and give the reins a good yank. Besides, I've made sure our agents are completely covered during all of this.'

'In what way?' North asks curiously.

'Just yesterday I got the okay from the Department of Justice that CIA agents will not be required to report drug trafficking by assets. If this thing goes sour at any point, so long as we say it's them and not us, we'll be fine,' Casey says with a wink.

Frowning, 'I have to admit, sir, it doesn't fill me with great confidence relying on people that aren't our own in order to give this campaign legs.'

Chuckling, 'Relax, Colonel, we're not going to be in the trenches with them. We're just using them to do the dirty work, and the quicker you do it the quicker it'll all be over. Which reminds me, get in touch with Dewey Clarridge today. He and Felix are putting together the final touches to that secret airbase in Ilopango. With that finally operational, it'll make flying weapons and supplies to the Contras in the jungles that much easier, as well as making them appear more than the collection of ragtag farmers most of them presently are.'

Looking pensively across the frosted lawn, 'You think we can trust that the traffickers are going to support the Contras enough to keep the FDN afloat?' the Colonel wonders.

Taking the cigar from his mouth, 'Aren't you listening, Ollie? We don't have to trust them. We just have to force them,' the Director states plainly. 'Aristides Sanchez seems certain that the FDN's close ties with traffickers will result in a sustainable amount of financial support for the time being. Remember, we're only letting these sonsuvbitches slide through until you and Major Secord can get the *Enterprise* up and running. In the meantime, what's important is we have the right people down there keeping tabs on things. Now, Felix can handle himself, just make sure he's got the support he needs and everything will be fine. In a year or two it'll all be over, Ollie. Don't you fret. You're doing a great job.'

* * *

Later that afternoon in North's office, the intercom on his desk beeps. Pressing on it, 'Yes?'

'Sir, Mr. Owen is here to see you,' the Colonel's secretary, Fawn Hall, says.

'Thank you. Send him in.'

Tentatively opening the door, a tall handsome young man wearing a plain navy suit and maroon tie walks in. With rosy cheeks, round wire-framed glasses, and not a whisker on his chin, Robert Owen looks as gentle as a choirboy.

'Good afternoon, sir.'

'Afternoon, Robert,' North says shaking his hand. 'It's good to see you again. Please, take a seat.'

Sitting opposite one another on matching cream-cushioned cherry-oak settees, North takes a brief moment to admire the kid.

'You know, just this morning I was talking with CIA Director Casey about you and he spoke very highly. Said you were loyal, hardworking, and dedicated.'

'Oh, thank you, sir.'

'How old are you, Robert?'

'Twenty-nine, sir.'

'Boy, to be in my twenties again,' North says warmly. 'You've done a lot for a young man, and being staff assistant to Dan Quayle is a pretty big deal. I've got a feeling he'll be Vice President one day. Are you sure about possibly leaving his office?'

'Well, sir, I've always been more interested in foreign policy. But if I may?'

'Please.'

Edging himself closer, 'What you're trying to do, sir, in Nicaragua, helping the Contras to free their people from the grips of Communism, to be a part of that would mean an awful lot, sir. It really would.'

'Is that so?'

'Absolutely, sir. I'm a proud American, and I believe in democracy, in personal liberties, and in freedom. And if that's what you are trying to secure for those poor Nicaraguans, and for the peace and safety of the American people, well then, tell me where to sign.'

'Just like that?'

'Absolutely, sir.'

'This is a serious transition, Robert. What the Security Council can and does is second only to the CIA.'

'I know, sir.'

'And what you'll be doing, what I'll be asking of you, may not be clear at first, it may not even appear morally right or even patriotic.'

Almost interrupting, 'It's okay, sir. I'm aware that I will be on a need-to-know basis. That there will be things I won't understand or be privy to full briefing. But that's because there is a bigger picture in play, a puzzle being pieced together whom only a select few are allowed to see all the moving parts. I accept that, sir. And I have faith in you.'

North raises his eyebrows.

'I have faith in our agencies and in the President of the United States,' Owen says empathically.

The Colonel squints, thinking for a moment, 'It's not going to be nice meet and greets down there, handshakes over steak dinners and sipping scotch. You're going to see things that may make you question that faith of yours. Just as my tours of 'Nam made me question mine.'

Lowering his head, 'Sir, I know I'm not a military man. I've never served and nor do I want to. And I know that makes me a coward in a sense. But I do want to help, help in ways that play to my strengths and not my weaknesses.'

'And what are your strengths?'

'Information, sir. Knowing where to be and when, who to meet and why.'

'Sounds like you want the job.'

Raising his eyebrows, 'There is nothing I would like more, sir,' Owen says keenly.

Impressed by the young man's eagerness, 'When would you like to start, Robert?'

With a twinkle in his eye, 'As soon as you need me to, sir.'

Smiling, 'Well, let's get down to business then.'

VII
THE MAN IN COSTA RICA

Standing in the shade of a rusty sheet-iron hangar, sweat beading his brow and chest, he watches a Salvadoran Air Force cargo plane come in to land. Swaying slightly against a warm mid-morning breeze, the aircraft descends out of a blue sky and over the rich green jungle that rings Ilopango air base. Felix swats at a bug crawling across his neck. Checking his watch, a thin gold casing and cracked tan leather antique from the '40s, he notices the second hand has stopped ticking. Giving the scratched face a few gentle taps, it starts moving and a wistful smile passes his lips.

Roaring loud and guttural, the twin-propeller C-47 lumbers along the runway taxiing towards the open hangar. Raphael Quintero steps out from the shade waving his arms at the pilot to stop and cut the engines. As the large propellers slow to a quiet spin, Felix walks out and stands beside his aid below the nose of the plane.

The pilot window opens, '*Hola, senores. Buenos dias.*'

'*Buen dia, capitan—?*' Felix replies.

'Aguado,' he says lighting a cigarette. 'Marcos Aguado,' the chubby man with heavily sagged eyes mumbles.

'How much do you bring, *senor* Aguado?' Raphael asks.

Unfastening his belts, '*Solo un poquito, senores.*'

Unlatching a small pilot door in the fuselage, the captain passes a clipboard to Raphael before hopping down onto the tarmac.

Scanning the inventory list he breathes a sigh of frustration, 'Hardly worth the fuel,' he says handing it to Felix.

A small military truck backs up to the rear doors of the cargo plane and half a dozen men in Salvadoran military greens begin unloading the supplies. Marked with *US Humanitarian Aid*, the heavy wooden crates are loaded onto the truck. Climbing onto the side and counting the crates and crosschecking the inventory list, Felix asks a man to open one of the cartons. Shoving a crowbar into its top, the crate reveals a pair of bazookas nestled on a bed of straw.

'At least they're American-made,' he says down to Raphael.

Rifles, machine guns, rocket launchers, grenades, Kevlar vests, knives, boots; weapons and equipment enough for a hundred men, maybe a little more. And yet not near enough. This is what Felix Rodriguez is overseeing, the CIA-controlled military half of Ilopango air base. A discreet pocket of aviation transportation and shipment ten miles from El Salvador's capital, an hour flight to Honduras, an hour-twenty to Costa Rica, and a mere two-and-a-half hours to Miami. Ilopango is also a protected airstrip where small Cessnas arriving out of Peru and Colombia and Costa Rica briefly stop to refuel before departing again, their payloads of white powder disappearing and returning, often within hours, as cold hard cash.

It frustrates Felix, an anti-Castro ex-Cuban who has fought and bled for political and social justice, seeing the unfathomable profits of drugs come and go right before his eyes. Millions of dollars funneling out of the United States and into the hands of criminals and murderers instead of to people and agencies trying to shape a better world. He can't help but be reminded of the failed Bay of Pigs Invasion; how Kennedy withdrew support for those on the beaches and how many died because of it. Now he is here in El Salvador, faced with a similar dilemma; the impossible task of trying to marshal and organize enough supplies to see the Contras equipped to fight a war that won't end in their own bloodshed. And every plane that arrives tells him he does not have enough, while every plane that departs is money going to a cause that is not his own.

'We are lucky,' Felix begins as he and Rafael watch the truck drive off, 'that there are only small skirmishes in the mountains. If a war were to start today, we'd be sending these men off to die.'

'Why can't the American people see that the best way to kill the snake is to cut off its head? Not throw fucking stones at it.'

'Because all the killing that goes on in this world is not on their soil and out of their sight. Chile, Bolivia, Cambodia, Vietnam. War is ugly and the people who are not there will never understand the things that must be done. That is why the people do not approve.'

'Out of sight? They cannot see Cuba? They forget Fidel wanted to drop missiles on their heads? Our beloved country ravaged by Communism. For two decades they try and kill Castro and fail. Now the Sandinista bring Marxist ideology to life in Nicaragua but remain reluctant to stamp it out? *Idiotas.*'

Felix remains pensive.

'They want democracy throughout the world,' Raphael continues, 'but aren't willing to fight to ensure it is achieved. Taking the moral high ground is of no use when your enemy speaks another ideological language,' he says spitting on the tarmac.

'You are not wrong, my dear Chi Chi,' Felix says patting him on the shoulder. 'Remember, I was there for the invasion. I saw our comrades shot, captured, and tortured. In Vietnam too. I know what it takes, but I also know when I am out of position,' he sighs. 'And we are out of position.'

Behind the hangars is a drab bullet-ridden concrete building. The facility, mostly empty, trickles with a handful of Salvadoran military personnel and the odd plain-clothed American military advisor or CIA agent. While in a small messy corner office, Felix watches through dusty Venetian blinds several duffle bags being loaded into the cargo plane before taking off, en route to deliver profits to someone far less deserving and of which, the FDN will no doubt receive a paltry portion.

Beneath a pile of papers, a phone starts ringing. Ignoring it he watches the plane ascend higher into the sky, reflecting on the limitations and frustrations of his posting. Finally wandering over to his desk and slowly taking a seat, he picks up the receiver.

'*Este es, Lasaro.*'

'*Good morning, Lazarus. This is, North.*'

Sitting upright, 'Good morning, Colonel.'

'*How're things?*'

Felix thinks for a moment, 'Problematic, sir.'

'*Go on.*'

'The weapons arriving here are in short supply. I have visited the camps around Danli in Honduras and the men there are marginally equipped at best. But as for the camps in Nicaragua, there is one rifle for every second man. Whoever is delivering those supplies is, well, not delivering, sir.'

'*Chrissake,*' he muffles. '*That's that Barry Seal sonuvabitch. I'll find out what's going on. Anything else?*'

'I have met with Commander Bermudez twice now. Sir, aside from the National Guard and ex-military, the fighters he has are practically peasants. We need more weapons, and they need training.'

After a long sigh, '*I know, Felix. Which is why you're not going to like what I'm about to tell you. After those little bombings you orchestrated in Managua and Leon last month, there's been resistance back home about continued support for this Contra effort. Now, I know we're already struggling but if I'm being honest, it may be about to get worse. A democrat from Massachusetts, Ed Boland, is cooking up an appropriations amendment to stop all funding for us and I'm being told he's likely to get the numbers.*'

'Goddamn it.'

'*I know. And with the Enterprise taking longer than we expected to start dealing with the Israelis, it seems we're in a spot of trouble. That's why I'm giving you the green light to do what needs to be done.*'

'Sir?'

'*The FDN, the traffickers, goddamn Escobar. We know they're moving the powder and as far as we can tell they're moving lots of it but the FDN isn't getting a dime on the dollar. We can't just sit back and watch. Especially not if this Boland Amendment gets passed.*'

'Turning a blind eye is one thing but directly facilitating is certainly another. I didn't realize we were going to involve ourselves so closely, sir?'

'Neither did I. But simply allowing it into our country and hoping the FDN is getting the kickbacks isn't sitting well with me. And certainly not with how ill-equipped the Contra forces are at the minute.'

'What do you want me to do?'

'Go see the FDN leadership in Honduras and Costa Rica, make sure they aren't being taken for a ride by the traffickers, or us for that matter. If the powder is coming in, which it is, then why isn't the directorate getting enough support? Now, if this amendment goes through, we are going to need to control the whole show, if you know what I mean.'

'If I may, sir, it's about time.'

'I'm glad you feel that way, Lazarus.'

'It will take some organizing though, sir.'

'Let me be clear. This is your objective now. We'll transition financial support over from the Enterprise when we can but it's this other business that seems to be the defining factor. We need money more than we need guns. That's why, Felix, I'm giving you the authority to get it in and out any way you can and with whomever you can do it with. Because if this campaign fizzles the next thing we know we're gonna have Commies storming the beaches and Democrats in the White House. And frankly, I just can't have either of those.'

'I understand, sir. Sir, forgive me for asking but is this coming from Director Casey? Do I need to report to Station Chief Clarridge?'

'You have Director Casey's approval to go on this and Dewey Clarridge has already been briefed on what we're green lighting you on. But truth be told, and there's no point in hiding it from you, this recommendation comes from your old pal, the Ghost.'

Felix smirks. Nowhere and everywhere.

'Lazarus, this is a code black operation. There will be no written reports, no sign-offs, no paper trail. You are free to move as you see fit. Am I making myself clear?'

'Crystal, sir.'

'Unless you are meeting senior officials eye-to-eye do not mention this operation or imply any complicit activities whatsoever. Of course, bring Quintero in on this *and whomever else you deem absolutely trustworthy. But if anything goes wrong, we need full deniability.'*

'I understand, sir.'

'All right. In the coming days I'll send you a cable with a list of protected military airbases and private aviation companies we're going to start using. Meet with the FDN, tell them we're taking over, for the good of the Contras. I know you're a good CIA man, Felix, but we're on the brink of losing this and things are going to have to get dirty.'

'Don't worry, sir. I know what it's like to be a rebel, to try and fight a Goliath and lose. I'll get started straight away.'

'Good.'

'Is there anything else, sir?'

After a moment, *'The Ghost said you might have some contacts in Colombia. Contacts that could be of use to us, directly.'*

'Say no more, sir. I'll do what I can.'

'Thank you, Felix. You're a true patriot.'

'Thank you, sir.'

'One more thing. I have sent someone down into the region to be my eyes and ears. He's already made contact with some of the FDN and he'll be in contact with you shortly. His codename is Bumblebee. Moving forward I would like you to communicate through him as much as possible.'

'I look forward to meeting him.'

'Listen, he's a little wet behind the ears, so he's on a need-to-know basis.'

'I see. And he doesn't need to know about this, sir?'

'That's correct.'

'Very good, sir.'

'Good luck, Felix. We're counting on you.'

His mind is ticking over before he's even hung up the receiver. Strewn across his desk are inventory papers, flight logs, supply-chain maps for sea and air, but all he sees now is the groundwork for another, larger operation, one that will tilt the scales in his balance for the first time since being stationed here.

'Chi Chi,' he yells out into the station through his open door.

After a moment, *'Si?'* his aide says poking his head into the office.

'Come, sit down. We have big news from the Colonel. Close the door.'

Quickly taking a seat across from Felix, 'What does he say?' he says leaning forward in the chair.

'He says things in the US may become more difficult for us. Less funding,' Felix says with a dubious raise of an eyebrow.

'Less! We barely have enough for the rebels as it is, let alone trying to support a full army.'

'I know, I know. But listen, the game is changing. All this coca flying in and out of here, getting our protection only to end up in the hands of people who care little for the Contras is at an end.'

'What do you mean?'

Felix smirks, 'The Colonel says that we are to procure the network of the traffickers. They want protection from the US Government, well, now it comes at a heavy price. We are to meet with the FDN leadership as soon as possible and ensure that profits are going directly to us.'

'Well, it's about fucking time.'

Felix chuckles.

'What is the strategy?' asks Raphael.

'The Colonel is securing airstrips and airline companies to transport the coca, while we are to secure its arrival, safekeeping, and departure. He didn't say anything else. He cannot,' he says nodding to himself. 'He has left this in our very capable hands, Chi Chi. We have full reign to make this happen, full authority to do what must be done.'

Smiling, 'When do we begin?'

'Now.'

Opening the top drawer of his desk, Felix retrieves a small black address book and begins flicking through its pages. Picking up the receiver and punching in a long series of numbers, he leans back in the chair and takes a deep breath.

'API Financial Solutions, this is Tiffany.'

'Hello, can I speak with Milian Rodriguez, please?'

'May I ask who is calling?'

'My name is Felix, from Operation Forty. He will know who it is.'

'Certainly. One moment please.'

As he is put on hold rather delightful music plays.

'Ah, Felix. My, my, my. What an unexpected call.'

'Indeed, it is. How are you, old friend?'

'I have my hands full, as I'm sure you can imagine... or not imagine seeing as you are a CIA hotshot in Latin America. But I am well. What country have they got you hatching schemes out of now?'

'Oh, today it's El Salvador, tomorrow it's Honduras, and next week it'll probably be Costa Rica. Listen, Milian, I must speak with you on very serious matters.'

'Am I in some kind of trouble?'

'No, nothing like that. I need your help.'

'Oh.'

'But I must speak with you in person. Are you flying through Central America any time soon? Miami is a stretch for me at the moment.'

'Well, you're in luck. I'll be in Panama in a fortnight. I have to see General Noriega about some business. Are you able to meet me there? Manuel will have me shacked up in a five-star hotel—might be a nice break from the sweatbox I'm sure the Agency has you sitting in.'

Laughing, 'You know me too well. Yes, Panama is not a problem.'

'Good, good. Call my office next week and I should have a schedule for you.'

'Wonderful. Thank you, Milian.'

'No, Thank you, Felix. We are long overdue.'

He hangs up the receiver.

'Who was that?' Raphael asks.

'Ramon Milian Rodriguez.'

Thinking for a moment, 'The money manager for the Medellin Cartel?'

'That's the one. I have known him for many years, since before I was recruited by the US military. He's not just a money manager for Escobar and Ochoa, he owns a big legal accounting practice in Miami and is on the board of several banks and trustees. There are very few people as well connected *and* clean as Milian.'

'What do you want to meet with him for?'

Raising his eyebrows, 'For his help.'

Rafael grins.

'Get in contact with Ferdinand Sanchez and set up a meeting as soon as possible. It's time we showed the FDN how to control a revolution.' Then, walking over to the window, 'It begins now, Chi Chi. A real push to extinguish the Sandinistas and their Socialist regime. And what we achieve here, with the Nicaraguans—if we are lucky—may just deliver the framework for another operation to kill that dog Castro, once and for all.'

'We can only hope.'

'Oh, we can do more than that. Much more.'

VIII
FREEWAY RICKY

Adjacent one another on the corner of 96th and Normandie are two hallmark establishments of the South Central area—*M&M's Soul Food* and the Holy Light Baptist Church—because the only thing that feeds the soul better than Jesus is twice-fried chicken and collard greens.

Rolling up in his pink Chevette, his fingers drumming to the beat of *Super Freak* on brown stuffing worn through the steering wheel, Rick checks out the spot before pulling over.

Opposite *M&M's* is a neat little apartment block with white walls, red rails, and a laneway at the rear. Normandie is a typically busy road, but with soul food in the air this particular junction has a lot of foot traffic, and now Rick understands what Ollie means by this being a good spot to move product.

Rick enters the diner to the jingle of a little bell and goes straight to the counter, 'Yeah, can I get a serve of the shrimp and grits, the chicken wings and waffles, two hamburgers with fries, and lemme see, a large serve of gumbo. Oh, and a couple of large sodas.'

A few minutes later he takes the food back across the street to his car, hides the half-ounce in the paper bag, and climbs the outdoor stairwell of the block. Making his way along the balcony, he can hear music jamming from one of the apartments. Sure enough, it's Goldie's.

He gives the door a kick and a foxy-ass black woman answers with red braids all stacked up on top of her head looking like Queen Nefertiti.

Blushing somewhat, Rick can only manage a smile.

Waiting, 'Well, who the fuck are you? A delivery boy?' Then turning inside the apartment and shouting, 'One of you little biznatches order *M&M's* and couldn't walk your ass over to get it?'

'Yo,' Rick says, 'it's me. Freeway Ricky. Ramone set us up.'

'You're Freeway Ricky?' she says disbelieving.

'Yeah,' he says smiling again.

Almost laughing, 'Well, come in then.' Looking at him from top to toe, his hands full with food and sodas and his big buckteeth grin, Goldie fights back a giggle, 'Nigga, you don't look like no gangbanger.'

'That's because I ain't no gangbanger.'

'But word is you moving coke by the kilo.'

'And who said you have to be a gangbanger to do that?'

A little speechless but smiling, 'What's all this damn food you got?'

'I didn't expect your spot to be so crowded and I didn't have anything to stash your product in. Plus, it's almost lunchtime, so I thought whoever was here might be hungry.'

Laughing again and peeking into the bags, 'What the hell you bring, boy?'

'I got some shrimp and grits, some burgers, some gumbo.'

Two young girls storm into the living area wearing an assortment of spandex, denim jackets, and hoop earrings big enough to put your hand through, 'What's all this hollering about?' one of them says.

'Freeway brought your lucky asses some lunch. Here, put it down. Rick, these are my two little sisters, Ladybug and Charmaine.'

'What kinda name is Freeway?' the younger one asks.

'What kinda name is Ladybug?' Rick says back, smiling.

The girls begin digging through the food when Charmaine pulls out a zip-lock bag full of ready rock, 'I know this ain't on the menu.'

'Oh damn,' Rick says embarrassed reaching for it, 'that ain't for you.'

The girl, fourteen at most, pulls away from him, 'Nigga, I know what coke is. What you think, we in the Palisades?'

The girls start laughing.

'I just never seen so much before,' she says holding the baggie up to the light.

'All right,' Goldie says, 'hand it over. Me and Rick gotta talk business.'

Blush pink walls, pink sofas, and pink fluffy cushions accentuate the lounge room. Goldie might be gangster but her home is the inside of a *Care Bear*. Sitting opposite each other with the bag of coke on the glass coffee table, Rick explains what he's giving her, the pricing structure, and how best to market rock cocaine.

'There's a lot more here than I thought there'd be,' Goldie comments.

'Oh, my bad,' Rick says leaning forward. 'I brought you four eight-tracks, not two. That's half an ounce. The second two is on credit.'

Goldie raises her eyebrows appreciatively.

'That's how I like to do business. Whatever you buy, I'll give you the same on credit.'

'Is that so? That's very giving of you, Freeway.'

'The way I see it, the more product people are moving, the more money they making. I don't wanna be the only one with cash in my pocket, while my homies are struggling. I wanna share it around so we can all get fat.'

Nodding and giving him a sweet smile, 'I like the sound of that.'

They stare at each for a few wordless moments and Rick gets the feeling maybe Goldie wants to hit something other than the coke. But as much as she is a fine piece of woman, he hasn't got the time to be fooling around. Getting attention from women is also something new to Rick. He has always been a little goofy looking, small and scrawny too. Funny, friendly, and with a good heart he's had a lot of female friends but never anything that eventuated into something romantic. Now that business is rolling, he thinks more and more about having a nice girl to come home to, but then again, he doesn't want anything to disrupt the ride either.

Clearing his throat, 'Anyway, I gotta get moving.'

'Oh, you're not gonna stay and eat?'

'Nah. I'll just take a burger for the road. I got a busy day.'

They walk to the door and she steps onto the balcony with him, 'Well, thanks for the hookup, Rick.'

'It ain't no thing. Lemme know when you wanna re-up, aiit.'

'No doubt.' Looking down into the car park, 'Where's your car at?'

'Oh, it's the Vette.'

Searching, 'I don't see no Corvette.'

'Not Corvette. The Chevette, down there,' pointing to his beat-up car on the street.

Laughing, 'Oh, boy. Freeway, you are some piece of work, I tell you.'

Back in the pink rust bucket, east on Century Boulevard, *One Fine Day* on the radio, south on Central Avenue, and right into Nickerson Gardens: Blood territory. Despite making tens of thousands of dollars a week now, Rick drives around in his busted Chevette because he knows not drawing attention is golden. He can have a hundred grand under the passenger seat or five pounds of coke in the trunk and ain't nobody even looking twice in his direction.

As he pulls up to Montel's house, homies across the street sitting out the front of their buildings start blooding him, not realizing who he is. It doesn't matter if he and Montel are in business together, this is gang turf and that counts for more than supplying good drugs to the neighborhood.

In Montel's front yard is a Mercedes 380 with big shiny rims, an Impala with a full chrome grill and moonroof, an Escalade, two BMWs, and a cherry red Acura. There's also music so loud the bass is shaking the front windows.

'So, that's where their money is going,' Rick says shaking his head. 'They spending all their profits.'

Rick presses the buzzer and after a few moments, the gate grinds open. As he walks across the yard, Montel steps onto the porch to greet him.

'Yo yo, Freeway. What up, my nigga?' Montel says revealing a front row of gold teeth.

Shaking hands, 'Nothing much, homie. I was just in the area and thought I'd come past, see what's up.'

Nodding, 'Cool, cool.'

'Sounds like you having a party?' Rick says.

Smirking, 'Party? Nah, this just a day in the life now, homie. Come in.'

Inside, Montel's home looks like something out of a rap video. Nickerson Gardens is straight-up ghetto but boy did he build a palace in a shithole. As they move through the house the floor goes from white tiles to plush carpets, leather sofas in front of a big screen TV with speakers six-feet high blasting music, and homeboys playing pool and girls snorting coke. All the homies are wearing brand new sneakers and sports jackets while shooting dice on the dining table with gold chains hanging from their necks, and the women are all looking fine with big hair, diamonds in their ears, and nails all done looking like they're about to be on a magazine cover.

Rick can't believe his eyes and Montel smiles when he sees his face looking around in amazement.

Passing a large kitchen littered with bottles of Alize, Hennessey, and half-filled glasses, 'You want a drink, homie?' Montel offers.

'Huh? Nah, I'm good.'

Montel walks Rick out onto the back patio where sitting in a bubbling Jacuzzi is Ramone wearing sunglasses and puffing on a cigar with two naked women beside him.

'Yo, Freeway, that you?' he says taking the cigar from his mouth.

'Yeah,' Rick says smiling his buckteeth. 'What up?'

'Pussy's what's up. And my dick,' Ramone says with a cackle as he puts his arms around the two ladies.

Taking a seat at a nearby table, 'So, what's what, Freeway?' Montel asks.

Scratching his arm, 'I was just wondering if you got any coke left? Because me and Ollie about to re-up again.'

Raising his eyebrows, 'That so? Yeah, I think I got like two or three kilos left.'

'That powder or rock?' Rick asks casually.

'Powder.'

'What he asking?' Ramone yells over the sound of the bubbles.

'He asking if we got any coke left,' Montel shouts back, his gold teeth glinting in the sunlight. 'Why, you want some to tie you over?' he asks Rick.

'Nah, nothing like that,' Rick says rubbing his chin. 'It's just, we buying bulk together at the same time but me and Ollie are moving it twice as fast.'

'Say what?' Montel says unimpressed.

Clearing his throat, 'I'm curious is all, don't you wanna make big money?'

Taken aback, 'What do you mean, do I wanna make big money? Of course, I fucking do. Shit, I already am, nigga.'

'What he say?' Ramone yells out again.

'He asking if we wanna make money or not?' Montel says bitterly over his shoulder without taking his eyes from Rick.

Cackling, 'Tell that little nigga, we already making money,' Ramone fires back.

'Don't get me wrong,' Rick says nervously. 'I can see you homies are living it up. It's just—'

'Just what?' Montel's mouth goes tight.

'Listen, we homies, so I'm just gonna shoot straight. When I brought you in with the Nicaraguan connect, I told you Nickerson Gardens can be like a cocaine supermarket, but it looks like you just happy leaving it a corner store.'

Frowning, 'Don't tell me how to run my shit, Ricky.'

Raising his hands, 'I ain't telling you how to run your shit, I'm just trying to figure out why you acting like this is the peak of the business when it's only just the beginning.'

'Nigga, look at us. Look at our setup. We rolling, homie. We're making ten, fifteen grand a week, easy. What do we need to keep hustling for?'

What Montel doesn't realize is Rick is making ten grand a day, *and* they are getting the dope from the same supplier. Right then he realizes he's surpassed Montel and Ramone—two big-time drug dealers—and that he won't need their money to resupply again.

'You know what,' Rick says tactfully, 'I'm sorry. I am telling you how to run your shit and that ain't right.' Taking a look around his crib, the homies and the women, the music, the drugs on tap, 'You got it going on here and I shouldn't question it. My bad, dog.'

What Rick doesn't say is the next time he re-ups from the Nicaraguans and gets a better price per kilo, he won't be passing on the discount to Montel and Ramone. If the homie says he's rolling then why should Rick bust his neck to get better prices for someone who doesn't give a damn about expanding?

Leaving Nickerson Gardens a little annoyed at Montel's inability to see the bigger picture, Rick knows there is an upside here too. He must be doing better than even he thought seeing as he is now passing guys who have been in the drug game a lot longer than he has.

Filling up his rust bucket at the gas station on Imperial Highway, in rolls a burgundy Pontiac Sunbird, the stereo loud and the young homeboys with their caps on backward trying to look fly. They're both wearing a lot of blue, which means they might be Crips members, so Rick keeps his head down watching the ticker on his pump click over.

'Hey,' one of the homies calls.

Rick pretends he doesn't hear.

'Hey, yo,' the voice yells again.

Rick's heart starts to race and he swaps the pump to his left hand so he can reach for the 9mm in his waistband, if he needs to.

'God damn. Yo! Freeway! You deaf or something? It's me, Little Petey.'

Turning around and looking over the sun-bleached roof of his car, he sees his old homeboy Petey with arms stretched out wide and a big smile on his face. Rick feels a wave of relief wash over him. Hanging up the pump and walking over they give each other some love.

'Shit, Petey, I ain't seen you since *Dirty Benny's.*'

'I know, I know.'

Noticing his blue LA Dodgers cap, blue shirt, and blue bandana hanging from his neck, 'Damn, you repping the Crips now?' Rick asks.

With a smug smile, 'Yeah. I'm rolling with the Grape Street Crips over in Watts. Oh, check it,' he says looking back to his car, 'that's my homeboy Benzo Al. Yo, Benzo! This my boy, Freeway Ricky.'

The passenger in the Pontiac gives a nod.

'So, what brings you across the 110?'

'You know, just some business,' Rick says smiling.

Looking at his Pink Chevette and laughing, 'Business must be booming,' Little Pete says jokingly.

'Hey now, looks can be misleading,' Rick defends.

'Speaking of business,' Pete says quietly, 'I'm in the PCP game but man, you hear about this rock cocaine niggas getting their hands on? Shit be spreading, fast.'

Little Pete and Rick go back to his car stealing days. After Rick took over *Dirty Benny's* chop shop when the old man went to prison for grand theft auto, he enlisted a number of his homeboys and cut-up men to sweep the streets between midnight and sunup for cars fitted with thousands of dollars worth of upgrades. The money was okay but the risk was high. After only six months the cops raided the garage and Rick lost everything: the shop, equipment, tools, and that was the end of that. Anyway, Little Pete was one of those homeboys and Rick knows he can trust him now as he did back then.

'Hear about it?' Rick says. 'Nigga, I'm the one delivering it!' he says with his trademark bucktooth grin.

Petey's face is in disbelief, 'You? You the one moving that shit through the hood?'

Thinking about how he left things with Montel, 'Not moving, homie, *supplying*. Check this out,' opening the passenger side door and reaching under the seat, Rick pulls out a brown paper bag with a fat roll of twenty-thousand dollars cash and two ounces of pure coke.

Little Pete has to look twice, 'Homie, you have got to get me put down,' he says seriously.

Laughing, 'Yeah, I got you. When you wanna hook up?'

'Fucking tonight.'

'Tonight? You that mad for it, huh.'

'Mad ain't even the start. How much can you give me?'

'How much you need?'

This is music to Rick's ears. He hears this same hungry tune over and over when people realize he's the one bringing ready rock to the streets.

'Nigga, I'll get Grape Street flowing by this time tomorrow. You get me whatever you think I need and I'll rustle up the homies right now to get you the cash.'

Rick thinks for a moment, if Little Pete is gangbanging then his distribution will hit the ground running. A gang will already have hustlers and dealers, enforcers, stash houses and drug houses. This is big and Rick knows it.

'Normally, I start people out with an eight-track or two,' Rick begins. 'But I know you a straight hustler, so I'm gonna cook you up a quarter pound. How's that sound?'

'Sounds tight. How much is a quarter pound though?' Little Pete asks.

Smiling and trying not to laugh, 'A quarter pound is four ounces and there are eight eight-tracks to an ounce.'

Little Pete nods but Rick can tell he doesn't know what these numbers mean.

'You're gonna get thirty-two tracks okay, and there are three-point-five grams per track.'

'And how much I sell an eight-track for?'

'No, you don't wanna sell an eight-track. You wanna sell grams and hits. Grams are about a hundred to a hundred-and-fifty. And hits are by the point, so try and get twenty bucks a pop, okay.'

'I feel ya.'

Smiling again, 'Don't worry, I'll go over it all tonight when you come pick up.'

'Cool. You still at your mamma's house on Figueroa?'

'Yeah.'

'All right, how much I need to bring you?'

'Three-gees an ounce. Four ounces makes—'

'Twelve thousand! God damn, nigga, you trying to rob me?'

'Hold the phone, man,' Rick says smiling. 'You only need to fix me up for half, the other half is on credit, aiit. Listen, you'll be paying three-seventy-five per eight-track but you should make anywhere from seven-hundred to eleven hundred off each one. So, you're either gonna double or triple your money.'

Little Pete breathes a big sigh.

'Trust me, homie, moving crack is like buttering bread. You and your homies ain't seen the money you about to make.'

Just then a black and white police vehicle pulls into the gas station.

Watching it, 'You cool?' Rick asks softly.

'Yeah my wheels ain't stolen, but I got heat in the glove compartment.'

'That's aiit, don't do nothing to give them a reason to search you.'

'I know.'

The cops pull up to the parking bay but leave the car running. One of the uniforms goes inside, while the driver gets on his radio.

'Looks like he checking your plates, homie,' Rick says.

After a few moments, the cop returns to the car and they drive off, staring at Benzo Al in the Pontiac as they go by.

'Mothafucking pigs,' Little Pete curses.

Smirking, 'Now you see why I drive this hunk of junk,' he says patting the door.

Little Pete can only shake his head and smile.

Later that evening after collecting what Junior finished cooking earlier in the day in Willowbrook, Rick finally gets home to show Tommy and Haney how to cook up. He's known the two since his Brett Heart Junior High days. Neither guy is gangster by any stretch but they are good kids with a lot of street rep. Like Rick, they never had any money and they aren't gang affiliated either, which is what makes them such hard workers; if they didn't earn, they didn't eat. Tommy and Haney started off splitting an eight-track between them, but now that they're doing a couple of ounces a week it's time to teach them how to cook.

'Okay, you see what I'm doing here, you see how I'm getting it all nice and gel-like?' Rick says.

'Uh huh,' Tommy mutters.

'That's what we want. That color, that thickness. See how it's all gooey?' Rick says pulling the fork out of the mixture and letting it droop back down.

'I see,' Haney comments.

In the garage of his mom's house, away from the gangbangers and drug houses of nearby streets, Rick has a neat little setup; a small kitchenette, a couple of sofas, a TV, and his own bathroom. This has always been his spot and everyone who comes here knows not to fuck with it. Sitting underneath the 110 Freeway, the home is as safe as safe gets in South Central, especially considering there is a hundred grand hidden in the walls.

'Okay, now we take it off the heat but we gotta keep stirring. Then we get some ice cubes, throw them in, stir it a little more, and that's it.'

'That's it?' Tommy asks.

'Yeah,' Rick says with a big grin. 'Now we'll let it cool, run some water over it when it's gone hard, and then we have a crack biscuit.'

Tommy looks at Haney and then back to Rick, 'Doesn't look too hard.'

'Yeah, but it ain't easy either,' Rick says. 'It's all in the touch, knowing when you've hit the right consistency. And that takes time.' Getting a fresh pot and another bag of coke, 'Okay, let's cook another ounce.'

An hour later they've successfully cooked up four ounces of ready rock. Yellow, chalky biscuits, clumped and hard. Money. Breaking apart the discs, Rick weighs the shards of rock cocaine on a triple-beam scale and bags up the crack for Tommy and Haney.

'Now,' Rick begins, 'you can't just keep cutting and cutting, okay. The dope will eventually give no high and you'll burn your loyal customers. Not to mention give ready rock a bad name.'

Just then Rick notices the headlights of a car pulling into his driveway. Both Tommy and Haney tense up, thinking it's the cops come to do a raid.

Rick can't help but laugh, 'It's all good, homies. Just my boy come to pick up.'

Going to the door and letting Little Pete in, Rick introduces everyone.

'You don't mind trading wares in front of my boys, right?' Rick asks Pete.

Tommy and Haney are dead quiet. They know a gang member when they see one.

'Hell nah, I don't mind,' Little Pete says cockily. 'The only thing I'll mind is if you step anywhere close to Grape Street, ya hear. That's Crips house, *my* house.'

Saving them from having to answer, 'Nah, these homies from Gramercy Park.'

Staring down at them for a moment, 'We cool then,' Pete says finally.

Reaching into the side pockets of his black *Raiders* jacket, Little Pete pulls out two fat rolls of cash held together by rubber bands.

'Three and three makes six-gees, homie,' he says slapping each stack into Rick's open hands.

Grabbing an orange *Nike* shoebox from the cupboard and handing it to Little Pete, 'Here you go, man. A quarter pound cut and bagged into eight-tracks, aiit.'

'Aiit.'

'Remember, a gram is a hundred bucks, at least. A hit is twenty. And if you wanna unload some eight-tracks as is, you're paying three-seventy-five a piece, so make on it what you will.'

'I feel ya.' After a handshake, 'I'll holla when I'm out.'

'Do that.'

'Good to see you, Freeway.'

'You too, Petey.'

Throwing Tommy and Haney a little shade before easing up, 'Be cool, little homies,' Pete says on his way out.

After bagging up a quarter pound each for Tommy and Haney and sending them on their way, Rick lays down on his bed, exhausted, headachy and a little high, but amazed at how much and how fast he's making money now. Today alone pocketed him about six- or seven grand. And hooking up Little Pete and his Crips connect is a huge move that hasn't even sunk in yet. Shaking his head thinking about Montel and Ramone already reaching their limit, Rick knows this is still only the beginning for him.

IX
CARLOS CABEZAS

A burning orange ignites the horizon, while a purple and blue darkness dotted with stars and a crescent moon dares to linger. It isn't the glory of a spring day he watches but the huge container vessel docked at Pier 80 unloading its plethora of wares under the cover of a retreating night. A light breeze gently tugs his canary-yellow robe as he stands on the apartment balcony on the corner of Texas and Sierra Street. Norwin owns the entire block though only the bottom floor is legitimately tenanted; the rest of the apartments being leased to fine up-standing fake identities who pay their considerable rent and fees always on time.

Stepping through the glass sliding doors are a pair of long legs and a brown skin body barely concealed beneath a white satin nightie, 'What are you doing, *papi?*' Sofia asks sleepily.

'Watching the docks, my love,' he says putting a heavy arm around her.

'And what are the docks doing?'

Smiling modestly, 'Delivering.'

Carlos's apartment, one of a few he lives in, is perched almost at the top of Potrero Hill on the east side of the peninsula, so it sees clear sunrises, sunny days, and the entirety of the Bay. Whenever a shipment comes in, he always stays here so he can watch the freighter unload with his own eyes. Within the next couple of hours, the following will take place: Several *South Beach Removal* trucks (one of Norwin's businesses) will enter the docks and be loaded with crates of designer furniture from Brazil. The trucks will then drive to various warehouses throughout the Bay area where the crates will be unloaded and opened revealing tightly packed blocks of individually wrapped one-kilo bricks of coca. Hundreds of them. Then, several stock-standard vehicles destined for any one of Norwin's car yards will enter the warehouses, collect between ten to fifty kilos of coca, and proceed to drive to a variety of safe houses throughout San Francisco and LA. The drivers will pull into the garages and backyards of these safe houses, turn off the ignition, leave the keys in the ashtray, and walk away.

'Then what happens?' Sofia asks, surprised by the intricacy and detail of the process.

'Then the distributors distribute.'

'And this happens—'

'Once a month.'

'*Increible*.'

Picking up a tiny pair of black binoculars Carlos rests his elbows on the rail and watches intently.

'Are you nervous, *papi*?' asks Sofia.

'I hate this moment. The coca is so close and yet still not in our grasp. And now it sits on American soil.' Taking a deep breath and bringing the binoculars away from his eyes, 'The Coast Guard and DEA heavily monitor the docks too. In San Fran, we can bring in the most in one shipment but it comes with the highest risk.'

'How much is down there?' Sofia wonders, indicating to the docks.

'About three-hundred kilos. Sometimes more.'

'Oh, my,' she says amazed by the volume. 'But Miami is easier?'

'*Si*. Several small shipping companies deliver coca every week to the Nicaraguan network there. Plus, it's protected.'

'Protected, by who?'

'The CIA.'

'Holy shit,' she whispers.

Smirking, 'Some of Norwin's coca is protected too. The stuff we get flown into Texas.'

'But why don't you just fly it all in if the CIA is protecting it?'

'Because the more coca that moves through the CIA the bigger the cut the FDN gets, and there's nothing Norwin hates more than giving away free money.'

'Wait, who is the FDN?'

'It's complicated. Remember how I said there was a revolution in Nicaragua? Well, money from the coca is going back to support it.'

'So, why doesn't Norwin want to help?'

Raising his eyebrows, 'Because he doesn't care what happens to Nicaragua. All he cares about is money. That's why he still wants to get his coca here on freighters, this way there are no payoffs. We fly a little through to keep the FDN happy, but if we can get three-hundred kilos in this way, why change?'

Barely following along with the confusing arrangements, Sofia can only shrug.

Peering through the binoculars again, 'Yes!' Carlos shouts.

'What is it?' Sofia says anxiously.

Pointing and letting her look, 'There, see the trees on the corner by the water, now move to your right just a little, that's the container yard, now just a little more to your right, what do you see?'

'Ah, oh! I see white trucks driving out of the dock!'

Breathing a long sigh of relief, 'That's it, *mami*. Arrived, safe and sound.'

Squealing with delight, Sofia throws her arms around Carlos, 'I'm so proud of you, baby. You're so clever,' she says tracing his jaw with her finger and pinching his chin, pulling him in to kiss her.

After a moment, Carlos moves to go inside.

'Where do you think you're going?' she says grabbing onto his robe.

'To shower. I have to make sure the goods are okay.'

'And what about these goods?' she says edging the spaghetti straps off of her shoulders and letting the nightie fall to the ground.

Raising his arms against the doorframe, Carlos lets his robe fall open revealing his now-awakened cock.

Smirking, 'That's what I thought,' Sofia says before dropping to her knees.

With the sky turning a pale blue and the streets mostly empty, Carlos pulls up to a warehouse only a few blocks away in Dogpatch. As he enters, out drives a grey Buick Regal, a brown Chevy El-Comino, and a navy Lincoln Mercury station wagon.

'You're late,' Norwin greets with a puff of smoke from his fat cigar.

A handful of guys are taking apart crates of furniture and unloading kilo bricks of coca into suitcases while idling with their trunks open are two white Cadillacs and a cherry red Fairmont.

'Sorry, Norwin.' Clearing his throat, 'What has gone out?'

Norwin waves a hand at Julio to come over.

'*Hola, muchacho*. Here,' he says handing Carlos a clipboard.

Looking it over the sheet is divided into three warehouses. Under each warehouse is a list of cars, registrations, which lot they are from, and a code number for where they are going. In the last column, there is a figure written after each of the cars—five, ten, twelve, twenty-two, forty, and so on—whatever the order amount is this month.

'The Buick, Comino, and Mercury just went out,' Julio adds.

'I know,' Carlos says scrutinizing the delivery sheet. 'Any breakage or damage?'

Clearing his throat, 'Yeah, only a bit. Looks like about fifteen or twenty kilos didn't make it on board.'

'And warehouses two and three, everything okay?'

'*Si*, Sebastian just called. So far, so good.'

With a puff of smoke, 'I'll be in my office,' Norwin says walking off. Then, without turning, '*Aqui, Carlos.*'

Julio gives his cousin a sympathetic look.

Entering the upstairs office, Carlos doesn't have to be a fortune-teller to sense Norwin is angry. And to make matters worse, Peña is standing silently over Chinco—one of the newer drivers—who is taped and bound to a wooden chair; his face beaten badly and his eyes swollen shut.

Carlos swallows but doesn't let his face give him away, while Norwin sits heavily in a brown swivel chair before re-igniting his chewed cigar, seemingly ignorant of the brutality seated next to him.

With a cigarette dangling from his lips and a fistful of Chinco's hair, Peña resumes punching and the only sound for what feels like minutes is the thud of hardened knuckles on pulpy, bruised flesh.

'Okay, enough, enough,' Norwin says reluctantly running his fingers through his hair to neaten himself.

Peña rips the duct tape from Chinco's lips and the man winces as two teeth tumble from his mouth. Grabbing a fresh scruff of his hair, Peña yanks down so the bloody face is looking skyward and whispers in his ear, 'Didn't your mother ever tell you not to bite the hand that feeds you.'

Leaning forward, Norwin picks up a letter opener fashioned in the form of an antique Spanish sword and begins picking at the dirt under one of his nails, 'Chinco,' he begins with a sigh. 'How did you not think I wasn't going to find out, eh? You can't steal from me; I own this city.'

The beaten man moans a reply.

Frowning, 'Chinco was skimming?' Carlos asks.

Raising his eyebrows, 'Peña caught him damaging bricks as he was loading them in the trunk. He did it last time, too.'

Chinco begins moaning again, more loudly this time before fumbling for actual words, 'Please... please, *senor* Meneses. I... I wasn't—'

'Shh, shh, shh,' Norwin says dismissively with a face awash with insult. '*Si*, you did, Chinco. You did. Now, be quiet, while I talk to Carlos about more important matters.'

Tossing the letter opener onto the table, Norwin leans back in the swivel chair, his hands cradled on his potbelly and cigar thick and smoking in the corner of his mouth.

After a moment, 'You were late this morning,' the little man mumbles.

Lowering his head, 'I know.'

'Why don't I want you to be late?'

'Because you do not want the coca sitting where you are.'

'That's right. I want it gone, out of the warehouse, away from my office, away from *me*.'

'I know.'

Interrupting through mumbled efforts to form words, 'Please, I didn't...' Chinco mutters.

Slamming his palm on the table with a bang, 'Ah!' Norwin cuts. 'I'm talking, Chinco. Don't make me more upset than I already am.'

Carlos and Peña exchange a glance.

Taking a puff, 'And why were you late?' Norwin resumes.

Carlos doesn't answer right away. He doesn't want to admit he was late because a woman came between him and his work, because he was fucking.

Chinco starts whimpering, quietly at first then louder. Norwin rolls his eyes dramatically before standing abruptly, snatching the Spanish sword letter opener laying in front of him and stabbing Chinco repeatedly in the throat. Thin fountains of blood squirt in all directions, spraying Peña in the face, showering the table, and even sprinkling Carlos's shoes.

Dropping the letter opener on the floor, Norwin looks down at himself aghast.

'Look at my fucking shirt. My new fucking shirt,' he says with dramatic disappointment at his blood-soaked garment.

Leaving Chinco to gargle his last breaths, Peña fetches a hand towel for Norwin. Sitting back down with a squeak and wiping his hands and face clean of blood, Norwin looks long and hard at Carlos.

'How is Sofia?' he asks finally.

'I—She is fine,' Carlos says plainly.

Chuckling, 'It's okay, Carlos. I'm a man with manly needs also. I understand. But don't let anything get in the way of business, *comprenday?*'

'Of course.'

'Good.' Then, after a moment, 'Has Henry called you?'

Frowning, 'No.'

Raising his eyebrows, 'Henry is your man, no?'

Before moving to LA, Carlos was briefly flying marijuana into the US for another drug trafficker named Jorge Morales, and Henry and Diego were one of his distributors. That was until Morales shifted into cocaine trafficking using his small fleet of Cessnas as a drug taxi service out of Opa-Loka, Florida. Unfortunately for Morales, he was selling one of his planes to an undercover DEA Agent and the aircraft he was showing him just so happened to have thirty kilos of cocaine in the back. Needless to say, Morales looked as surprised as the Agent. Evidently, one of Morales's pilots parked the wrong craft in the wrong hangar and now Morales is looking at sixteen years. This aside, once Carlos found himself in California selling Norwin's cocaine, he naturally reached out to Henry and Diego to make moves in LA on his behalf. Henry was always involved with drugs despite coming from a decent family. He could never keep his mouth shut and that's what made him good at making connections, but that's also what got him in trouble. Was Henry Carlos's man? Perhaps. But not if his life or business were at stake.

Swallowing, '*Sí*, he is.'

'Then how is that I'm telling this news?'

'What news?' Carlos says worriedly.

'Diego is in hospital and they're not sure he's going to make it,' Norwin says unemotionally.

'Holy Christ, what happened? Gangbangers?'

Norwin shrugs his shoulders, 'Who knows, who cares. But Danilo says he is going to need a hand, so I need you to go to LA. With Diego dead or dying, that *puta* Henry is the only contact to the blacks and that Freeway kid now.'

'I'll leave today.'

'Good.' Taking a long puff of his chewed cigar, 'Danilo says Henry has started smoking. Says he saw the pipes at his house.'

Raising his eyebrows, 'He's bored, he has no friends in South Central. Aside from the restaurant, Diego does all the leg work down there.'

Leaning forward, 'He wanted the black pussy, Carlos. But Henry is a *puta* and the blacks can smell a *puta*.' Sitting back and cradling his hands again, 'He's unreliable.'

'I know,' Carlos says.

'And you know we cannot have unreliable people in our business.'

'*Sí*.'

'Very good. Go to LA. Do what Danilo needs. And straighten Henry out.'

* * *

Beneath an afternoon sky of orange and purple, a yellow cab pulls up to the Centinela Hospital in Inglewood. As Carlos gets out an ambulance screeches into the emergency bay, likely delivering another statistic of the gunshot, stabbing, or drug overdose variety. Walking the hallways of this magnificently underwhelming cream-brick monstrosity and ignoring distant wails of pain and nurses rushing past with gurneys and crash-carts, Carlos sees Danilo sitting on a chair outside of a recovery room.

'Hola, amigo.'

'Hola,' Danilo says standing and shaking hands.

Peering through a small window, Diego is motionless, white and sickly looking, with tubes coming out of his mouth.

'How is he?' Carlos asks.

'He had surgery this morning. He broke his spine so he'll be paralyzed.'

Carlos winces, 'Terrible. Diego is a good man. Do you know what happened?'

Crossing his legs, 'Well, apparently Diego is quite the ladies' man around here, has a few girlfriends on the go, that sort of thing. Unfortunately, one of those girlfriends also happens to have a boyfriend, a big one. Last night Diego was caught in bed with this woman by the big man who threw him out of the window.'

Looking confused, 'Diego got thrown out of a house window and broke his spine?'

Shaking his head, 'It was a fifth-story apartment. He landed on the roof of a Buick, which broke his fall otherwise he'd probably be dead.'

'Jesus,' Carlos whispers.

'Anyway, thank you for coming down so quickly, Carlos.'

'Of course.'

'Listen, I have my hands full here,' Danilo starts. 'I don't have time for this, and especially not for Henry. He's smoking the crack now. He's loose, paranoid, can't keep appointments.'

Frowning, 'I know, Norwin told me.' Sighing, 'It's my fault. I should have seen this coming when I stopped making trips to LA. What do you want to do?'

'Well, we still need him for the black connect now that Diego is finished, but he needs fixing.'

Nodding, 'I'll take him to Honduras.'

'And kill him?' Danilo asks curiously.

'No. Let him sober up.'

'Oh, *si*, good idea.'

'I have business in Honduras coming up, so I can drop him at Puerto Cortes, put him in a nice resort, give him rum, women, beaches. That'll stop him thinking about smoking.'

'Very good,' Danilo says making a note of it in his black diary. 'Listen, I'm extending our distribution to San Diego, so I can wear the loss to the black connect for the meantime.'

'Are you sure?'

'*Si*. Look at these negroes, they aren't going anywhere. Besides, Diego is only doing ten kilos a month to that Ricky boy. It's good but not that good. I have more pressing matters of concern than trouncing around these black neighborhoods.'

Carlos takes another long look through the window shaking his head in dismay.

'First things first,' Danilo says, 'we need to go see Henry. The idiot thinks this woman's boyfriend is going to come for him next. We need to cool his head down. I've been using his restaurant as a safe house and his home to stash some coca. He's sitting on about twenty kilos and half-a-million dollars, so I need to make sure he doesn't do anything stupid.'

'*No problema.*'

Closing his diary, '*Vamanos.*'

Leaving the hospital, they climb into Danilo's black Cadillac Fleetwood. Poppy, the driver, is an old battle-scarred Nicaraguan of few words and bone-chilling glances. With slick grey hair, thick mustache, a glass eye, and hands that can break arms (and have), he is Danilo's bulletproof vest.

'Poppy, take us to Henry's, *por favor.*'

Despite it being only a short drive to *Fiesta Bar & Grill*, Danilo is eager to talk business.

'Listen, Diego was overseeing the connect in San Diego. Our in there are two Italian brothers, Jerry and Richie Dominelli. They're big real estate investors. Flashy guys with big *cojones* and a lot of fun. I'll need you to go down there and handle things.'

'Handle?'

'Explain to them the misfortune that has befallen our dear Diego and that you will be taking over. This Jerry man is a high roller and he's in touch with very big players down there.'

'Like who?'

With a shrug, 'The mayor Roger Hedgecock and Larry Remer who runs the newspaper; both have a healthy appetite for strippers and whisky. Vincent Miranda is a gay Portuguese hustler and owns a bunch of adult movie theatres, restaurants, and bars. A lovely man, energetic and lively and always smiling. The San Diego elite look squeaky clean from the outside, God-loving and conservative, that sort of thing, but they love nothing more than drinking and smoking cigars at parties with pretty young showgirls sitting on their laps.'

'I see.'

'When are you off to Honduras?'

'Next week, Thursday.'

'Excellent. Plenty of time to go down there and have some fun with the Dominelli's.'

'So, what do you want me to do with them?' Carlos asks curiously.

'For the most part, simply go have a good time. Dinners, parties, shows; that sort of thing.'

Raising an eyebrow, 'You should have sent Julio for this job.'

'If we sent Julio he wouldn't come back,' Danilo says jokingly. 'No, let them see we are favorable businessmen with a very keen interest in San Diego.'

Frowning, 'I didn't realize we were interested in San Diego,' Carlos remarks.

Smiling, 'Norwin is. Well, the real estate that is. San Diego is primed for development and the Dominelli's are hustlers who are going to make it happen. Norwin wants to be a part of that.'

Making an agreeable face, 'Okay, and what's the coca situation down there?'

'Vincent Miranda, the club owner. Now, he's not a supplier but he gets a couple of kilos every week or so.'

'If he's not a dealer then what does he do with the coca?' Carlos asks a little confused.

Raising an eyebrow, 'He hosts a lot of parties. He is a very well-connected and loved man in the Gaslamp District, and he is very generous with a lot of people; performers, adult stars, employees, and of course fellow businessmen in the city. That is how we wound up meeting the Dominelli's.' Then, making his tone very clear, 'But the Dominelli's do not know that we are in the coca business, okay? Only Mr. Miranda does. It is very important that Jerry understands us to be legitimate investors, *comprenday?*'

'Si, no problema.'

Handing Carlos a business card, 'To get Mr. Miranda's coca to San Diego, I have set up a small rental car business. Three locations here in LA and one in San Diego. Whenever we need to make a delivery, we simply fill out a log sheet and drive it down.'

Looking at the card, 'And how is LA going?'

'Very good. We have a dozen business fronts all operating smoothly now, and distribution is steadily increasing.'

After a moment, 'Norwin doesn't seem particularly satisfied.'

Danilo chuckles, 'Is Norwin ever satisfied? No, he wants to be as big in California as the Medellin Cartel is in Colombia. Plus, the FDN makes contact every other week asking for more money.'

Thinking about his meeting with Ferdinand Sanchez next week, 'Norwin is making a lot of money now, you'd think he wouldn't mind supporting the Contras, you know, for the sake of Nicaragua.'

After a moment, 'Yes and no. All of the major traffickers are getting loose CIA protection at the moment, and sure, that has allowed us to increase the amount we can get into the US. But this is a volatile enterprise, Carlos, things could change in the snap of one's fingers. So, why should we jeopardize so much of what we have worked so hard for? All of these businesses, all of this real estate, it needs a steady flow of income for many more years to keep it viable. It's in our interest to prolong our financial obligations to the FDN for as long as possible, or even forever if the Contra revolution fails,' Danilo finishes casually.

A little taken aback, 'And why would it fail?'

'Well, who are the Contras anyway? Aside from the old National Guard, they are mostly peasants and farmers. Sure, Aristides is saying the FDN has US backing and also the CIA's, but Nicaragua has been wrecked socially and economically by the revolution. Why should we support so heavily a cause whose triumph would equate to what exactly?'

'For one, the return of our country from Communists,' Carlos says incredulously. 'Individual freedoms and liberties for proud Nicaraguans that have had them stripped away. Lands and businesses returned to their rightful owners.'

Smiling, 'And how many people were stripped of those civic rights and ownerships under Somoza? And if the FDN really has US backing then whoever takes power from the Sandinistas will just be another American puppet.' Chuckling and patting Carlos's knee, 'Don't take offense, my friend. I know what you are saying but you only have to glance at a history book to see that when a country's government is toppled it takes many years for the ship to right itself. The FDN, the Contras, Washington's war in Nicaragua, it won't achieve its goals overnight. No, more likely it will take years.'

Carlos doesn't reply.

'Don't get me wrong, I too want a fair and democratic system back home, with international trade and foreign investment, with healthcare and education for our children. But the revolution has come at a cost and I am not ignorant to the damage it has caused our beloved country, whatever our hopes may be.'

Arriving at *Fiesta Bar & Grill* the conversation has left a sour and sad taste in Carlos's mouth, while Danilo's curt appraisal of the situation in Nicaragua is hard to argue with. The spirit of the people has been crushed despite the reformations the Sandinistas and their supporters hope to achieve. In war there are only victims; even the winners have all lost something. And what is gained is often not something tangible but a mere idea, and ideas come and go like the wind.

Making their way through the restaurant they find Henry in his office having just snorted a line of coca as white powder lightly coats his left nostril.

Startled, 'Hey! Oh, oh, Danilo, it's you,' he says wiping his nose and sniffing in an attempt to hide the hit. 'And Carlos! Oh man, Carlos, am I happy to see you,' he says standing from his chair and reaching for a hug.

Embracing Henry, he reminds himself the poor man is weak and lonely. 'It is terrible news about Diego,' he says sincerely.

Henry's face tenses, 'I know. He threw him, he threw him right out of the fucking window,' he says grabbing a fistful of his hair.

'*Como estas?*' Carlos asks gripping him by the shoulders.

Sniffing, 'Yeah, yeah, I'm okay. Where have you been? I haven't seen you in like, three or four months, man.'

Henry's eyes are bloodshot and sagged with dark bags.

'I know, I know. I have been busy in Frisco and now,' looking at Danilo and back to Henry, 'now Danilo runs LA, so it is hard for me to get down here.' Looking around at the clutter, 'May we sit?'

'Oh yeah, yeah of course. Where are my manners?'

Quickly brushing food crumbs from one chair and grabbing a stack of papers from the other, Carlos and Danilo take a seat.

'Henry,' Danilo begins, 'you need to calm down, everything is going to be okay.'

Looking serious, 'Is it? How do you know? Diego was banging a gangbanger's girl, man. And she knows all about this shit, all this,' whispering suddenly, 'coca business.'

'Henry, listen, nothing is going to happen to you,' Carlos softens.

Henry's eyes dart across his desk and then to the safe in the wall, 'But, but I've got all this money here, and at home.' Then, whispering again, 'I've got coca at home, lots of it. And she, she's been to the house, man,' he says fearfully.

'That's why I'm here,' Carlos continues, 'I've come to make sure nothing happens to you. Danilo and I are going to take the money and we're going to move the coca from your house too. Okay? You have nothing to worry about.'

Rubbing his temples and breathing a long sigh of relief, 'Good, good. Because, you know, we don't know what that bitch is thinking. She could be telling the gangs about everything or the boyfriend could be coming here right now to hurt me too.'

'He's not coming here,' Danilo says losing patience. 'Diego was smart about how he conducted business.'

Henry's eyes widen, '*Was*. Is Diego dead? Tell me he's not dead, please tell me he's not dead,' he moans while doing the cross repeatedly.

'No, Diego is not dead,' Carlos says soothingly. 'Are you listening to me, Henry? He had surgery this morning and he is going to survive. He may be paralyzed, it's still early days, but he is alive.'

'Oh, Lord. Thank you, thank you, Lord.'

Danilo and Carlos exchange a look.

'Listen,' Carlos continues, 'next week I have to fly to Honduras and I want you to come with me.'

Looking worried, 'Huh? You're not cutting me off, are you? Carlos, please. Don't cut me off, man.'

Leaning forward in the chair, 'No, don't be stupid. You're not being cut off, not at all. We need you very much. You're still one of my guys and you're still our connect into the negro neighborhoods, yes? I just want you to come with me for a week or two, get you out of here,' he says waving a hand at the restaurant. 'You and Diego have been doing a lot of work, a lot of hard work, and now with this shit that's happened, I just want to give you a break from it all. Clear your head, get clean.'

Hanging his head, Henry starts to whimper.

'*Gracias,*' he whispers. '*Gracias, gracias, gracias.*'

'I have to go out of town for a few days but I'll be back next week and then we'll go, okay? Can you hang on a few more days, *muchacho?*'

Rubbing his eyes, '*Si, no problema.*'

Standing up, 'Okay, now open the safe,' Danilo says sternly.

***

A blouse ripping open sends buttons flying revealing a pair of bikini-tanned tits so plump her hands can barely contain them. A happy scream turns into a squeal of laughter as the bare-chested brunette is mounted by a young blonde starlet, the two disappearing beneath sofa cushions and body parts. Popping loudly, a champagne bottle shoots a splurge of foamy white spray across nearby partygoers too drunk to tell the difference between sweat and French bubbles on their skin as backstage of the *Hotel San Diego* bakes beneath a ceiling of squiggly red neon, dawn a few hours off, and the Walnut crew boogying to Prince's *I Wanna Be Your Lover* as alcohol, cigarettes, and cocaine course through their veins.

'You see, look at him. You take the man out of his pompous mayoral position and he's as scandalous and uninhibited as the rest of us,' Vince Miranda says with a laugh.

Sitting at a quiet end of the long oak bar, as far away from the drunken revelry as to have a private conversation, Carlos and Vince perch on round leather stools watching a typical night for these friends and colleagues—and occasional lovers—spiral into a drug and alcohol-fueled orgy. It may appear to be a dingy den of debauchery, smoke-filled and seedy, but the basement bar is also a place of late-night refuge where Vince and the gang let down their hair and surrender themselves to Downtown's frivolous and frolicsome afterhours splendor.

'Roger Hedgecock,' Vince in his tight white suit continues theatrically, 'Mayor of San Diego City, happily married, father of two, nostrils filled with coke, and a hooker on each leg. But, *shh*, don't let him know they're working girls, *that* might be crossing the line.'

'You don't like the man?' Carlos asks.

Squinting, 'Like him—I despise him. Or at least who he pretends to be.'

'Then why is he here?'

With a sad face, 'You have come to San Diego at a difficult time for me, Carlos. All that I have built here is slowly being taken from me. Hedgecock there and the City Council want to clean up the Gaslamp District. My district. George and I put Downtown on the map. Now they're trying to condemn my properties one by one. And why? Because I show adult films in my theatres? Because I bring vibrancy and nightlife and a little *gusto* to this city?' Taking three gulps of his scotch, 'Twenty-six properties I own here. Theatres and hotels and bars, all bought with my own hard-earned money. And what would they be if I hadn't?

Parking lots and strip malls.' Sighing, 'I don't know, I think if I can make that man happy,' he says pointing his cigarette at the mayor, 'maybe I can keep the pricks at bay.' Taking a long drag and raising his eyebrows, 'Then again, maybe I'm denying what's right in front of me.'

'Hey, don't talk like that VM baby,' the barman says refilling their glasses of scotch. 'You're doing a fine-ass job. This city owes you a fucking debt.'

Smiling modestly, 'Thank you, Mr. Whitehead, you're too kind.'

Waiting until he goes back to the other end of the bar, 'That's Dan, my projectionist. He's been with me almost two decades and I love him to pieces.'

'And what about him?' Carlos gestures his drink towards Jerry Dominelli, curious to know more about the man he's here to charm.

'Ah, the Dominelli brothers. Those two are the future of San Diego, apparently,' he says taking another gulp of scotch. 'Look at them. You could cut a swathe through this room. Jerry and his brother Richie in their fine suits and their women wearing clothes from Rodeo Drive. Even at four in the morning, they uphold an air of patronizing class. What for, I say?' he says disregarding.

Carlos gives him an understanding smile.

'Forgive my melancholic state,' Vince says patting him on the knee. 'Perhaps they are the future, the next big real estate guys and I just don't want to admit my time is over. I came from nothing, Carlos. I was just an immigrant like so many others and yet I have millions in my pocket. But my heart and soul are in these walls. You take these properties away from me and you take away what I live for.' After a moment, 'I am a good judge of character, Mr. Cabezas, and those two spell trouble for this city, I can feel it.'

Nodding, 'I understand too well what you are feeling, Mr. Miranda. I have already lost everything I held dear to me back in Managua. It is true what they say,' Carlos says thoughtfully, 'that you don't realize what you have until it's gone. Don't get me wrong, America is a fine country but sometimes I wonder what I am doing here. This business I have gotten myself in, it is not what I intended to be.'

'Well, we always have a choice. So what, you bring cocaine into the country. It liberates people, makes them feel king or queen of the world for a night. People are still free to choose whether to bump it or not. Me, I put sex on the big screen so people realize their dark little fantasies aren't really that dark at all; quite the opposite in fact. We all just want to love and feel loved, you know.' Taking a long drag of his cigarette, 'Of course, life takes us down unwanted paths now and again but the sun is always shining somewhere.'

Raising his eyebrows, 'So too the darkness, then, no?'

Giving Carlos an endearing smile, 'See, look at you. A stranger to me until tonight and now we are talking matters of the heart and life as though we're old pals,' Vince says clinking glasses with his newfound Nicaraguan friend.

They sit quietly watching the fun and fury of a wild night reaching untethered—and unclothed—heights before Vince leans close, 'Listen, I know you are here to maintain amicable relations with the Dominelli's but tread carefully with them, you hear me.'

At that moment Jerry looks over and raises his glass, giving Vince and Carlos a subdued smile.

Returning the gesture, Vince says with a ventriloquist-like grin, 'Yes, cheers, you conniving wop. Enjoy my liquor and my hospitality,' before downing the rest of his scotch.

Vince signals for the barman to come and fill his drink again.

As Whitehead begins pouring the scotch, 'Hey, VM, you know I don't like sticking my nose where it doesn't belong but is everything all right with you and Georgie?'

Feigning a smile, 'Mr. Tate and I are just fine, Mr. Whitehead.' Then, inclining his head, 'But thank you for asking.'

'You got it, VM,' the barman says with a wink before moving off.

Clearing his throat, 'George Tate, he is your—?'

'Business partner, lover, a husband without the legalities,' Vince rattles off looking over at the stout man in a peach floral shirt, his balding blonde head beading with sweat while flirting with a doe-eyed slender kid who appears barely of legal drinking age.

'And the young man?' Carlos asks.

Pursing his lips, 'Oh, just a pup from Beverly Hills who's getting his first real taste of drugs, sex, and rock n' roll,' Vince says offhandedly.

Walking towards them with her arm around a man's waist, 'Vincent, baby,' the woman says with a yawn, 'Tom and I are calling it a night.'

'Just so,' Vince says warmly. 'What time is it?'

Checking his watch, 'Just gone three-am, Vinnie,' the rugged man with thick mustache answers.

'Thank you, Tom. Oh, pardon my rudeness. Donna Martin, Tom Wimbish, allow me to introduce my new friend, Mr. Carlos Cabezas all the way from sunny Nicaragua,' Vince says as though calling someone to the stage.

Smiling, 'Also known as San Francisco,' Carlos says shaking hands.

'And what brings you to San Diego, Mr. Cabezas; business or pleasure?' Tom asks.

Looking at Vince before answering, 'I think a little of both.'

Biting her lip, 'So, we'll be seeing more of you then?' Donna asks flirtatiously.

'I certainly hope so,' Carlos replies coolly.

'Lucky for us,' Donna says with a wink before tugging Wimbish along. 'Good night, Vincent,' she calls from over her shoulder as the two stumble towards the stairwell.

Pushing his scotch away, 'I think it's time I call it a night too, Mr. Cabezas.' Standing from the stool and reaching into his pocket, 'They say you shouldn't get high off your own supply, so here's a taste of my own vice,' Vince says handing Carlos a ball of white powder wrapped in plastic.

Looking it over, Carlos isn't quite sure what it is.

'It's not coke, darling. It's heroin. And the good stuff.'

'Oh. Thank you but I'm afraid I don't do needles,' he says offering it back.

Ignoring him and waving for a couple of girls to come over, 'Good boy. Neither do I. This you can snort but go easy because it's as pure as the stuff you bring over.' Straightening his jacket, 'There isn't a rush like coke but when it hits, you'll feel warm and fuzzy like you never have. And if one of these pretty babes happens to have their mouth around your cock, well, you might just think you've gone to heaven.'

Carlos inspects the bag of heroin as two women, hot and breathless from dancing, arrive at the bar.

'Girls, Carlos here is a very special guest and I want you to show him a good time, okay,' Vince says politely. Then, pinching Carlos's chin gently and smiling, 'Welcome to San Diego.'

* * *

Holding in a burp that he isn't certain might be vomit, Carlos is struggling to deal with a three-day hangover courtesy of Vincent Miranda's unrelenting hospitality made worse by the one-hundred percent jungle humidity and midday sun belting down on him.

'Wow. You look like shit,' Ferdinand says impressed.

'I feel like shit.'

Greasy, unshaven, and with clothes creased and sweat-stained, Carlos can't remember if he's showered anytime in the last couple of days or not.

'What happened to you?'

'Three days in San Diego happened,' Carlos says hoarsely.

'What's in San Diego?'

Peering over the top of his sunglasses, 'Women. Alcohol. Coca.'

Ferdinand raises an eyebrow, 'Maybe I should visit this, San Diego.'

Carlos looks at him blankly before throwing a couple of aspirin into his mouth and washing them down.

Safely easing a burp out, 'Then I had to go back to LA to pick up one of my guys,' Carlos continues. 'Then fly to Teguz, then to Tela, drop him off in Sula before finally flying to Costa fucking Rica,' he says slouching with his head hanging off the back of the chair staring skyward.

Singing its way out of the kitchen in spits and spats is the sizzle of pork frying; the smell carried by a warm midday breeze floating through the little roadside open-air eatery. It's lunchtime and the cookhouse is busy with laborers and farmers and wives briefly escaping the heat and hardships of the day. Liberia is the last large town in northwest Costa Rica, nestled below the jungles and mountains that form the border with Nicaragua. It also happens to be an FDN stronghold not only for Contra camps but also for the safekeeping of coca making its way out of Colombia.

'Well, you better sharpen up real quick,' Ferdinand says casually.

'Why's that?' Carlos asks without changing position.

'Because someone important is meeting us.'

Slowly leaning forward and dragging his sunglasses to the tip of his nose, 'And who the hell is that?'

'I have not met him.'

'Him?'

Shrugging, 'The CIA's man in Costa Rica.'

Carlos's face spasms in disbelief, 'Are you fucking kidding me?'

'Relax, *amigo*.'

'Relax? He's CIA.'

'And we're the FDN.'

'No. *You're* the FDN. I'm a cocaine trafficker living in the US. Jesus Christ.'

'He's on our side. He wants what we want,' Ferdinand insists.

Removing his sunglasses and pinching the bridge of his nose, Carlos can't believe what Ferdinand is telling him. The fucking CIA.

Shaking his head, 'You play politics, I don't,' Carlos says bitterly. 'Once the CIA knows who you are you're finished. Your name gets put down in a file somewhere never to be forgotten. Then, if you don't cooperate with them, one day out of the blue the DEA or the FBI or Customs comes knocking on your door.'

'Hey,' Ferdinand says sternly, 'we don't have a choice here. The FDN is nothing without the US's backing. And the FDN has one intention, to remove the Sandinistas from the seat of power in Managua, do you understand?'

Staring long and hard at the rebel leader, '*Si*. I understand.'

Calming his voice, 'Besides, you signed up for this remember, to help save Nicaragua.'

Signed up? Carlos remembers being put in a compromising position, despite which, he has successfully been redirecting small amounts of Norwin's cocoa to the FDN in Miami. A deadly game that could cost him a hand or an eye should Norwin find out, and yet a feat that singlehandedly appeases Aristides and the Sanchez brothers, the Contras, and even Norwin who sees the dope being flown in as a hedged bet against his other import means, and the CIA who get to see the utility of their secret airbase being used as it intended.

After a moment, 'And what is it that he wants?' Carlos asks.

Standing at the table wearing a Hawaiian shirt and khakis, 'I want to ensure profits go directly to the Contras and don't end up in someone's pocket,' the man says smoothly. Then, removing his mirror aviators, '*Hola*, gentlemen. I am Max Gomez.'

Ferdinand and Carlos exchange a look.

'Now, let me guess,' he says rubbing his chin, 'You are *senor* Sanchez, cousin to Aristides Sanchez of the FDN directorate and brother to Troilo, yes?'

Ferdinand nods.

Then pointing casually towards Carlos, 'Which makes you *senor* Cabezas, formally of the National Guard and now a resident of San Francisco working under the tutelage of Norwin Menses, correct?'

Carlos raises his eyebrows in reply.

Taking a seat at the table, '*Bien.*'

As a waitress passes Felix calls for her, '*Disculpe, senorita*. May we have three beers and a serve of *casado* for myself.'

'*Quieres pescado o chuletas de cerdo?*'

'Oh, the pork chop, of course. And for my friends,' he says inviting Ferdinand to order.

'*Chifrijo, porfa,*' Ferdinand orders.

And then gesturing to Carlos.

Squinting at the menu, '*Ah, gallo pinto,*' Carlos mumbles.

Slapping the table Felix gives a burst of laughter, 'Nursing a hangover are we, Carlos? Too good, too good.'

'*Algo mas?*' the waitress asks.

'That'll be all. *Gracias,*' Gomez says still chuckling.

Carlos shifts uncomfortably waiting for the Agent's amusement to subside.

'Forgive me,' Felix starts, 'perhaps I shouldn't have insinuated your identities so presumptuously. It implies an advantage of knowledge that people find unnerving. I know you but you do not know me.'

Carlos gives Ferdinand a look.

Smiling, Felix continues, 'Look, don't be surprised, or concerned for that matter. It's my job to know whom the FDN is dealing with. I assure you, I am a pleasant man to work with. After all, our goals are the same, are they not?'

'Yes,' Ferdinand says agreeably, 'they are.'

'Good. Now, I know this meeting comes as somewhat of a surprise to you, *senor* Cabezas, and for that, I apologize. You come to Costa Rica on one of your scheduled trips to meet with *senor* Sanchez here, also to meet your suppliers to discuss production and deliveries and so on, and then here I come, arriving barely announced and without prior introduction.'

Appearing with the beers the waitress clinks them down on the table. Freshly popped, a light foam rises in their necks as the bottles drip with condensation. Taking one Felix downs the cold amber liquid almost to finishing, relishing the crisp coolness of the beverage against the sweltering humidity of the jungle air.

Wiping his mouth, 'Now, the question on the end of your tongues should be, what did I mean about ensuring profits go directly to the Contras, correct?' Waiting for Carlos and Ferdinand to nod before continuing, 'We in the CIA are under the impression this is supposedly already happening. However, our intelligence tells us that a considerable amount of cocaine is entering the US and yet what we figure the FDN to be receiving is simply not adding up.' Taking another long draught of his beer, 'It is, for this reason, the CIA, along with the FDN directorate, would like to establish a more secure network of funding for the Contra forces.'

Leaning forward, 'You mean control our supply of coca and take your own cut,' Carlos says cynically. 'In other words, the CIA would like to become cocaine traffickers. Does that sound about right?'

'No, no, no. The CIA will do no such thing and for the record nor does it condone such illegal activity. We're not going to touch the cocaine, we don't even want to see it. What we do want is for you and Norwin Meneses to exclusively use the Ilopango airbase.'

'But we are already going through Ilopango,' Carlos offers coyly.

'Please, don't insult me, *senor* Cabezas. You are flying but a paltry amount in. Thirty to forty kilos a week is well shy of the hundreds we know Norwin Meneses is distributing in California.'

Carlos's eyes flash to Ferdinand, wondering how much of what he agreed to has already been divulged to the CIA man.

'Listen,' Felix says, 'for the protection and allowance of your cocaine into the United States to continue we require your passage of transport to move through Ilopango. As simple as that. There is no need to waste your time continuing with alternate routes, and especially not with the painstaking delivery via sea.'

Ferdinand nods agreeably.

'In Ilopango,' Felix goes on, 'the money will be distributed directly to where it is needed and spent on the most important effects; not furnishing the inside of mansions,' he says with a chuckle.

Leaning back in the chair, 'I see. And do we have a choice in this matter?' Carlos asks.

'No, not really.'

Closing his eyes, he gives a capitulating nod.

The young waitress arrives with their food, steaming and smelling delicious.

'*Ahh, maravilloso,*' Felix bellows shoveling food into his mouth immediately. 'Don't worry, Carlos, this isn't bad news,' he says between mouthfuls. 'You're going to get more cocaine into the US than you ever imagined. The kickbacks handed over at Ilopango will be negated by the substantial increase in volume.'

Looking at Ferdinand, 'Norwin isn't going to like this.'

'Well, I am afraid that is too bad, *senor* Cabezas,' Felix cuts in. 'But if you would like to enlighten me as to an arrangement that better suits the criminality of what you are doing, please go ahead?'

Giving Gomez a dry look, Carlos doesn't offer an answer.

Smirking, 'That's what I thought. Now, it goes without saying that this friendship between the CIA, the FDN, and businessmen such as yourself needs to be kept a very private relationship.'

'I imagine so,' Carlos says with a sigh.

'Ferdinand here will leave you with a list of private airbases you are to use. Additionally, your plane registrations and flight paths will be CIA sanctioned should DEA or Customs question or seize any aircraft.'

'And for what business will these planes be arriving and departing in the US?' Carlos inquires.

'For humanitarian aid and military supplies, of course,' Felix says with a smirk. 'After unloading whatever it is that you will be unloading in the US, you are to resupply with munitions that you will fly back to Ilopango for us.' Stuffing a spoonful of pork and rice into his mouth, 'You scratch our backs, we scratch yours,' Felix says cheerfully.

Carlos nods reluctantly.

Wiping his mouth with a napkin, 'As we understand it, the successful movement of cocaine is not so much about supply and demand but simple logistics,' Felix says thoughtfully. 'The difficulty arises from getting the pilots, the planes, and safe passage from point A to point B. Well, *senor* Cabezas, here it is. Tell your suppliers to ante up. We have a war to fund.'

X

FREEWAY RICKY

Hanging up the receiver with a slam, Rick stares desperately at the phone on the wall.

'Still no answer?' Ollie asks.

Fuming, 'No.'

'What are we gonna do?'

Shaking his head, 'Man, I dunno.'

No word from Henry or Diego in over a month, *Fiesta Bar & Grill* closed down and boarded up, and Mr. Fisher so drugged out he doesn't know what day it is let alone where Henry might be. Since the Nicaraguan connect has been so solid, running out of cocaine isn't something Rick ever thought he'd hear himself say, and here he is, days away from being bone dry.

Sure, other small-time suppliers are floating around South Central, but none Rick knows well enough to do business with on the scale he needs. Plus, their product would be cut to high hell *and* he'd probably pay through the nose for it too.

Running dry, even for a week or two, poses a big problem for Rick. Over the last several months his distribution has gotten so far and wide hustlers and dealers are moving his product that he's never even met or seen before. Guys are coming up all over South Central and all making bank from his coke, whether they know it or not. But it's the very middle layers of this depth of distribution that allow for guys beneath Rick to become rivals at any given time. With their own networks and customers, switching from one supplier to another is of little concern, so long as they are getting coke in. As for Rick, he *is* the supplier, and if his source disappears, there's no replacing it at his level.

Of course, cocaine from Mexico or the east coast still makes its way into LA, nowhere near as good as Rick's but cheaper and for that reason marketable. Not that this ever bothered Rick, realizing early on that product drives the market and so long as he had Henry and Diego he would stay on top. Now, all of a sudden Henry and Diego weren't picking up.

Rick gets on the phone and calls some of his old dealers. The conversations are quick, not just because they aren't the type of thing you should be discussing over the phone but because the prices are way too high or the amount available to purchase would last Rick a day, maybe two.

'Hold up,' Ollie says, 'what about Tony?'

'Tony who?'

'Tony, you know that Nicaraguan cat we met once at Henry's restaurant.'

'Oh, yeah. But we don't have his number. And he wasn't a dealer neither, he was just one of Henry and Diego's buddies.'

'Exactly. He might know where Henry and Diego are,' Ollie says keenly. 'And I know we don't have his number but remember he said he owned a small clothing and manufacturing shop in Montecito Heights.'

'Oh, yeah, he did.'

'Montecito ain't a big neighborhood, homie. Surely, this Tony guy can't be that hard to find. I mean, how many Nicaraguans gonna own a clothing store in Montecito?'

'Damn, Ollie, you right!' Rick says excitedly. 'Let's jet.'

Mid-afternoon they trek across town and descend into the old suburb of colorless buildings populated mostly with Latino and Asian laborers. Sure enough, after asking a few shop owners about the whereabouts of a fat Nicaraguan clothes seller in the area, they find Tony on the corner of Broadway and Workman Street. He remembers them immediately and greets them well.

'Hey, Tony,' Rick says, 'you know where Henry and Diego at? We ain't heard from them in over a month.'

'Oh, you didn't hear?' Tony says with a sad look. 'Diego got thrown out of a window.'

'Out of a window!?' Rick and Ollie say together.

'Yes, yes. Something to do with his girlfriend and her husband, I'm not sure.'

'Oh, shit. Is he okay?' Rick asks.

'Not really. He is in a very bad way, I hear. He's paralyzed and is now in a—how you say—rehabilitation center somewhere.'

'God damn. And you don't know where?'

'I'm afraid not. I didn't know him too well, you understand. I only met him and Henry a few times at the restaurant through some of our mutual friends.'

'And what about Henry?'

Shrugging his shoulders, 'No one's heard from him since Diego went into the hospital.'

Rick and Ollie give each other a disappointed look.

Clearing his throat, 'I assume this is about, you know, business,' he says with a wink.

'Yeah, actually it is,' Rick says.

Whispering, 'You need the *cocaina?*'

'We do. You know somebody?'

'Yes, of course. Fellow Nicaraguans. I think maybe they are getting the same stuff as Henry and Diego. The coca is not my thing but let me make a call for you.'

Rick and Ollie's eyes light up as Tony picks up the phone and begins dialing a number.

Turning away slightly and speaking in whispered Spanish, Tony begins brokering a deal.

Taking the phone from his ear and covering the mouthpiece, 'Okay, my friend says the price is sixty-thousand a kilo. He has three kilos on hand and can deliver tonight.'

Pulling Ollie away from the counter, 'Shit, sixty is top dollar,' Rick says.

'It is. But we don't have anything else. And at least this is probably pure if it's coming from the same source as Henry and Diego.'

'But we don't know that it is.'

'We'll test it first,' Ollie suggests.

Rick thinks for a moment, a look of concern across his face, 'I guess if we've lost Henry and Diego, we gonna need to start somewhere. We need coke for our dealers, that's most important.'

Nodding, 'The price may be high now but we can work it down if they become our regular.'

Rick rubs the back of his neck anxiously, frustrated that things have taken a sudden turn and in the worst possible way. Losing your supplier is spot number two on your worst-case scenario list. Number one is getting busted and being put in jail.

Turning back to the counter, 'Okay. Tell your man we'll buy the three keys he's got,' Rick says.

Putting the phone to his ear, Tony again speaks in soft Spanish.

Hanging up the receiver, 'Done. Come to my home at seven-thirty tonight with the money, and the guy will bring the coca.'

'Damn, Tony!' Ollie says, 'Did you get us out of a jam or what.'

'Yeah, thank you, Tony,' Rick adds. 'We owe you. I won't forget it.'

Counting their lucky stars they drive back home, which is now on 88th and Grand in the pocket neighborhood of Century Palms. Rick moved out of his mamma's garage a couple of months ago. She figured he was in the drug game and didn't like it, but she didn't know how deep until cleaning out a closet in a spare room she discovered a little over a hundred thousand dollars stashed in shoeboxes. Rick also had a hundred-and-fifty-thousand hidden in the garage, another hundred-and-fifty-thousand spread across three or four stash houses, and about sixty- or seventy-thousand out on consignment. Not that anyone would know of course because he still drove his pink Chevette and didn't flash any jeweler. He wasn't sure if telling his mom he had made even more money than what she found was a good idea, so he kept quiet. She gave him a big old Jesus speech about right and wrongs and doing the Lord's work, but he can't forget how poor they were back in Arp, Texas when he was a kid. The town had about eight-hundred people in it, mostly farming folk, and their two-bedroom cracker box house sat on the outskirts where no one visited. Sometimes he went to school, sometimes he didn't. No one cared. Rick and another black kid from down the road would catch rats for fun or play in the vacant building on the lot next to theirs. Then when Rick moved to South Central to live with his aunt and uncle and their five kids, he and his mom had to sleep on the sofa. Then they went on welfare. He remembers going with his mom to fill out a job application in a whites-only restaurant and they had to enter from the back alley because blacks weren't allowed through the front door. When he was six, they lived with Uncle George and his wife Bobbi Jo. His uncle was a mean alcoholic and used to beat Bobbi Jo almost every night. One night when he had the devil in him, he was ready to beat her bloody for something she didn't do. Rick's mom shot and killed Uncle George that night, in self-defense. She still went to jail and Rick realized three things: fuck being poor, fuck not having your own roof over your head, and fuck the Lord for not doing shit about it.

Rick moved around the corner into a big corner-block house on the other side of the 110. It was Ollie's mamma's house but she passed away a few years ago. It's a little worse for wear now; salt damp in some of the walls, bad electrics in one half of the house, a split beam in the roof, that sort of thing, but it's theirs. With five bedrooms, two large living rooms, and a big yard, homies are always over hanging out.

When they get back to the house, they tell Redmon and Lonzo—their personal muscle—what's going down. The plan is to take two cars to Tony's so they can split the coke between them in case the cops pull one of them over on the way back. Fortunately, Tony's house is on the corner of Vermont and Washington, just across the I-10 in what's known as the Salvador Corridor, and just a fifteen-minute drive straight up the 110. They'll be there and back in no time, and with three kilos of dope to give them some breathing room.

After collecting and counting one-hundred and eighty-thousand dollars, Rick calls his homeboys Hermes, Fat Joe, and Chuck over for added protection should the deal go sour, and tells them to pick up two clean cars. Rick isn't expecting anything tricky though seeing as Tony gave his home address, so he and his crew head out for a quick bite of pizza at *Dr Munchies* before the deal goes down.

With the sun close to setting, the sky a bruised purple, and their bellies full of thin-crust pepperoni, it's finally time to head off. Rick and Ollie sit in the back of a grey Buick with Redmon and Lonzo up front, while the other three take a black LeBaron.

'You nervous, homie?' Ollie asks Rick who's gone unusually quiet.

Raising his eyebrows, 'It just hit me we barely know Tony and know nothing about his homeboy with the coke. Now, we driving over to his house with almost two hundred grand,' he says.

'I hear you. But this Nicaraguan cat probably knows Henry and Diego if they all taking pieces from the same pie. One would think they should be as cool as each other.'

'One would think.'

'Besides, Tony wouldn't tell us to come to his home if things weren't straight.'

'I know,' Rick says still unconvinced.

Grinning, 'Besides, look at the size of these motha fuckers,' Ollie says gesturing to Redmon and Lonzo. 'Ain't nothing gonna go down without these big chicken-eating homies breaking bones and letting off the heat.'

Cracking a smile, he knows Ollie is right. They're bringing five guys with them and all homeboys who know how to handle themselves. Plus, this is Tony's home they're meeting at after all. No one brings boys from the hood to their house if they're going to set somebody up.

Next to a car wrecker on the corner of Vermont and Washington runs a tight little avenue. They pull up to a house with windows aglow beneath a terracotta porch, big cacti sticking out of the ground, and a pink tricycle on the lawn. As Rick and Ollie walk to the front door, children talking Spanish and the smell of Latino home cooking carries its way out.

'See,' Ollie winks. 'Nothing to worry about.'

'I hope so,' Rick says tucking a 9mm pistol into his waistband.

Ringing the doorbell, they hear Tony's voice speaking quickly and after a moment the door opens.

'Gentlemen, good evening,' he says warmly. 'Come in, please.'

Rick turns and signals to the two cars parked out front that they're going in. And if you're wondering why Tony is being so accommodating to this little transaction, it's because he stands to make a few thousand dollars on commission.

Ushering them into a small living room near the front door, Tony hurries off to the kitchen and brings back two cold beers.

'Please, a refreshment,' he says a little nervously.

Rick can tell this is Tony's first rodeo. He was like that too in the beginning. The first time he handed over ten grand to Buddy the top few notes were wet from his sweaty palms. Then his first fifty-thousand dollar deal he was so nervous and his mouth so dry he practically mumbled over every word he said. By the time he started dealing directly with Henry and Diego, he was a lot more comfortable handing over that much cash. Then, after purchasing a hundred grand's worth of product every week the edge completely wore off, and seeing so many stacks of cash day in and day out changed what money looked and felt like. That said, even though tonight's deal was only for two hundred grand, it was with someone Rick had never met before and he could feel those old nerves coming back again.

'So,' the Nicaraguan clears his throat, 'that is the money?' he says looking at the brown paper bag under Rick's arm.

'Yeah,' Rick says coolly.

'Oh, very good.'

Ollie and Rick eye the room; family photos cascade the walls in thick wooden frames, two silver Spanish-looking ornamental swords cross each other above a small television set, and an oak buffet draped with a Nicaraguan flag has its shelves lined with vinyl records.

'Smoke?' Tony says offering them a cigarette.

They decline.

The Nicaraguan lights up and takes a long drag before scratching his moist forehead.

Untouched, the cold beers drip and fizz on a glass coffee table; Tony forgetting to put coasters beneath them.

'So, where's your boy at?' asks Ollie.

'Oh, any minute now, any minute,' Tony says reassuringly.

There's a knock at the door and their host jumps up to get it. Some pleasantries are heard before he returns to the living room and introduces the man with the dope.

'Gentlemen, this is Freddy. Freddy, this is *senor* Rick and *senor* Ollie.'

Wearing jeans and a white tee shirt revealing tanned sinewy arms and veins like electrical cords, Freddy is tall and stick thin with long black hair pulled into a knot.

'What up?' Ollie greets.

Nodding, 'Where's the monies?'

'Where's the coke?' Rick shoots back.

Tony is about to speak but refrains.

Looking from Rick to Ollie and then back to Rick again. Freddy holds up a plastic *Safeway* shopping bag with a large mass of powder cocaine wrapped up in the bottom.

No one speaks.

Something isn't right; normally there's some kind of chitchat first to break the ice, lighten the mood like before making love, that kind of thing. When there's no chitchat, it means someone's about to get fucked.

Tony, licking his dry lips, looks back and forth between Rick, Ollie, and the Nicaraguan dealer.

'Please,' he begins sensing the sudden uneasiness, 'just give him the monies, *senor* Rick.'

After a moment Rick gives a nod but doesn't get up off the sofa. Freddy hadn't fully come into the living room, so Rick doesn't want to appear weak going to him.

Looking almost pained, 'Gentlemen,' Tony says to no one in particular.

Eventually, Rick holds up the paper bag for Tony to make the swap.

Shuffling around the coffee table, he takes the money and hands it to Freddy, while firmly taking the coke in his other hand.

Passing Rick the plastic bag, the weight feels good. But as soon as he and Ollie peer into it, they can tell right away it isn't cocaine. Before they even look up Freddy is running out of the house like a man on fire, and Rick and Ollie leap from the sofa giving chase.

Out on the street, Freddy is striding across the lawn like Carl Lewis.

'Yo!' Rick yells to his men, 'Get that motha fucker!'

The Buick and LeBaron are parked out front but they're both on the same side of the street, while Freddy jumps into a waiting car facing the other direction and immediately speeds off.

'Shit!' Ollie shouts. 'That motha fucker's gettin' away!'

Both of the cars struggle to do a u-turn on the narrow avenue and Rick is standing on the sidewalk yelling at them because it's taking so long. After knocking over a mailbox and hitting two parked cars the LeBaron finally screeches off.

'You stay here with, Tony. And call the homies!' Rick tells Ollie before jumping in the Buick and joining the chase.

Redmon is barely on Chuck in the LeBaron, and Chuck is barely on whatever car Freddy is in. Sixty down Washington, Seventy on Vermont, now eighty down West Adams Boulevard. This is bad. Rick and his closest men in cars packed with heat running red lights, swerving through traffic, chasing after almost two hundred grand. North through University Park, beneath the 110, right fucking past California Highway Patrol of all things, and poof, Freddy's gone, disappearing somewhere in Downtown.

'God damn it, you stupid motha fuckers!' Rick hits the back of the headrests of Redmon and Lonzo in front.

Looking worriedly in the rear-view mirror, 'What the hell happened?' asks Lonzo.

'That snake motha fucker sold us god damn cake mix, that's what the hell happened!'

Redmon and Lonzo exchange a look before pulling over down a side street and waiting for the other car to join them.

'You stupid stupid fucking motha fuckers. How in the hell you let this happen, huh? Tell me motha fuckers because I'm dying to know!' Rick yells furiously.

None of the homeboys dares to open their mouths. Instead, they all look at one other playing the blame game with their faces.

Rick's eyes are set to bulging. With his mouth open and wobbling, 'What, ain't no one know how y'all let this shit happen? Cat got all your motha fucking tongues? Someone speak up, so help me God,' he says seething.

Redmon starts nervously, 'We, we didn't see anyone else in the car, Rick. The guy who drove up was the one who got out and went inside. There, there must have been someone else hiding in the front who crept in the driver's seat.'

'And, and we didn't realize it was still running, Rick,' adds Lonzo.

'Didn't you think to go check? What the fuck I paying you for?'

'Man, he was in there for like five minutes, Rick,' Redmon says cautiously. 'We thought shit was gonna take a lot longer.'

Shaking his head, 'Yeah, well you thought wrong, nigga. Y'all thought wrong!'

Everyone is quiet again and Rick slumps into the seat seething, not believing he's just lost a hundred and eighty-thousand cash.

'God damn it!' he says slapping the leather upholstery. 'Take me back to Tony's place.'

A few minutes later they arrive at Menlo Avenue and on the front lawn silhouetted by a porch light the fat Nicaraguan is being beaten like an oversized piñata.

'Why you do us like that, Tony?' Ollie is yelling in his face. 'Why you do us like that!'

Moses and Jamal are taking turns knocking Tony's teeth out with their fists sounding like they're smacking cold meat as they pound into his soft pudgy face.

He's not even resisting. Moses holds Tony's head up by the scruff of his hair, while Jamal punches. Then they swap over and the beating continues.

When Rick gets out, they let Tony go. Slumping headfirst into the grass he doesn't have the strength or consciousness to put out a hand to break the fall.

'Did you get Freddy?' asks Ollie desperately.

'Hell no we didn't get Freddy. That motha fucker long gone.' Standing over the barely conscious Nicaraguan, 'You hear that, Tony. Your boy done run away with my money!'

Tony moans.

His wife and children can be heard screaming and crying somewhere in the house.

'Don't worry,' Ollie says, 'I told her if she calls the cops, we gonna put a bullet through her head.'

Kneeling down in the grass, 'Tony? Wake up, Tony,' Rick says.

Moaning, he tilts his head in Rick's direction but both of his eyes are fat and closed over.

'You know where Freddy lives, Tony?' Rick asks.

'P-please... don't kill me, *senor* Rick.' Coughing up blood, 'I-I didn't know... I—'

Rick squeezes his bloody and swollen face by the cheeks, making his mouth pucker up and ooze blood, 'You know his address, Tony? His address?'

'*Si,*' he squeaks.

'How far?'

'N-not far. Picfair Village.'

Letting go of his face and standing, 'All right, get him in the car. Let's go.'

Picfair is just west of Mid City, less than a ten-minute drive from where they are. No one speaks the whole trip over. Tony is the only one who makes a little noise, whimpering quietly sandwiched between Rick and Ollie in the back. When they get to the small two-bedroom house there are no lights on and no car in the driveway. Rick and Ollie stay in the Buick with the Nicaraguan, while Redmon and Lonzo case the house. To their surprise, the front door is unlocked and they go in. After a couple of anxious minutes, they come back out.

'Ain't no one here no more, man,' Lonzo says back at the window of the car.

'What you mean?' Ollie asks.

'Fridge is full of food, cupboards too, but ain't hardly anything left in the bedroom. Closets and dressers been emptied real quick. Draws half open, only a few bits of clothing lying around. That motha fucker checked out.'

'Please, *senor* Rick, I didn't know.'

Ollie slaps him, 'Shut the fuck up, fat boy.'

He starts whimpering again.

Frowning, Rick knows Tony had nothing to do with the dirty deal. Besides not being in the drug game himself, he'd never have held the meeting at his own house with his wife and kids there. He got duped, just like Rick. But it's his own fault at the end of the day, Rick realizes. He reached out to cats he didn't know, set up a deal with someone he'd never met, and handed over a bag of cash like he was passing gravy for a Thanks Giving turkey.

'What are we gonna do with this double-crossing motha fucker?' Redmon asks. Pulling the slide back on his 9mm with a *chink* that makes Tony shudder, 'We can take him inside this here house and empty his brains out in the bathroom. Then at least this Freddy bitch will have the police snooping after him.'

'Yeah, I like that,' Lonzo says nodding.

Tony starts to cry.

Ollie slaps him again, 'You hear that, fat boy. You fucked us and now you about to be dead.'

Redmon opens the door to pull Tony out but the Nicaraguan grabs hold of the front seat and starts screaming for his life.

'Hold on!' Rick shouts. 'Hold the fuck on!'

Pulling Tony back down into the seat, Rick gathers his thoughts. 'This ain't on him. This on us.'

'What?' Lonzo says shocked.

'It's on me. It's on Ollie. And it's definitely on you two motha fuckers,' he says eyes wide and accusing at Redmon and Lonzo standing outside of the car.

'So, this punk ass bitch gonna get off scot-free?' Lonzo says.

Tony's face is smeared with blood, his nose bent out of shape, eyes purple and fat, and he's missing three of his front teeth.

'He look like he got outta this without a scratch?' Rick says to them.

Ollie's face realizes what Rick is saying, but Redmon and Lonzo shake their heads.

'Get in the car,' Rick says. 'Let's get the fuck outta here before the cops come.'

Back on Menlo Avenue as Rick walks Tony to his door, the fat Nicaraguan begs for forgiveness.

'I'll sell my shop and give you the money, *senor* Rick. I'll, I'll sell my car, my furniture, my clothes and pay you back,' he says, tears squeezing out of slits where his eyes should be.

'Forget about it, Tony. You don't owe me anything.'

Whimpering, 'I'm so sorry, *senor* Rick.'

With the rage now out of him Rick starts to feel bad for the man. His face is beaten to a pulp and his wife likely thinking she just lost her husband.

'I'm the one who should be sorry. Go inside to your family.'

Bowing his head and praying with his hands, 'Thank you, *senor*. Thank you, thank you, thank you.'

The drive back to 88th and Grand feels like it takes forever. The mood is somber and the car devoid of conversation. Back at the house, Ollie and Rick sit in the living room shocked and angry at what has just transpired.

'Man, when I got up this morning, I thought things couldn't get worse,' Ollie says. 'Now twelve hours later, we still don't have any product and we lost two hundred thousand in the process.'

Laying on the sofa with his head looking skyward, 'A hundred and eighty,' Rick says distantly.

Frowning, 'What?' Ollie says.

'We didn't lose two hundred, we lost one-eighty.'

Ollie gives Rick a curious look.

'Don't count what you haven't made, and don't count what you ain't lost.' Then, sitting up and looking at Ollie, 'You and me started this game with three-hundred dollars, you remember?'

Raising his eyebrows, 'Yeah, I remember.'

'Imagine what twenty-gees would have been to us back then, Ollie. Yeah, we lost a hundred and eighty tonight, but we still got over four hundred thou on hand. We'll get back on track, homie. But right now, I got to lay the fuck down before I kill somebody.'

The next morning Rick wakes to the phone on his bedside ringing.

'Yo?' he says hoarsely.

'Rise and shine, Freeway.'

'Who this?'

'Buddy, homie. And today's your lucky day.'

Well, Rick thinks, anything short of going to jail has got to be better than what happened last night, so the bar is set pretty low.

Buddy explains that one of his boys, a major coke dealer from Jacksonville, Florida, named Chinese Dave, just got out of prison and has some serious cocaine connections out of Miami. Evidently, Buddy disclosed roughly how much product Rick was moving, which didn't sit well but it was done now, and that this Chinese Dave can definitely hook him up with big weight from the east coast. Buddy also says the coke is coming from some high-up Central Americans. Despite being burned last night by a sly Nicaraguan, Rick knows that if Buddy is saying this hookup is legit, then it is. He doesn't need any more persuading and heads straight over to his house to meet this Chinese Dave cat.

It's ten in the morning and Buddy twists open a bottle of *Olde English* malt liquor and pours himself and Rick a glass. He lives in Pacific Palisades, a flashy neighborhood next to Santa Monica and Rick can see the ocean from the window. He didn't think homies would ever live this far from the hood, then looking at the forty-ounce in Buddy's hand he realizes a nigga from the street can stray wherever he likes but he'll always have the hood in him. Still, it is the nicest house Rick has ever stepped foot in, even nicer than Montel's.

'So,' Buddy says, 'what's good, Rick? I ain't seen you in a while. Business must be booming if you out of product.'

Rick has to tread softly, the only reason he and Ollie were able to buy coke from Henry in the beginning was because Buddy was generous enough to bankroll their first few kilos. But Buddy sold pure powder to high-roller homies, while Rick cooked crack and in a matter of a couple of months sold three times as much as what Buddy was. That's when Buddy suggested Rick hook up with Montel so they could start buying ten kilos at a time and get a better price. Fortunately, Buddy was cool about Rick no longer needing him to get the coke, but Rick always felt funny about making more money than those who helped him get his start.

'Yeah, business is aiit. I'm still trying to come up though, you know.'

Laughing, 'I don't know who you trying to fool, Freeway; everyone else or just yourself.'

'What's that supposed to mean?'

'Every hustler worth a damn in South Central knows you moving a couple keys a week, and yet you drive nothing but beat-up cars and look like you on damn welfare.'

Flashing his bucktooth grin, 'Yeah, well, business comes first for me.'

Sipping his beer Rick stares towards the ocean, remembering when he and his cousins would ride for an hour on their bikes to Playa Del Rey in the summer.

Sometimes they'd go to Venice Beach too and watch ballers shoot hoops and hustle. Rick loved watching them smack-talk each other and make money from nothing but their game. He hasn't been back to the beach in years though, and coming to Buddy's place and seeing the water makes him realize this is what he's working so hard for, to have something like this, a flashy home filled with nice things. And close to the beach too, yeah, he likes the sound of that.

Ding-ding-dong.

Putting his drink down, 'That'll be Chinese Dave,' Buddy says going to the door.

Returning to the living area Buddy is accompanied by a crazy-looking guy; hair wet and permed, skin blacker than ink, and wearing so much gold bling Rick has to squint every time the homie shifts around.

After a quick introduction, they get down to business.

'So, how much you in for?' Dave asks.

'Depends on the price?'

Buddy is an original gangster and Rick knows he can trust him, which means he can trust Chinese Dave. He's also desperate for product so he can't risk pussyfooting around.

'Forty-thousand a kilo. Just under thirteen hundred an ounce.'

Rick's poker face is strong but Buddy's eyes light up. These prices are unheard of to anyone not dealing in heavy pounds and kilos. To put it in perspective, the wholesale street price for an ounce is anywhere from two-and-a-half to three-thousand dollars. This is less than half that, and uncut if Dave is telling it true.

'Aiit,' Rick nods, thinking. 'I should be able to rustle up six-hundred-thousand, so put me down for fifteen kilos.'

'Nice,' Chinese Dave says. 'I'll be in for five. Need to get my own business rolling again.'

Nodding, 'So, what's the plan?' Rick asks.

'Simple,' Dave says coolly. 'We fly us and the cash to Pensacola. The airport there is smaller with less security. From there we get a rental car and drive to Miami. It's a long drive but safe because we'll have Florida plates. When we get into town, I'll buzz my connect and he'll tell me where the drop is. We take the cash, check the product is good, and if it is then we finalize. Bang bang and the deal's done.'

Rubbing his chin, 'And how we getting the coke from Miami to LA?' asks Rick.

Shrugging, 'The only way; drive it back.'

Rick's eyes bulge with disbelief, 'We driving from Miami to LA with twenty keys of coke in the back?'

Giving him a dirty look, 'Would you rather we fly, homie?' Dave says.

Rick hadn't considered how Chinese Dave got his coke from the east coast to the west coast, but he was hoping it was something better than this.

'Damn, how you normally get your keys back here?' Rick wonders.

'I ain't normally buy up so much weight at once. Anyway, you need to chill the fuck out, looking this gift horse in the mouth and shit.'

'Who you calling a gift horse?' Rick says getting up from the sofa.

Standing as well, 'Me, nigga!' Dave shouts.

Rick doesn't understand what the hell Chinese Dave is saying.

'Aiit, aiit!' Buddy says calming everyone down. 'Cool all your jets, homies. I ain't tolerating no bickering in my house, you feel me?' he says eyeballing both men.

After a moment, 'Good,' he says. 'Now, Dave, I'm assuming that's the only way you can get that much product back to LA?'

'Not just the only way, but the safest,' he says knowingly.

Turning to Rick, 'Well, that settles it. That's how the deal's done, Freeway. Are you in or are you out?'

Pursing his lips, he's not happy but he also has no other choice, 'Yeah, I'm in,' Rick says sourly.

Finally, they shake hands; Chinese Dave's wrist gold-laden, and Rick's bone thin and skin-cracked.

* * *

Two days later at Terminal 3, Gate 34, the placard reading *Delta Airlines* flight D771 LAX to Pensacola, Rick and Chinese Dave shake hands once again.

With Rick is Ollie and Lonzo, while Dave has brought his man, Nevel, who Rick is a little dubious of for reasons he can't quite pick other than the man's appearance: droopy eyes, a weak chin, and always looking around nervously. Rick was hoping Dave would dress down a little seeing as they are smuggling almost a million dollars in cash across state lines but oh no, here he is looking as though he just got off stage at the Grammy's with his hair permed and flashing jewelry like Prince.

'You all set, homeboy?' Dave asks.

'Yeah.'

Leaning close, 'Got all your paper, I hope. There ain't no layby when we get to Miami.'

Rick smirks, 'Nah, we ready to shop.'

With six-hundred-thousand dollars stashed in luggage, stuffed in carry-on bags, and taped to their bodies; Rick doesn't show it but he's nervous as hell, not just for leaving LA with almost every dollar he has, but for flying with it. For a year and a half, he's been grinding day in and day out to make this money and he's crossing his fingers and toes that this deal comes off.

Despite his nerves, the flight goes smoothly; the *Delta* jet sailing across the mid-west, dropping low over Alabama before touching down in Pensacola. With their baggage collected without a hitch, they hit the road in a rented four-door Lincoln Continental, Miami-bound. The drive is long and uneventful, passing nothing but green farmland for hours until they head south on the turnpike and cross the endless sea of bogs and marshes of central Florida. Everyone takes a turn napping except for Chinese Dave who periodically snorts coke hidden inside a large diamond-crusted Jesus cross hanging from his neck. Rick wants to tell him to cool it with all the blow but knows this is his setup so lets him be.

Lonzo's at the wheel when they enter the first beachside city. None of the guys except Chinese Dave have been to Florida before, so they drop the windows and soak in the tropical air.

'It's kinda like LA, ain't it?' Ollie reflects.

'You only saying that because of all the damn palm trees,' Lonzo jokes.

'No, it ain't,' Ollie says. 'Just a whole lot flatter though, and ain't no smog like back home, that's for sure.'

Cruising through West Palm Beach, Lake Worth, Pompano Beach, and Fort Lauderdale they're all staring out of the window like kids on their first road trip and hollering at each other every time they see something fancy. Only Rick is quiet, smiling his big grin as warm air rushes through his mop of dreadlocks, happy seeing places new and different from the ghettos of South Central.

'Hey!' Ollie yells, 'Check it, they got a Hollywood here, too!' Laughing, 'See, I told y'all this place is just like LA.'

At long last, they descend into Miami, the city gleaming under a mid-afternoon sun, green palms swaying in a soft breeze, and a thick smell of cigar smoke and brassy Latin music filling the air of East Little Havana. This is Nicaraguan territory and Chinese Dave has booked the *Tower Hotel* for them right across the street from Domino Park where old Cuban men with grey hair, yellow teeth, and potbellies play dominos and argue about Cold War politics.

After checking in Dave makes a call and says the deal will go down tomorrow morning, so they all head out to scope the scene. Riding around town with the stereo bumping, they drive across the bay and hit Miami Beach for some fun. They check out where *Scarface* was filmed, and walk along Ocean Drive with its magical backdrop of pastel-colored hotels before stopping at *Big Kahuna Burger* for burgers and sodas.

As the sun disappears behind building tops to the west, South Beach lights up. Bars embellished with neon glow in bright blues and pinks, while disco music funks its way out of every club along the strip: *Bee Gees, Diana Ross, Earth Wind & Fire, Rick James*, you name it. Scantily clad women, fags, and hustlers in floral shirts and fedoras litter the street, while white guys so tanned they look Latino and Latinos wearing clothes so expensive they look white. With alcohol, drugs, and sex on the tip of everyone's tongue, the little island roars into party mode.

Rick, Ollie, and Lonzo stay out for only a couple more drinks. Suddenly feeling out of place in unfamiliar surroundings—especially with what they're here for—makes them decide to call it a night. Still, they had a blast and roll back to Little Havana with the windows down hollering at cute girls and blasting the stereo.

After a long day of traveling all the guys settle in for the night, readying themselves to be sharp for tomorrow's deal. What happened with Tony only a few nights ago is still fresh in Rick's mind. Almost more concerning than that major fuck up is the fact they aren't strapped for this deal either, and this makes Rick more than worried. He and Dave have an argument about not having any guns when they get back to the hotel and it's Nevel that comes between them. Another reason not to trust him, Rick thinks afterward.

The next morning they're all up early but no one is saying much. Nerves. Everybody is feeling it; you get dressed, put on your shoes, and brush your teeth, all on autopilot. Watch some news on a small television set without taking in a word the newsreaders are saying. You find yourself staring at wallpaper or curtain fabric or a couple of birds on the telephone pole through the window with a face that says you haven't slept a wink but your mind is going a million miles an hour, thinking about how the deal is going to go down, what the room will look like, how many guys there'll be, how strapped, whether they're going to slide across a suitcase filled with the most perfect coke you've ever seen or whether you're going to be handcuffed to a shower rod, while some Nicaraguan who can't speak English drives a chainsaw into your chest.

Piling into the Continental, the sun a ball of fire on the horizon of a picture-perfect day, they drive to a little powder blue apartment building a few blocks away. Ollie, Nevel, and Lonzo stay in the car, while Rick and Dave walk to a second-story room with a suitcase worth just shy of a million dollars.

When they get to the door, they're both still before Rick asks, 'Hey, what's this cat's name we meeting?'

'Octavio Cesar. Why?'

'Dunno. Just thought I should know his name is all.'

The homeboys both take a deep breath before Chinese Dave gives the door a gentle knock.

'*Pasale,*' a voice calls from inside.

Turning the brass doorknob worn down to brushed steel where a million hands have gripped before, they enter a dark room veiled in cigar smoke and close the door behind them.

Five minutes later they walk out, the deal done.

It's fast and clean and Rick can't believe how easy. And just like that they have themselves twenty kilos of uncut cocaine straight from the jungles of South America.

Back in the car they drive straight to the *Tower Hotel* to get their things and get the fuck out of Miami.

'One guy?' Lonzo says in disbelief. 'These cats leave one guy sitting on twenty keys of coke to make a deal.'

'Yeah, I can't believe it either,' Rick says still feeling the rush.

Chinese Dave is looking out of the window but Rick can see a smug little smile creasing his lips. He earned serious respect from Rick for the way he handled himself. As soon as they walked in Rick could tell straight away, he was a veteran of transacting big weight. And despite his appearance, Rick admired Dave's cool demeanor and confidence, a side of him Rick couldn't see before, blinded by glittering rings and a dripping perm.

With the score complete and twenty-kilos of cocaine sitting in the trunk, they still have to get it back to California. Rick makes a call to Redmon and Moses in LA; the plan for them is to drive a motorhome and meet the rest of the guys in Dallas. With them on their way, Rick, Ollie, Lonzo, Nevel, and Chinese Dave head to Georgia in the Continental and start the long journey home.

Rolling into a crappy *Motel 6* just outside of Atlanta after nine-and-a-half hours of driving, they order pizza and watch television on a twenty-five cents-per-hour set. In the morning Rick and Chinese Dave go car shopping; with another twelve-hour drive to Texas to go, they need something more comfortable than the Continental, plus they need to ditch the rental with Florida plates. Dave picks out a Toyota van and splits the ticket price with Rick who wasn't expecting to buy a car straight off the lot on this trip, and despite having over a million dollars worth of coke on him, he's down to the last few hundred dollars he brought. Still, with every passing hour, he knows he's that much closer to being back in LA, and that makes him very happy.

Traveling in the van makes life more comfortable for everybody, who all take turns driving, sleeping, or playing DJ on the radio. They stop for lunch at a barbeque diner called *The Little Dooey* in Starkville, Mississippi famous for its smoked meats and homemade hot sauces; the men relish the opportunity to gorge themselves on perfectly slow-cooked rib-eye opposed to junk food takeout which is just what they need to prepare themselves for the eight-hour leg to Dallas.

Arriving late at night they stay at another *Motel 6* in Fort Worth, a half-hour out of the city. Taking the last rooms available they're one bed short, so Rick takes the sofa while letting Lonzo and Ollie sleep in the singles. Despite Rick's recent claim to sudden wealth, it hasn't shaken him from his meager roots, and sleeping on a sofa for a night brings a smile to his lips, reminding him of how far he's come.

The next morning at seven-am, the entire *Motel 6* building is awoken by a loud air horn from the parking lot. Jumping from the sofa, Rick rushes to the window and pulls the blind back to find Redmon stepping out of a large brown motorhome with orange racing strips running up the center and shiny chrome hubcaps.

Opening the door, 'Shit, nigga, the fuck you think you doing?' Rick yells in a hushed angry voice.

'What?' Moses says from the driver's window. 'You don't like your limo, homie?'

'Hey, shut the fuck up down there!' a voice shouts from the second floor.

'Yeah, some of us still sleeping, assholes!' someone else yells through a window.

With a smile on his face, Redmon walks up to Rick and gives him a big hug, 'Fuck these crackers, Freeway. Let's get your ass back to LA where you belong.'

Twenty minutes later, Rick, Ollie, and Lonzo load up the RV, while Chinese Dave and Nevel jump in the Toyota. Hitting the road like a negro version of *National Lampoon's Vacation*, they cross almost fifteen-hundred miles of grace land with twenty kilos of pure Colombian coke, which, once cut and cooked into ready rock, will turn Rick's six-hundred-thousand into two-million dollars; and that is a business model well-worth the risk.

XI
THE MAN IN COSTA RICA

'*Disculpe, senorita,*' Felix calls to the waitress. 'Two more beers, *por favor.*'

He and Ferdinand watch Carlos climb into a cab and disappear down the dusty road.

'Don't worry, he'll come around,' Ferdinand offers.

Frowning pensively, 'We may seem to want the same thing but our agendas are different nonetheless. *Senor* Cabezas serves Norwin Meneses, first and foremost. And Norwin Meneses only cares about one thing, cocaine. The FDN on the other hand only cares about fighting the war. And what lies in the middle? Money.'

Nodding, '*Si*, it does.'

Turning to Ferdinand, 'Do I need to be worried about him?'

After a moment, 'Have you seen where the coca is made, Agent Gomez? The farms in the jungles?'

'No, I have not,' Felix says a little reluctantly.

Smirking, 'If what you say is true, that the traffickers can really use this airbase in Ilopango for safe passage into the US, then you have little to be worried about.'

'Is that so?'

Smirking, 'You have no idea how much coca they're making. Tons, every day. That is why the night the FDN was formed Norwin Meneses was there, sitting

151

amongst some of the most powerful and patriotic Nicaraguans alive today. Meneses was also there so Aristides Sanchez could ask him for financial support.' Chuckling, 'That was a year-and-a-half ago and only now you *Americanos* finally realize coca is the commodity that will save Nicaragua.'

Arriving with the beers the waitress clinks them down on the table.

Watching the white bubbles fizz and pop, 'And this is why *senor* Cabezas will come around, you say?' Felix asks thoughtfully.

'*Si*. You are opening floodgates, Agent Gomez, floodgates that will change the tides of history. But look, they are businessmen, not a charity. Your demands will at first seem an imposition, but if all that coca in the jungles finds its way over to the United States, rest assured Norwin Meneses will sing a different tune.'

Sighing, 'Norwin Meneses doesn't care about Nicaragua, but I can make him care.'

Curious, 'What's that supposed to mean?'

Raising his eyebrows, 'Imposition or not, he and *senor* Cabezas are drug traffickers,' Felix says firmly. 'And if they don't cooperate, I can make life very difficult for them.' After a long draught of beer, 'Anyway, I've also come here to let you know that myself and another agent are going to be more hands-on with the FDN down here. The CIA has had enough sitting around.'

'Oh?'

Swatting a bug on his arm, 'The FDN needs help and that's what I'm here to ensure,' Felix says matter-of-factly. 'My superiors are eager for the FDN to rid Nicaragua of the Sandinistas at all costs, and that's exactly what I plan to do.'

'Well, Aristides will be most happy to hear that,' Ferdinand says warmly.

Checking his antique watch, the second-hand ticking, '*Bien*, I have a plane to catch.' Standing from the table, 'Oh, you'll be hearing from the new agent very soon.'

'What's his name?'

'Bumblebee.'

Frowning, '*Abejorro?*'

Shrugging, 'Because he always knows where to find the honey. *Hasta luego, senor Sanchez.*'

* * *

Gently stirring an icy *mojito*, warm sea air drifts across the rooftop pool of the *Simon Bolivar Hotel* in downtown Panama City. The crystal blue Bay twinkling in the distance framed by tall buildings and the lush green *Cinta Costera* hugging the coastline before disappearing into the cobble-stoned *Viejo District* to the south.

'Well, I'm glad to hear things have been so favorable for you, my dear Felix,' Milian says licking the end of an ivory stirring stick. 'If the *Americanos* know one thing, it is to reward those who show them loyalty.'

Felix smiles and nods before sipping his beer.

A prestigious accommodation, the *Simon Bolivar Hotel* is occupied by foreign politicians and dignitaries, businessmen and millionaires visiting the city less so for work than they are for pleasure. The pool area buzzing with girlfriends and mistresses lazing beneath a blue summer sky, bikini-clad and sun-kissed, while their potbellied and cigar-smoking men gather in small chuckling clusters or doze in a Jacuzzi.

'But enough pleasantries,' Milian says after a salt-crusted sip of his cocktail, 'you have come to talk about serious matters, so please, go ahead.'

Sitting beneath an umbrella at a secluded table overlooking the city, Milian sits back in his fine linens and awaits Felix's proposition.

'Well, as you would know there is a war going on in Nicaragua.'

Raising his eyebrows, 'A war? I know of a revolution, but that has been and gone,' Milian says coyly.

Clearing his throat, 'Yes, I suppose you are right,' Felix corrects. 'The CIA *wants* a war. We want to remove the Sandinistas from power.'

Shrugging, 'But of course, they are Communists.'

'Indeed. *The Fuerza Democratica Nicaraguense* is leading counter-revolutionary forces throughout the region to hopefully within the next year or two lay siege on Managua.'

'*Si*, I know of the FDN.'

'Good. What you might not know is the CIA, in the interest of our own national security, is funding the FDN and helping to arm and train these troops.'

Smirking, 'Ah, the *Americanos*, always sticking their noses where they don't belong.'

Felix continues, 'The problem is Congress does not support these military actions. They do not support the destabilizing of foreign governments.'

'Naturally, they do not want another Vietnam,' Milian says sipping his drink.

'That is correct, but the situation in Nicaragua is dire. The fledgling forces are scattered throughout the jungles and are low in supplies, in equipment, in weapons. They need to be brought together, at any cost.' After a brief pause, 'And so I have been authorized to seek financial support for this operation through other means.'

Smiling, 'I see.'

'So, as the account manager for the Medellin Cartel, I was hoping we could come to an arrangement that sees both our interests benefitted.'

Rubbing his chin thoughtfully, 'Who has approved such actions? Surely, not the CIA.'

'No. Someone else.'

Waiting, 'And who is that?'

After a moment, 'The NSC. A very small arm of the Presidential Office that has a lot of power.'

Raising his eyebrows, 'Okay. And what is this mutually beneficial arrangement?'

Taking a deep breath, 'I am requesting a financial contribution from the Medellin Cartel for use by the Contras. In return, I can guarantee safe pipelines for cocaine to enter the United States.'

'How much money are we talking?'

'Twenty-million dollars delivered on a per-need basis.'

Milian's eyes flicker as he crunches numbers in his head, 'And these pipelines, will they be pipelines you control?'

Felix shifts in his chair, 'I have airbases and airstrips you are welcome to use, or I can ensure your existing supply routes receive complete protection.'

'How?'

'Simple. I flag your people and companies as CIA assets assisting with the Contra effort. If DEA or Customs detain anyone or any vehicle, they call a number and we tell them you are working undercover as part of a top-level operation.'

Nodding, 'You know, every country from Bolivia all the way up to Mexico receives payoffs from Medellin coca. Government officials and agencies, armies, police, customs, storage yards, shipping companies, everyone. But the CIA, they are something else,' Milian says thoughtfully.

'I have been approved to move as I see necessary,' Felix continues. 'There is no one to answer to on this, not for you anyway. This would be a completely private agreement between you and I. And Milian, I need this, I need this bad.'

Taking a few gulps of his *mojito* before crunching on a cube of ice, 'I am here in Panama on business with Manuel Noriega. Now, Manuel gets away with what he does because the *Americanos* need him so badly. But one day they will pull the rug from beneath him, of that even I know.'

'What are you saying?'

Stirring his cocktail, 'You are playing with fire, Felix, and I'm trying to ascertain whether that means I am too.'

Felix sips on his beer but tastes nothing, and despite his mouth being parched the amber liquid fails to refresh it. His dry tongue feels thick and clumsy, and the only flavor on it is the distaste of forcing himself to do something he wishes he did not have to. Something that one day he may come to regret. Milian is a friend and compatriot, a Cuban exile from the '60s who fought and fled the same oppressions Felix did. Now they find themselves staring at one another from opposing sides of the law, only this is politics and in politics all laws are breakable if the cause is just.

'Without money, we cannot do anything to oppose the Sandinistas,' Felix says. 'And if Communist ideology spreads throughout Central America, that spells bad news for the likes of Escobar and Ochoa, does it not?'

Stirring his drink, 'All men can be bought,' Milian says thoughtfully. Then, smirking, 'Even CIA men, it seems.'

Felix swallows hard.

Laughing and reaching across the table patting Felix's hand, 'It's okay, my friend. Of course, I will help you. I am certain my employers will relish the opportunity to receive assistance with our international operations.'

On the table are a notepad and a diary. Taking a pen, Milian begins writing, 'We'll begin with these two. *Frigorificos de Punta Arenas* is a Costa Rican seafood company that ships to Miami weekly.'

'Who runs it?' Felix asks.

'A Cuban by the name of Luis Hernandez.' Still writing, 'This is the other company I would like to see have additional protection. A private cargo airline company that goes by the name SETCO. Now, there are three co-owners, one of whom you surely already know of.'

Felix raises an eyebrow.

'Juan Matta Ballesteros.'

Wincing, 'Jesus Christ. One of the biggest drug dealers in Central America,' Felix says sourly.

'I know, I know. Don't worry, he rarely leaves Honduras and when he does, he only goes as far as Mexico.'

Shaking his head, 'And the other owners of this SETCO?'

'Frank Moss, an American pilot. He's the North American point of contact, but I believe the DEA has a file on him already.'

'For what?'

'What else? For trafficking coca.'

Closing his eyes and squeezing the bridge of his nose, Felix is starting to question the cost of getting into bed with the Medellin Cartel. But no, these are desperate times and when a man is starving, he must take food from whoever offers it if it means he gets to fight another day.

'Come on, my dear Felix. You know this is how the world works. The drug business is worth billions and it stimulates economies in ways you cannot even imagine,' Milian implores.

Frowning, 'It also kills people and corrupts governments.'

'*Si*, it does. Just like *Marlborough* and *Coca-Cola*.'

Felix looks at him blankly.

Chuckling, 'The third owner is Mario Calero. Ring any bells?'

'No,' Felix says with a little uncertainty.

'What about his older brother, Adolfo Calero?'

'Of the FDN?'

'That's the one.'

'And what does his brother do, this Mario?' Felix inquires.

Smiling, 'Everything Adolfo cannot.' Putting the pen down, 'Adolfo has always been in the political limelight, rubbing shoulders with Colonel Bermudez, Aristides Sanchez, the Somoza elite, and whoever else. But because of that he has always had to play a straight bat. I see Adolfo now and again at dinner parties and political functions in Miami, and I can tell you he knows what goes on in the jungles. But Mario is a clever, clever man and has his fingers in all the pies.'

Leaning forward, 'How so?'

'Just being good friends with Juan Matta should suggest enough. He's ex-Nicaraguan Air Force so he knows how to fly. He's been a middleman for coca and marijuana in Central America for years and has contacts and holdings throughout the Caribbean.'

'How has he stayed off the radar?' Felix wonders.

'As I said, a clever man. He partners up with the right people and does as little of the heavy lifting as he can. Anyway,' Milian says sliding the notepad across the table, 'get started with these two companies. When can I inform my people of your assurances?'

'Give me a few days.'

'*Bueno.*'

'Milian,' Felix says hesitatingly, 'I may need some funding right away.'

Smiling, 'Of course. Leave me with the address of this airbase of yours and I'll ensure a down payment is sent immediately.'

'Thank you, my friend.'

'Say no more, Felix.' Raising his *mojito*, 'To Cuba.'

1983

XII
CARLOS CABEZAS

A cold sea breeze blows up the rugged cliffs ruffling his thick brown hair. Waves crash against the rocky shore of Thornton State Beach in southern San Francisco, while the wind howls its late-winter chill. In the pitch dark of a moonless night, the sky indistinguishable from the black ocean, a red signal light flashes meekly atop a cargo ship. Sitting a half-mile out from shore the enormous freighter *Ciudad de Cuta* awaits dawn before entering the Bay and completing its thirty-two-day voyage from Port Tumaco, Colombia.

From the dirt car park of the *Mar Vista Stables* perched on the ridge, Carlos leans his elbows on the roof of a burgundy Cortina and peers through small binoculars, following the foamy wakes of three inflatable dinghies as they approach the starboard side of the ship.

'Are they there yet, *papi?*'

Without removing his gaze, 'Almost,' he says softly to Sofia sitting in the car.

Over the last few months, the hauls of coca have been collected out here at the mouth of the Bay. Still reluctant to fully cooperate with the FDN and CIA, and seeing as the coca has been arriving by the ton-load without hitch, Norwin continues to exploit the protection the drug traffickers are receiving despite the strongarming by that Agent in Costa Rica. They need to beg, not threaten me, Norwin told Carlos after what happened. And seeing as the Contra effort in Nicaragua is achieving next to nothing, perhaps Danilo is right in holding off committing so generously to the cause. That said, a prudish and skeptical man, Norwin was weary of continuing to unload at the docks and so now, Carlos organizes his men to meet the freighters at sea where duffle bags full of cocaine are thrown overboard.

Against the hull of the ship, white flashlights wave back and forth signaling to the deckhands to drop the bags.

'Here we go,' Carlos says quietly.

Black shapes move around rising and falling where the water bangs against the hull. The duffle bags are tied to buoys so they don't sink and are easily fished out. A few moments later the flashlights click off and the little inflatable boats pull away, heading back to shore.

Taking the binoculars from his eyes Carlos breathes a sigh of relief.

Then, the unmistakable sound of a helicopter chopping through the air. Carlos turns to see it cutting less than a hundred feet in the air, while in the water black Coast Guard speedboats rush towards the dinghies. Sirens blaring and lights flashing across the water they come from both directions along the coastline. Hovering directly above the dinghies the helicopter shoots its bright spotlight down on his men.

'This is the DEA. Cut your engines. You are now under arrest,' the speaker booms.

In shock, 'Holy fucking Christ,' Carlos whispers.

'Carlos!' Sofia shouts. 'The cops!'

Looking south along the ridge to where the vans are parked at the Presbyterian Church, he can see the swirling flashes of red and blue coming down the road long before he hears the sirens.

'Carlos! We have to get out of here!'

Banging the roof of the car, 'God damn it!'

Climbing in, Carlos starts the engine but doesn't turn on the headlights. Panicked and breathing fast, Sofia watches out of the rear window for any other cop cars. Driving down the dirt service road with no lights on, Carlos pulls onto Skyline Boulevard and hammers it toward the city.

'Fuck!' Carlos yells punching the steering wheel. 'Fuck, fuck, fuck!'

'Holy shit, Carlos,' Sofia whispers, almost in tears. 'What the hell was that?'

'That was a fucking bust,' he says through gritted teeth.

'But, but I thought you said you had protection?'

'I thought we did too. I have to call Norwin,' Carlos says planting his foot on the gas and thundering down the freeway.

Pulling over at a gas station in Sunset, Carlos rushes to a pay phone.

'The DEA got us,' Carlos says before Norwin even says hello. 'They got the fucking coca.'

Emotionless, *'I know.'*

'What? You know?'

'Si. Aristides Sanchez just called me, not five minutes ago.'

Rubbing his forehead, 'Aristides Sanchez, in Honduras? I don't understand.'

'You are safe?'

'*Si*. I always go separate to the vans, you know that.'

After a moment, *'Come here, now.'*

Nodding, 'Okay. Wait—I need to call Julio. And Sebastian. Tell them to make sure they have nothing on them or at their houses.'

'Don't bother, it's too late. Julio's already been arrested.'

'What?'

'Him. Sebastian. They raided two of the warehouses as well.'

'Fuck. Which two?'

'The empty ones.'

'Thank Christ.'

'Fuck Christ, that was four-million dollars' worth of coca!'

Carlos pulls the phone away from his ear.

'Just get here. Now.'

'Of course.'

Getting back in the car, Carlos is confused and still in shock.

Grabbing his arm, 'What did he say? What's going on, Carlos?' Sofia asks.

Staring at the steering wheel, Carlos tries piecing together the fragments of information, 'We were tipped off,' he says distantly.

'By who?'

Turning to her, 'I don't know. But head of the FDN in Honduras knew it was going to happen. He tried to warn Norwin.'

After dropping Sofia at his Potrero Hill apartment, Carlos arrives at *Cesar's Auto Shop* on the corner of 26th and Van Ness. Inside the dark apartment, Norwin sits at the dining table beneath a glowing light, a half-drunk bottle of scotch in his hand and a chewed cigar smoldering in his mouth.

Walking to the table Carlos's heart is racing but quickly realizes Norwin's mood is sedate. There's also a .357 revolver sitting off to the side, unnerving him even more.

'Please, sit,' Norwin says pouring two glasses of scotch and spilling some.

Gulping his shot down, 'Aristides Sanchez said it was this Gomez guy. That the tip-off was a favor, and a warning,' Norwin says dubiously. 'He can either protect us or punish us for going around the CIA.'

Shaking his head, 'So, it was him? He tipped off the DEA?' Carlos asks.

'No, the tip-off was from someone here in San Fran, but Gomez said he could have stopped the raid, if he wanted to.'

'So, he still let it happen?' Carlos says incredulously.

Seething, 'Just because we're not going through their fucking channels in, in, where is that fucking place?'

'Ilopango.'

'Ilofuckingpango,' Norwin says darkly. Then, chewing his cigar for a moment, 'The fucking FDN is fucking my business!' he says slamming the table and making their glasses jump.

Carlos doesn't speak. He's seen this before; this bottled rage and it usually ends with someone dead. Swigging his scotch, he hopes it's not him.

'Who is this Gomez guy, anyway?' Norwin asks.

Shrugging, 'He's just the man in Costa Rica.'

'Well, the man in Costa Rica just lost me five-hundred kilos of coca.'

Carlos nods before finishing his drink, 'And six of my best guys.'

Refilling their glasses, 'How much money do they want from me? Every month I give them tens of thousands and this is how they repay me? This is an outrage,' Norwin says painfully.

'It's Reagan,' Carlos offers. 'And the CIA down there. They want another Somoza to lead the country only the US government won't let them spend any money to make it happen. So, now they squeeze it from any means they can.'

Norwin's eyes are bloodshot and glassy. He doesn't respond.

Clearing his throat, 'So, what did Aristides say to you?'

Raising his bushy eyebrows dramatically, 'He calls and the first thing he says is, I'm sorry, there was nothing I could do. Says someone tipped off the DEA about the shipment coming in. Peoples in the DEA told peoples in the CIA, and word travels to this Gomez guy. He calls Sanchez and says, tell your friend Norwin in San Francisco that if he wants to stay out of jail then he better listen.'

'Unbelievable,' Carlos says softly before downing his drink.

'I said, you gotta be kidding me. If this CIA *puta* wants money so badly then why the hell isn't he protecting my coca?' Closing his eyes, he finishes his glass of scotch. 'Aristides says, that's just it, the CIA will give protection so long as they are getting their share. Says they aren't waiting around any longer. That for the Contras to stay together, money must come from somewhere and it's time the traffickers paid their way.'

His hand wobbling, Norwin tops up their glasses again.

'It really makes me sick,' he continues, 'all these snakes in the grass, hiding in the shadows waiting to strike me. Don't they see who I am? What I'm trying to do here?' Knocking back the scotch he throws the glass across the room, shattering it against a wall.

Reaching over he drags the revolver across the wooden table and begins twirling it. Then, picking the gun up and pretending to fire it one by one at figures lined up in the dark, he makes a shooting sound; *pow, pow, pow*. Around the room he goes until his gun is pointing at Carlos. Squinting through cigar smoke he waits, thinking, then cocks the hammer back.

'What exactly did you agree to when you met this Agent last month?'

A bead of sweat traces its way down the side of Carlos's forehead, 'Nothing, I told you.'

'Nothing?' Norwin echoes.

'I've only done as you instructed; increased the amount we fly through their airbase to one-hundred kilos, while giving contributions directly to Troilo in Honduras.'

'And?'

'And that's it,' Carlos says nervously. 'I told you he wanted everything to go through Ilopango, that he meant business,' he pleads.

Raising his bushy eyebrows, 'That's what you told me?'

Carlos swallows hard watching the dark end of the barrel staring at him like a narrow tunnel ready to suck him into oblivion.

'*Si*. That they had enough of the traffickers going around them and that was months ago. I mean, this is the fucking CIA after all,' he says defensively.

Puffing on his cigar and keeping the gun pointed at Carlos, 'Well, I guess the time has come then,' Norwin says before clicking the hammer closed. Looking down at the gun as though it's a harmless paperweight, 'What other choice do we have now? If this is how far this *puta* can reach then Ilopango is where we have to go.'

Carlos's chest heaves with relief.

After a sigh, 'Max Gomez better be right,' Norwin continues. 'If we use this airbase, we better get all the coca in the jungles of South America through there. Then we'll see just how worthwhile it is being in the CIA's pocket.'

Frowning, 'How do you mean?' Carlos asks.

Taking the cigar from his mouth, 'Gomez told Aristides that if any of my high-ranking guys got busted to make sure they say they are working for the FDN. Any drugs and especially any money found in their possession, they are to specifically tell the authorities that it is for the Contra effort in Nicaragua.'

'I see.'

'But that's not all I'm upset about,' Norwin says chewing his cigar. 'Donald Barrios called me yesterday asking how come the negroes from California are coming all the way to Miami to score coca when they should be getting it delivered to their doorsteps in LA?'

Carlos shifts uncomfortably, 'That, that is Danilo's territory. When I got rid of Henry after what happened to Diego, he said he could wear the loss to the black connect.'

'Yeah, well, the black connect is buying twenty kilos at a time from my Miami competitors. Twenty-kilos, Carlos!' he says squeezing the cigar in his fist and smothering it into the table. Looking at the ash pressed into the palm of his hand, 'Get him back. Get Henry back and get him selling to the negroes again.'

'*Sí*, of course.'

With a disappointed look on his face, 'I am a superstitious man, Carlos. You know that. And I know bad luck comes in threes.' Leaning forward with his elbows on the table and cradling his hands, 'This is now two misfortunes that have befallen me. When the third one comes, someone is going to get a bullet in their head,' Norwin says plainly.

Swallowing, '*Sí*, I know.'

The next morning, Carlos goes early to see Julio who is being held at the Daly City Police Station. Appearing drab beneath a grey sky, the interlocking square buildings look prison-like with their cement ribbing and featureless decor. As Carlos climbs the red-brick steps he feels a wave of nerves washing over him, daring to walk into a cop station only hours after almost getting busted himself.

* * *

Behind Perspex glass with a phone to his ear, he awaits Julio to enter the visiting room. This is the first time anyone from their network has been arrested, so he's uncertain how much trouble his cousin is in or how wide the DEA's net has been cast.

Wearing an orange jumpsuit, in walks Julio with bags under his eyes and a dour look on his face.

'*Hola, hermano,*' Carlos says affectionately.

'*Hola,*' Julio says hoarsely.

'Are you okay?'

Shrugging, 'I am fine. But what the hell happened last night?'

Looking around the room, 'We were tipped off,' he whispers.

Frowning, 'By who?'

Carlos leans close to the glass, 'We don't know. But that CIA agent, Max Gomez, called Aristides last night to warn him it was happening. He could have stopped it.'

'That *bastardo*.'

'I know.'

'Why didn't he? Isn't he meant to be on our side?'

'Supposedly. But this was a warning to us, for not going through Ilopango.' After a sigh, 'I guess he knows a lot more about what we're bringing in than we thought.'

'Yeah, well, what the fuck is going to happen to me?'

Changing ears, 'Tell me what happened last night?'

'What's to tell? Me and Luci were sleeping and the next thing I know my front door is getting kicked in. DEA and cops were in the bedroom before I could find my underwear.'

'So, what have they arrested you on?'

'Conspiracy to traffic cocaine, a little drug possession.'

'What's a little?'

'About an ounce.'

'Nothing. That's okay.'

'And possession of forty-thousand cash. Proceeds of crime I heard the cops calling it,' Julio says with a raise of an eyebrow.

Frowning, 'Where was the cash?'

'On my bedside. I just picked it up from Pedro in Oakland earlier in the night.'

'But it wasn't with the coca, right?'

'No, the coca was on the coffee table in the living room.'

'Good good, then legally they won't be able to connect the two. Have you made a statement yet?'

'No, of course not.'

Nodding, Carlos thinks for a moment, 'Okay, this is very important, Julio. You need to tell them the money is for the FDN back in Honduras. Now, if they were raiding your house at the same time that they were catching us picking up coca at sea, then they will have investigative evidence that you are involved with cocaine trafficking.'

'Fuck me.'

'Listen. That is why you must stick to the story that the coca you were conspiring to traffic was specifically to raise funds for the FDN. Use those words.'

'What, and that's supposed to get me out of trouble?'

'Yes.'

Julio looks unconvinced.

'Norwin,' Carlos continues, 'is sending over a lawyer today. He'll arrange documents from the FDN directorate attesting that this is true.'

After a moment, 'Will I do time?' Julio says pained by the possibility.

'I don't know. It depends what they have on you. But Aristides told Norwin that all we need to do is stick to this story, say the right names, and the right people will keep us out of serious trouble.'

Nodding, 'Okay. So, everything was for the FDN.'

'Exactly.'

After a long sigh, 'How much did we lose last night?'

'Five-hundred kilos.'

Shaking his head, 'If they connect me to that five-hundred kilos—'

'Don't worry, they won't.'

'You're certain, *hermano?*'

'I am certain,' Carlos says with a warm smile.

'Who else got busted last night?'

'Sebastian at his home, same as you. And the guys in the boats. They might be in a little more trouble though.'

Nodding, 'What happens now?'

'You'll have an arraignment most likely tomorrow. You'll plead not guilty and post bail.'

Julio's eyes light up, 'You mean I'll be out of here?'

'*Si*, of course. Whatever the bail amount is Norwin will pay. Then you just have to come back for pre-hearing. The prosecution will offer a plea bargain. Normally, you don't take these.'

'How come?'

'Because they're bad. But this is where our CIA connections should intervene. And of course, the fact that you were performing services on behalf of the FDN.'

Julio smiles for the first time.

'Don't worry,' Carlos reassures, 'you'll be all right.'

A guard walks over to their window and informs them that they have two minutes left.

'What are you going to do?' Julio asks.

'I'm going down to San Diego for a few days, lie low.'

'Every couple of weeks you're there now. What are they feeding you? Pussy?'

Chuckling, 'No, no. There are just some good people down there.' After a pause, 'And it's nice not to have to worry about all this,' he says indicating the police, the coca, the trafficking, and everything that comes with it.

Smirking, 'Maybe I should come with you one of these days.'

'Any time, *muchacho*. Okay, I have a flight to catch. I'll call you when you're out.'

'Sounds good, man.'

* * *

That evening as a soft orange sun sinks into the Pacific and a light breeze pulls across the ocean making the air cool and salty, bow-tied waiters serve champagne on ice, crème fraiche caviar on blinis, and tight rolls of Iberico *jamon* stuck with toothpicks of green olives to San Diego's elite as Jerry Dominelli's sunset soiree hits full swing. His beachfront mansion on Neptune Place in the ritzy suburb of La Jolla boasts one of the best views in all of California, while an invitation to such an evening often elicits convenient mingling of the right people looking to broker business deals of varying legality.

Beneath hanging lights glowing against the ensuing twilight, Jerry is explaining to a small group of guests his recent road to success since relocating to San Diego from Chicago. Sitting at the round white marble table are local business owners, real estate players, Roger Hedgecock the Mayor, radio commentator, and all-round Mr. San Diego nice guy George Mitrovich, Carlos Cabezas, and standing at Jerry's shoulder in a black slip dress is Nancy Hoover, his trophy girlfriend.

'It's funny,' Jerry says, 'we tell the working Joe's of the world to save their pennies, as though holding onto cash will somehow propel them into financial freedom.' Chuckling, 'But what they don't realize is that every single rich person in the world is heavily invested in stocks, bonds, metals, real estate, you name it. And that's why me and Richie came to this fine city filled with hardworking Joe's because we saw an opportunity here, an opportunity that the Joe's can't see or touch because it's beyond them. You see, some people in this world have to make big money, they just have to. It's in their blood. Just as most people—the Joe's—whose ideas are small and who lack the courage or smarts to create big plans, have to work little jobs to keep everything going. I mean, we all can't be rich otherwise nothing would get done.'

They all laugh.

'I'm a rich man because I have to be,' Jerry continues. 'It's in my blood. The world needs people like me. It needs my ideas, my plans, and my ability to spend money on things to keep the Joe's employed. Isn't that right, baby?' he says patting Nancy Hoover on her firm backside.

As a young bow-tied waiter quietly offers canapés to his audience, 'I'll have another Long Island too,' Jerry says before continuing his speech. 'The fact of the matter is America is the land of opportunity. It was built on the backs of salesmen and swindlers, on dreamers and their believers, by hucksters selling snake oil and the suckers who paid for it with their blood and sweat. And it's what has made America great,' he says clenching a fist. 'The right man summons the right idea from deep within himself and he transforms his world.'

'Even if that success comes at the cost of someone's blood and sweat?' Court Connors, a local real estate guy who owns a bunch of houses in Carmel Valley, asks, uncertain of Jerry's crude point of view.

Giving a wry smile, 'Kings and queens, my friend. What matters is we build the tall buildings, the great bridges, the ships to haul fine goods from one part of the world to the other so the rightful can enjoy the fruits that they deserve. Look, nobody remembers the Joe's who broke their backs carrying bricks and steel all their life or who keep the streets clean or cut my hair, and that's just the way it is. All people want, without realizing it of course, is to feel like they're a part of a great society, even if that means spending all their life propping up that splendor for more important people. So long as they get their weekly paycheque, can shop at *Sears,* and watch baseball on the weekend, they think they've got it good. Am I right or am I right?'

'You're not wrong, Jerry. Not wrong, at all,' Roger Hedgecock says gruffly.

Noticing Court's unconvinced expression, 'Still not seeing what I'm saying?' Jerry asks.

'Well, I just don't think the hard-working people of America really live a life too dissimilar to ours,' Court offers. 'Sure, there are differences but fundamentally we all want the same things and for the most part go about it the same way.'

'That so?' Jerry says unimpressed. 'Okay, how about this; do you like the taste of that ham you're eating?'

Looking at the roll of fine meat in his hand, 'Yes,' Court says.

'Would you say it's delicious?'

'Of course, it is.'

Raising his eyebrows agreeably, 'The best ham you've ever eaten?'

Chuckling, 'You know, I think it is.'

'Good, because that ham is from a certain part of Spain where the pigs graze in oak forests right before they're slaughtered. Now, am I right in thinking that you've never had it before?'

Clearing his throat, 'Well, no I haven't,' Court admits sensing a trap.

'That's right, you haven't. And you wouldn't have ever tried this fancy Spanish ham if it wasn't for me. And that's my point. Without people like me in this world, people like you wouldn't know such nice things. I am the fruit and you are the labor,' Jerry says slowly.

Court fondles the ham in his mouth with his tongue which has suddenly lost taste.

'What about the champagne, Jerry, where's that from?' Bradley Moore, a loud-mouth penny stocks investor, blurts.

'I don't know, fucking France somewhere. Who gives a fuck about the French?'

They all laugh again.

'Look, there's always going to be winners and losers. It's just the way it is,' Jerry says smugly.

Calling from the balcony, 'Oh, but one has to care, Mr. Dominelli,' Vince Miranda offers. 'One has to care about his fellow man. If we simply ignore the misery of others then what does that say about ourselves?'

Twisting over the chair and giving the club owner a dry look, 'A wolf doesn't concern itself with the opinions of sheep, does it, Mr. Miranda?' Then, turning back to the group, 'Now, one can't care about the whole world, can he? It's not even possible. Roger, you care about the city of San Diego. Nancy, the district of Del Mar. Mr. Mitrovich, you care about your wonderful radio listeners. But outside of that, outside of your reach,' Jerry makes a capitulating gesture, 'you have no control, so what does it matter.'

Raising his glass of whiskey in agreement, 'A bitter truth too few have the intestinal fortitude to swallow, I'm afraid,' Hedgecock says forthrightly.

'Well said, Roger,' Jerry compliments before glancing back at Vince, 'Do you care about the bums and junkies that litter your sidewalks in Gaslamp, Mr. Miranda?'

Feigning a smile, Vince doesn't offer a reply.

'That's what I thought,' Jerry says darkly before turning back around. 'Now, where's my fucking Long Island?'

Later, as the party spills inside where amongst odd-shaped furniture, erotic sculptures, and massive *art nouveau* paintings, party guests form small inebriated clusters. Glamorous women in expensive cocktail dresses have begun revealing more of their tanned San Diego skin, while cigar smoke hangs heavy as men in fine suits laugh to obnoxious levels.

Standing at the end of the bar, Carlos is having his glass of rum refilled when Jerry appears keen to discuss more personal matters.

'Having fun, Carlos?'

Feigning a smile, 'Yes, of course. You have a lovely home.'

'Home?' Jerry says with a chuckle. 'It's a fucking mansion. Have you seen such views?' he says indicting moonlight bouncing off of the endless expanse of the Pacific Ocean.

'It is quite something,' Carlos offers.

Leaning an elbow on the bar, 'Isn't this what you and Norwin and Danilo have come to America for, to make yourselves rich?'

'Actually, we had it quite good in Nicaragua, before the revolution, that is.'

'As good as you have it now?'

'Danilo and Norwin, very much so. They had businesses and big houses on the beach, ranches in the country with cattle, that sort of thing.'

'I can believe that. I like the way Danilo talks business; he's a man who knows how to make money. He has an appetite for it, which is why he's eager to invest in San Diego. He sees what I see here, the opportunity to turn a dime into a dollar.' Crunching on a cube of ice, 'But with you, I don't quite get the same feeling.'

Carlos raises his eyebrows.

'You come here to make sure that the business relationship between Danilo and myself stays favorable, plus you bring in a little blow for Vince Miranda,' he says discretely.

Carlos's face remains unmoved.

'Don't worry, your secret is safe with me. Business is business and I'm the last person in the world to have anything against the need to turn a profit.'

'Money is money after all,' Carlos says swirling his glass of rum.

'That it is, my friend. And I think that's what I find interesting about you, Carlos. You're here to make money but money is the one thing you never seem to talk about.'

Smirking, 'Talking about what Norwin and Danilo wish to invest in San Diego is not why I have been sent here.'

'But that doesn't mean a man is not to talk about business.'

'I'm afraid my priorities aren't the same as Danilo's.'

Surprised, 'You don't care about making money?' Jerry asks.

'No, of course, I do. But I also care about what is happening back in Nicaragua.'

'This revolution thing?'

'Many thousands have perished and the country has been turned upside down.'

'So what? Soldiers' die, that's what they do.'

Soldiers are fathers and brothers and sons as well, Carlos thinks.

'I don't mean to be unsympathetic,' Jerry continues, 'but ask yourself, what are they fighting for?'

'For social and political freedom,' Carlos says thoughtfully.

'That's right, they're fighting for something better than what they have. Isn't that worth dying for?'

Furrowing his brow, 'I think fighting and dying are two different things.'

Shrugging, 'Maybe. I don't know shit about war. But what I do know is you can't make an omelet without breaking some eggs.' Leaning close, 'Every day people die. That's not what matters and yet most people fail to understand this. What matters is you make the fucking omelet. You're not in Nicaragua anymore and you can't be in two places at once, Carlos. You're in fucking San Diego and just look at what is being offered to you,' he says turning towards the upper-class guests mingled throughout his home. 'Caviar parties, high-class pussy, and mansions overlooking the goddamn Pacific Ocean,' Jerry finishes spreading his arms out wide.

Carlos feigns a smile but is unmoved by Jerry Dominelli's pitch.

'Speaking of high-class pussy,' Jerry says from the corner of his mouth as Nancy Hoover interrupts them.

'Now, what are you two boys talking about so quietly by your lonesome?' she says teasingly.

Putting his arm around her tight waist, 'Oh, Carlos here, was just telling me how the lights and glamour of San Diego don't attract him,' Jerry jokes.

'You mean to say that there is nothing in our fine city that fancies you, Carlos?'

Smiling, 'There are some things here that are nice.'

'Just nice?' Nancy says faking hurt. 'Then we're clearly not doing a good job of convincing you of the treasures our beloved city has to offer, are we?'

'Don't be too hard on yourself, baby. Carlos has sore eyes for Nicaragua.'

'Nicaragua?'

'Yeah, there's a revolution going on—'

'Yes, the Sandinista Government assumed political control a couple of years ago, if I recall correctly.'

'You know about the struggles in Nicaragua?' Carlos asks.

'Just a little. It was the Somoza family, I believe, who ruled the country for the last few decades before the new Government took control. But wasn't *that* the revolution?'

'It was. Now there is another trying to take the country back again.'

Laughing, 'No wonder these fucking places never get anywhere.'

'Jerry,' Nancy reproaches. 'That's Carlos's home you're talking about.'

'Get out of here. America is his home now; he just doesn't realize it yet.'

Smiling, 'America is a wonderful place but I didn't choose to come here. I was an officer in the National Guard; if I stayed the Sandinistas would have put me in front of a firing squad.'

'Oh my, that's terrible,' Nancy consoles.

'And yet, here you are drinking expensive champagne and rubbing shoulders with some of the most important people in San Diego,' Jerry says dryly. 'I'd say that is a rather fortunate turn of events, and a rather fortunate set of circumstances in which you find yourself.'

'And what circumstances might that be?' Nancy inquires coyly.

Smirking, 'Business, baby. The chance to turn a dime into a dollar. Isn't that right, Carlos?'

'That's right,' Carlos agrees. 'I am in a position most are not, especially for Nicaraguans. You are right about what you said earlier; it is in Danilo and Norwin's blood to be rich, but it is in my blood to help my people in some way. If that comes at a cost to the business I'm involved in, then sobeit.'

'How very noble of you, Carlos,' Nancy says.

Raising his eyebrows, 'I'm not so sure Danilo and Norwin would be very happy to hear that,' Jerry remarks.

'Well, it's a good thing they didn't hear it then,' Carlos answers.

Chuckling, 'I like you, Carlos. There's something about you, but I fucking like it.' Then, seeing Roger Hedgecock and Vince Miranda in a heated conversation across the terrace, 'Now, baby, see if you can convince Mr. Nicaragua here, what a fine city San Diego is and why it needs his boss's money. I need to go put out a fire,' Jerry says walking off.

Reaching over the bar and grabbing a bottle of champagne, Nancy fills her glass.

'Jerry takes a little getting used to,' she says before sucking the foamy bubbles before they spill over the rim.

'I'm sorry?' Carlos says curiously.

'He says what he thinks and that makes people uncomfortable.'

'I am not uncomfortable, Miss Hoover. I am used to dealing with people who think they have *grande cojones*.'

'*Cohonies?*'

'Confidence.'

'Oh.' Taking a sip of her champagne, 'Then why do I get the feeling you don't want to be here?'

Smiling, 'Jerry was only joking when he said I did not like San Diego. This is a lovely city with lovely people. In fact, I'm beginning to enjoy my time here more than I do in San Francisco or LA.'

Nancy raises an eyebrow.

'But I am from a different walk of life, a different place,' Carlos adds.

'That's a little extreme, don't you think. I mean, we barely know each other and we get along swell. Besides, who's to say where we end up isn't where we're meant to be? And the same goes for the people we meet along the way. That's how life works doesn't it? It just happens to us, while we're busy making other plans.'

Carlos smirks but doesn't offer a reply.

'See, you may want to be somewhere else but you're here now, standing next to me,' Nancy says with a wink. 'But the real question is, why would you want to be anywhere else?' she asks intriguingly.

Chuckling, 'I can see why you're the Mayor of Del Mar, Miss Hoover. You're much sharper than you look.'

'Oh really? And how do I look, Mr. Cabezas?' she says pretending to take offence.

'You mean aside from looking like Gia Carangi?'

Almost spitting her sip of bubbles out, 'Gia Carangi; that is quite the compliment,' Nancy says beginning to blush.

Smiling, 'I hope I haven't made you uncomfortable, Miss Hoover?'

Clearing her throat, 'No, because I know you're lying,' she says coyly. 'Us brown hair and brown eyed girls are a dime a dozen. Everybody knows blondes have more fun.'

'Maybe in America, but we see things differently in Nicaragua.'

'Is that why you want to go back?'

'I think it's more that I don't want this: mansions, fancy parties, everyday making business deals and the asses you have to kiss to make them happen,' Carlos sighs.

'Then why are you here?' Nancy asks seriously.

'Because I have to be.'

'Then maybe it's meant to be.'

Shaking his head and smiling, 'I think I was wrong about you, miss Hoover.'

'And how's that, Carlos?'

Looking around the room, 'Jerry, these people—'

'Yes?'

'I—'

Out of nowhere Vincent Miranda threads his arm through Carlos's, 'Save me,' he begins theatrically, 'save me from these absolute windbags, *please*. Oh, no offence, Nancy baby.'

'None taken, Mr. Miranda.'

'What's the matter, Vince?' Carlos asks.

'What's the matter? If I hear one more remark about what's right for the country or good for the people, I'm likely to turn Protestant for Christ's sake.' Sinking the rest of his scotch in one gulp, 'I need to get out of here. Carlos, will you walk me to my car?'

'Of course.' Then, giving Nancy a warm smile, 'Please, excuse me.'

'By all means,' she says with a smile.

Holding onto the Nicaraguan's arm, Vince and Carlos walk down Jerry's marbled hallway and across the front yard where Mercedes Benzs and BMWs are parked at varying angles. Vince's car is a dark green MG with a tan soft top, and he's accidentally parked it in the rose garden.

'You know, I could literally wring Roger's neck. Wring it. The pompous asshole,' Vince fumes.

Chuckling, 'Why are you here, Vince?' Carlos asks gently. 'Why do you come to these parties if you loathe them so much?'

Sighing, 'You've asked me that before, Carlos.'

'*Si*. And still you come.'

Fumbling for his keys, 'What do they say? Keep your friends close but your enemies closer.'

Carlos smiles, waiting for the little Portuguese man to explain himself better.

With a laugh, 'Come now, one never reveals all his cards at once. A man as clever as you should know that.'

They both smile.

'Listen, tomorrow morning I want to discuss something with you. Will you meet me?' Vince asks seriously.

'Of course.'

Smiling, 'Good. Six-five-five Fifth Avenue, nine-am.'

'I'll be there. Are you all right to drive, Vince?'

Smirking, 'Cheating death is half the fun of living, darling.'

XII
FREEWAY RICKY

Spinning precariously on the rim, a worn *Spalding* basketball decides whether to drop in the basket or not. Homeboys pressing against each other beneath the ring, their muscles bulging and skin gleaming with sweat in a midday sun as they jostle for position to get the rebound, while sweatbands, NBA singlets, flattop afros, gold chains, and seventeen-hundred dollars rides on a Manchester Park pick-up game that's reaching cataclysmic heights as the ball dances around the iron ring, ignorant of the drama it's causing.

Finally, a delicate *swoosh* as the ball passes through a chain net.

'Yes, motha fucker! Point game,' Raymond shouts, all two-hundred pounds of him.

Holding the ball under his arm, 'Point game? Shit, negro, your damn foot was on the line,' Kenny says with a scrunched-up face, his scrawny body lost beneath a *Lakers* jersey three-sizes too big.

'Nigga-what?' Raymond says incredulous. 'I took that jump shot two-feet behind the three-point line. That makes the score *nine*-eight, ours.'

'Oh, hell no you didn't,' Kenny says shaking his head. 'Look at me, look how short my ass is.'

Frowning, 'And?' Raymond says confused.

'And I'm half the distance to the ground compared to your giant black ass,' Kenny explains. 'I seen your Sasquatch foot halfway over the line.'

'The hell it was,' Raymond says angrily.

Unworried by the size of the man, 'Listen, Big Foot, there ain't no way it's nine-eight yours. If it is I'm gonna go home and kill myself.'

'Well then, you better go kiss your mamma goodbye,' Raymond says dramatically.

'What the *hell* you just say?' Kenny says throwing the ball at him.

Stepping in, 'Alright, alright,' Rick says separating them. 'You two need to chill the fuck out, getting all puffed chest and shit. We playing ball is all. Damn.'

'Yeah, ball with seventeen-hundred bills riding on it,' Raymond says seriously.

'Freeway ain't pissed because seventeen-hundred dollars is like seventeen-cents to this nigga,' Kris, who's on Rick's team along with Kenny, chimes in.

Everyone chuckles.

'Check it, he ain't even broke a sweat on this game yet,' JoJo remarks, poking Rick's forehead searching for traces of perspiration.

More laughing.

Knocking his hand away, 'Sweat! Man, I'm running the show for my team!' Rick defends. 'I should be wearing that damn Isaiah Thomas singlet.'

'Jim Paxson more like it,' Jojo says back.

Rick's eyes go big, 'Jim Paxson is a cracker!'

The court is crowded with kids, teenagers, fly women, hustlers, gangbangers, you name it, and everyone is doubled-over laughing. Rick doesn't mind being the target of their jokes. He was always the class clown growing up anyway, plus he'd rather homies joking and teasing than getting mad with each other for real. Even though this is Manchester Park and a neutral zone between gangs, fights still break out time-to-time and you'd be kidding yourself if you didn't think half of these homies weren't strapped.

'Aiit, so what's the count?' Raymond asks.

'Shit, Raymond,' Kenny says, 'you behind on your rent again you need this money so bad?'

Rick jumps in before Raymond's blood pressure explodes, 'The score is nine-eight, theirs.'

'What?!' cries Kenny.

'You right, Kenny,' Rick says. 'Raymond's Sasquatch ass almost landed on me when he hit that jumper and I was all the way out here,' indicating well past the three-point line. 'Which means it had to be a three-ball,' Rick says regrettably.

'What the fuck I tell you,' Raymond says eyeing Kenny before snatching the ball and taking it out past the line to start the game again.

A tense hush settles over the asphalt court as sweaty bodies push against each other once again. As the play starts the crowd begins to cheer and suddenly all the smack talking has disappeared with the seriousness of the game now at finishing point.

After a series of quick passes, Jojo and Raymond run a well-rehearsed high pick-and-roll play at the top of the key that catches Rick and Kenny off-guard and leaves Big Foot completely unguarded. Jojo tosses the ball into the air with a delicate touch allowing Raymond to leap completely over Kenny—knocking him over in the process—and slam-dunking the ball with such ferocity the backboard almost breaks.

'There it is, there it is!' Raymond yells giving his teammates high-fives. 'Pay day mother fuckers.'

Bending over with hands on his knees Rick is breathing hard.

Still lying on the ground, Kenny winces, 'God damn, I think my hip is broke.'

Laughing and giving him a hand up, 'Nah, the only thing broke is your wallet, homie,' Raymond says, the fire of the game now extinguished.

Despite being a little pissed at losing, deep down the guys are content being a part of one of the best pick-up games had at Manchester in a long time. The crowd spills onto the court and high-fives and hugs are given.

Standing on the sideline is Redmon and Lonzo and Rick calls for them to come over.

'Here,' pulling a stash of fifty-dollar bills from beneath his spandex undershorts, 'take this, go to *Dr. Munchies* and get twenty pepperoni pizzas and twenty Gatorades for everybody.'

Rick isn't about bailing homies out if they lose on a game of pick-up, or dice, or betting on the pro-league. It's their choice to tout their money like that; don't gamble what you can't afford to lose he always thought. But these are his homies, his neighborhood, his Manchester Park and he wants to see everyone happy. So, spending a hundred-dollars on pizza and Gatorades is a gesture that's no sweat off of his nose but goes a long way in the community.

All of a sudden, a couple of cars screech into the car park and everybody freezes thinking, *drive-by*, but out jumps Ollie and he's stressing.

Running over, 'Yo, Rick, you gotta come quick! The cops is raiding our spot on 82nd Street!'

Pulling over down the street a way, they sit and watch a dozen uniform cops and DEA agents wearing bulletproof vests drag homies out onto the lawn, some face down being handcuffed and others just sitting cross-legged like they're in grade school.

'Damn,' Rick says quietly.

It isn't the worst thing that could happen. This is a crack house, sure, but with only a small amount of dope inside and most likely not too much money either. Runners take cash from crack houses every half an hour to avoid situations just like this. The cops will be furious. Still, Rick hates seeing his homies being ruffed up and getting arrested. He'll have them all bailed out by tomorrow, but this is the first-time serious heat has come down on one of his main crack houses.

Breathing a sigh of relief, 'At least it's only Shrimp's spot,' Ollie says.

'Don't matter whose spot it is, that's our dope, our customers, our money,' Rick says thoughtfully.

Ollie nods.

'We need to step up our security,' Rick states. 'If this was Mumbles joint on 81st, we would have lost five-times as much as they seizing now.'

'True that,' Ollie says raising his eyebrows.

Despite being a raid, there doesn't seem to be a lot of commotion, which tells Rick the cops must have found hardly any crack in the house. Half an hour later, the cops clear out and take four guys to jail: Shrimp, who runs the spot, Young Stevie his helper, and two of their homeboys who Rick doesn't know by name.

'Alright, let's go to Aunt Mary's so we can get her organized to bail these homies out,' Rick says eagerly.

Mary previously worked as a bank teller for thirty-three years until her son, Peach, broke it to her that he was dealing crack and making her entire salary every couple of weeks. Well, Mary quit her job the next day and became Rick's full-time money-counter. She's got a mind like a steel trap for numbers and because of her clean record and trusted work history, Rick set up a business front for her to operate out of which includes bookkeeping, personal taxations, and most importantly, dealing in bails and bonds. Every time a homie needs to get bailed out, Aunt Mary files the paperwork, writes a cheque and moseys on down to the courthouse in her Sunday's finest and springs the poor sucker.

Meanwhile, defense lawyer Alan Fenster is on Rick's payroll too. Now, he's a legitimate attorney and all but it just so happens he specializes in petty crimes and drug convictions, and Rick conveniently provides him with a never-ending stream of clients. Together, Mary and Mr. Fenster, see to it that the doors of the local courthouse and remand center remain a revolving one.

On the corner of 88th and Broadway, Ollie and Rick arrive at a little white-brick single-room office slotted next to a Laundromat, pawnshop, and corner-store selling cigarettes, magazines and longneck bottles of alcohol. Wearing a purple dress-suit with shoulder pads like a defensive lineman, breasts like watermelons, and an ass like a rhino's, Mary cackles her gravely laugh as they walk in.

'Ricky-boy, Ricky-boy, what trouble are you bringing me today?' she says jokingly with a huge smile.

'Well, good morning to you too, Aunt Mary,' Rick says feigning hurt.

'Oh, hush now,' she says standing and becoming serious, knowing all too well that when Rick or Ollie walks through her door it's usually because someone's just gone to jail. 'What's the problem, sugar?'

Putting a small gym-bag on her desk, 'A couple of our boys just got done over on 82nd street,' Rick says seriously.

'Hmm hmm, first timers?'

'Yeah, I think so.'

'How many?'

'Four arrests.'

'Okay. Do you know how much they were caught with?'

'Nah, but it can't be much.'

Turning around and flicking through a filing cabinet, Mary is already retrieving bail paperwork, 'And how much have you brought with you?'

Ollie unzips the bag revealing wads of cash, 'There's forty-gees here. Hopefully bail is only five or ten each.'

'Hmm hmm. Have you spoken to Alan yet?'

'Not yet.'

Sitting back down and dabbing a pen to her tongue, 'Don't fret, I'll call him. Ollie-boy, please be so kind as to put that there bag in the back room and then you kids be on your way.'

Ollie quickly drives them back home so Rick can phone all of the spots and tell his people to lay low for the afternoon. Twelve calls and twenty-minutes later Rick hangs up the phone with a big sigh. No other crack houses have been raided and Mr. Fenster is already at the courthouse checking on Shrimp and the other homies.

Not a moment later the phone rings and Rick gives Ollie a look.

Picking it up, 'Yo?'

'*Hola, Ricky. How are you, my friend?*'

'Henry?! That you?' Rick says disbelievingly.

'*Si, of course. Who else would it be?*'

Jumping up, Ollie puts his ear to the phone.

'Where the hell you been, Henry?' Rick says incredulously.

'*Me, oh, here and there, holiday, business, back and forth, you know how it is.*'

'Holiday? Man, you couldn't have called a brother, let me know you were leaving town and shit? Goddamn, things went real bad real quick a couple of months ago.'

'*Oh no, that is terrible, my dear Ricky. Please, forgive me. You are not in any trouble, are you? You are still moving the coca, yes?*'

'Shh! The hell's wrong with you. Oh, oh, you mean coconuts. Yeah, I love me some coconuts. Why's that, you back selling fruit again?'

'*Not quite. I've decided I don't think the Californian air is for me, but before I leave there is someone I would like you to meet.*'

'Oh really?'

'*Yes, yes. He's, ah, my uncle. Yes, that's it.*'

'You're not trying to set me up now are you, Henry?'

'What, no! How long have we been doing business, Ricky-man? Two years, three years. Come on.'

'What makes you think I wanna meet this uncle of yours?' Rick questions.

'Because, Ricky-man, he showed me everything to do with the coconuts from South America, and he is very eager to meet you.'

Rick's eyes bulge with excitement and Ollie whips his shoulder with delight. 'Well, let's meet him then.'

'Ah, very good. There's just one thing, Ricky.'

'Yeah, what's that?'

'There is a small cost to make all these arrangements happen.'

Chewing his lip for a moment, 'Yeah, well, I know nothing in this world is on the house. What's the fee, Henry?'

'Eighty-thousand.'

'Eighty-thousand dollars!? Damn, Henry, you smoking the coconuts or something? What makes you think I need to meet your uncle that bad?'

'Well, for starters, he lives here in LA.'

'And?'

'And that means you won't have to keep driving back and forth to Miami, Ricky.'

Rick pulls the phone from their ears and covers the mouthpiece, 'Shit, how he know that?'

'These damn Nicaraguans man,' Ollie says, 'they connected as fuck.'

'Are you there, Ricky-man?'

'Yeah, I'm here.'

'Listen, my uncle Danilo, he is responsible for all the coconuts in California. You think what you and me were doing before was a lot? Well, it's nothing compared to what he can do for you.'

Eighty-thousand dollars isn't a great deal of money to Rick seeing as he's earning anywhere from twenty- to thirty-thousand profit a day. But eighty-thousand just to meet somebody, even Rick has never paid that much before. Henry is right though; collecting their dope from Miami is a route he'd like to close as soon as possible. And if this uncle is Henry's supplier, then Rick will be going straight to the source by the sounds of it.

'Aiit, Henry, when can we catch up?'

'How about tomorrow?'

'Yeah, I can do that.'

'Bueno. Meet me at Taco Pete's in Morningside Park at eleven-am.'

'Aiit, no problem, Henry.'

'With the monies, yes?'

'Yeah, with money.'

'Excellent, my dear Ricky. Trust me, you won't regret it.'

'I better not. See you then,' Rick says hanging up the phone.

'Hot damn, Rick,' Ollie says excitedly, 'no more driving to goddamn Miami.'

Rubbing his chin, 'Not just that, but we'll be able to go a step above Chinese Dave too.'

Since their first fateful trip to Miami almost two months ago, Rick and Chinese Dave have done another six visits, each time increasing the weight of dope they're bringing back and each time Dave's confidence growing to the point of pure arrogance. Nothing bad has happened, yet, but it's been on Rick's mind to make a move away from him. He's too loud, too flashy, and thinks the sun shines out of his ass, even on a cloudy day. The only problem is their coke connect in Miami is unrivalled. There has always been a little Nicaraguan cocaine floating around LA, even after Henry went missing, but the volumes are so small Rick has never bothered to chase down who was bringing it in. Now it didn't matter.

Later that night near Midtown Crossing—where Venice, Pico, and San Vicente come together—groups of fly homeboys and homegirls gather along the sidewalk. Looking like they're about to appear on *Soul Train* they line up to enter a huge red, orange, and yellow-brick building. *World on Wheels*. Rick is taking a rare night off. For the last two-and-a-half years it's been all work and no play for Freeway and he's finally eager to meet a girl. Aside from a handful of booty-calls in that time, he hasn't come close to having a girlfriend. He's always been a bit goofy looking and he knows it, with a rough beard and buckteeth, and his head a mop of dreadlocks, and despite being okay with girls finding him more fun than fly, lately he's been thinking how far up he's come, this little can't read or write, poor-ass homie now worth over three-million dollars, and yet he's still sleeping in an empty bed. Well, it's time he changes that.

Old habits die hard though as Rick arrives in a stock silver Buick wearing clothes so plain that when he sees the crowd he considers driving home and getting changed. But it's too late, standing by the entrance Tommy and Haney see Rick and holler him over. Haney is a real good-looking kid and now with all the money he's making, he's wearing the latest Nike's, a sweet Raiders jacket fresh off the shelf, and so much gold around his neck he's likely to fall over. Oh, and the other thing about Haney, he has all the flyest girls after him.

'Damn shame about what happened to Shrimp today,' Tommy says.

'Could have been worse,' Rick states. 'They'll be out tomorrow. I always look after my hustlers.'

'Speaking of hustling,' Haney begins, flashing his *Old Spice* commercial smile, 'man, are we meeting some dynamite tonight.' Putting his arm around Rick's shoulder, 'Let's go get it.'

Inside *World on Wheels* disco lights flash and twirl, the bar is jamming, the roller rink is full, and the DJ is spinning all the hits: Cold Crush Brothers, Afrika Bambaataa, Run-DMC, Kurtis Blow, Spoonie Gee, The Treacherous Three, Trouble Funk, Boogie Boys, Debbie Deb, and even some Beastie Boys.

After grabbing a drink, they do a lap of the place and Rick loses count of how many people come up to Haney and Tommy to say what's up. Old, young, fly, nerdy, gangster, straight, it doesn't matter, these young cats know just about everybody it seems. This is good, Rick realizes, this is why these two boys have come up so fast. It isn't just that they're nice looking or have some street credential, it's that not only are they rolling in money but they're showing it off too. And this is something Rick has never brought himself to doing.

Young homies wanted to be like them and fly girls wanted to be with them. Funnily enough, almost every person coming over to show love to Haney doesn't so much as blink an eye at Rick and he can't believe it.

'Man,' he says with hands on his hips.

'What's wrong?' Haney asks worried.

Shaking his head, 'I knew I laid low but damn not this low,' Rick says desperately.

Tommy and Haney give each other a look before laughing.

'Ain't nobody even know my name,' Rick says disbelieving.

Wiping a tear from his eye and slinging an arm across Freeway's shoulder, 'Oh, believe me, homie,' Haney comforts, 'they know your name. What they don't know is what in the hell you look like.'

'Besides,' Tommy says, 'you don't want nothing to do with these girls anyway. They into homies that can bench press two-hundred pounds or play football. And they only care about this,' he says thumbing one of his gold chains.

'Yeah, and this,' Haney says grabbing his dick.

Despite what his boys are saying, Rick can't help but feel a little dejected.

With his arm still around Rick, Haney sees someone in the distance, 'Nah, what you need ain't no girl. What you need,' he says slowly, 'is a woman.'

Off in the distance, beyond the crowd, arcade machines, and folks tripping over themselves on skates, is a fine-looking woman with big hair, wearing a white singlet and tight *Levi* jeans, hoop earrings, and nails painted gold and sparkling.

Rick swallows, 'Who that?'

'That my homeboy, is Marilyn.'

'And who is Marilyn.'

Smiling, 'Well, allow me to introduce.'

As they walk over Rick is suddenly nervous, like the first time he bought coke from the Nicaraguans or when his uncle was after his mamma and aunt Bobbi Jo. Funny how fear works, no matter what the situations is it always feels the same whether you're staring at the girl of your dreams or staring down the barrel of a gun. You go cold and stiff and your hands go all clammy. When they get closer though the nerves seem to wash away, and if there's such a thing as a magic spark or love at first sight, Rick is feeling it.

Marilyn sees Haney coming towards her but plays it cool, leaning back against the bar and slowly drawing a cigarette to her lips.

Flashing his *Old Spice* smile, 'Hey, Marilyn. How you doing girl?'

After a puff of her menthol, 'Oh, hey, Haney,' she says turning towards the three of them. 'I'm good, baby.'

If Marilyn is older than these girls climbing all over Haney and Tommy, it can't be by much. Regardless, Rick has never seen a woman so fine in his life.

Fortunately, this temporary spellbind is keeping him from scaring her with his bucktoothed grin.

'Yo, check it, I want you to meet my main man, Ricky,' Haney says.

Hinting a smile, Marilyn extends her hand.

Taking it softly, 'Marilyn, that's a beautiful name,' Rick says before giving the back of her hand a soft kiss.

Haney and Tommy burst out laughing but Rick never takes his eyes from her. And as pathetically chivalrous as kissing a girl's hand may be, Marilyn doesn't take her eyes from Rick either. When the two homies realize whatever is happening is mutual, they cough back their laughter.

'Aiit,' Haney says clearing his throat, 'we gonna go for a scout, Freeway. We'll clap back at you later.'

After they leave Marilyn looks Rick up and down, 'So, you're Freeway Ricky, huh?' she says coyly.

'Suppose I am. That alright with you?'

It's rare to find someone who opposes the drug game in LA. At least a black person anyway. Most of the time it's all that these communities have to put real food on their table and money in their pocket. But the ugly truth is that money is being taken from somebody: a kid, a wife, a mamma, and every now and again you find someone who realizes it.

'A homie's gotta do what a homie's gotta do,' she says with a smirk.

Marilyn isn't one of them.

'That's the truth.'

And neither is Rick. Life has always been hard, from being born in dustbowl Arp to moving to LA and sleeping on sofas and living off of food stamps and seeing dead bodies in the street. One could argue that for a lot of black folks around here the likelihood of amounting to anything is pretty fucking low, so how else does one succeed in a place like this except to cut a living from selling drugs? In school, on television, on the news, all you hear is how you're meant to get a good job, have money and a nice house and car, but how are you supposed to get all that when the schools are falling down and there are no social services and no one giving a damn about black folk? Well, drugs is how. It's the only commodity a school dropout can get his hands on and double his money or build a six-figure business. In fact, if you go high up enough, the drug game becomes a very complex enterprise with wholesale distribution, market share, competitors, a fluctuating customer base, product quality and marketability, and everything else you find in a free market industry. The only difference is it being illegal and you don't go to school to learn about it; the education comes from the streets.

'So, what brings you out of the hood, Freeway?'

'Oh, you know, everyday I'm grinding and it makes you forget about the finer things in life.'

'The finer things, huh?' Marilyn says sucking on her menthol with shiny red lips.

Resting his elbow on the table, 'Yeah, when you put business first for so long you lose track of more *personal* needs.'

Turning towards him, 'Is that a fact?'

With his head cocked to one side and nodding, Rick's playing it cool, 'Factomundo.'

Narrowing her eyes trying to get a read on the peculiar figure standing before her, 'I must say, your reputation proceeds you. Everybody thinks Freeway Ricky is some high rolling badass drug dealer.'

'Yeah, well, looks can be deceiving.'

'I can see that.'

Taking a sip of his drink, 'But that's exactly what I'm after. Why do I want everybody to know who I am or know what I got?'

Intrigued, 'Is that so?' Marilyn asks.

Raising his eyebrows, 'If I wanted to be famous, I would've become a sports star or something.' Then, crunching on an ice cube, 'Nope, I want to be able to do what I want when I want. That's why I work as hard as I do.'

'Anything?' she inquires teasingly.

'Well, almost anything,' Rick says with a cheeky smirk.

Moving closer Marilyn stands square in front of Ricky, 'You know what you are?' she says thoughtfully, 'You're an enigma.'

A little concerned, 'What's an enigma?'

'Something special.'

Rick grunts, 'Man, I ain't never been called special in all my life.'

Silently staring at one another, while colored lights and flashes from a disco ball dance across their faces, Marilyn leans forward and kisses Rick, slowly at first before working her tongue into his mouth. Rick hasn't felt a kiss with such passion for longer than he cares to remember.

After half an hour of conversation about their childhoods, the vast array of jobs they each have worked, and who they know in the hood, Rick offers to get them some food. The snack bar at *World on Wheels* is at the far end of the skating rink, so Rick leaves Marilyn at the bar and goes off. After purchasing a couple of hotdogs and a jumbo slushie, Rick turns around and sees a face he'd rather not see: Wayne Honcho Day, a true original gangster from the streets. The last time they stood opposite one another was when Rick was new to the game and a cat named Richie Rich shafted him on half an ounce of cocaine. Well, one stolen Cadillac, a punch-up at a pool hall, and a drive-by later, Honcho was the hired muscle to oversee the dispute. Honcho didn't have a stake in this drama, but he certainly didn't care much for Rick either, who at the time was just a skinny kid with zero street credential.

With two hotdogs in one hand and a slushie in the other, Rick contemplates his options, which he quickly realizes isn't many. A long history of violent crime, repeated stints in jail, and now a shot caller for the Grape Street Crips, nobody fucks with Honcho. With a thick afro coming all the way down to form a pair of lamb chops on his jaw, arms popping, and a chest like a gorilla, he is a mean looking man.

After what feels like minutes, finally Honcho opens his mouth, 'What up, cuz?'

Acting as though he only vaguely remembers him, 'Oh, hey, Honcho,' Rick says. 'Been a long time, man.'

Standing with the burley gangster is another Crip named Chubb, and even though Rick has never met him he knows exactly who he is: an enforcer. It's funny how the higher up a gang member climbs the less dirty work he actually does; the steady stream of up-and-coming thugs keen to represent themselves with a gang are more than happy to do all the dirty work; beatings, drive-byes, car-jackings, territory takeovers, you name it.

Honcho hasn't changed his expression and Rick notices his mouth has gone dry.

'I done heard you're the man, now,' the gangster finally says in a deep voice.

A wave of relief washes over Rick. Honcho's words essentially translating to can he get hooked up, without explicitly asking, of course.

'Yeah, I'm doing alright,' Rick says casually.

Smirking, 'That's not what Little Petey says.'

Rick may have forgotten that Little Pete is a low ranker for the same Crip set, but he hasn't forgotten the most fundamental element of business; supply and demand, and demand for ready rock is as big as ever. That said, Rick has always believed it was only a matter of time before gang leaders would start approaching him asking for direct access to sell crack. And by them coming to him, Rick can avoid having to align himself with one particular gang, and in the process avoid cutting himself off from all others. He's been waiting for this moment to happen. And with Little Pete buying as much as five-pounds a day, Honcho being the first gang leader is now no surprise.

Continuing, 'Little Petey making all his niggas come up and we done know it was from his coke connect. Now, we getting our cut and all but Petey just a low ranker, Freeway, and I wanna make Grape Street blow up. Ya feel me?'

Slowly, Rick's big white buckteeth begin to appear as a huge smile parts his lips.

For the next twenty minutes Rick and Honcho walk around the rink as he explains the product, quantities, and potential profits. When he's done, Honcho offers him twenty-grand to be shown how to cook and make crack, and says he'll buy fifty-thousand dollars' worth of ready rock the next day. And just like that, without lifting a finger Rick had just acquired new hustlers and with them entirely new markets to move his crack cocaine.

After saying goodbye to Honcho, Rick realizes he's left Marilyn waiting all this time. Rushing back to the bar, she's nowhere to be seen. Rick finds Tommy and Haney over by the DJ booth and asks if they've seen Marilyn. They haven't. Then someone taps Rick on the shoulder.

'Marilyn!'

Wearing a crop black leather jacket and her bag slung over her shoulder, she looks like she's ready to leave.

'Damn,' Rick says hastily, 'I got caught talking business and I—'

'It's okay,' Marilyn says calmly. 'I saw you walking with Honcho and figured that's what's up. Business is business.'

'You're not mad?'

'No,' she says plainly.

'Oh,' Rick's eyes dart nervously, 'so, you fixing to leave or something?'

'Yeah,' smiling cutely, 'with you.'

'With me?' he says with eyes big with confusion.

Giggling, 'Yeah, stupid.'

Grabbing him by the sleeve she pulls him along. Rick turns back towards his homeboys and makes a face a mix between joy and trepidation.

As they make their way towards the exit, Rick asks, 'So, where we going?'

'I dunno, you tell me?' Marilyn says cheekily.

When they get outside Rick is perplexed and excited and has no idea what to do next. It's been so long since he has had to make decisions with a girl on the fly. He starts thinking how much easier booty-calls are because both of you know what the deal is. But this is all different, and even though he's only just met Marilyn, he can tell he has feelings for her and doesn't want to screw it up.

'Okay. Umm,' Rick starts. 'You still hungry because I forgot to get you your hotdog?'

Giggling, 'No, I ain't hungry.'

'Okay, okay,' he says scratching his head looking down the street for an idea to pop. Frowning, 'What about catching a movie?'

'Uh uh.'

Rick puts his hands on his hips in a gesture that says he has no idea what to do.

Pulling him close, 'Alright, I've got an idea,' she says softly. 'I wanna see the master cook.'

'You wanna see me cook?'

Biting her lip, 'Yeah.'

'Crack?'

'Yeah!'

'Why?'

Shrugging her shoulders, 'Because you must be good at it. And I wanna watch you do it.'

Cook, Rick thinks, now that's easy. Laughing, 'Well, let's go then.'

They ride in the Lincoln back to Rick and Ollie's house. Normally the place would be teaming with homies smoking weed and drinking but for the last few months the property has been undergoing significant renovations; adding bedrooms, extending the downstairs living area, a new patio, a swimming pool going in, *and* putting in a three-car garage. When they arrive, Rick takes Marilyn by the hand, guiding her through timber frames and across plastic drop sheets.

Neither Rick or Ollie do much cooking, the food kind that is, but the kitchen has just been remodeled and is so flashy it looks like the set for *Yan Can Cook*. Marilyn sits cross-legged on the bench sipping a glass of Hennessey admiring how seamless Rick's knowledge of the fine art of cooking crack is as he simultaneously measures water levels, sets temperatures on the stove, and weighs baking powder on a triple-beam scale.

Like any respectable drug dealer Rick has pure cocaine on hand at all times, and from the drawer below where tea towels and oven mitts are kept, he retrieves about half a pound of white powder and dumps it on the bench next to Marilyn.

'Is that what I think it is?' she says in disbelief.

Grinning, 'What else you think it's gonna be?'

'But, but it's so much.'

Licking his finger and pressing it into the mound of coke, Rick rubs his teeth and gums, 'That right there is the finest coke money can buy.'

Carefully, eyes focused and concentrated, Rick begins the process of turning cocaine into crack. Fascinated by his careful movements and mesmerized by his hushed voice, Marilyn edges her way closer to observe arguably the best cook in LA make the magic happen. Softly and rhythmically, Rick turns the bubbling white goo with a silver fork, folding it back and forth on itself like egg whites for Pavlova, while every few moments describing to her the subtle transformations he's looking for in order to create the perfect biscuit.

Rising steam caught in the orange glow from the range hood, a gentle warmth from the open flames, and Marilyn now standing at the stove pressed against his shoulder, Rick can't help but feel like he's dreaming. After twenty-minutes, Rick switches off the burners and dumps cubes of ice into the saucepans.

Facing her, 'And that is how you make ready rock.'

'You're amazing,' she says softly.

Rick grins.

Marilyn closes her eyes and takes a long deep breath.

'Ah, you okay?' Rick asks worriedly.

Looking towards the ceiling and exhaling, 'I feel... kinda tingly,' Marilyn murmurs.

'Oh, you're just a little contact high from the fumes. I guess I'm used to it but you must be—'

Opening her eyes, Marilyn launches forward and starts kissing Rick wildly. Before he knows it, she squats down and unzips his pants pulling his cock out and straight into her mouth. She's moving so fast he hasn't time to think about what she's doing. Rick can only tilt his head back and feel himself start to lengthen as her tongue performs its own kind of magic.

High, horny, and both feeling the thrill of hooking up with someone for the first time has them squirming around half naked right there on the kitchen floor. It's incredible how impassioned spontaneous sex makes the human body ignore the most uncomfortable of surfaces and positions. With his bony shoulder blades pressed against cold tiles, his pants tangled around his ankles, Marilyn guides Rick inside her, squeezes her tits and begins slowly grinding on him; and in that moment Rick realizes he's in love.

XIV
THE COLONEL

'Five-hundred kilos! Are you fucking kidding me!' Duane Clarridge yells. 'We thought they were bringing in a quarter of that, God. Now I *know* we're being had by these goddamn traffickers.'

The CIA Station Chief's soft white cheeks turning pink with rage. Despite Clarridge looking more like a grade school teacher with neat greying hair, a pudgy build, and a gentle face, he's a career man with the Agency and any misperceived appraisal of his appearance is likely intentional.

'Get your shit together, Ollie! Don't you see they're taking you for a goddamn ride!'

The Colonel sits stoic with his arms crossed, 'I'm a busy man, Dewey.'

'Yeah, with what?' Clarridge says spitefully.

'With the Saudi's, with Khomenhi, training Afghan rebel fighters, flying back and forth to Paris to meet that CIA lap dog,' North says with a shrug.

'Who?'

'Who else—Ghorbanifar.'

Rubbing his forehead with a laugh, 'Ghorbanifar, Jesus. We're giving you access to everyone aren't we?'

Crunching his molars, 'It's not my idea. I'd rather not be dealing with a rat that stinks as much as he does.'

'Oh, pucker up Ollie, don't be so sensitive. If you need backdoor lines of communication into Iran, he's your man. Besides, he's a big-time private arms dealer and that'll make Bob McFarlane feel better about approving all of these weapons sales for the Contras and Bob McFarlane is the one man that stands between the President and keeping you on his good side, don't forget,' Clarridge says suggestively.

'I'll have to keep that in mind,' North says dryly.

They're silent for a moment before Clarridge says softly under his breath, 'Five-hundred kilos.' His anger seemingly revitalized, 'I've got my agents busting their guts down there for you, giving you contacts and businesses and pilots on a silver platter.' Counting them on his fingers, 'Barry Seal, R&M Equipment, Juan Matta, hell I've even got General Bueso Rosa donating Honduran taxpayer money to the FDN. What more do you need?'

Almost obtusely, 'Remind me again who Matta is?'

'Aren't you up to speed on any of this?' Clarridge says in disbelief. 'What are you going to do when Casey pulls me out of Latin America?'

'Don't give me that,' North frowns dismissively. 'You know that my portfolio is equally focused on our interests in the Persian Gulf. I can't keep up with every drug dealer that comes and goes through South America. One minute they're a big deal and the next some rival cartel has gunned them down in a damn whorehouse. Besides, I don't know why you aren't staying? We're only in the middle of all this.'

'The middle is goddamn right,' Clarridge's cheeks flare up again. 'I told Bill Casey one week, one week after becoming head of Latin America that I had two objectives and two objectives only: one, take the war to Nicaragua, and two, start killing Cubans. And I can't believe we're smack bang in the middle of nineteen-eighty-fucking-three and the Sandinistas are still in power *and* Castro's head isn't stuck on a spike somewhere.' After a deep breath, 'Regardless, I couldn't stay even if I wanted to. Director Casey is hell bent on moving me into Lebanon after the US Embassy got bombed last month by those Hezbollah sonsuvbitches. Besides, this thing in Nicaragua has a few more years written all over it, and if you don't know who the hell Juan Matta is then prepare yourself for that time to be an uncomfortable one, Colonel.'

'You really think it has several years on it?' North asks uneasily.

'If the struggle for funds is going to continue then why wouldn't it? And if it does indeed start to drag out then you need to up your game, Ollie. That's more bombings, more political sabotage, more propaganda. You need to create as much unrest for the Sandinistas as possible and on all fronts. They have to be perceived as failing, and not just to their own people but to an international audience as well.'

North, overwhelmed as well as bored of Clarridge's tirade, gives the CIA Chief a look saying as much.

Crossing his arms, 'Do you at least know SETCO?' Clarridge says patronizingly.

'Of course. The Honduran airline company who along with that Costa Rican seafood shipper, what's it—*Frigorifcos de Punta Arenas*—received the first State Department aid contracts to transport supplies from the US to the Contras.'

'Right. They were both Felix's finds. And who owns SETCO?'

Oliver has to think, 'That ex-Navy pilot, Moss, Frank Moss.'

'And?'

'And what in the hell does it matter?' North says losing patience.

Unperturbed by the Colonel's frustration, 'And Juan Matta, Ollie. Juan Matta is one of the largest drug dealers in Latin America. Ever since he and Miguel Gallardo used their drug profits to overthrow the Honduran president back in '78 and bring to power General Paz Garcia, a Somoza sympathizer might I add, the CIA has been very friendly with the man. Why do you think SETCO even received aid contracts in the first place?'

North crunches his molars.

Leaning forward, 'Do you even know who runs *Frigorificos*?'

Narrowing his eyes, 'If you can tell I don't know then why are you asking?' the Colonel says slowly.

Realizing he's perhaps labored his point, Clarridge eases his tone, 'What I'm trying to get you to see, Ollie, is these are the types of individuals you have at your disposal and you're letting them walk all over us, the NSC, the CIA, the goddamn White House. You're sitting in the driver's seat but I'm not seeing much driving. It makes me sick we had to give that rat Meneses in San Francisco a tip-off only to discover they're the ones pulling the wool over our eyes, the damn CIA!' Calming himself down, 'Look, my advice to you is get a good handle on what's going on down there, because at the moment there's a lot of you-know-what coming into this country and not a lot of fighting going on in Nicaragua.'

'Hearing you loud and clear, Dewey,' Oliver says coldly. 'Are you about finished?'

Sitting back, 'Don't be upset with me, Colonel. I'm just laying it all on the table before I move out of the region in a few months. And no, I'm not finished. Frank Moss has been tagged as a drug smuggler by the DEA since '79. Now, he's receiving our cover and all but word is a DEA agent named Zepeda out of Honduras is about to officially launch an investigation into SETCO. Whether you realize it or not, and I stress not, certain branches of the Contras in the Honduran mountains have been depending almost solely on Matta's contributions.'

'Great. Isn't Ed Heath head of DEA Latin America? I thought he was cozy with the CIA?'

'He is, which is why you need to get on the phone with him as soon as and squash this thing.'

Both men are quiet for a moment before Clarridge changes the subject, 'How's our boy, Barry doing? You got him on a tight leash?'

Oliver's molars begin grinding. That drug running sonuvabitch is a complete and utter maverick. A career flip-flopping between TWA pilot and CIA asset since the '70s, he and his team of cowboy pilots have become an integral component for resupplying the Contras. Based in Mena, Arkansas, Seal's fleet can deliver a full supply load of weapons and be back on US soil in less than eight-hours. The only problem is the fleet's undisclosed reloading of dozens of duffle bags of Colombian cocaine, which they drop over Mena farmland to waiting trucks. Sure, some of it finds its way to Nicaraguan exiles turned FDN leaders, but for the most part, Seal's profiteering is just another uncontrollable branch of the drug trade that North and the Contras can only barely get a piece of. And worse still, Seal is using his protection to move all sorts of other illegal substances throughout the region on behalf God knows who.

Lying, 'Sure do,' North says firmly.

'That's good because he's a wild one.'

Clearing his throat, 'We've recently added Terry Reed, a former Air America pilot out of Thailand and Laos, to our Mena outfit,' the Colonel offers, changing the focus of their conversation. 'We're building a training facility for Contra fighters in the Ouachita National Forest, ten miles north of the ranch we set Seal up with. Apparently, Reed and Seal are buddies from way back.'

Nodding, 'What's Reed's role?'

'He'll be training pilots on how to perform resupply missions, night landings, precision airdrops, and such. We'll also be training field commanders on guerrilla warfare and showing them how to use advanced weaponry that they'll soon be getting from the Enterprise.'

'Well, look at you, Ollie. Maybe you do have your hands on the wheel, after all.'

North gives the Station Chief a dry look.

'And what about Pastora?' Clarridge asks. 'We're still sending him supply drops now and again don't forget, it would be nice if he showed us good favor at some point.'

Shaking his head, 'You don't need to tell me,' the Colonel says with frustration. 'We're doing our best to persuade him to join the Contra effort but communication with him is infrequent. We know he's commanding his own troops against the Sandinistas near the Honduran border but he seems cold on teaming up with Adolfo Calero and Aristides Sanchez, and us by association.'

'We need to be careful with him, he's a hero to a lot of Nicaraguans,' Clarridge says thoughtfully. 'You may need to consider taking him out to prevent an uprising of his own; there's a lot of Contra camps scattered throughout those jungles and it would be disastrous if they defected to his leadership.'

'I'll have Bumblebee keep a close eye on it.'

'Do that. And that double agent of ours down there, he providing anything worthwhile on the Sandinistas?'

'Worthwhile is being generous.'

'Well, he is just a photographer after all, what more can he do?' Clarridge says with a shrug.

'Barely more than a tourist with a camera.'

'Since the fall of Somoza we haven't had time to work an agency man inside, so he's all we've got, I'm afraid.'

A gentle knock on the door makes both men look over. Peaking her head in is the Colonel's secretary.

'Excuse me, sir, but Director Casey is looking for, Agent Clarridge,' Fawn Hall informs.

Turning to North, 'Great, good news, I'm sure,' Clarridge says dryly.

'And Mr. Owen is also here, sir,' the secretary adds.

'Thank you, Fawn. Send him in.'

'Listen, Ollie,' Clarridge says, 'I don't want to be a snake in your boot but you need to be doing a better job of pulling these pieces together, all right. Get these assholes flying through Ilopango and let them know who the hell they're dealing with.'

'Understood,' North says crunching his molars.

'Good,' Clarridge says standing. 'Well, I better go find out why my ass is about to hurt.'

Walking to the door to leave, the Agent bumps into Robert Owen who drops a stack of dossiers in the process.

'Oh, excuse me, sir,' Owen apologizes as he begins collecting strewn files. 'I—I didn't see you, sir,' he says from his knees.

Giving North a quick glance, 'No problem, Mr. Owen,' Clarridge says. 'Nothing top secret there I hope.'

'Oh, no, sir. Absolutely not, sir,' Owen stammers nervously.

Chuckling, 'Well, there better be soon,' Clarridge jokes before stepping around Owen and leaving.

Picking up the files and smothering them against his chest, the flustered young messenger makes his way over to the cherry-oak settee and takes a seat.

Looking up suddenly, 'Oh, may I sit down, sir?' Owen asks.

Smirking, 'Yes, of course, Robert.'

Between them is a slender oak coffee table with a square crystal carafe filled with whiskey. Taking a matching crystal tumbler and filling it with the amber liquid, North gestures if Owen would like a glass.

'Oh, no thank you, sir,' he says rearranging his documents into their previous order.

Smelling his drink, 'When did you get in?' the Colonel asks.

'This morning, sir.'

After getting lambasted by Clarridge the Colonel is eager to hear something positive, and from the look of Owen's frazzled eagerness he may be in luck.

'Great news, sir,' Owen says handing the Colonel a manila folder. 'I made contact with a ranch owner by the name of John Hull in northern Costa Rica, right along the border of Nicaragua.'

'An American?'

'Not just an American, sir, but a proud red, white, and blue Republican hailing from Evansville, Indiana.'

Without looking up from the dossier, 'Go on.'

'A month ago Hull reached out to Senator Dan Quayle, of all people, about supporting the Contra effort seeing as he has some rather enthusiastic opinions about these stinking socialist Sandinistas.' Clearing his throat, 'His words, sir. Evidently, Hull has been a longtime friend and financial backer of Senator Quayle's and flew to Indiana along with a low-ranking Contra captain by the name of Luis Rivas to express his desire to help.' Retrieving another small file from his lap and handing it to North, 'Rivas has only a short history with the FDN but he shows up on Aristides records as being an exile arriving out of Colombia and donating a significant pledge to the FDN, likely to secure a place as an officer. From what I gathered in the meeting, Rivas appears to be romantically involved with Hull's daughter.'

Scanning the document, 'And in what capacity does he wish to help? Money donations?' the Colonel inquires.

'Not quite, sir. It seems Hull has been in Costa Rica for nearly two decades and in that time has formed some very close relations with business tycoons, government officials, and even several old Somoza hands. Basically, he's more than happy to open his property up to anyone, official or otherwise, to support the war and ferry weapons in and out of.'

'Ferry weapons?' North asks curiously.

'His ranch has an airstrip that'll handle anything up to a DC-4,' Owen says enthusiastically.

'Well, that is good news. Good job, Robert.'

Blushing, 'Thank you, sir.'

'Can you inspect his ranch anytime soon?'

'He's already offered me an invitation. I'll be there in a fortnight.'

Tossing the dossiers onto the cushion next to him, 'Excellent. Thoroughly check his willingness to comply with the Contras, and verify the suitability of his ranch. Once I get your approval, I'll put him on the payroll.'

'Absolutely, sir.' Then, putting another folder on the coffee table, 'And here are the inventory logs you asked for.'

Taking a gulp of whiskey, 'Thank you. Now, tell me, Robert, are you enjoying your time in Central America?' the Colonel asks.

'Oh, very much so, sir.'

Smiling, 'Not too hot for you?'

Chuckling, 'Well, it is a little humid, but no, sir, it's not too hot for me.'

'That's good because unfortunately things may be about to get a whole lot hotter down there. With this whole Boland Amendment coming into effect next year it'll mean we're going to have to appropriate more funds on our own. And that means relying on more of those bastard businessmen who don't give a damn about peace and democracy but only the money that lines their pocket,' North sighs reaching across the table to refill his glass.

'You don't have to tell me, sir. I can see that happening clear as day down there,' Owen says dumbfounded.

Frowning, 'Oh, really. How do you mean?' the Colonel asks.

Clearing his throat, 'Well, take Jose Robelo for instance; a prominent member of the FDN with ties to organized crime syndicates and cartels in Central America, who we now suspect as having sold equipment and weapons provided by the US Government. I mean, we're struggling to arm the Contras as it is let alone the FDN selling the damn equipment.'

Uncrossing and re-crossing his legs, 'Well, hang on just a minute there, Robert. Now, I know Central America is a corrupt political mess but we aren't certain Robelo even sold those missing weapons. Not to mention that Robelo is one of Adolfo Calero's close associates, and Adolfo Calero is arguably the most important leader of the FDN, and one of the few installed by the CIA might I add.'

Giving a bashful look, 'Yes, that's true, I suppose. It's just when you're down there, sir, and you're watching the trucks pull up to the planes and they're all speaking so fast in Spanish and one lot of crates goes this way, while another goes that way,' Owen says exasperated. But before the Colonel can alter the line of conversation, the messenger continues, 'And speaking of Adolfo—and I appreciate what a vital role he plays for the FDN—I can't help but get the feeling that he also cares about how he can personally profit from this revolution.'

Crunching his molars, 'How do you mean?' North asks.

'Well, someone he is in very close contact with is Sebastian Gonzalez who, although isn't directly part of the FDN, he is heavily involved with moving within its network. I have gathered information on Gonzalez regularly flying between Panama, Miami and San Francisco. My gut feeling is he's laundering money from somewhere,' Owen says with eyes wide and unblinking.

North shifts uncomfortably, 'And how do you reckon that?'

'Because Gonzalez also engages with Mario Calero, a lot. And Mario, oh boy, is he something special. Like a Latino James Bond except not working for the good guys. Almost everywhere I go down there it seems Mario has just been. I can't believe we don't have a detailed file on him already considering who he's involved with.'

'Such as?' North says suppressing his frustration not only at the caliber of individuals associated with the FDN but also with their relentless opportunistic meddling with the Contra effort.

'The aviation company SETCO Felix arranged last year to receive aid contracts and fly weapons over, well, I have reason to believe Mario is a part owner of it. Sure, Mario has a clean record but Gonzalez has a lot of communication with SETCO's other owners Frank Moss and—'

'Juan Matta,' Oliver says sharply.

'Oh, so you're aware of Moss and Matta's personal histories?' Robert says, a little surprised that the Colonel would knowingly operate with individuals with such questionable backgrounds.

Crunching his molars, 'Unfortunately, I'm all too aware, Robert.'

Owen's eyes begin to fidget nervously and there's suddenly an awkward uncertainty in the air.

Realizing he may be getting into muddier waters than he can handle, North gulps down his whiskey and changes tact, 'That's fine work, Robert. Fine work, indeed. And you're right, it's a shame and an absolute concern that we have to deal with the likes of Gonzalez and Matta and who knows how deep Mario Calero goes or God knows how many others.' Slamming his empty glass on the coffee table before sitting back and casually stretching an arm across the settee, 'But that is the unfortunate reality of our plight at present. Our hands are tied, Robert; shackled by Congress and the Democrats and the damn liberals who want their freedoms but aren't willing to fight for them. If only they knew. If only they knew the challenges we face, you, me, the CIA, the agents down there, the challenges of reaching end goals but all the while lacking the clear and necessary navigation to get there. If only they knew how hard it is, to do what we do, to marshal an entire people, to train them all, to deliver equipment and supplies so they don't go hungry or get sick, to gather intelligence, to gather counter-intelligence, to form alliances, to cut them, to persuade politics and presidents, to give people hope and freedom, to win, Robert. If only they knew it wasn't so easy, that sometimes, often times, you have to do things that don't appear right to make right happen.'

Robert Owen is quiet, overwhelmed and emboldened by the Colonel's commanding rhetoric.

Narrowing his eyes, 'Now, let me ask you something serious, Robert,' the Colonel says sternly. 'Do you still believe in the cause? That destabilizing the Sandinistas is the right thing to do?'

'Yes, sir, I do.'

'To what lengths?'

'I'm sorry, sir?'

Dusting lint from his pant leg, 'What is justifiable in all of this? Is political sabotage, okay?'

'I would say yes, yes it is, sir.'

'What about damaging or destroying Nicaraguan trade and supply chains so that we may weaken them, starve their spirit?'

'I—I suppose so, yes.'

'What about using artillery say, to target their factories or broadcast stations?'

Owen opens his mouth but no words come out.

'How about civilians? Women and children? What if some were to have the misfortune of getting killed in the middle of this revolution?'

Swallowing, 'I'm sorry, sir, but I don't believe I'm in a position or qualified to answer that.'

'But it makes you feel uncomfortable though, doesn't it?'

'Well, yes, of course it does, sir.'

'And so it should,' Oliver says approving of the young man's uneasiness. Leaning forward, 'But what if it's for the greater good, you see? What if a town gets burned down, or an office building gets bombed, or a market place getting shot at is the thing that turns it all around? What if a handful of dead civilians is a catalyst for an entire nation to realize they're rooting for the wrong team?'

Owen doesn't reply.

'I know, I know, when you think about it too hard and you see their faces, by God it doesn't seem right. I know it and I've been there. But when you stand back and you think of the thousands upon thousands of lives saved because of one bad deed, well, you understand that it's okay. You see that no matter how horrible something is, if it saves everyone else then it really isn't that horrible. How can it be?' After a moments pause, 'And now just remember that the other side is willing to do the exact same thing to you. Or worse.'

Owen looks uneasy, but after collecting himself he says something that surprises the Colonel.

'Sir, when I sat in this room on this very sofa almost eighteen-months ago, I told you that there would be things I wouldn't understand, things that a person of non-military background wouldn't be able to appreciate. And although I've now seen my share of dead bodies lying in the mud over there, I'm still no better at deciding whether the loss of life was in vain or not. But, I also sat here and told you that I trusted you. And that, sir, hasn't changed not one bit. I want to serve my country with steadfast dedication, and the manner in which I am able to do that is by serving you, sir.'

A faint smile creases the Colonel's lips, 'That's damn good to hear, Robert. And you know what, I'm going to get on the phone to Felix tomorrow and make sure he keeps a close eye on everything down there.'

Smiling warmly, Robert Owen nods as though he received a heartfelt sermon from his father about life and God and fighting the good fight.

'Now, the reason why I really asked you here today,' the Colonel says keenly. 'How would you feel about coming over to this full time? None of this, half advisor to Dan Quayle, half NSC liaison officer. I mean really get you looking after what I need in the region?'

Swallowing, 'Only if you think I'm ready, sir?'

'Absolutely you're ready. Look at you, finger on the pulse, giving me information I otherwise wouldn't have.'

Owen's cheeks begin to blush, 'I'm at your service, sir.'

'Well, all right then. Now, up until recently you've been gathering intelligence, connecting with Contra leaders, appraising the condition of military camps and bases, and relaying that important information between myself and agents in the area.'

'Yes, sir, that's correct.'

Standing and walking over to his desk, 'Well, I think it's high time to get you looking after some more important matters.'

Owen raises his eyebrows.

Picking up three dossiers, North hands them to the young messenger before taking a seat, 'I would like you to start overseeing fund allocation from the State Department contracts these private companies are receiving, as well as NHAO aid money going to companies like *Frigorificos de Punta Arenas*. Then, I want you on weapons detail. As of now there is one main company delivering arms from within Central America. It's called *R&M Equipment* located in Tegucigalpa, Honduras and it's run by a couple of American boys: Ron Martin and James McCoy. However, in the coming months the Contras will start receiving supplies from *Stanford Tech*, a company more familiarly known as the *Enterprise*. Recently retired Major General Secord is a good friend of mine and runs the outfit. Acquaint yourself with the two companies, their supply chains, and so on. We need them to be running as smoothly as possible; no more of this offloading of our supplies, you hear me. Now, I would also like you to meet and communicate with Moshe Arens, the Israeli Defense Minister, Menachem Meron who heads the military attaché for Israel here in DC, and Ahmed Saleed, the Defense Minister for Iran. These three men are crucial to the Iran-Contra supply of weapons.'

Receiving the file, 'And what is it you'd like me to do specifically?' Owen asks.

'Firstly, I want you to be there when the deliveries arrive and ensure they go directly to the Contra camps. Secondly, I want you to oversee the transfer of funds from Iran to Israel and into our bank accounts in the Bahamas. And lastly, I'd also like you to personally verify that fund allocation is going to the right Contra leaders. Understood?'

Scanning the documents, 'Yes, sir. Absolutely.'

Frowning, 'I'm losing track of how many people down there are on the NSC or CIA payroll.' Then, shaking his head, 'Things are only going to escalate from here, which is why I need people I can trust and believe. And you, Robert, are one of those people.'

Smiling, 'Why, thank you, sir.'

Sighing, 'I'm afraid the NSC and CIA are going to have to implement a variety of subversive tactics in the coming months. Small calculated confrontations so that we may weaken the Sandinista resolve.'

Owen looks worriedly at the Colonel over his round wire-frame glasses.

'And I'm only telling you this because I want you to know that I'm being honest with you, Robert. That, refraining detail, I'll be as open as I can with you about how we navigate our way through this mess.'

'I—I understand, sir. Thank you, sir.'

Sliding forward to the edge of the sofa and resting his elbows on his knees, 'You're going to be privy to some very clandestine and classified activities,' the Colonel says in a hushed voice. 'And I need you to be okay with that.' After a pause and an unflinching gaze, 'Are you okay with that, Robert?'

Owen swallows hard.

'Everything that I'm doing has been given the okay from the President himself,' North continues quietly. 'These activities, these problems, are of the utmost national importance and security, and there is nothing you need to worry about.'

Owen nods slowly at first before gaining reassurance.

'Now, one of those problems that needs fixing is a man called Eden Pastora.'

XV
THE MAN IN COSTA RICA

Black smoke plumes high into a blue sky and machinegun fire cracking in short bursts echoes from beyond the tree line ahead. Felix and Rafael, quiet and vigilant, bounce along a dirt road in an open-top jeep trailing a supply truck heading towards the source of the blaze. Commander Enrique Bermudez has been pushing his troops across the Nicaraguan border, harrying newly established Sandinista forces each time they attempt to secure a base. This morning, somewhere atop the La Montana ridgeline a skirmish broke out.

Felix watches the lush greenery blur past before closing his eyes and inhaling the rich jungle air, searching for a calmness he knows exists in spite of the chaos and carnage of war.

'*Ah, puta,*' Rafael complains struggling to crunch the jeep into second gear as the dirt road tunnels beneath a canopy of trees.

As they enter a clearing more errant squirts of gunfire go off, while Contra soldiers appear jovial and laughing. Felix surveys the battleground: burning tents, a shelled cinder block building engulfed in flames, blood-spattered vans riddled with bullets, and dead bodies scattered about the place being undressed and looted.

Skidding to a stop behind the supply truck, several sweat-stained men in military khakis smoking cigarettes and AK47s hanging from their shoulders wander over to greet the arriving vehicles. From the rear of the truck two medics jump out carrying field packs, while soldiers begin unloading fresh water and food stuffs.

Marching towards the jeep is a short stocky man in military uniform and cap, '*Hola*, Agent Gomez. What brings you out here?'

Stepping out of the jeep, '*Hola*, Commander. I was in Teguz checking a weapons shipment when we heard you had initiated an offensive this morning. We drove straight here.'

Removing his cap and wiping sweat from his brow, 'A long way to drive to see dead men.'

Watching soldiers looting dead bodies, 'What are they doing?' Felix asks.

Sucking air sharply through his teeth, 'Spoils of war,' the Commanders says with a shrug.

After a moment, 'Did you lose any men?' Felix asks.

'No, today we were lucky.'

'*Bueno*.'

Looking around, 'This was not a permanent camp but an outpost,' Commander Bermudez says. 'They are guarding the border here east to west, directly south of Danli. The Sandinistas know that's where I am now.'

Nodding, 'You plan to relocate then?'

'*Si*.'

'Where to?'

'Either south to Choluteca or east to Las Mangas.'

Enrique Bermudez is a serious and measured military man with a wealth of experience in jungle warfare. Despite his high rank and importance to the FDN, he cannot bring himself to stay away from the fighting. He knows there is too much at stake. Bermudez also links the military arm of the FDN to Aristides Sanchez's political arm, and in turn connects Adolfo Calero's financial campaigning in the US. Together the men are affectionately known as the Iron Triangle.

Noticing that the Commander appears frustrated, 'You seem displeased, Commander Bermudez?' Felix says.

Sucking air through his teeth again and shrugging, 'What happened here is not the war that needs to be fought. *Sí*, we chip away at Sandinista forces but for the Contras we waste precious munitions.'

Watching the Commander carefully, Felix gives him an understanding look but refrains from saying anything, aware Bermudez wants more supplies despite Felix's inability to deliver.

'How much time do you have, Agent Gomez?'

Checking his antique watch the second-hand has stopped ticking again, 'As much as you need Commander.'

'There is a town about an hour's drive from here. I want to show you what is left of it.'

Frowning, 'What's left?'

'*Sí*. It was attacked a week ago and burned to the ground.'

Felix gives Rafael an uncertain look. 'By who?'

'Who else? Captain Pedro Ortiz,' the Commander says bitterly.

A convoy of three jeeps rumbles its way along a dirt road, stopping periodically to check for Sandinista patrols that may be further down in the valley. Passing acres of abandoned farmland whose operators have likely fled the war—this one or the last—or simply had their land taken by the new government, they see barns sitting on a lean, tractors left to rust, houses dilapidated and vacant; desperation and ruin scarring the landscape. Before long, with the sun high in the sky, they enter a small town whose outbuildings have been blown to pieces by mortar shells. Felix barely searches for indications of what kind of skirmish took place when he sees bloated and rotting bodies lying in the street.

Not much further the jeeps pull over. Exiting the vehicles, soldiers wander over to a cupola shaded by a large almond tree and light themselves cigarettes.

'Come with me please, Agent Gomez,' Commander Bermudez says, leading Felix and Rafael through the town on foot.

Rounding a corner they disturb a cluster of crows pecking at the entrails of a fat woman not yet fully putrefied. Only the two soldiers accompanying them react to the grisly sight, while Felix, Rafael, and the Commander are all too familiar with the gore of war.

'Every building has been torched,' Rafael remarks.

'*Sí*,' Commander Bermudez answers.

Behind what appears to have been the town hall, where the soil is soft and grass grows, a series of shallow pits have been dug with a dozen or two bodies partially concealed by dirt. Men, women, a few elderlies.

Letting the CIA men take in the sight for a moment, 'They made them dig their own graves before slitting their throats,' the Commander says. Then, sucking air in through his teeth, 'No waste bullets. At least you have taught them well, Agent Gomez.'

Felix doesn't respond.

Continuing, 'This is the work of field captains with no experience of battle, just the CIA showing them how to pillage and torture,' the Commander says bleakly. 'Come with me please.'

Leading them across the street they enter a plain building blackened by fire with the roof fully burned away. Beneath their feet ashy debris mounds like sand dunes as what was once tables and chairs and cupboards has been reduced to rubble.

Felix frowns when he notices charred bodies huddled together at the far end, 'What is this?'

'This was the school, Agent Gomez,' the Commander says flatly. 'And they are children,' he says pointing.

Crossing himself, Rafael quietly mumbles a prayer before walking back outside. Felix conceals a sinking feeling of despair and slowly glances around the building, taking in the devastation long enough for Commander Bermudez to not think him cowardly before too making his way out.

Back in the blaze of sunshine the three men are quiet for a moment.

'Did you notice anything in particular about this town, gentlemen?' the Commander asks.

Rafael says dryly, 'Not a single dead soldier.'

'That's right. The threat of this town was that it supported the Sandinista Government. When I questioned Captain Ortiz why he did this, he told me the men here could have raised arms against Contras.' After a moment, 'Captain Ortiz is a *chilote*, remember.'

'Green corn?' Rafael asks.

'*Si*, a *campesino* highlander. They are rural workers from the mountains who originally fought against the Somoza's, then after the overthrow turned against the Sandinistas too. The *chilotes* have had it bad, I'll give them that; losing their land, livestock, even their children when they had no food to put in their bellies. But Captain Ortiz goes too far for his revenge. If only he realized an eye for an eye would leave the whole world blind.' Raising his eyebrows, 'But this is what happens when men are made captains and commanders by the CIA, told to blindly follow that manual you handed to them, and who lack the necessary military teachings such as those who were once a part of the National Guard.'

Felix gives the Commander a stern look, 'And what do you want me to do about it?'

Shrugging, 'Perhaps there is nothing you can do, Agent Gomez. In any case, this is not the war that needs to be fought. But this town lies directly between two-thousand Contra fighters in the mountains and the city of Esteli to the south. After that is Matagalpa and then Managua. Of course, I cannot condone such activity, *senor* Gomez, but I understand this is a revolution after all. If we are to ever lay siege upon the capital, we are standing upon the road that will take us there and such atrocities as you see before you will no doubt happen again for these are the soldiers the CIA have gathered.' After a sigh, 'I wanted you to see this, to see what your Agency is encouraging, what it is responsible for.'

Choosing his words carefully, 'I understand this is not ideal, Commander, but the Contras are outnumbered and outmanned in this fight,' Felix says. 'There is no excuse for killing women and children, but the men here were not just civilians, they were dissenters, wolves in sheep's clothing. And sometimes they are more dangerous than an enemy wearing a uniform holding a gun.'

Sucking air through his teeth, 'You wish to kill the man before he becomes bad, in case he becomes bad?' Smirking, 'This is an *Americano* tactic, Agent Gomez. And I understand it, killing is easier than persuading, and faster too.'

Looking off towards the jungle, 'Sometimes, Commander, people need to be pushed in the right direction, so they can see whose side they should be on.'

Spitting in the dirt, 'I'm only showing you what happened here because this is not your country after all. They are not your children in there, but mine. It is one thing to have a political cause but something else to ensure it is realized.' Raising his eyebrows, 'My point is, we must be careful not to become more monstrous than that which we are revolting against, no? Such blemishes can only be hidden for so long.'

'Indeed, Commander.'

'*Bueno*.' Whistling to his men, 'We should be going, it is not safe for us here.'

As the convoy bounces north back towards the Honduran mountains, their conversation continues.

'Don't get me wrong, Agent Gomez, the FDN sincerely appreciates your efforts to support and supply the Contras, but the path that lies ahead is a difficult one. We need ten-times the men we currently have, and the means to train them. The longer this takes the deeper Sandinista ideology takes root.'

'Don't worry, the Colonel in Washington is working very hard to increase the flow of weapons to you, along with more financial assistance. In the meantime, the Agency will continue to pursue non-combative strategies within Nicaragua.'

'Ah, more *Americano* tactics,' the squat Commander says with a smirk. 'You are a Cuban, yes? Then let us bear in mind that propaganda, political sabotage, and assassination squads did not exactly work in your country either.'

Rafael frowns but Felix remains steady, 'Would you prefer the CIA to stop disrupting the Sandinista ascension to power and control of your country, Commander?'

'I did not say that, Agent Gomez. All I am saying is be careful because the strategies you think are the easiest often come back to bite you.'

Having had enough of playing diplomat, Felix presses the reality of their situation, 'Let us speak frankly, Commander.'

'I thought we were.'

Smiling, 'Yes. Nicaragua and Cuba are not the same. Castro has held the country underwater for decades, and so Cuba is not in a position to be merely swayed politically. Nicaragua on the other hand only needs to be shifted from one side of the revolution to the other. Somoza fractured the country, tore the classes apart. All this country needs is stability, money, and a democratic system to quickly bring it back together. It's not that the people want a socialist government necessarily, they just want a government that isn't ruled by a dictator.'

'That simple, eh?'

'No, you are right. We are getting ahead of ourselves, trying to solve tomorrow's problems today. Right now, the concern is the Contras. What they have, what they need more of, what tilts things in our favor. Agreed?'

'*Si.*'

'Good. And that is why I've come to visit you, Commander, to try my hardest to give you what you need so that we do not have to resort to such underhanded tactics.'

Commander Bermudez raises his eyebrows in agreement.

'Now, there are some matters that I would like to crosscheck with you. Recently I was able to arrange certain financial contributions to make its way to Danli through Ferdinand and Troilo Sanchez. I initially had some minor setbacks securing this channel but I hope things have been more reliable over the last few months?'

Furrowing his heavy brow, 'As far as I can tell, they appear to be.'

'As far as you can tell?'

'*Senor* Gomez, all the money that comes into Danli for the Contras goes through Aristides Sanchez and Horacio Pereira, you should know that.' After a moment, 'But yes, in recent months I would say Pereira has organized the delivery of several military trucks, general supplies, as well as better quality weapons to the frontlines.'

'*Bueno.*'

'However, it is worth noting the weaponry is coming from *R&M Equipment*, while the supply drops directly from the US, from what my captains are telling me, are becoming less frequent and the log sheet often does not match what is on board.'

Shaking his head, Felix gives Rafael a worrying look.

'This is your man, Barry Seal, no?' Bermudez suggests.

'I'm afraid so, Commander. He has been a vital asset in getting supplies deep into the camps but more recently I feel his *cojones* have gotten too big for his pants.'

Bermudez looks unmoved.

'Have you seen him recently?' Felix asks.

'*Si*, I have seen Barry. He flew into camp last week along with Adolfo.' Turning and spitting out of the side of the jeep, 'Maybe you should remind Calero the war is here and not in Miami, eh.'

* * *

Closing his eyes and taking a deep whiff of a *Twinkie* fresh out of its wrapping, Felix licks his lips before plunging the soft spongy cake deep into his mouth. With yellow crumbs dusting his chest and whipped cream smearing into the corner of his mouth, Felix rejoices in this little slice of American heaven. It's been two years, three months and seventeen-days since he has stepped foot on US soil, and so personal deliveries such as a box of *Twinkies* or packs of *Big Red* gum become gifts of indescribable pleasure.

Leaning back in a chair, his office a sty of folders and ledgers and maps, Felix is savoring a moment of tastebud joy when from beneath a pile of papers on the desk a phone rings.

Wiping his mouth, '*Hola?*'

'*Hello, Lazarus, this is North.*'

Sitting up, 'Sir. This is a surprise.'

'*I know, I know, but I have some things we need to discuss personally.*'

'Of course.'

'*There's an American civilian by the name of John Hull living in north-east Costa Rica. He owns a ranch out there with an airstrip and he's eager to aid the Contras.*'

'I see. Do you need me to do a background check?'

'*No, it's already been done. He checks out. Bumblebee is on route to confirm the status of his property, and Clarridge is processing Hull as a CIA asset and getting him on the payroll.*'

'Very good, sir. And how do you want to utilize this asset?'

'Well, he's out there in the mountains somewhere so it's pretty isolated. My thoughts are to open a supply channel between him and the US, if you understand my meaning. Similar cover profiles and protections as the others.'

'Understood, sir.'

'Good. Now, who can you get to fly in and out of there that we don't mind cutting loose if things go pear-shaped? Ideally, they'll need to be connected to the Contras in some way, shape or form so we can keep all of this in-house. Remember, we need plausible deniability at all times.'

'Indeed. Let me see who we have on a watch-list, one moment, sir.' Rummaging through documents on his desk, Felix finds a file listing imprisoned or indicted drug traffickers that could be offered deals and incorporated into a supply program.

Scanning a document, 'This looks good, sir.'

'Go on.'

'Jorge Morales, a Colombian-born resident of Miami, is looking at sixteen-years for cocaine trafficking. He ran a small aviation outfit based out of Opa-Loka airport, Florida. He's a known associate of Popo Chamorro, already a CIA asset in Miami, and Donald Barrios who we know makes ongoing contributions to the Contras and is a friend of Adolfo Calero.'

'That is good.'

After reading more of the file, 'That's interesting,' Felix says.

'What is?'

'Two of Morale's ex-pilots are already running humanitarian aid flights for the Contras. Geraldo Duran and Marcos Aguado are Salvadoran officers. Ferdinand Sanchez put them forward to us when things were just getting started.'

'Well, they'll already by acquainted with operations then. Can you move them across to support this, Jorge Morales?'

'I don't see why not.' Then, with a little concern, 'Sir, Morales is a serious drug man.'

'So? Seems everybody down there is a goddamn trafficker. Make it happen, Felix. I'll get Owen to hand-deliver logistic maps once he's finished surveying Hull's ranch.'

'Thank you, sir. I'll speak to the Justice Department and get Morales a deal. And I'll arrange for agents to contact Chamorro and put him in touch with Morales.'

'*Sounds good. Now, Felix, I'm about to send Bumblebee into the region full-time but,*' after a sigh, '*I still don't think he has the sack to handle us being involved with the powder business.*'

'I see.'

'*Don't get me wrong, he's a patriot and understands that in times of war even the good guys have to do things that would otherwise go against their moral fiber.*'

'Say no more, sir.'

'*Good. And speaking of moral fiber, have you laid eyes on that Seal sonuvabitch?*'

'Not in a few weeks, sir, but Bermudez has.'

'*Is that right?*'

'And he has serious concerns about his reliability of late. Seal appears more concerned with helping Escobar and Ochoa than he does about helping the Contras.'

Felix can hear the Colonel grinding his teeth through the receiver.

'*Don't worry,*' North continues, '*I know. I'll explore options to cut him out as soon as I can.*'

'Very good, sir.'

'*What else have I got for you? Oh, you'll have a couple of new pilots coming in and out of Ilopango, Lazarus. Both former Air America pilots, Terry Reed and Bill Williams. They're going to be heading up a training camp over in Arkansas, teaching groups of Nicaraguans and Salvadorans how to fly, but they'll also be making supply drops to you.*'

'Very good, sir.'

'*One last piece of news. We're going to be making a move on Pastora. He's too much of a liability to the FDN now that we're going to be building a southern front using Hull's ranch as ground zero. We can't have that snake roaming the jungles and potentially undoing all our hard work.*'

'Pastora is not an easy target, sir.'

'*I know. Look, this isn't happening tomorrow. We're still gathering intel on his movements and considering a plan of attack but it'll be soon. With how fractious the Contras are already, unification is paramount.*'

'Indeed it is, sir.'

'*Sorry to drop such a heavy load on you at once, Lazarus, but I only do it because I know you can handle it.*'

'Think nothing of it, sir.'

XVI
FREEWAY RICKY

Blinking his blurry eyes open, morning light filters in through grey venetian blinds. Stretching his wiry body beneath a black satin quilt, Rick realizes he's alone in bed and for a panicked moment wonders whether last night with Marilyn was all a dream. But as if on cue, the soft hum of a woman's voice muffled by the stream of a shower drifts out from the bathroom.

Blinking his eyes and almost coming to, he takes a deep breath, 'We just became the kings of LA.'

Sitting up and rubbing life into his cheeks, Rick's bucktooth grin spreads across his face. A woman, a fine ass woman, is in his shower, naked, singing. Damn, life is good, he thinks.

Checking the time on a bedside clock, 'Shit!' Ten-am; an hour until Rick has to meet Henry.

Jumping out of bed, Rick pulls a pair of stripped drawers on and tiptoes into the bathroom.

'Hey,' he says tentatively, 'Marilyn?'

The singing stops and pulling the shower curtain aside just enough for her to poke her head out, 'Well, good morning, Rick,' Marilyn says with a smile.

Leaning against the vanity, 'I didn't hear you get up. Did you sleep okay?'

Pulling the curtain closed, 'Oh, I slept like a baby,' she giggles.

'That's good.' Scratching his head, 'Hey, umm, I forgot I got some real important business to take care of this morning.'

'Oh,' her tone changes. 'Well, I'll be out in a minute or so.'

'No, no, it's not like that. You take as long as you want.' Rubbing the back of his neck, 'It's just, I didn't expect you to come home with me last night and, and if I'd known then I wouldn't have had this business I need to see to is all.'

Marilyn is quiet for a moment, 'That's fine, I understand.'

Having hit it off so well with her Rick's only concern is that last night was just a booty call for her, while being something much more for him.

Clearing his throat, 'So, umm, are you glad you, you know, you came home with me last night?' Biting his lip, 'I mean, what I'm trying to say is, did you have fun last night, you know, with me?'

Turning the water off and holding her arm out from behind the curtain, 'Towel please.'

Rick scrunches up his face like he's blowing this as he feeds a fluffy towel into the shower.

A few seconds later Marilyn steps out, her body wrapped, and faces the mirror checking for smears of mascara or eye-shadow she may have missed washing off, 'What do you think?' she says plainly.

'Look, I ain't one of them guys that says how a woman should act,' Rick says timidly. 'For me, a woman can do as she pleases and if she just pleases to hook up with a homie then she has every right to. But about last night—'

Turning around to face Rick, she gives him an expecting look.

Swallowing hard, Rick finishes his point nervously, 'I—I'd hate for it to have been just a hook-up because, well because—'

Marilyn's face is cool and unflinching, and her hands clutch tightly at the knot in the towel above her breasts.

Rick swallows again.

'You wanna know if it was just a one-night stand, huh?' she says.

He nods.

Undoing the knot in the towel, Marilyn slowly lets the towel drop to the floor. Stepping forward and cupping Rick's face with her hands, 'Well, I hope this answers your question,' she says teasingly before moving her hands to the top of his head and guiding Rick down to her pussy.

Twenty minutes later Rick is showered and dressed and strutting his way downstairs like Richie Roundtree in *Shaft*. As he enters the large living area, Ollie, Redmon and Lonzo, Moses, and Kenny all turn.

'Rick,' Ollie says dismayed.

'What?'

'What in the hell you doing a cook up last night and leaving crack all over the kitchen for?' he says shocked.

Rick completely forgot about the cocaine on the counter and the biscuits sitting in the saucepans. Rubbing his neck with a dubious expression on his face, his mind goes back to what happened in the kitchen and can only muster a dopey smile in response.

Ollie gives the homies a concerned look before turning back to Rick, 'What's the matter with you? You done slip in the shower and fall on your head or something?'

The creak of footsteps coming down the stairs makes everyone look.

Marilyn enters the room unfazed by the staring homeboys and puts an arm around Rick's waist, 'Hi, I'm Marilyn,' she says with a certain sass.

Despite being fresh-faced she has an undeniable natural beauty; big eyes and long lashes, high cheekbones and juicy lips, and still wearing last night's clothes she maintains a sexiness uncommonly seen at ten in the morning.

'Yo, Moses,' Rick interrupts the gawking, 'Give Marilyn a ride home, aiit.' Then turning to her, 'I'll call you, okay.'

Putting a hand on his cheek and kissing him, 'Yeah you will.'

After Moses walks Marilyn out, 'Who in the Cosby kids was that?' Ollie asks dismayed.

Raising an eyebrow, 'That's Marilyn.'

Giving a series of fast blinks, 'I don't know who Marilyn is but damn she is fine.'

Laughing and shaking his head, 'You ain't gotta tell me, man.'

'Hold up,' Ollie's eyes squint, 'she ask for any coke?'

Smiling, 'Nope.'

'Any free crack?'

'Uh uh.'

Squinting so hard his eyes almost shut, 'She ask for money?'

Laughing, 'Not a dollar.'

'Well, god damn, Freeway,' Ollie says with a huge smile, 'you done found yourself a woman?'

All the homies start hollering and whistling making Rick blush a little. He can feel butterflies in his stomach still and knows he's found something special in Marilyn despite only meeting her last night. And he must be giving off a vibe about it too because even the guys can tell something is different.

Getting a little embarrassed, 'All right, all right. Y'all acting like I never been with a girl before,' he says feigning a tough guy act but keen to change subjects. 'Now, we going to meet Henry or what?'

'Yeah, in a minute,' Ollie says. 'We just waiting on Shrimp and his boys to get here so we can sort them out for getting run in yesterday.'

The doorbell rings and Redmon gets up to answer it.

In walks Shrimp, a tall skinny homie with dreadlocks, Young Stevie who's about five feet tall on a good day, and Clyde and his little brother Doc both with matching flat-top afros; all of them sporting scuffs and scratches, and Shrimp a swollen black eye.

'What up, what up, what up?' Shrimp greets everyone jovially, proud to have done a night in the slammer.

Once they've sat down, 'So,' Ollie asks, 'How'd you go in holding overnight?'

'*Pshh*, it won't ain't no thing, O. Them pigs only booked us on misdemeanor and intent to sell because we had fuck all in the spot. Doc there had just done a cash run not ten minutes before and we were waiting for a re-up from the stash house.'

'That's real good,' Rick says.

'Yeah, that lawyer of yours, Mr. Fenster, he came and spoke to us in the afternoon and told us everything was gonna be cool.'

'They ask you any questions?' Ollie asks routinely.

'Yeah.'

'And what'd you say?'

'I told them the crack fairy comes every night at midnight to bring us the goodies.'

All the boys snicker.

Shrimp continues, 'That's when they gave me this,' pointing to his busted eye. 'But check it, have I got news for you,' he says turning to Rick.

A wash of concern grips Freeway. Despite going to painstaking lengths to stay under the radar, he is one of the biggest, if not *the* biggest coke dealer in LA, and even he's unsure what kind of information law enforcement have on him.

'We got put in a holding cell with about twenty other brothers,' Shrimp begins. 'All arrested yesterday or the day before. Aside from a couple of Crips most of them were just peddlers and street hustlers. But get this, these two beefy white cops come into the cell and start eyeballing everyone real slow. They ain't saying nothing, just coming up to your face and acting all tough. Anyway, one of them comes up to me and says, you, are you Freeway Ricky? I was like what? Hell nah I ain't Freeway. I don't even know who that is. Then across the cell, the other cop goes to another brother, what about you, are you Freeway?'

Ollie and Rick exchange a confused look.

'The cops do this to another four or five guys,' Shrimp continues, 'just asking the same question. At first, I thought it was because I got dreadlocks like you, but they were asking cats of all different shapes and sizes if they was you. These cops, man, they know your name but they ain't got a clue who the fuck you are.'

Ollie starts to chuckle, and so do Redmon and Lonzo. Then everybody is doubled over laughing. Rick feels a wave of relief rush over him and shakes his head smiling. Once everyone has calmed down Ollie becomes serious.

'Well, if our spots are gonna get hit now, what are we gonna do to protect our crew?' he asks the group.

'I already thought of how,' Rick says meditatively.

Everyone looks at him with quiet attention. He may be a high school dropout but Rick is as street-smart as they come and they know it. Even his partner and best friend Ollie concedes that Rick is clever in ways he'll never be, and doesn't mind being the brawn, while Rick is the brains.

'When I was driving home last night, I noticed one of them duplex houses down the street was having a party,' Rick explains. 'One side was all lit up, lights on, music bumping, barbeque smoking at the back, but right next door the lights were off, and ain't nobody home.' Nodding to himself, 'That's where we gonna move our spots to.'

A little uncertain, 'To the house down the street?' Ollie asks.

Scrunching his face, 'No, into those duplexes all around the place; the ones that are joined down the middle. We'll have a stash house on one side and leave the other side empty, then we're gonna bar-up the windows and put extra locks on the doors so it takes longer for the cops to get in.'

'What good is that gonna do if the homies are stuck inside?' Kenny says confused.

'Don't you get it? The cops can't raid your neighbors just because you live next to each other,' Rick says. 'That's where the duplex comes in. Inside a cupboard or a closet, we gonna cut a secret passage that leads into the next door. This way the homies can sneak out, while the cops are trying to get in, then, by the time they do bust in, our guys can just walk out onto the street and stand with everybody else watching the cops look like fools busting an empty house.'

'I'll be damned,' Kenny says softly, 'that is some serious David Copperfield.'

Smiling, 'Like I always say, goddamn genius,' Ollie adds.

Rick is grinning from ear to ear, 'What's a hundred dollars a week in rent if we're gonna have to bail out crew all the time? Oh, speaking of,' he gets up and grabs a small gym bag from the dining table. Unzipping it he takes out four stacks of cash held together with rubber bands.

Standing in front of the youngsters, 'All right, Shrimp, ten-kay,' he says slapping a thick wad of bills into his hand. 'Young Stevie, seven-and-a-half. Clyde and Doc, five grand each.'

They all look down at the cash in their hands before giving each other confused looks.

'It's a goodwill gesture, homies,' Rick says.

'Y-you don't need to do that, Freeway,' Shrimp says hesitantly. 'We're your boys, man.'

'Yeah, I do. You getting sweated by the cops because you're moving my dope. That makes me half at fault. So, this is a thank you gift. Plus, that's strike one. One more strike and you're out of the dope game, so I wanna make sure you're properly compensated. Ain't none of my homies gonna get three strikes and life, while I'm running things.'

'Damn,' Shrimp whispers gratefully, while Clyde and Doc stare at the cash in their hands having never seen so much at once that is all theirs.

After a moment, 'All right, now go on and get outta here. We gotta book. Ollie will organize a new spot for you in the next couple days, aiit.'

The young homies all stand and shake hands before filing out of the house before Rick and Ollie double-check the amount of cash in the gym bag and head off to meet Henry.

It's a sunny but crisp spring day and the cherry red billboard of *Taco Pete* gleams bright. A humble window-serve Mexican spot that does ninety-nine-cent tacos on the corner of Manchester and Second Avenue in Morningside Park, just around the block from where Henry used to live. Bustling with customers, the small eatery enchants locals with its retro stonework walls and yellow and red coloring, taking people back to the '60s when fast food first kicked off.

Sitting at a bench on his own, Henry is bent over eating when Rick and Ollie approach him.

Seeing them Henry jumps to his feet and quickly licks his fingers clean, 'Ricky man,' he says hugging him. 'And Mr. Ollie,' smiling and hugging him too. 'Please, sit down, sit down.'

'So, Henry,' Rick begins, 'How you been, man?'

While finishing off a fish taco, 'Me? Oh, good and not so good,' he mumbles. 'Listen, gentlemen, I have to apologize for disappearing unannounced many months ago. My mother was very sick you see, in Honduras, I had to fly out straight away and be with her. I should have said something but I didn't have time. And then the nasty business that happened to Diego,' Henry stops eating to do a cross.

'Is Diego getting better?' Rick asks.

Dropping his taco into a paper basket and wiping his hands with a napkin, 'No, I'm afraid not,' he says sadly. 'He is in a very bad way. Paralyzed and weak, he needs twenty-four-hour care. When he's a little better he will be going to Costa Rica, likely for the rest of his life.'

'Damn, man. Well, we're sorry to hear it,' Rick says.

'Yeah, give him our best wishes when you see him next,' Ollie offers.

'I will, I will.' Wiping his hands clean Henry eyes the gym bag sitting between Rick and Ollie. Clearing his throat, 'Is that what I think it is?'

Rick puts his hand on top of the bag and nods, 'Eighty-gees.' Looking around, 'but I don't think this is a spot you wanna count it.'

Smiling, 'Oh, I don't need to count it, Ricky man. You and Mr. Ollie are not strangers but businessmen and friends, and we have known each other long enough, yes.'

'That's true,' Rick says, 'but there's just one thing missing from this handover, Henry. Where's your uncle Danilo?'

Turning around and looking into the parking lot behind *Taco Pete*, a black Cadillac Fleetwood is parked in direct view of them. Standing by the driver's side door is a thickset man with slick grey hair and a bushy mustache.

'Is that your uncle?' Rick asks.

'No, that is Poppy, my uncle's bodyguard. Danilo is in the back seat waiting for you.'

Standing, 'Well, let's get this show started.'

As they walk over Poppy opens the passenger door and inside the Nicaraguan bookkeeper awaits legs crossed in a fine black suit.

Henry goes suddenly shy, '*Hola*, Danilo.'

Tilting his head, 'Henry.'

Clearing his throat, 'I—I guess I'll be on my way then,' Henry mumbles before rather awkwardly hugging Rick and Ollie at the same time, one arm around each man's neck. 'My bag, Ricky man?' he says holding out his hand.

Rick looks slowly from Poppy to Danilo and knows these cats are the real deal despite Henry's strange behavior. He hands over the bag and Henry backs away nodding and thanking them.

'Please, *senor* Ricky,' Danilo says from inside the car, 'take a seat so that we may talk.'

Rick spots Redmon and Lonzo in the parking lot who are packing heat and ready and waiting should anything go wrong. He climbs into the back seat, while Ollie stands outside the car with Poppy.

Before either Rick or Danilo speaks, they both curiously watch Henry half walk half run to his car before screeching off.

'What's up with Henry,' Rick asks.

Shaking his head, 'He is embarrassed, you see, because he only agreed to hand you over to me if I paid him eighty-thousand dollars.'

'What! You too? Damn, Henry charged *me* eighty grand to meet you!'

Closing his eyes and smirking, Danilo pinches the bridge of his nose.

Despite eighty-thousand dollars being roughly a good day's work to Rick, he's still surprised at Henry's handiwork, 'Man, why would your nephew do you like that?'

'Nephew? Henry said I was his uncle?'

'Yeah.'

Chuckling, 'Oh dear. What else did he say?'

'The reason he disappeared the last few months was because his moms got sick in Honduras.'

Now laughing, 'His mother?' Danilo says slapping his thigh, 'That *puta*, Henry, he was smoking the crack. We sent him to Honduras to get him clean only to realize we no longer had any use for him. Well, there was one thing we needed from him. You, *senor* Ricky.'

'Shiiit.'

'Well, you can't blame him for trying one last score before being cut loose,' Danilo says. 'Anyhow, let us rejoice that we have met at long last. It would seem you and I have actually been business partners for quite some time only Henry stood between us.'

Nodding, 'His coke was your coke.'

'That's right. And even the coca you have been so arduously getting from Miami is still coca coming through the Nicaraguan network.'

'For real?'

'Indeed. Now, despite it belonging to the broader Nicaraguan connection, it is fair to say that you are buying from my competitors, which is a grave injustice to you when you consider the same product is sitting right here in Los Angeles.'

'And I'm thinking at better prices too?'

Smiling, 'I imagine so.' Opening a small black diary on his lap, Danilo looks overs his notes, 'As far as I can tell you're getting fifteen to twenty kilos a week through Miami at roughly forty- to forty-five-thousand a brick.' Looking at Rick, 'You don't have to answer. I may be off here or there but that is what I figure.' Closing his diary, 'What I would like to offer you is thirty-thousand a kilo starting with thirty kilos a week. How does that sound?'

Rick's heart skips a beat. The bookkeeper is bang on with what he's moving out of Miami but he doesn't care how he knows. All Rick can think about is making an extra nine-hundred-thousand dollars a month without having to do anything different. No, with having to do *less* by not having to ship his coke all the way from Miami to LA. On top of that not only wouldn't he have to partner up with Chinese Dave any more, but with the price being ten-grand less per key he'll be able to turn any competitor in LA into a customer.

'You got yourself a deal,' Rick says keenly.

Patting Rick on the knee, 'Very good. Now, as you can tell, at this quantity I care more about volume then price. Are you confident you can move such weight per week?'

Smiling his bucktooth grin, 'At thirty-thousand a key, the only problem I'm gonna have is running out.'

Chuckling, 'Oh, *senor* Ricky, I don't believe we'll be running out for many years to come.'

'Well, when do you wanna start?' Rick asks.

'How about right now?'

Rick looks around, 'We ain't sitting on thirty kilos, are we?'

'No, don't be silly.' Leaning forward and resting an arm on the front seat divider, 'You see that brown Honda parked over there?'

Squinting, 'Yeah, the two-door Silverfish.'

'Thirty kilos in the trunk. Keys in the ashtray,' Danilo says coolly.

Looking at the tubby Nicaraguan a little speechless, 'Man, I don't know what to say.'

Smiling, 'Say, you're welcome, because it is you who is also doing me a favor don't forget it.'

'I'll just say thank you, thank you a lot, Danilo. What about the car, where do I return it?'

'You don't. This is how our deals will be done. Each week a new car, coca in the trunk and keys in the ashtray.'

'And how do I pay you?'

Taking a slip of paper from his diary, 'This is my address in Carson. It's a small office building with an underground parking lot. Deliver the money in a clean car, park it, and—'

'Leave the keys in the ashtray,' Rick finishes.

Nodding and smiling, 'Just so, *senor* Ricky.' Handing him the piece of paper, 'This here is my phone number. You can call me any time, day or night. On occasion I am in San Francisco for business, but this is only for a few days at a time.'

'Aiit, sounds good.'

'I look forward to this being the beginning of a long and fruitful partnership, one in which we both prosper handsomely from our efforts.'

'Me too, Danilo. Me too.'

'Well,' gesturing a hand towards the parked Honda, 'your chariot awaits, *senor* Ricky.'

They shake hands and Rick climbs out. Poppy gives both men a steely look but says nothing before getting in and driving off.

'What'd he say,' Ollie asks eagerly.

Slowly, Rick looks around; at the sky, at *Taco Pete*, at people walking on the street as if seeing it all anew.

'Yo, what happened, Rick?'

XVII
CARLOS CABEZAS

Jutting out from a faded blue-brick building, the old *Aztec Theatre's* three-line marquee hangs cracked and discolored. Large retro neon letters, bulbless and broken, are held in place by bolts so severely rusted they've stained the paneling brown. A stiff breeze whips bits of trash down the Fifth Avenue sidewalk, while the lifeless vacancy declares Gaslamp seedy and hungover.

Blowing warmth into his hands, Carlos shrugs off a crisp morning chill.

Looking fondly up at the marquee, 'Don't ask me why but the *Aztec* is one of my favorites,' Vince says tenderly in a pressed white suit.

Along the wall old show posters in the process of peeling away reveal the acts they replaced, and those before them, while windows and doors are boarded up and graffitied in fading colors. In the doorway a faint smell of urine hangs but Vince appears unbothered.

With no electricity running through the building and a windowless foyer, the men walk into almost pitch darkness.

'Mind your step, darling,' Vince calls to Carlos as he makes his way knowingly through the gloom.

Pushing open two swing doors Vince leads them into the small theatre, while their feet crunch unswept dirt and debris as they walk down the aisle towards the stage. Filtering in through small windows high up near the rafters, grey light catches dust motes floating through the shards. Up a creaking staircase and across a wide timber catwalk littered with cables and disused lighting equipment, the men enter a bare room framed by a dirty wall-to-wall window overlooking the city. At the far end a pair of brown leather armchairs sit opposite each other with a small wooden side table between them and an ashtray overflowing with old cigarette butts.

Taking a seat Vince retrieves a silver cigarette case from his inside pocket, pulls a smoke and taps the tobacco end gently on the lid, 'This is my quiet place, Mr. Cabezas. Where I come to brood.'

Standing with his hands on his hips in front of the glass, Carlos quietly surveys the city.

Lighting the cigarette and drawing deeply on it, 'I'll say it so you don't have to. Yes, George is fucking that kid.' Rubbing his temple, 'That Beverly Hills shoe salesman.'

Carlos glances at Vince but says nothing.

Sighing, 'George and I have been together a long time and we've been through a lot. He's a reserved man but he has ambition and gusto when he needs to. Me, I'm a hustler with flare and a fine suit. I know what I want and I know how to get it.' Dragging on his cigarette, 'Welton Jones did an article on me last year and asked how much I was worth. I guessed around twelve-million.'

'Guessed?'

Smiling, 'That's what he said. If you can count how much you have then you can't have that much, can you?' Vince says knowingly.

Carlos raises his eyebrows in agreement.

'I'd be lying if I said I could have achieved all of this without George though. I would have done all right but not this good. Him on the other hand would have very little if it weren't for me. So,' he says drawing on the cigarette, 'he can have his toy boy, I don't care. We've both had our share of affairs.' Smirking, 'One of the perks of being gay is the obscene number of lovers you can negotiate in and out of your life. With no wife or children to blur things, having the occasional tryst damages little.' Rubbing his temple again, 'But for the first time I can't see what's in front of me, Carlos. And it's making me nervous.'

Carlos takes a seat in the leather chair, 'You said when we first met that your life is in these walls. If you're not in San Diego, what will you do?'

With a careless shrug, 'Retire back home to our walnut farm in Encino, drink scotch for breakfast and watch the sun rise over the horizon through the haze of my cigarette, I suppose.'

'That doesn't sound like you?'

'I'll be fifty next month and I have no idea where the years have gone.' After a pause, 'We all want to go somewhere peaceful before we die.'

Carlos hints a smirk, 'Are you giving up the fight?'

'I didn't think I was but perhaps I am. There is only so much George and I can do to ward off the Committee. They want to clean this place up and we are the gay trash in the way. The city's occupancy rate is in decline and hotels are struggling all over the place. But not my hotels, no, they're always close to full. And do you know why, Carlos? Because I have the attractions that keep people coming to Gaslamp. And when Downtown is bustling people need a place to crash, so pick a hotel, I don't care which one because I own them all. *Mr. Penn's*, the *St James*, the *Hotel San Diego*, you name it.

'It's not my fault the city has a plug up its ass, that they're too straight to have a little nudity on a big screen. I mean this is a damn navy town after all; how many sailor boys are fucking their wives and daughters and sons for Christ's sake? But no, they want to clean it up, sweep us all out and build malls and department stores and ice-cream parlors. And how long will that take, ten years? And what happens in the meantime? What happens to all the hardworking Joes that built this place, that give it life and energy and character? They want, nay, need to enjoy the fruits of their labor,' Vince scoffs. 'They brag about Gaslamp being the historic district but they're happy to tear down its history and replace it with shiny junk. Wolves, Carlos, wolves they are. And who are we to the rest of the city's developers, huh? Just a couple of fags who no longer belong, who don't fit the sales brochure of the new San Diego. There, see those cranes, Carlos? That's the new *Horton Plaza* going up. A two-hundred-million-dollar development. We can't compete against that.'

'There's always a bigger fish,' Carlos says distantly, strangely thinking of Norwin and the power the little man has over him even from afar.

'Quite right. I do the best I can. My theatres get closed down or I close them, rename them, reopen them,' shaking his head tiredly. 'I lose one, purchase another. It's a game I know I'll eventually lose, but if I can take a few of the bastards down with me, by God I will.'

Watching him quietly, Carlos knows when a man is speaking to heal himself and not because he wants to be heard, so he stays silent and lets more of Vince's pain surface to the top.

Continuing after a moment, 'I thought maybe, just maybe, I'd have at least one hotel that was all mine, and a couple of theatres too. Ones not just for smut but for real shows with dancers and singers and all the rest. But they just don't want us here anymore the damn wolves. The Committee, the mayor, hell, even Jerry despite how hard he kisses my ass.'

'And yet you are always together, you and these wolves,' Carlos inquires.

Smiling and lighting another cigarette, 'All this time, my dear Carlos, you keep asking why I go to his parties when what you should be asking is, why am I being invited?'

Carlos immediately realizes his misjudgment.

'You see, Jerry wants this building.'

'The *Aztec?*'

'Not just the theatre, darling, but the shoebox *Fox Theatre* next door and the *Casino Theatre* next to that. It's all one title. Sure, he's a condescending prick to me in front of his friends but when we are behind closed doors, he turns on quite the charm. Naturally, I know he's full of shit but I let him believe he has the wool over me. So, he continues to invite me to his obnoxious soirees and I indulge him by going.'

'Okay. And why does he want this building?'

Stretching out his arms, 'Because it is a rundown forty-thousand square-foot gold mine. I may look like a silly fag immigrant to these big shots, but I started from nothing, Carlos. And anyone who starts from nothing and is able to build what I have is not someone you can pull the wool over.'

'Are you finally showing me your cards?'

Smiling, 'I know the Dominelli brothers are up to no good. They are taking invested money and shysting people. Of course, it'll be years before any of the poor souls realize that Jerry and his brother and their harem of girls are off spending every dollar. Yes, it'll come crashing down eventually but even the

Dominelli's aren't that stupid.' Sitting back and crossing his legs, 'You see, when you are a major property owner here in San Diego you are given proposal documents for any new developments that could affect your business assets, and this has included everything Jerry has started or says he will.'

'And what have you found?'

Leaning forward, 'Every project that has monumental foreseeable delays is licensed to what I believe are front corporations. Corporations that, should the projects go bankrupt, Jerry and his brother appear only as consultants of. These are the companies that I just know they're stealing peoples' money from. Now, every piece of property or development that has actually gone up belongs to another company, one that lists the Dominelli's on the board of trustees. And the proposition papers he has offered me for this building is from precisely that company.'

Nodding, 'Clever. But that does not explain how you are going to screw him over.'

'Well, this theatre is owned by *Walnut Properties*, as are all of our other assets, however there is something special about this building. We first purchased it in our private names before handing it over to *Walnut*, but because of its lucrative size we added in a ninety-nine-year ground lease in the original contract.'

'What is a ground lease?'

Smirking, 'It means whoever buys the building doesn't own the land that it's on. They can develop whatever they want and not only do I get paid a monthly fee but it comes with all sorts of juicy eviction rights.'

Frowning, 'Won't they notice this ground lease when they purchase the building from you?'

Pinching the pleat in his suit pant and straightening it, 'Like I said, Jerry and Richie are shysters. They want to steal from people, dupe them and take what isn't theirs. It's in their nature.' Narrowing his eyes, 'He invites me to his parties so I can see how badly the city's players don't want me here, how seriously my time is at an end. And the snake does it so I will jump at whatever offer he presents me for this building. Remember, I am not selling, he is buying. He has already tried to purchase it from me with a verbal contract and a handshake can you believe. No, no, no, he'll present me with a barely legal document that practically steals this place from me, and while feigning capitulation I'll reluctantly sign it. They'll pay me real money, not like the rest of their Ponzi schemes, and when they finish building whatever they plan to build here I'll expose them as frauds by flicking the first domino that'll knock over everything they have ever touched in this beautiful city.'

Nodding, 'Bravo, *senor* Miranda.'

Vince rolls an arm in front of his chest before bowing slightly in the chair.

'So, this is it, your last move before leaving your beloved San Diego?'

With a forlorn look, 'It may be. I don't want to go, of course. My blood is in these walls and my soul in the streets,' Vince says with vigor. 'But my theatres are closing one by one and I've been fighting criminal charges since the early '70s. I've lost some, won others, and lost again. This is nothing new. The only difference is I'm getting old, Carlos, and my heart wants peace.'

'I know what you mean.'

'Yes, you do, which is why you spend so much time here now isn't it? You've come to love this city, just as I did all those years ago. You can feel its warmth, its pulse, you, a real man of real appetites knows what thrives here. You can feel it under your skin, coursing your veins. It's the salt in the air, the heat of the sun, liquor in the bars, and pussy in your face. Or in my case, cock in my mouth,' he says jokingly.

Carlos chuckles looking down at his hands.

Leaning forward, Vince softens his tone, 'I see you are torn between worlds, my dear Carlos. The longing for your home in the jungle, the drug business in LA, your woman in San Francisco, and Dante's *Paradiso* you've found here in Gaslamp.' After a pause, 'It would seem you too are on the precipice. You too must look into your heart and choose.'

Now it's Carlos's turn to brood.

Draping an arm across the back of the chair and lighting a cigarette with his other hand, 'I know what you're thinking, how do you start over again without leaving it all behind?' Then, taking the smoke from his mouth and exhaling, 'I'm not sure you can. I'm not sure you're supposed to.'

* * *

Looking at his reflection in a smeared bathroom mirror of *Studio West* nightclub, the music muffling its way downstairs and voices yelling from the corridor, Carlos stares expressionless. Laughing, a couple of skinny glam boys burst out of a cubicle together. Seeing the small bag of coke and a line racked and ready to be inhaled, one of them bites his lip preparing to ask for a bump. His friend however, recognizing the Nicaraguan in his linen grey suit and silk floral shirt not being a typical guest of the west San Francisco club thinks better of it, pulling him away.

Oblivious to the spectacle behind him Carlos hunches over and snorts.

Despite being the men's room, in come a trio of women; two brunettes and a blonde, all with big hair, heavy eye-makeup and wearing fishnet stockings, a bit of leather and not much else. Two squish into a cubicle squealing gaily, while the blonde notices Carlos's coke and struts over.

Running her fingers across his broad shoulders she crooks a smile at him in the mirror, 'So, are you gonna keep all this blow to yourself or do you wanna make a girl's night?' she whispers in his ear.

Stuck in his own world, Carlos barely notices her, 'I'm sorry?'

'The blow, daddy, can I get a hit?'

Looking down, 'Oh. Have it,' he says rubbing his nostrils and walking away.

Confused, 'What, all of it?' the blonde calls out.

Striding down a dimly lit corridor, the heat and volume of *Studio West* ramps up. Pressing against the wall he passes a guy and a girl making out, followed by two girls doing the same only with a little better technique. Further down the raucous of thirty women yelling over the top of one another is deafening as they cue for the ladies bathroom. The passageway stifling with the smell of cigarette smoke, body sweat, and a concoction of countless perfumes and colognes. Up a dark stairway, the DJ spinning *Gimme the Night*, and a huge blast from a smoke machine greets Carlos as he enters the club's main floor. Squiggles of red neon spell the venues name on a huge brick wall, while blue and green lasers cut across the vaulted ceiling of the two-story warehouse, and dancers in white leather groove atop catwalks and podiums that ring the iridescent dance floor.

Standing on the edge and watching, Carlos eyes a cute redhead in a gold sequin dress dancing feverishly in a world of her own. With every twist of her hips and shake of her tits her outfit sparkles and shines, bringing on his high. Taking a deep breath he feels a kind of giddy feeling bloom in his chest; a result of the serotonin starting to skyrocket. Mesmerized by the shimmering dress, his vision tunnels and the energy in his solar plexus turns to liquid and courses his veins. Running his fingers through his hair, Carlos takes a deep breath and squeezes his way into the hot sweaty throng of disco fever. Rubbing against warm bodies, faces appear clear and faultless before suddenly melting into a Dali or fracturing like a Basquiat. Women twist and tease and men rub and grope; the *Studio West* dance floor is sex with clothes on.

Out of nowhere, a slender hand grips the back of his neck and pulls him down. Soft lips press against his own, while a wet tongue briefly enters his mouth.

'Thanks for the blow, daddy,' the pretty face says before disappearing back into the orgy.

Barely registering the experience, Carlos smiles to himself and squeezes further into the dancefloor.

'Hey, my man, Cabezas!' a voice yells from behind. Rocking a black perm and sunglasses with two scantily clad women under each arm, it's Pedro, the strip club owner from Oakland. He's wearing an open brown fur coat so big it looks to have been a Grizzly, but topless underneath save for a thick gold chain and black leather pants so tight you can see the contour of his cock. 'Man, is it good to see you.'

Carlos smiles and nods, not yet ready to materialize words.

'Where's your drink, man?' Pedro says looking at his empty hands.

If a face could mumble then that's what Carlos's does.

Possessing a lavish appetite, Pedro is of course sporting two drinks. Handing one to Carlos, 'Here, *chicano*.'

Taking a big gulp, it's a coke and whiskey. Not Carlos's liquor of choice but the ice-cold liquid is like mana from heaven pouring into his overheating body. Taking a breath and licking his lips, Carlos bottoms up the drink.

Laughing, 'See, I know that face, it says, I'm fucking high as a mother fucker but damn I'm thirsty.'

'What brings you across the Bay, Pedro?' Carlos says slowly.

'What else, pussy,' he says squeezing the women at his side. 'Nah, everyone knows the best clubs are on this side of the bridge. But what gives, brother? I haven't seen you in ages. Julio says you moving to San Diego or some shit?'

'No. Maybe. I don't know.'

Smirking, 'Well, there must be something there to leave all this behind.'

Avoiding the topic, 'How's business, good? Julio keeping on top of things for you?'

'Keeping on top of things? Man, you guys are getting it in faster than I can move it,' Pedro says with a laugh. 'I've opened up two more spots since I last seen you. Come over to O-Town next time you're in Frisco, you can have a taste of my wares,' he says with a quick double raise of his eyebrows.

'I will, I will,' Carlos says affectionately knowing he never will.

'Alright, be cool, Cabezas. I see your ass soon,' Pedro declares before moving off.

The conversation with the strip club owner snaps Carlos from his high. Looking up to the second floor he sees Sofia sitting with the others and is jolted back to the discomfort of San Francisco, of his fraying relationship, of Norwin, the FDN, and organizing the never-ending flow of tons of cocaine from one country to another and all the people who need to be made happy along the way. His high sinking like a stone in a pool, thinking, maybe he shouldn't have given that bag of coke away.

A steel staircase leads Carlos up to a mezzanine floor and back to their private booth. Around a glass table strewn with an assortment of drinks, Sofia, Lucile, Charlie, and Luna are in typical party spirits. Well, all except Lucile whose been nursing her Ramos Gin Fiz for the last hour, her mood persistently sour ever since the raid last month.

'You're back, *papi?* You were gone so long I thought maybe you went back to San Diego,' Sofia says with bitter sarcasm.

Leaving her question alone, Carlos squeezes into the booth and sucks the rum-coated ice in his glass before signaling to Julio standing at the bar for another round.

Sofia gives him a lingering look that he's become all too familiar with. He knows he deserves it. He knows it's the quaintness of San Diego, Tijuana a mere forty-minute drive south where he can speak Spanish again, it's Vincent Miranda and Donna Martin, and dare he admit Nancy Hoover. These places and these people revitalizing something inside him, a fondness, a pleasure unspoiled by war or drug deals, and yes, perhaps it's a fresh start he never thought he'd have.

Looking down and stirring her drink, 'I don't understand why the cops came to our house,' Lucile says quietly to Carlos. 'How did they know to go there?'

The question catching him off-guard, 'Well, they were tipped off,' Carlos offers. 'Who knows how long they could have been following Julio. Or the other guys for that matter.'

'But not you?' she says resentfully.

Frowning, 'Excuse me?'

Tossing her straw onto the table, 'No, you didn't get in any trouble because you're never here anymore. Just Julio to take all the heat,' Lucile sulks.

Carlos watches her carefully, not knowing where this is coming from.

'If Julio was in San Diego,' she goes on, 'he wouldn't be in any trouble. It's not fair.'

With the cocaine he snorted still rifling through his brain Carlos is too spaced out to deal with a high-strung headcase and stands from the table.

Arriving with two rums on ice and seeing Lucile fighting back tears, Julio's face turns to confusion, 'Hey, what's a matter with you?' he says to her. Then to Carlos, 'What did you say to her?'

'Me? Nothing. She just went off about you getting arrested last month.'

Julio makes a tired face before leading Carlos back to the bar.

Putting the drinks down, 'Man, Luci has been breaking my balls. I get she's upset with the cops kicking our door in but she's really been shaken up by it. She ain't no Sofia, that's for sure.'

'What's that supposed to mean?'

Shrugging, 'Sofia gets off on the fact that you're a big-time coke dealer but Luci can't stand it. Plus with you spending so much time in San Diego lately and me picking up the load here, now add to that getting arrested and that I'm gonna have to do a stint in jail,' Julio makes a pained face and leaves his point unfinished.

'It'll be six-months at most,' Carlos says.

Shaking his head, 'Doesn't matter, she wanted me out of the business *before* the bust, now you can imagine what she's like. You should have seen her when she came to visit me at the station, yelling about the DEA coming after the wrong people. She got so worked up she almost fainted.' Taking a sip of rum, 'She's like Jekyll and Hyde, man. One day she's angry at me, angry at Norwin, and the next she's crying saying how she messed up and got it all wrong.'

'Got what all wrong?' Carlos asks.

'Falling in love with me, a bad boy coke dealer,' Julio says with a cheeky grin.

Frowning, Carlos sighs at the situation, knowing it's never good for business having someone so emotional so close.

'Don't worry, *hermano*, I'll make her okay,' Julio reassures. 'I'm gonna have to lay low for a while now anyway.'

Carlos gives his cousin a concerned look before leaning on the bar and sipping his drink, 'Speaking of Norwin, how do you think he'll feel about me leaving San Fran, permanently?'

'Permanently?' Julio says raising his eyebrows.

'Come on, don't act so surprised.'

'I know, I know. You love it down there, I get it. But what about the business here we've been trying to build for the last two years? What about Danilo in LA? Hell, what about Sofia?'

Looking over his shoulder towards the booth, 'That's just it, you have San Fran sown up, Danilo has LA, and Sebastian is doing more and more of the leg work in the jungles. What do I need to be here for anymore?'

Grabbing him by the neck and shaking him gently, 'When did this happen, Carlos? When did you change, man?' Julio says with a comforting smile.

Looking into his drink, 'I don't know, *hermano*. Maybe it's not being able to go back home to Managua. I feel like I'm just floating around.' Taking a sip of rum, 'Then there's Norwin, he's a madman and because of him we're in the FDN's pocket, and because of that we're in the CIA's pocket now too. And then, the people I've met in San Diego,' shaking his head, 'they're different, they're outside all of this and they make me forget about it. They care about different things, want different things and I like that.' After a deep sigh, 'Sofia loves the power, it makes her feel invincible, but I don't want that, not the power or the fear hiding underneath it. And I sure as hell don't want to owe anybody, least of all my life. We've already lost too much, *hermano*.'

Julio whistles a long note, high to low. '*Dale pues*. Well, as we say back home, you make the road by walking on it.'

Carlos raises his drink, 'And eyes that see do not grow old.'

They chink glasses and gulp down the rum.

Leaning his elbow on the bar, 'But, what are you going to do about her?' Julio gestures at Sofia. 'She's got bigger *cojones* than most guys I know.'

Looking at her pensively, 'All things in this world must come to an end, Julio.'

With dawn approaching, the drive back to his Protero Hill apartment is quiet and uncomfortable. The plight of Carlos's predicament encumbered further by his Colombian high finally starting to wane, while Sofia, whose seething resentment is merely a daily add-on—like applying eye-liner or blush—is now only half drunk, the half that is bitter and jilted and looks how smeared mascara might feel.

Neither of them is willing to start a conversation on the way home, not even something hollow that would get them started at least to what is to come. Both filled with ammunition and argument and counter-argument to what the other will say, if they said it, if only someone would say a word. Just one. But neither of them does. They're still silent as Carlos pulls into the parking garage; the screech of the roller door grating like fingernails on a chalkboard. Echoing through the garage tires squeak as rubber turns on polished cement. Turning off the ignition Carlos remains quiet, pausing for a brief second before giving up and reaching for the door handle. The outsole of Carlos's wingtip shuffles across the cement of the parking garage, too tired to be lifted properly for each step, while Sofia's bare feet pit-pat on the cold ground, but still no words. The ding of the elevator and the grind of the doors opening, a slow heavy push on the button for the twelfth floor followed by a long sigh. That's all.

Exiting the lift he walks faster than her down the hall, an unconscious reaction to his frustrations. This is why he wants to leave, this fakery and dishonesty and the struggle for power; between her and him, and he and Norwin. When will it end? Never, he supposes. And that's why he knows he must go. They are his wolves and they are eating away at him.

Sitting on the end of the bed in darkness, Carlos begins unbuttoning his silk shirt.

'You're never here anymore. I never see you,' Sofia says quietly leaning on a wall.

His fingers stop working and he sighs, 'It's work. It's Norwin, he wants me down there. What am I supposed to do?'

'Yeah, that's not what Lucile says.'

Turning and frowning, 'And what would Lucile know?'

'She talks to Julio, and Julio says you're choosing to be down there, that you have new friends and probably new pussy too, huh. Is that it?' she says starting to whimper.

Standing, 'No,' he lies, to which part though? Walking over he stands in front of her but doesn't touch her, 'I—I don't know what to say, *mami.*'

'Don't call me that,' she sulks. 'You don't get to call me that any more,' she says wiping a tear with the back of her hand.

Carlos gently puts his hands on her shoulders but Sofia slaps him.

'You come and you go as you please but you don't think about me, you don't think about how hard you make my life here,' she says full of spite.

Stepping back, 'Hard? Yeah, because your life is so fucking difficult with all your free clothes and free apartments and free money.'

'Hey,' she says pointing at him, 'remember who was the one bringing in your coke in the first place.'

Fighting back a laugh, 'Oh yes, how could I be so stupid? Your couple of kilos a month two years ago is what pays for all the warehouses and businesses and pay-offs. Where would we be without you?' he says sarcastically.

Glaring at him, 'Fuck you, Carlos.'

'Yeah, fuck me. That's all you do, spread your legs and hold out your hand waiting to get paid.'

Enraged, Sofia leaps at him slapping and swiping but his size make her efforts futile. Grabbing her arms he gently pushes her away from him.

Breathing heavily and her hair a mess, 'Don't you treat me like shit, Carlos. Don't you dare. I know too much, remember that. I know all about those warehouses and businesses and pay-offs,' Sofia says coldly.

She's drunk and knows that's his only weakness. His criminal life is at the same time his Achilles heel and the well that supports her lavish lifestyle.

Carlos stares at her.

Mistaking his quiet for being trapped, Sofia continues, 'That's right, don't forget how much I know about your business, about Danilo and Norwin—'

Lunging at her, Carlos grabs her by the throat and slams her against the wall making a picture drop and a lamp on the buffet topple. His huge hand gripping around her neck and chin.

Whispering in her ear, 'No. Don't even pretend to do that. Don't even joke.'

Tears streaming down her cheeks Sofia only whimpers in response.

It may be Carlos's weakness but that doesn't mean she can poke it.

'Do you understand me?' he says with a slight squeeze.

Sofia manages a slight nod.

Letting her go she slumps to the ground and begins sobbing.

Carlos grabs his jacket and car keys before walking over to her, his mind racing. After a moment, 'You can keep the apartment,' he says emotionless before leaving.

1984

XVIII
THE COLONEL

A thin veil of glistening dew rests atop the White House lawn, while the southern portico remains a washed-out painting of greens and greys as an early autumn chill grips the Capital. His gaze is stony and sharp and his molars are grinding, visible against his freshly shaven cheeks. Wearing a woolen coat and moleskin gloves, he makes a fist and squeezes until he can hear the stretch of leather against his knuckles. This is where he stood last time, on the gravel path by the trickling fountain. He can't believe it's been two years. What has he done? Has it been enough? Iraq is at war with Iran, the Soviets are pursuing their invasion of Afghanistan, Castro is still commanding, and the Sandinistas are still in power. No, perhaps not, he thinks.

Staring boldly into the greying sky he waits patiently for the National Security Advisor and CIA Director to arrive for their secret meeting; a meeting they can't have inside a building should their conversation be overheard or recorded.

Stepping out of a black sedan by the western gate is a squat man layered in a black coat, scarf, and wool fedora. Marching along the gravel path and puffing a thick cigar, Bill Casey looks like a bulldog chewing what's left of a leather shoe.

'Good morning, Colonel,' he says gruffly.

'Morning, Director.' Peering towards the West Wing building, 'Well, Robert still isn't coming, so how do you want to play this thing?'

Taking the cigar from his mouth, 'Play what? Bud was in for bombing those harbors as much as you and I were.'

'Yes, but we both know he was under the impression the attacks were going to be far less dramatic.'

Frowning, 'So? It was a paramilitary operation,' Casey says firmly. 'What does he think, the CIA were going to post letters asking the ships to leave Nicaraguan waters?' Putting the cigar back in his mouth, 'Of course vessels were going to get damaged,' he mumbles, 'we were using bombs for chrissakes.'

Oliver raises his eyebrows in agreement.

After a moment, 'How's Felix going?' the Director says with a puff.

'He's going just fine. That southern front is developing much quicker than we expected, thanks to Hull and the prime positioning of his ranch. The Contras in those jungles are able to receive supply airdrops quicker than the camps spread out across the Honduran border.

'Good, good. Plus with George Doubleya in Panama working on General Noriega to let us use his military bases for training and his ports so we can spy on the Sandinistas, I'm sure that rapscallion rat will be more than obliging to smuggle weapons and money into Nicaragua for us.' Squinting through the smoke, 'And the move on Pastora?'

'Rob Owen is in the region now and will rendezvous with the team when we get a green light.'

Chewing on the cigar, 'And we're still going with a press conference attack.'

'It makes the most sense. A public place, live to air. The angle is to make it look like a gutless Sandinistas attack to murder dissenters within their own ranks.'

'Very good.'

A door slamming in the distance makes both men look towards the West Wing.

Storming through the Rose Garden is Robert McFarlane, a thin pencil of a man with a shorter than normal gate making his legs move quicker than they should. Shoulders hunched with his hands in his pockets and his breath steaming in front of him he looks furious.

'Morning, Bud,' Casey offers.

'Don't you morning me, Bill. Are you men crazy? They were Dutch and Russian boats you almost sank. We're trying to prevent war, not start it!' McFarlane blasts.

'Oh, put a lid on it,' the CIA Director says disregarding. 'We've got bigger fish to fry than some damaged ships.'

McFarlane's eyes go white, 'Put a—put a lid on it? The papers are going wild with this. And Congress, boy oh boy. Do you realize reports are spreading that the Contras are killing women and children in the countryside? Is that true?' he says looking at the Colonel.

Frowning and shaking his head slightly, 'I'm afraid there is just no evidence whatsoever that such things are happening,' North says plainly.

Casey makes an unimpressed face.

'Don't you roll your eyes at me, Bill. Let me tell you something,' McFarlane says pointing a bony white finger, 'Congress has revealed what your little Contra budget is going to be next fiscal year.'

Both Casey and North's eyes focus.

'A big fat zero.'

'Zero!' Casey says whipping the cigar from his mouth.

'That's right, zero. Nothing. They're done with all this unsanctioned covert subterfuge you and your agents are up to. They've had enough and quite frankly so have I. Now, I've tried to sell the importance of the Contra effort but enough is enough. The Sandinistas are no danger to the United States. They have no resources, no exports of interest, and pose no military threat to anyone.'

Tossing his cigar away angrily, 'And what happened to keeping the Contras together, body and soul?' Casey says, his jowls beginning to flare.

'Look, I'm not saying the CIA can't be down there keeping an eye on things, but as far as tax payer money goes, and certainly as far as bombing foreign vessels, you're about one grenade shy of this thing coming to a grinding halt.' Taking a breath, 'Now, I'm all for selling weapons to Iran, especially seeing as it makes for the perfect cover to say we're doing it to get all these American hostages out of Lebanon, but I'm working my ass off in the Oval Office pushing that this is the best way to support the FDN. As for you, Colonel, you better start towing the line because the stuff I'm hearing,' McFarlane shakes his head, letting his point go unfinished.

Oliver's molars crunch.

'I don't know what you're upset about, Colonel,' McFarlane continues. 'You sit there in the Executive Office, a mere few hundred yards from Ronald, and you're off doing God knows what under his Presidential approval. I don't know who you think you are but you better rein it in.'

Glaring at the man, 'Perhaps I should remind you. I am a veteran of war. I have commanded platoons into battle. I have been shot by men and I have killed them in return. I have been awarded the Silver Star, the Bronze Star, and two Purple Hearts. And as of right this minute I am the military advisor of the National Security Council, which gives me the authority to protect this country in ways that I see fit.'

McFarlane swallows despite trying to remain resolute.

'Okay, okay,' Casey says calmly, 'zip it up, Ollie, we all know what you're made of and we're damn lucky to have you.' Breathing a deep sigh, 'Look, Bud, as a man of office it's difficult for your kind to appreciate how delicate and perilous the position we have to put our agents in. Agents that may be a codename to you but are husbands or fathers or friends to Ollie and I. Now, there's nothing I'd like more than to be discreet about what we're doing in Nicaragua but if you could for a moment realize how tenuous our position is. We've got the damn Soviets invading the hell out of the Afghans, we've got that madman Saddam at war with Iran with all the oil in the free world at stake, and as minor as the situation in Nicaragua looks in comparison, a successful turn to socialism by the Sandinistas completely undermines Operation Condor and what we've been trying to execute in the Southern Cone for the last decade.' After a moment, 'If we lose Nicaragua to left-wing ideology then how long until we lose Venezuela, Bolivia, Brazil, Argentina,' he says counting the countries on his fingers. 'The list goes on, Bud.'

McFarlane chews his lip conceding how important the Contra situation is on paper.

Seeing this, Casey continues tactfully, 'Look, I agree mining those harbors was perhaps a little too heavy-handed but if you want the truth, we're not doing enough, not damn near enough.'

Rubbing his temple, 'God damn it,' McFarlane says under his breath. 'So, where do we go from here?'

'If you're telling us that Congress is going to give us nothing then the CIA and NSC are just going to have to do more, and the more we do the less you're going to want to hear about it.'

'Well, that sounds reassuring,' McFarlane says unimpressed.

'Relax, this is our job,' Casey reassures. 'It isn't pretty but it keeps the free world ticking.'

Putting his hands on his hips, 'What do you want me to tell Ron?'

'Tell him everything is under control. And to let the CIA and NSC do what they're designed to do: operate, conceal, infiltrate, and destabilize.'

After a sigh, 'I thought this whole Contra thing was going to be an easier ride?' McFarlane says to no one in particular.

'So did we,' North says seriously. 'But funding a national revolution is an expensive project, and having to secure financial aid from ulterior sources is tricky if not time consuming.'

'That's why it's drawing out,' Casey adds. 'We've got to put our trust in CIA assets and exiles and goddamn traffickers to get weapons and money into the country for chrissake. Hardly the situation we want to be in.' Then, after a pause, 'Zero funding from Congress, unbelievable.'

McFarlane puts his hands back on his hips, 'Another thing,' he says with renewed frustration, 'What in the hell is going on with Barry Seal? Isn't he one of yours, Colonel? I've got the DEA up my ass asking how deeply involved he is with the CIA.'

'Seal is a liar and a thief,' Casey mutters.

North clears his throat, 'He was part of our resupply outfit but the man was also smuggling drugs for the Medellin Cartel.'

'Jesus. And whose bright idea was it to use him?'

Glancing at Casey, 'It was the early days of the Contra effort and Seal and his men were the best pilots we could find to do the job,' North offers.

Frowning, 'So what does he know?' McFarlane inquires.

'Nothing we can't deny,' North states. 'Besides, Bill is right, he's a liar and a thief, and his testimony isn't worth a dime. We bailed him out a few times for the extracurricular cargo he was bringing back into the country but when he got caught a couple of months ago in Fort Lauderdale with two-hundred kilos of marijuana we cut him loose.'

McFarlane closes his eyes, 'I'm going to pretend I didn't hear that.'

'Why the interest in Seal?' Casey asks.

'Well, the DEA want to use him for some sting operation and get Escobar and Ochoa on film loading up cocaine.'

Shrugging his shoulders, 'And?' asks North.

'Apparently, Seal has suggested to do it at a Nicaraguan airbase just outside of Managua to show the Sandinistas are trafficking drugs.'

North and Casey give each other a surprising look.

Smirking, McFarlane continues, 'Looks like Seal is trying to get into y'all good books and save himself from doing ten years in prison. Two birds with one stone, as it were.'

'That is interesting,' Casey mulls.

'Should we intervene?' North asks the CIA Director.

'Why should we? If the DEA want to pay for it and put in the man-hours then they can go for it. I'll keep a close eye on how it develops. If Seal manages to get this thing to go down on Nicaraguan territory it could prove very useful to our cause.'

All three men are quiet, each bothered by their own knowledge and frustrations with trying to keep this country not just safe but in power.

Casey breaks the silence, 'Look, gentlemen, the upside is the longer it takes for a country to regain its power, while at the same time depending on Uncle Sam for help, the deeper they get into our pocket.'

McFarlane appears unimpressed by the statement, 'Yes, well, officially the American Government fully supports a democratic Nicaragua and the liberating of its people from a Socialist regime, and we will continue to provide *humanitarian* aid to freedom fighters.' After a sigh, 'Unofficially, I don't want to know and neither does Ron. But can you at least stop making it look like it's us doing all this stuff down there?' McFarlane implores.

'It's not like we aren't trying,' Casey states.

'Well, try harder. Please.' Checking his watch, 'All right, I need to get going. Good day, gentlemen,' McFarlane says cordially before marching off towards the West Wing.

Watching him go, 'I don't know how a man so weak can hold such a critical position,' Casey says disappointedly. 'How can you not explicate the vital importance of the Contra effort to Congress. Zero funding,' he utters again in disbelief.

'Maybe it's not so bad,' North reasons.

'And how's that?'

'Direct Congressional funding comes with briefings, aid contracts and approvals. A paper trail, as it were, that taxpayer money is being suitably spent. If there's no funding then there's no paper trail.'

Casey squints pensively, appraising what the Colonel is implying.

North continues, 'If we don't have to worry ourselves with providing covers for where money is going then it's open house about who gets our support and how much, while preserving complete deniability that the NSC or CIA know anything about where it's coming from.'

Retrieving a fresh cigar from an inside pocket, 'You may be right, Colonel,' Casey says inspecting the tip of the stogie. 'But don't underestimate how difficult building a dependable supply chain worth tens of millions down there will be, even with all that other stuff going on.' After a moment, 'Then again, with everyone watching Afghanistan, the Soviets, and the Iran-Iraq war, I imagine there's no better time than now to go full steam ahead.'

The Colonel smirks.

'But listen to me, keep it off the books.'

'Of course, sir.'

'No, all of it,' Casey says seriously. 'Only use assets you can cut-off or kill, use the banks we have in the Bahamas, no American ones. This may be your one and only opportunity to go full throttle here but I want none of it coming back to bite the CIA's ass when it's all over. Central America may be a corrupt shithole but when those presidents topple, they love nothing more than to spill the beans if it means saving their neck.'

'I understand,' the Colonel says confidently.

XIX
BUMBLE BEE

Humming smoothly high above a lush jungle blanketed in broad-leaf palms and irregular mountaintops, a small white Cessna cruises imperceptibly through a perfectly blue sky. The tiny craft, one of a thousand criss-crossing the Caribbean, carrying with it vital cargo that keeps the western hemisphere on tilt: money, drugs, and occasionally information.

Looking closely at a map and cross-checking their location on the instrument panel, Jorge Morales squints towards a mountain ridgeline ahead, while far below a wide river, brown and turbulent, meanders like a great serpent.

'I think we're almost there, *primo*. We're going over the San Juan River now which means three-clicks past that ridge and we should see it on our starboard.'

Gary Betzner, a slender man with neat brown hair and a bushy moustache nods. His sharp chestnut eyes pierce the treetops, while his hands remain delicately poised on the controls. They're flying over the south-west corner of Nicaragua and have been informed to stay on high alert for military outposts that could have anti-air weaponry.

Folding and putting away the map, 'Thank you for helping me, Gary,' Jorge says seriously.

Betzner smiles, 'Think nothin' of it,' he replies with gentle southern drawl. 'Just like old times, anyways. A couple'a scorpions in a lunchbox with wings lookin' for a food fight.'

'No, I couldn't do this without you. If I'm going to slip this drug charge I gotta make the CIA happy, you know.'

'Without me?' Betzner smirks. 'How many pilots you got flyin' out of Opa-Loka? Fifteen? Twenty?'

Laughing, 'Yes but not a single one nearly as good as you, *primo*.'

'Ain't that the truth,' he says with a wink.

Looking out of the window to the jungle below, 'I still remember the look on the faces of my guys when I told them you were a crop duster from Arkansas. They laughed so hard tears came out of their eyes.'

Betzner chuckles quietly.

'Little did they know you were ex-Navy, eh. The best pilot I ever seen,' Jorge adds reminiscently. After a moment, 'How many of my planes you crash flying in and out of the jungles, *primo*?'

'Not one.'

'How much cargo you lose?'

'Zip.'

'And why's that?'

'Because I can fly a single-prop bug-catcher up a goffers butthole with my eyes closed.'

Smiling warmly at his American pal, 'It is good to be back in the cockpit with you, old friend.'

Betzner's eyes dart across the avionics, 'Two-and-a-half clicks, *Hor-hay*. Remind me again who we're meetin'?' he asks.

'Okay. An old *Americano*, John Hull. It's his ranch we're landing on. Then there's Mario Calero, he's a big-time player and an old friend of mine. His brother is part of the FDN directorate. And a young *Americano*, Robert something. He's in with the CIA.'

Betzner whistles, 'The CIA, the FDN, covert supply drops. Sounds more serious than our days drug runnin' for them cartels.'

'Don't let a few capital letters scare you. More serious just means bigger contracts and more money.'

Smirking, 'I ain't scared, just prefer it when the government ain't keepin' tabs of us flyin' in and out of them here jungles.' After a moment, 'So, what you gotta do to make them CIA boys happy campers?' Betzner asks.

Morales raises his eyebrows, 'Weekly supply drops of guns and munitions, and a million a year in contributions to the FDN.'

Frowning, 'One-million,' Betzner says hesitantly. 'That's it?'

'That's it, *primo*.'

Both men burst out laughing before Betzner leans on the controls and banks the Cessna towards a barely noticeable clearing in the jungle.

* * *

Standing on the edge of a dirt runway and squinting expectantly, Robert Owen watches a small craft descend out of the sky. His dark hair stuck to a sweaty forehead, his shirt soaked under the arms with perspiration, and his cheeks and neck red from spending too long in the sun. Not a man built for the tropics, or for national security fieldwork in Central America either, Owen stands out like kid in a cantina at midnight. Fortunately for him word has spread that he is an important courier not just of information but of money moving between the CIA, FDN, and all those on the fringe.

'Is that them?' Owen yells back towards a tent. 'They're late.'

'Relax, son. This is Costa Rica and in Costa Rica there's no such thing as late, only still on the way,' John Hull shouts back, much to the laughter of the men sitting with him. Men with machine guns hanging from their shoulders and cigarettes dangling from their lips; Costa Rican, Salvadoran, even Argentinian, and all ex-militia, mercenaries, or bodyguards for political parties and cartels that no longer swing power.

Puffing on a chewed cigar, Hull dabs at his sweaty sun-spotted and balding head with a white handkerchief. Wearing a short-sleeved shirt pulling tight around his pot-belly, neat brown linen pants, and large square glasses windshield-thick, John Hull looks more like a retiree of *Del Boca Vista* south Florida than a Central American landowner with undisclosed black-market connections.

Someone else who appears out of place is Mario Calero sitting legs-crossed in a peach silk shirt, pressed white slacks, and tan leather boat shoes. Looking more like a model than pilot, the varied and often exaggerated stories of the man—business owner, polo player, speedboat racer, gambler—are all, unbelievably, true.

'Is it just me, *senor* Hull, or is there something odd about that man?' Mario says deliberately looking over the top of his black sunglasses.

Chuckling, 'I've never seen a CIA Agent so jumpy,' Sebastian Gonzalez remarks.

'That's because he ain't no Agent,' Hull says dabbing his neck. 'He's just a staffer, a bookworm who's never seen shit in his pants is all. Personally, I think he's a queer. Damn has to be.' After a puff, 'Then again, if he was, I doubt his boss would have given him this job. Hell, Ollie North is as American as apple pie on the fourth of July.'

Kicking a rock impatiently with one hand on his hip and the other gripping a manila folder, Owen watches the plane come in to land. Swaying as it descends, the Cessna hits the dirt runway and bounces its way towards the tent in a cloud of brown dust.

Betzner parks the craft and cuts the engine, while Jorge squeezes past the tightly packed cargo and opens the cabin door.

'Greetings,' Hull says when they step out, 'welcome to *Casa de Hull*.'

'*Gracias, senor,*' Morales says offering his hand. 'I am Jorge and this is Mr. Gary Betzner.'

'Pleasure to meet you boys.'

Clearing his throat, 'Good day, gentlemen. I'm Robert Owen, your CIA contact.'

'And this is Mario Calero and Sebastian Gonzalez,' Hull says finishing the introductions.

Something about the way Mario and Jorge shake hands gives Owen the sneaking suspicion that they already know each other. An observation he'll take mental note of. Fully aware of how important this assignment is, meeting real assets in the field and overseeing their engagement with the mission, the young courier is eager to ensure he fulfils his task: to be Colonel North's eyes, ears, flesh, and blood.

Peering over the top of his sunglasses, 'Is this a piston engine or turboprop?' Mario asks.

'She's a turboprop *Pratt & Whitney*,' Betzner replies.

'Which would make it a 208 Caravan, yes?'

'Not quite. It's a 208B making it one-point-eight meters longer than the 208 and turning it from a nine-seater into a thirteen-seater. Or in our case increasing the payload by three-hundred kilos.'

Raising his eyebrows, 'But still a three-blade McCauley I see.'

'With full feathering and reversible pitch. You know your planes, *aymeego*.'

Hinting a smile, 'Only a thing or two.'

Clearing his throat again, 'Speaking of, where is the other plane?' Owen questions.

'Oh,' Betzner says looking into the distance, 'If I'm not mistaken, that's them now.'

The men all search the sky blankly unable to see or hear the craft.

Frowning, 'Where?' Owen asks.

'There,' Betzner points to a clear blue sky.

Nestled in a low valley, Hull's ranch is walled in by two long sloping peaks. After a few uncertain seconds, a small grey Cessna appears from behind one of the faces, banking hard having seen the landing strip late.

Shielding their eyes as the second craft pulls up, the group make their way over to its rear door where two Latin men step out.

'*Hola, amigos*,' Jorge greets them. Then, turning to Hull and Owen, 'Please, allow me to introduce my other pilots: *senor* Geraldo Duran and *senor* Marcos Aguado.'

After brief pleasantries are exchanged, Hull whistles to a group of military looking men lazing in the shade of a nearby tent. One of them hops in a flatbed truck and turns the ignition. Slowly backing it up to the two aircraft, men begin grabbing crates from the cargo hold and loading them in the truck.

'Excuse me!' Owen shouts to the men. '*Disculpe, por favor*, I need to count those crates.' Then, turning to Jorge, 'Do you have your inventory sheet?' he asks hurriedly.

'Yes, of course,' Morales says reaching into the cockpit and retrieving it.

Climbing onto the side of the truck, Owen checks each crate as it's being loaded making sure it corresponds to what's on his log sheet, 'Sixty units of M-16s, forty units of M-60s, twenty-five units of C4, twenty-three landmines, eighty units of grenades, and ten units of rocket launches,' he says quietly, ticking each line of his inventory sheet.

Watching Owen go about his inspection, Morales gives Hull a look.

'Yeah, the kid's a real stickler for procedure,' the old man mumbles through his cigar.

After the truck is loaded it rumbles off the runway and disappears down a dirt road. A moment later two white dirty vans appear with stickers on the side reading *Equipo Humanitario*. Pulling up next to the planes, the men in military khakis begin loading crates on board.

Quickly checking his documents, 'Wait, what's all this?' Owen says confused.

'Humanitarian supplies, sport,' Hull says.

'Humanitarian supplies?'

'Toilet paper, kiddo. You ask Max, he knows it's coming,' Hull reassures.

'That's right,' Jorge adds. '*Senor* Gomez said sanitary supplies are in urgent need. Soap, bandages, talcum powder.'

'Talcum powder? What for?'

'For chaffing, *senor*.'

Frowning quizzically, 'Chaffing,' Owen mutters to himself.

'Don't get yourself in a pickle, junior,' Hull says taking the cigar from his mouth. 'Maxi knows all about it.'

Clearing his throat, 'Right. Well, I'll be sure to check that with him,' Owen says scribbling a note down in his folder. 'And Mr. Morales, may I ask where you are headed to with it?' he asks, while looking down at his papers.

'That's where it's going, to Max at Ilopango. We're loading up on a shipment of guns to take to General Bermudez in Las Mangas, and then it's back home to Fort Lauderdale.'

Snapping his folder shut and smiling, 'Perfect.'

'Yeah, perfect,' Hull repeats, his cigar wedged in the corner of a half grin. Then, shielding his forehead from the sun with a handkerchief, 'Jorge, Gary, I don't mean to be inhospitable but I'm afraid I'll need to head off. Young Robert and I have some business that needs attending. But now you know where my little hamlet is I'm sure I'll be seeing a lot more of you,' he says with a wry smile.

'That you will, *senor* Hull,' Jorge replies warmly.

Mario Calero and the other pilots watch as Hull and Owen climb into a jeep flanked by guards and disappear into the jungle. Once they are out of sight Mario removes his sunglasses and turns to Jorge laughing before embracing the pilot.

'*Como estas, hermano?*' Mario says.

'*Me va muy bien*. No, better than great—look at us,' he says spreading his arms wide and motioning to the jungles around them. 'We're flying the planes, delivering the coca, and making the monies.'

Smiling, 'That we are, my friend.'

Lighting a cigarette and mumbling, 'And finally with channels backed by the US Government,' Marcus Aguado adds watching the last of the crates being loaded onto the two Cessna planes.

'I heard you got caught with a lot of cocaine,' Mario continues. 'Thought you were facing ten-years?'

'Sixteen more like it,' Jorge corrects. 'Good thing I own a lot of planes and know a lot of pilots, eh.'

'And the CIA cut you a deal, just like that?'

'*Si*. Put me in touch with a couple of FDN guys out of Miami: Popo Chamorro and Octavio Cesar.'

'Is that so? They are close associates of Donald Barrios whom I know quite well.' Mario looks to the ground thinking before raising his eyebrows, 'Seems the *Americanos* are getting desperate. Sixteen-years to drug running is quite the bargain.'

'Hey, I'm not complaining.'

'And nor would I,' Mario says with a chuckle. Eyeing the other men accompanying Jorge, 'You look familiar, *senor*,' he says to Aguado. 'Where would I know your face from?'

Answering for him, 'Marcos here, is a Salvadoran Air Force pilot, but he's also Norwin Meneses's link to the Cali Cartel,' Gonzalez says. 'He's been flying most of Norwin's coca into the US for the last few years.'

'Ah, Norwin, how is the old rat?' Mario says with a smirk.

Shrugging, 'The same as he's ever been,' Gonzalez says casually. 'Angry and with an asshole so tight if you stuck a lump of coal up there, he'd shit out a diamond.'

All the men laugh.

'And how is that you have been able to fly his coca in all this time?' Mario asks Aguado.

Taking the cigarette from his mouth and squinting his heavily sagged eyes, 'I got an early humanitarian aid contract to fly weapons to *R&M Equipment*; some *Americano* warehouse in Honduras. Then, I would go to Colombia, fill up on coca and fly right into a military base in Texas. No customs, no checks, no nothing. Half the coca went west to California and the other half east to Miami. Bingo bango.'

'But you're not anymore?' Mario asks.

Blowing smoke, 'About a year ago, maybe a little longer, all my flights started going through Ilopango so the CIA man could keep better track of things. That was until last month when Gomez asked me to help Jorge out.' Flicking his cigarette into the dirt, 'Now, he's a funny one,' Aguado muses. 'An ex-Cuban and Government Agent asking Felix Milian of all people for handouts, and now he watches coca go out and cash come in. *Extrano, no?*'

Shrugging, 'All the *Americanos* care about is winning,' Mario says simply. Then, looking at Gary Betzner but asking Jorge, 'And who's the *gringo?*'

Raising an eyebrow, 'My *primo* and my best pilot.'

A simple nod from Mario says that is all he needs to know about the man. In the drug business your word is your bond, and how far you go in the trade is determined by how well you can be trusted. A small lie will see you lose a finger or an ear or maybe your beloved pet, but screw over someone important enough and you'll find yourself staked to a chair with a car battery electrocuting your nuts until your eyes bleed and your heart stops ticking.

'I'm curious though,' Jorge continues, 'what brings you out into the middle of the jungle? The only people getting more coke into the US than you are Pablo and Ochoa.'

Smiling, 'Yes but coca on a plane is worth three-times as much than on a boat because of how quickly it arrives. And this coca is protected, which means the volume we can get into the US is like nothing we've ever seen. Not even Pablo.'

'But this Gomez, he is taking a heavy cut for the Contras, no?'

'*Si*, of course. But as dirty as the CIA wish to play it is nothing compared to how dirty the traffickers are. You see your plane, *hermano*, has the coca the *Americanos* think we're bringing in, while your plane, *senor* Aguado, has the coca they have no idea about. That's hundreds of kilos per flight, per day that they know nothing about.'

'But isn't their man at Ilopango overseeing it all?' Jorge questions.

Chuckling softly, 'The CIA oversee what we want them to oversee,' Mario says sliding his sunglasses on. Then, putting his arm around Jorge, '*Vamanos. Tiempo para una cerveza, hermano.*'

* * *

Sunlight creeps through drawn venetian shades and smoke from Hull's cigar thickens the dark room with a haze of *Cohiba*, peppery and earthy. Tinking quietly in the corner a small iron-blade fan offers little reprieve from the sticky humid air of the third-story French-colonial suburban villa and CIA safe-house. Luxuriously appointed with art deco furniture, hanging rugs, an enormous oil painting of a young Juan Santamaria torching a hostel at the battle of Rivas in 1856, Spanish guitars gathering dust in a corner, and a wall-to-wall library of antique leather-bound books makes the location feel more like an affluent private residence than it does government-owned property.

'We are overseeing everything now, Agent Holtz,' Robert Owen says confidently despite the sweat beading his brow. 'All the weapons, the supplies, the funds coming from the Israelis, you name it. It's messy, that's for sure, but the Colonel knows exactly what he's doing, sir. You can count on that.'

Squinting, Station Chief Philip Holtz gives Owen an unconvincing look, not because he doesn't believe the young courier's sincerity but because everything that the Colonel puts in motion feels like a stick of dynamite waiting to go off.

Holtz, a wily veteran with grey eyes and bone white hair gives the appearance of a sophisticated man in his twilight years: a retiring sociology professor, or perhaps surgeon working for an NGO, maybe a missionary even. However, his graceful aging is a mask, a con and fortunately for Owen, Holtz's disdain for Socialism runs as deep as the Colonels.

'You don't need to tell me what I already know, Mr. Owen,' Holtz says calmly. 'My concerns are that circumventing Congressional approval is going to land us all in hot water.'

Rolling up his sleeves, 'But the NSC isn't required to secure Congressional approval, that's the beautiful part.'

'Beautiful,' Holtz's eyes narrow. 'That's not a word I'd use to describe what we do, Mr. Owen.'

Clearing his throat and sliding his round glasses back up his nose, 'With all due respect, if we let the Sandinistas retain power in Nicaragua then what kind of signal does that send to the rest of the region.'

'You do not to remind me what's at stake. I've been in Central America since before your career started.'

'Sir, it's all under control,' Owen says a mix between pleading and persuading, fully aware Holtz is a senior Agent and yet on the other hand reminding himself that he's speaking on behalf of the Colonel.

After a brief uncomfortable silence, 'I've seen it myself, Phil,' John Hull says leaning across a teak dining table. 'The kid's got a real knack for it, keeps tabs on just about everything coming and going.'

Holtz cradles his hands under his chin and takes a calming breath.

'May we continue, sir?' Owen asks keenly.

After a nod Robert Owen runs through a checklist of various tasks as though ticking off his grocery list, a list that includes materials for upgrading Hull's runway, erecting Contra outposts, storage depots for weapons and other supplies, and newly revised propaganda literature personally revised by the Colonel for agents to distribute in Costa Rica; each point a meticulous cross-checking followed by fastidious scribbling in one of Owen's several folders he's always carrying.

'All right, and lastly the matter of Eden Pastora. Where are we up to?' Owen looks up expectantly.

Clearing his throat, 'Are you aware of our double agent in Managua, Mr. Owen?'

'Torbinson, the Swedish photojournalist? Yes, I'm aware of his cooperation.'

Holtz raises his eyebrows as if to say, this kid is on a too long a leash. If the Sandanistas caught him he'd spill the beans before yanking out his first tooth with a pair of pliers.

'Right,' Holtz continues, 'Torbinson is close to Tomas Borge of the Sandinista Interior Ministry and they want eyes on Pastora at all times. They're still eager to convince him to re-join the Sandinista Government and be an asset rather than a threat.' Sliding Owen a folder, 'Felix has arranged the triggerman, an Argentine spy named Roberto Gaguine who'll pose as a Danish journalist.'

'An Argentine posing as a Dane?' Hull asks after a puff.

'He speaks perfect Danish, plus he's one of those fair-haired Argentines. His cover name is Anker Hansen.' Standing from the table and walking across the room, 'Two of our assets will accompany Torbinson and Hansen, making sure they make it to Pastora's press conference in La Penca next month.'

Noting it down, 'Very good,' Owen remarks, 'and when are we making contact with these assets?'

Holtz picks up a telephone and after a brief moment says, 'Come on up.'

Muffled sounds from the floor below, a door opening and closing followed by footsteps coming up the stairs make Owen shift uncomfortably. Twisting around on the chair he watches the figures enter the room.

Wearing a white tee shirt and ripped jeans, '*Hola, senores,*' a handsome Latino man says before wandering over to an ornate black-iron liquor cabinet and pouring himself a glass of rum. While a Middle Eastern man, ignoring any social niceties, sits heavily in a brown leather chair and lights a cigarette.

'Gentlemen,' Holtz begins, 'this is Mr. Robert Owen, a liaison to the NSC.'

Smelling the rum in his glass pensively, 'NSC? I am unfamiliar with this one, *senor* Holtz.'

'It matters none. But Mr. Owen here connects the dots between the Contras and certain people in Washington. This here,' the station chief pointing towards the man refilling his glass of rum, 'is Felipe Vidal, an ex-Cuban.' Then, motioning towards the sofa, 'And that one there is Amac Galil, an Iranian assassin.'

'Well, it's a real pleasure to make your acquaintance, gentlemen,' Owen says warmly.

Felipe fights back a smile before exchanging a look with John Hull, while Amac draws back on his cigarette with disinterest.

After a moment, 'Oh, and yours, *senor* Owen,' Felipe says gesturing his glass.

Looking around, 'Where's Gaguine?' Holtz asks curiously.

Cutting off his gulp, 'You mean, Hansen.'

Bounding up the stairs and entering the room loudly, 'Never fear, Martin the Englishman is here.'

'Excuse me, who are you?' Owen asks, confused.

With sandy-blonde hair, a bony face and sharp blue eyes, 'I'm Roberto Gaguine.'

'You mean, Hansen,' Felipe corrects pulling the glass from his lips.

Still confused, 'Then who's Martin the Englishman?'

'Me, of course,' Roberto says with an enthusiastic smile. 'What good is a spy if he does not go by several names, no?'

'Right,' Owen says with a gentle smile. Checking his watch, 'May we get down to it, I have a plane to catch.'

Crossing his arms, 'Floor's yours, Roberto,' Holtz says plainly.

Closing his eyes, Felipe shakes his head with restrained frustration.

Lifting a silver hard-shell briefcase into the air like a magician theatrically presenting his top hat to a crowd, Gaguine gracefully moves to the dining table before gently placing the case down and unlatching its locks. Nestled in a grey foam cut-out is a small video camera, the kind a television cameraman would use for recording material in the field. The Argentine spy lifts the recording device out, shows his audience each side of the camera indicating its authenticity before placing it on the table.

Owen watches with bated breath awaiting the big reveal,' Well?'

'Well, what?' Roberto questions. 'That's it.'

'That's what?'

A warm smile creeps across Roberto's face, a gesture full of kindness for the young courier's innocence and naivety. Then, pressing the tape eject button a compartment opens revealing a stick of C4 wired into the camera.

Patting Owen on the back, 'Why, it's the bomb, my good man,' Roberto says softly.

Leaning forward, Owen's eyes go wide staring at the rigged device with awe, 'So this, this is what's going to get Eden Pastora?'

Chuckling, 'Yes, my friend, that's the plan,' Roberto says kindly.

Taking the cigar from his mouth, 'Kid's still a little wet behind the ears,' Hull says apologetically.

Confused, Owen curiously touches the soft skin of his earlobe, while Felipe smirks from behind his glass of rum.

Butting out his cigarette, 'It means, you fresh out the pussy,' Amac says spitefully.

XX
FREEWAY RICKY

Morning sunlight gleams off of the windshields of freshly washed and buffed sports cars at the *Felix Chevrolet* car yard on the corner of Figueroa Street and Jefferson Boulevard. Since hooking up with Danilo and completely shoring up LA with coke, Rick is finally out shopping for his first real car.

'You've never seen anything like this before, sir,' Jerry, the car salesman begins his pitch. 'With over two-hundred horse power, a liquid crystal display, pop-up headlights, computer activated transmission, fourteen instrument readouts each updated sixteen times every operating second, and *Bose* stereo for sound out of this world, this is the most advanced operating car on the planet.'

Squinting with thought, 'Aiit, I'm sold!' Rick says rubbing his hands together. 'Take off the plastic and start her up,' he adds with a bucktooth grin.

'Fantastic,' Jerry says. 'But you do realize we don't have one available here right now?'

Taken aback, 'What do you mean, right now? You just sold me the damn car?' Rick says incredulously.

With an uncertain smile, 'But this is the demo model, sir. You can't have this one. Plus there's paperwork we need to fill out first, a credit check and loan application.'

'Credit check? I don't need no loan, Jerry, I'm paying cash money.'

'That's great, sir, that's really great but I'm afraid there just isn't a C4 on the lot you can have. I mean, you have to go on a waiting list to get one of these,' Jerry chuckles nervously.

Furious, 'A wait list to get the car I'm staring at?' With his hands on his hips, 'And how long is the wait?' Rick asks.

'Oh, it's short, sir. At the moment I believe it's about two-months.'

'Two-months!'

'Sir, you have to understand this is the most advanced operating car—'

'On the planet, yeah yeah, I hear you, Jerry,' Rick finishes unimpressed.

Then, pulling up in front of the sales office as if purposely to insult Rick, a freshly polished silver Corvette rumbles deep and guttural. Climbing out, a stocky salesman swings the key on his finger and enters the building. Looking long and hard at the sleek machine Rick can't believe his luck; the first flashy purchase he wants to make for himself and he can't even get it.

Still standing with his hands on his hips, 'Why can't I have that one?' Rick asks.

Swallowing an anxious laugh, 'Because that one has already been purchased by the gentleman sitting inside, sir.'

Storming into the sales office and interrupting, 'Hey yo, is that your car out there?'

Taken by surprise, a guy in a blue button shirt and yellow sweater tied around his shoulders sinks into the chair.

'Excuse me, sir, what do you think you're doing?' the stocky salesman says standing from the desk. Then, as Jerry rushes into the office, 'Jerr, what the hell is this guy doing?'

Flustered, 'I'm sorry, Ron. This man didn't realize there's a wait list for the C4?'

'You,' Rick says looking at the buyer, 'the ticket price is forty-grand. I'll give you eighty-grand cash for your car right now. You can buy two.'

Stammering nervously with a confused look on his face, 'Ei-eighty-thousand dollars?'

'Sir!' Jerry interrupts.

Reaching into a small purple *Lakers* backpack slung across his shoulder, Rick pulls out thick wads of cash and tosses them onto the table.

'Sir!' Ron tries to intervene again. 'Jerr, go get security for Christ's sake.' Then, speaking to the gentleman sitting down, 'Marty, I'm terribly sorry about this—'

'Marty,' Rick interrupts, 'make it a hundred-thousand and some change. You can buy three,' he says pulling out more wads of tightly rolled notes and smiling his bucktooth grin.

'Ron,' Marty says after a swallow, 'cancel my paperwork.'

Thundering down the 110, screeching sideways through Avalon Gardens and looping back through Gramercy Park like a street racer playing for a pink slip, Rick finally pulls into the driveway of Ollie's house on Figueroa, the breaks steaming and clutch stinking.

On the porch are Kenny and Moses who come rushing over.

'Damn, Rick,' Kenny says, 'this is tight! I can't believe you got one of these. There's a wait list and everything.'

Smirking, 'Not for me,' Rick says using the bottom of his tee shirt to clean finger smudges from the door. 'The most advanced operating car on the planet,' he adds reflectively.

Whistling, 'How much it set you back, Freeway?' Moses asks.

Feeling a little embarrassed that he paid as much for a Corvette as he would have for a Porsche or Mercedes, 'Oh, like a hundred or something in the end,' Rick mumbles.

Squinting at the car Kenny seems to be wondering why it cost so much, 'A hundred grand? Ain't these like forty-gees, Rick?'

'Yeah, but money ain't the point,' he says quickly. 'A homeless man can kill for some shoes in winter even though a pair only costs six-dollars at *Wal-Mart*.'

Kenny and Moses give him a confused look.

What Rick can't quite communicate is that in this world money gives you choices and that's all people really want. Money may not buy you happiness and neither can it solve all of your problems but without money you're stuck, trapped inside an invisible cage where real options are taken away from you and in its place is only the illusion of choice.

Rick walks through the fully remodeled house that looks like it belongs more in Beverlywood than it does under the shade of the fourteen-lane wide 110, with its Italian tiled flooring, plush carpets, built-in bar, and huge sunken living room with wrap-around sofas. Eating a bowl of *Lucky Charms* at the kitchen bench is Ollie reading the paper, while Redmon and Lonzo argue over how to use a *Jack LaLanne* juice extractor.

'Where you'd go this morning?' Ollie asks through a mouthful of milk and marshmallows. 'You dropped your girl off but you ain't come in.'

Before Rick opens his mouth Moses answers, 'This swish nigga just got himself a fresh Corvette C4.'

'You got a new Vette?' Ollie says dropping his spoon in the bowl with a splash.

Flashing his buckteeth, 'Most advanced operating car on the planet.'

'Well, damn, look at you,' Ollie says smiling. 'Finally letting your dreads down and enjoying the fruits of your labor, huh.'

'And about time, too,' Rick nods. Grabbing the box of cereal and pouring himself a bowl, 'Marilyn cool?' he says squinting into the backyard.

Picking up the paper, 'Yeah, she cool. Just been in the pool all morning,' Ollie says.

'So, what's happening in LA today?' Rick asks.

'Oh, you know, the usual,' Ollie begins. 'They spending all this money for the Olympics but ain't none to help the black folk,' he says giving the newspaper a flick. 'Then them sand niggas at war with each other in the Middle East, and Reagan looking ready to go for President again.'

'Yeah, yeah. What about the Dodgers, they win last night?'

Turning to the sports section, 'Nope. Lost to the Padres four-nine.'

'Damn, we can't even beat the Padres?' Rick complains. After a spoon full of charms, 'I swear, when the Lakers lost to the Celtics last year all our teams went downhill,' he mumbles.

'Speaking of the Lakers, looky here,' Ollie says reading from an article. 'Magic Johnson signs one of the longest and richest contracts in sports history.'

'My man!' Rick says excited, 'How much he making?'

'Says, Magic signed a million-dollar deal.'

Scrunching up his face, 'A million a week?'

Scanning the article, 'Nah, a million a year,' Ollie says.

'A million dollars a year! Damn, that homie is in the wrong game,' Rick chuckles.

'Yeah, but you hear about his house parties, right?' Redmon says from the kitchen. 'Every weekend it's sex and champagne over in Bel-Air.'

'Not just sex, nigga throws orgy parties,' Kenny adds. 'All the finest honnies in LA are there and at midnight if you ain't got a piece of pussy under your arm then Magic throws you out.'

They all laugh.

'Apparently, he runs around the house making sure everybody's getting busy, don't matter where they are,' Redmon continues. 'In the pool, in the kitchen, hell on the sofa in front of everybody. Magic just loves pussy.'

Surprised by this apparent common knowledge, 'How come I didn't hear about these parties?' Rick asks.

'Because you love money more than you do pussy,' Kenny jokes.

They all laugh again.

Walking to the glass doors with his bowl of cereal, Rick watches Marilyn floating in the swimming pool on a pink blow-up mattress; her body oiled and glistening, her head bopping to music coming through her *Sony Walkman* headphones, and the small mound in her belly getting bigger every week. He loves Marilyn and their baby too, but making money is his drug and he can't get enough. Since hooking up with Danilo almost a year ago Rick has been buying up to one-hundred kilos of coke from the Nicaraguan and turning over half a million in profit every week. With over thirty crack houses across LA and two rental car businesses to drive cash and coke all over the country, things couldn't be better.

'I'm gonna go see Danilo today,' Rick says thoughtfully.

'Yeah? Everything alright?'

Walking back to the breakfast bar, 'I been thinking, I wanna send pure coke directly to my cousin in St Louis and teach him how to cook.'

Putting the paper down, 'But Dennis is already doing twenty-pounds a week of crack.'

'And how many pounds of crack we doing in LA per week?' Rick asks knowingly.

With a shrug, 'Two-fifty?' Ollie answers.

'Three-hundred. Sometimes three-fifty in a good week.' Letting those numbers sink in for a moment to make his point, 'Ain't no twenty-pounds, is it?' Pulling up a stool, 'When we first started out you asked me how long this ride was gonna last. You remember that? Well, I didn't know then and I still don't know now. But I remember a hundred-grand back then was like a million dollars to us. Now we sitting on millions so what's to stop us from making tens of millions?'

Raising his eyebrows, 'I feel ya, Rick, but when's enough? We've got LA locked down for good, ain't no one gonna come along and take what we built here. Plus you got a little one on the way. When you gonna chill, homie?'

Chewing his lip, 'Enough is when I know my kids won't have to ever work a day they don't want to in their life. When they can go to a good school and college. Enough is when their kids are setup too. When they can dream whatever they wanna be and actually have a shot at it.'

'Damn, Rick,' Kenny says, 'You want white kids or something?'

They all laugh again, except for Rick. He knows there are two types of people in this world: the ones who see it all set in concrete and just play the game as it's dealt to them, and then there are the ones who want something different, something better than what has been handed to them and are willing to fight for it.

* * *

Sitting behind an oak desk inside a small office of plain furnishing, a potted palm in a corner, and the unappealing view of Carson through a wide window, Danilo considers Rick's request.

'You can trust this man, Dennis?' the Nicaraguan says after a moment.

'Trust him? He's my cousin, course I can trust him.'

Shrugging, 'Then I don't see why not. The more coca we move, the more money we make, no.'

'Damn straight.'

'Where is this, St Louis?' Danilo inquires.

'St Louis? It's in Missouri.'

'And where is Missouri? Forgive me, this country is a big place with many names. Anything outside of Florida, New York, and California is a stretch for me.'

'That's cool.' Rick thinks for a moment, 'You heard of Kansas City?'

'No.'

'Nashville?'

Danilo shakes his head apologetically.

Scrunching his face, 'Arkansas?'

'Arkansas, yes!'

Raising an eyebrow, 'Of all the places you don't know, you know Arkansas?'

Chuckling, 'One of my coca supply chains lands in Arkansas. How far is it from there to St Louis?'

'Depends where in Arkansas.'

'A little town called Mena.'

'Mena? I ain't never heard of Mena.'

'It's not far from Little Rock. Do you know Little Rock?' Danilo says, excited about his remote knowledge of Middle America.

Rick's eyes go big, 'Yeah, I know the Rock! When I was a kid living in Arp, Texas me and my mom would drive to St Louis every Thanks Giving to spend it with family. Now, to get from Texas to Missouri you drive right through Arkansas passing Little Rock on your way to Memphis, then it's straight up the 55 to St Louis.'

Nodding, 'And how long is the drive?'

'Only about five or six hours.'

Smiling, 'Well, that is lucky for us, *senor* Ricky. When would you like to begin?'

'Well, I wanna fly up there and teach him how to cook, so whenever the next shipment arrives from the jungles is good for me.'

Opening a black diary, Danilo scans its pages, 'The next shipment into Mena is the early hours of Wednesday morning, which means I can have the coca in St Louis by lunch time.' Looking up, 'How will that do?'

'Perfect. I'll be there Wednesday night.'

'Very good. And how much weight can your cousin handle?'

'I'm thinking ten keys to start with.'

Nodding and making a note in the dairy, '*No problemo*. Let me speak to my peoples and make the necessary arrangements.' Closing the ledger and leaning back in his chair, 'You have an appetite for money, Ricky.'

'That a problem?'

Chuckling, 'No, I like it. You want to grow, and a man needs to grow.'

Standing from the chair Rick walks to the window. Squinting against the bright day and grey building tops he thinks hard about his situation.

'You know why I want money so bad, Danilo? Because I didn't have a dime growing up. I wanna have what I was never given a chance to get.'

Danilo nods, 'I can understand that.'

Putting his hands on hips with his gaze fixed on the concrete jungle before him, Rick continues thoughtfully, 'I'm living a life I never expected to live. Actually, I'm living a life society never *wanted* me to live. Negroes ain't meant to have what I have. That's not how we're brought up or what we're told to believe. The only way to get out of the hood is to be an athlete, and then they don't mind you living in big fancy houses and marrying white girls. The only other way is to sell drugs but man, if you black and you get caught with a couple rocks you looking at three years, and that's for your first offence; and three years is enough to break a man.' Turning and facing Danilo with a sigh, 'I'm working so hard to make as much money as I can so I can get out, but I don't know where to. What's a negro from the hood who can't read and write meant to do with a few million dollars in his pocket?'

Watching Rick quietly Danilo leans back in his leather swivel chair with his hands cradled under his pudgy chin, 'Do you know why I am able to get so much coca into the US?'

'Because people wanna make money.'

'Yes, of course. But also because there is a war in my country and a certain amount of profit goes back to our people, our revolutionaries so that we might one day get our home back.'

Raising his eyebrows, 'No shit.'

'Listen, there is always a reason behind what people do but not always a purpose. Let us call it action versus reaction. The majority of people live a life of reaction, merely responding to the day-to-day throes of their situation. Few, however, live a life of action, of independence, of freedom. You, *senor* Ricky, have shifted from reaction to action and that makes you uncertain despite all that you have.'

Rick is quiet.

'What you have is money but what you lack is purpose because, as you say, you are living a life society never expected you to live. The purpose behind the coca, well some of it, is to fund a revolution. The purpose behind the revolution is to liberate Nicaragua from Socialism. And the purpose behind that is because *Americanos* are afraid of Communism. They love nothing more than believing they are free and yet the vast majority live a life of complete servitude thinking they are temporarily displaced millionaires. It's quite comical, really.'

Frowning, 'What's servitude mean?'

With a wry smile, 'It means slave, *senor* Ricky,' Danilo says pointedly.

'People are slaves without realizing it? Yeah, I can believe that.'

Danilo's chair squeaks as he leans forward, 'And what is a slave to do once he is freed?'

With an empty look on his face, 'I guess that's the million-dollar question, ain't it?' Rick offers.

Smiling, 'And you, *senor* Ricky, have a million dollars.'

* * *

Rick spends the next three days in St Louis eating and drinking and cooking crack cocaine. During the day Dennis takes him into Soulard, a historic suburb a stone's throw from the mighty Mississippi River filled with barbeque restaurants, crawfish, and blues bars. Dennis graciously pays for every meal and every drink as a means of thanking Rick for turning him from a used-cars salesman into what is likely to be a millionaire by this time next year. By night, however, Rick painstakingly teaches Dennis the fine art of cooking crack and before long they turn ten-kilos of pure coke into over eighty-pounds of ready rock; four-times the amount his cousin was previously doing and all it took was the snap of Rick's fingers to make it happen. Rick also gives his cousin a crash course on the best ways to move so much weight; from wholesale distribution tactics to increase market reach, staggering retail prices, ways of turning competitors into customers, and renting small apartments to keep cash in and others for crack. The information vital and the hook up invaluable. It's taken Rick years of hard work to rise this high, of trial and error, of deals gone bad, of losing coke, money, and dealers to understand how the intricate and complicated world of drug trafficking operates.

Living in Tower Grove East, Dennis's drug territory covers four lucrative black neighborhoods: Gravois Park, Dutchtown, Bevo Mill, and Carondelet. But in order to sell almost a hundred-pounds of crack in a week Dennis has to establish a network north of the city into blocks like Wells-Goodfellow, Walnut Park, Jeff Vander Lou, and Baden. These areas sprawling with gangs, hustlers, drug dealers and drug addicts. The trick to expanding into territories that you don't run is not to simply setup shop and become another competitor; that'll get your hustlers and dealers shot real quick. In fact, it's the opposite. You approach the suppliers directly offering your product to them, while making minimal profit. At this weight per week what you care about is volume of sales rather than sales by value. A McDonald's cheeseburger costs sixty-five-cents and sells for a dollar but take out of that rent, wages, and franchise percentages and the storeowner only cuts maybe five- or ten-cents per burger. It isn't much but when you're selling a couple of thousand cheeseburgers a day the economy of sales tips in your favor. And with an endless supply of the best coke coming into the country this is precisely what Rick explains to Dennis before he leaves; worry about making sales, not money, and the profits will come.

Arriving back in LA on Friday afternoon, Rick catches a cab to the new house he bought when he found out Marilyn was pregnant. Set back a couple of streets from Inglewood Avenue, Rick can jump on the 105, thunder east and be at Ollie's in Century Palms in less than fifteen-minutes or at any one of their crack houses scattered either side of the 110. He bought the house because it's in Hawthorne, a predominately black and Hispanic neighborhood of fine working-class people. It's also a subtle move west and *almost* out of the hood. A modest powder peach home ringed in stone cladding and with a big ironwood tree in the front yard, Burl Avenue is a nice street, clean and tree-lined with green verges and friendly neighbors. Even though Rick can afford ten of these houses, he knows this isn't a forever home. It's just a safer place to be for when they have their baby, and until he works out what the future holds for a drug kingpin with no education.

Walking in the door he finds Marilyn on the sofa, her feet in fluffy white slippers resting on the coffee table and her tee shirt pulled up to her breasts.

'Quick baby,' she says.

'Not even a hello?' Rick asks.

'The baby's kicking!'

Rick drops his bags and rushes over. Taking a seat he puts his hand over her navel.

After an anxious moment, 'There, did you feel that?' Marilyn says excitedly.

'Nah, I missed it!'

'Okay, okay.' Putting her hand on top of Rick's and moving it further around the side of her belly they wait wide-eyed and quiet for another kick, 'There! You feel that one?'

'Damn! Is that her?'

Laughing at Rick's excitement, 'That's her, that's our baby.'

Cupping her stomach with his hands Rick puts an ear to her belly, 'Hey yo, baby girl, it's your daddy,' he shouts. 'I'm gonna make sure you have everything you want in this world, you hear me. Swimming pool, Barbie dolls, hell I get you a pony if you want one, okay.'

Laughing, 'And where in the hell we going to keep a pony, Rick?'

'We'll get her one of those little ponies, the ones that grow to as big as a dog.'

'You're so stupid,' Marilyn says giggling.

After kissing each other Rick checks his watch, 'It's almost six-o'clock, we gotta get going to Ollie's or we'll be late for the party.'

Putting her arm across Rick and resting her head on his chest, 'Stay a minute and talk to me, I've missed you.'

'Aiit,' Rick says slouching deeper into the sofa.

'So, how was St Louis, baby?'

Breathing a big sigh, 'It was good, real good. Got Dennis cooking no problem and I just flooded the place with the best crack they've ever seen.'

'Yeah?'

'Yeah, and man, St Louis got a lot of potential.'

'Tell me, baby?'

'See, we're delivering crack cooked here in LA all the way to Denver and Dallas, but if I can shore up Dennis in St Louis with pure coke and have him cook from there, then that opens up the entire east coast to us. I'm talking Chicago, Cincinnati, Atlanta, Jersey, Philly, even maybe New York one day.'

'And Danilo has enough coke for you to do that?' Marilyn wonders.

'You know how much coke I get from him?' Rick asks seriously.

'A lot,' she says with a giggle.

'One-hundred-kilos a week. And I know he's delivering to cats in Florida and who knows where else.'

'Damn,' Marilyn whispers.

Closing his eyes and leaning his head back on a cushion, 'Nah, he has plenty because there's a war in Nicaragua or some shit.'

'A war, huh? And what's that got to do with the coke?'

'Profits, baby. When you're moving that much powder you best believe people are getting their share.'

'And what are we doing with our profits?'

Rick opens one eye, '*Our* profits?'

With a smirk, 'We together, I ain't going nowhere, so what's yours is mine.'

Raising his eyebrows and smiling, 'Well, *we've* been busy the last six-months buying properties and scaling-up our street sales in LA as an insurance.'

'Insurance for what?'

'So no matter what happens to the rest of our network we'll always have LA making drug money for us.'

'And what if the coke does eventually dry up, what are we gonna do?'

'Well, we already own a rental car business, a bunch of liquor stores, and a licensed bail bonds. Those alone make more money than most people could hope for.'

'But?'

'How'd you know a but was coming?'

Smiling, 'Because I know you.'

'Well, what I really wanna do is open up a chain of motels,' Rick says thoughtfully.

'Motels?'

'Yeah, you ever played Monopoly? There's a lot of money in motels, and not just the business side of it but all the real estate you own too. I realized that when me and Ollie bought all those houses and apartments to store cash in. Property goes up in value over time, so I was thinking what better way to own more land than to build some motels.'

'Look at you Mr. Businessman,' Marilyn says impressed. 'And then what?'

'Then we'd get rich without having to work or move drugs and we could do whatever we want, live wherever we want.'

Lifting her head off his chest, 'Live wherever we want? What's wrong with living here, everybody we know is here?'

'Yeah, but it's the hood.'

Frowning, 'And?'

'And ain't nothing good in the hood except drugs and violence.'

'That so,' she says standing from the sofa. 'What about your family, Rick? Your friends? What about me, huh? We all from the hood.'

'Come on, I didn't mean it like that. I just want us to have a good life, I want our baby to have a good life and not have to grow up seeing the shit we've had to.'

'And where's that? Where's this magical place where people don't judge us by the color of our skin or the school we went to or the way we talk, huh? And why the fuck you think I wanna live there anyhow when everybody I know lives between Gardena and Compton, and Inglewood and Florence?' Marilyn says angrily.

Rick is quiet, partly because he's tired and partly because he wasn't expecting this conversation to turn into an argument. He does want to leave the hood but aside from the obvious he doesn't really know why and even less so how to make it happen. And Marilyn has a point too, everyone he's ever known and loved is here in South LA but that doesn't mean he has to be. Action versus reaction, right?

Marilyn stares at Rick for a moment before narrowing her eyes, 'Is that why you bought this place in Hawthorne?'

Not ready to acknowledge that he does in fact plan to leave, 'Hawthorne is still the hood!' Rick protests.

Putting her hands on her hips, 'The hell it is!'

'It's right next to Holly Park,' Rick argues.

'And?'

'And Holly Park is right next to West Athens and that's ghetto as fuck. Plus Hawthorne got their own Crip sect, they're customers of mine.'

Storming into the bedroom but continuing the argument, 'Don't you think I don't know what you're doing, Ricky,' Marilyn yells out. 'Just on the other side of the 405 is North Redondo and next to that is Hermosa Beach, Redondo Beach, and Torrance Beach.'

Crossing his arms, 'I don't know what you talking about.'

Returning to the living room in a loose green polka-dot dress, 'Boy, you've been dreaming about the beach since I first met you. Talking about how you always used to ride your bike to Venice as a kid and then how one of your original coke connects lives over in Pacific Palisades and how nice it is there.'

'Baby—'

'Don't baby, me. We're having a child, Rick,' she says disappointedly. 'If you have these grand plans you need to tell me about them. It ain't just you anymore.'

Rick chews his lip uncertain of what to say because he's uncertain about what he actually wants.

'We need to go, we're already late,' Marilyn says flatly.

Riding in Rick's new Corvette with a gooey orange sun setting behind them, they drive in uncomfortable silence. Rick rumbles off of the 110 into Magnolia Square taking the back streets to Ollie's house. Tall palm trees sway in an indigo sky, while kids ride their bikes laughing as they catch the remains of daylight. Houses are aglow with families just happy it's the weekend as they sit down to watch the *Cosby Show* with foil-wrapped TV dinners. When it's like this it's easy to forget how bad this place can be, and Rick can't help but think about the innocent people here who aren't doing anything wrong; just caught up in world with no real chance of escaping.

Sitting in the back of a black Mercedes a few blocks away, two men load magazines into Uzi's and rack the slide back loading the chamber, while the driver pulls leather gloves tight over his hands before adjusting the rear-view mirror. A helicopter flying past the 110 makes them all look nervously skyward, but it continues northeast disappearing into the purple darkness.

'Aiit, you niggas ready?' the man in the back asks.

'Yeah, Dave,' the one sitting next to him says softly.

The driver only nods.

After a moment, 'I said, you niggas ready or what?' this time more forcefully.

'Yeah, we ready,' they both say loudly.

'Good. Remember, Nevel, you're out your window shooting over top, I'm out my window, and Skinny you get two clean shots off with your sawed-off shotgun but don't you dare fucking crash this car, you feel me?'

Flexing his hands around the steering wheel, 'I feel you.'

'You can drive slow because these niggas will think we're just their homies coming to the party, so make sure you spray the shit out of the place. But most important, when you see that Ricky mother fucker, I want all your shells going at him, aiit.'

Taking a deep breath they pull black ski masks down over their faces, wind down the windows and get into position. Slowly pulling onto Grand Avenue, the street is full of parked cars and they can already see people standing around the front of Ollie's house.

'Okay, now, Nev,' Dave tells his partner to climb out of the window and take aim across the roof.

Two women walking towards the house see the car and the men with guns and scream. Everyone in the open garage and front yard looks at the Mercedes with a hollow expression because that brief moment before a drive-by happens is too fast to be fully comprehended. Then the triggers get squeezed and within seconds bullets spray with lethal indiscrimination, hitting walls and windows and arms and chests and faces. People scramble and dive for cover behind tables and chairs and each other, while screams of fear and agony are drowned out by the automatic squirt of gunfire tearing through the night. Brass casings rain down on the Mercedes and onto the street as the car rolls slowly along. Someone shoots back at the Mercedes puncturing holes in its side. Squeezing his last buckshot before dropping the shotgun in his lap, Skinny grabs the wheel with both hands and plants his foot on the pedal.

Screeching around a corner, Dave grabs Nevel by his belt pulling him into the car.

'Oh, shit.'

'What? What happened to Nev?' Skinny shouts.

Seeing that he's taken a bullet through his forehead, 'Nev's dead,' Dave says flatly lifting the balaclava off the man's face, revealing a small black hole oozing with blood.

'Fuck!' Skinny says hitting the steering wheel.

After sliding around a few more corners, 'Aiit, drop your speed, we don't want the cops pulling us over,' Dave says calmly.

As the black Mercedes approaches a small traffic intersection, stopped at a red light is a brand-new Corvette C4 with an unmistakable driver at the wheel. Pressing on the gas, Skinny crosses to the oncoming lane and slams on the breaks in the middle of the street.

'What the fuck you doing, Skinny?!' Dave yells.

'It's Freeway, nigga!'

'Where?'

Pointing to the Corvette in front of them, 'There!'

Sitting at a red-light Marilyn finally breaks the silence, 'I know you love the beach, and I get you want to leave the hood but, Rick, who are we if we don't recognize where we come from? You think moving a couple of neighborhoods over is going to change who you are but it isn't.' After a moment, 'I want our baby girl to go to a good school and have nice things too, but that doesn't mean we have to leave the city either.'

Before Rick can respond a black Mercedes screeches sideways into the middle of the intersection and a guy wearing a ski mask jumps out.

'Rick!' Marilyn screams.

Seeing that he has a silver revolver already pointed at them, 'It's okay, baby, just be cool,' Rick says calmingly.

Approaching the driver's side window, 'Out! Get the fuck out!' the man shouts.

Rick slowly gets out of the car holding his hands half up.

Smirking, the guy in the ski-mask aims his gun at Rick's forehead.

'You want the car?' Rick says. 'Take it. I ain't gonna stop you.'

'The fuck I want your car for, nigga?'

Rick's mouth is dry but he tries to remain calm, 'Then what do you want?'

'You,' the gunman says slowly.

'Me?' Rick says confused. 'Do you know who the fuck I am?'

'Yeah, I know who the fuck you are, why you think I got this gun pointed at your head?'

Squinting, Rick finds something oddly familiar about the gunman. Then, seeing the gold chain on his wrist, 'Chinese Dave, that you?'

Shaking his head and sighing, 'You just had to get too big for your boots didn't you, Freeway.' Pulling the ski-mask up over his face, 'Yeah, you at the top but you can't see who you've stepped on to get there, homie,' Dave says spitefully.

'I ain't stepped on no one,' Rick defends. 'If homies can't keep up with how much I move then that's on them. Everything I got has come off my own back.'

'Fuck that. You wouldn't have shit without me.'

'Without you? Nigga, if we were still getting coke from Miami all this time we'd be in jail by now. I made coke in LA what it is.'

Smirking 'So you did. And now I'm about to take it back.'

They stare at one another for a tense few seconds before Chinese Dave pulls the hammer back on his gun. Rick is frozen, remembering how he felt when his mamma shot his uncle, how loud the gun was when it went off, how fast the bullet travelled and how quickly it took the man's life. Now it's his turn and he feels sad and empty that everything he did wasn't enough to prevent his life from ending up this way, like so many others in the hood do, and how nobody really remembers who they are after, just forgotten victims of society, victims of gangs and drugs and violence, victims of being black and growing up in poor black neighborhoods where dying before the age of thirty is a likelihood. We're all innocent, Rick thinks, even the ones who pull the trigger. We're all just reacting to this hard world. It ain't no one's fault and yet at the same time it's all our fault for not trying hard enough to change the game. Even Rick wanted to conquer it, rise above it, escape it and yet here he is, staring down the barrel of a piece of metal that will take away everything that ever meant something to him.

'Time's up, Freeway,' Chinese Dave says coldly.

Headlights suddenly beam across Rick's face making him squint and then the screech of tires makes Chinese Dave turn just in time to see the grill of a cream Buick slam into him. Cartwheeling over the hood, smashing the windscreen and flipping into the air like a ragdoll, he lands in a crumpled heap twenty-feet away.

Crashing into a row of newspaper racks, the Buick comes to a stop on the sidewalk, steam pissing out of the engine, while the Mercedes tears off, snaking its away down the street and around a corner.

Redmon stumbles out of the Buick holding his bloody forehead and Rick blinks at him blankly before coming to the realization that he's not dead. Walking over to Chinese Dave and standing over his twisted body, one of his eyes is twitching and only the white is visible in the other.

'When you come at the king,' Rick whispers, 'you best not miss.'

Sobbing, Marilyn climbs out of the car and walks tentatively towards Rick.

Between gasps, 'Ri-Rick, are you okay? You-you're not hurt, are you?' she asks.

Turning to her slowly, 'You see this, this is why I wanna get the fuck out of the hood,' he says to her gravely.

XXI
CARLOS CABEZAS

Cutting through dark silence the phone on the bedside rings sharply. Rubbing his eyes Carlos rolls onto his arm, sighing when he sees the green neon lines on the clock read three-twelve-am.

Picking up the receiver, 'Hello?' he says hoarsely.

There's no response, only heavy breathing.

'Talk,' Carlos says firmly.

After a deep breath, *'It's me, darling.'*

Frowning, 'Vince? What's wrong?'

The little Portuguese man grunts, *'Everything. I—I need something, someone,'* his voice breaks.

Sitting up and changing ears, Carlos turns on a brass lamp, 'Someone? You're not making any sense, Vince.'

'No, I'm not.' Taking another labored breath, *'I'm afraid, Carlos. I'm afraid I might do something stupid. Can you meet me?'* he says with a timbre in his words, an uncertain fragility.

'Of course. Where?'

'The Aztec, upstairs. You know the spot. I'll leave the doors unlocked.'

Vince hangs up and Carlos stares worriedly at the phone in his hand.

'Is everything okay?' Nancy Hoover asks softly from beneath the sheets.

Frowning, 'I'm not sure, I've never heard him like this.' After a moment, 'I have to go.'

Reaching out and grabbing his arm, 'Wait.'

'Vince needs me,' he says gently.

'I know, but I need you too.'

Carlos sighs before rolling back into bed and clasping her hand. They are both quiet, uncertain of how protective to be of one another. Nancy is still with Jerry after all but her feelings for the Nicaraguan have become unbearable. As for Carlos, he has found in her everything he didn't know he wanted or needed and yet she belongs to someone else.

'Listen,' he begins, 'it won't be much longer until we can leave and start our life together. You just have to be patient.'

Nestling into his chest, 'Tell me again how it'll be,' she whispers.

'As soon as I wrap things up in San Francisco I'll be free, then when your term as mayor is finished, we can go, like we said.'

'To Miami?'

'To the Keys, yes. We'll sail to the Bahamas, to Jamaica, to Mexico. There's a little island not far from Cancún called Holbox. There are no cars or roads there; just villas on the sand and flamingos in the water.'

'You promise?'

'I've made my choice, Nancy, and you're it.'

A small smile creases her lips, 'Oh, Carlos, why do I feel like I've known you my whole life?'

Cupping her face and kissing her, 'I have to go, baby.'

Lighting another cigarette Vince stares vacantly at the crane-lights blinking atop the almost complete Horton Plaza. His eyes are bloodshot and sagged, and the bottle of scotch he's been drinking is half gone.

Carlos reaches for Vince's glass.

'Best not darling, I—I have this nasty cough,' Vince complains. 'Here,' he says offering him the bottle.

Taking a long swig and wiping his mouth with the back of his hand, 'Okay, tell me, Vince, what's going on?'

Pinching the bridge of his nose and giving a sigh, 'It happened. The one thing I swore to never let happen, happened.'

Carlos waits.

Raising his eyebrows and giving a capitulating smile, 'I've lost everything.'

Frowning, 'What do you mean, lost everything?' Carlos asks.

After an anxious giggle, 'George—he, he has secretly sold all of my assets to the Dominelli brothers.'

'What? How?'

Shaking his head, 'Jerry wasn't inviting me to his parties to assuage my reluctance to sell the *Aztec*, he was stringing me along so George could pull the rug out inch by inch.'

'But your name is on the titles, no?'

'Yes, but you see, a homosexual couple is not considered a legal relationship in this country. So, to protect ourselves we each gave the other the power to dissolve or sell *Walnut's* assets on our own in the event of an unforeseeable tragedy.'

'But there has been no tragedy, you are alive and well. Why would George do this?'

Gulping his scotch and looking solemnly into the purple night, 'That Beverly Hills toy-boy,' Vince says quietly. 'George is making a break for a new life.' With a shaky hand he refills his glass, 'Can't say I blame him, look at me; I'm a shadow of what I once was.'

Leaning forward in his chair, 'Can't any of this be stopped?'

Drawing deeply on his cigarette, 'I don't think so. I saw the contracts earlier tonight, the deeds, the asset transfers. They've all been finalized and the cooling-off periods have all expired. It's been going on for almost a year and I had no idea.'

'This is unbelievable,' Carlos says standing. 'And where's George now?'

'In LA. He called me, spoke very cut and dry, you know, like you would if you just stole everything your best friend built and loved.'

Carlos rubs his chin, 'I can have him, you know,' he says making a gunshot motion to the side of his head.

'And what will that solve, darling? It won't give me back my theatres and hotels. It won't give me back my life's work,' Vince says with a sardonic smirk.

Clenching his jaw, 'This is an outrage. How are you so calm?'

Looking up at the Nicaraguan with wet eyes, 'I'm not,' he says flatly. 'I feel devastated and destroyed. Everything I've built dismantled piece by piece behind my back. I'm seething, I'm mad, I'm lost and empty and helpless.' Looking at his glass of scotch, 'I'm just drunk,' he says as a tear rolls down his cheek.

Calming himself, 'What are you going to do?' asks Carlos.

After a moment, 'I still have a couple-hundred thousand in a private account and the house in Encino. So, I suppose call an early retirement,' the words making his chin quiver. 'But it appears I've been beaten, hustled out of my own home.'

'You can't let this happen, you can't let it all go to waste, Vince,' Carlos urges.

Chuckling into his glass of scotch before downing it, 'And how do you propose I stop it, Mr. Cabezas? Ask Jerry to just sign everything back over to me?' Shaking his head, 'It's over. I've finally lost the battle.'

Looking out through the window, dawn approaching in the distance, Carlos searches for solutions, 'What about insurance policies?' Then, turning, 'What about the ground lease at least for the *Aztec*?' he says eagerly.

Feigning a smile, 'There's nothing, Carlos. The power of attorney George and I gave ourselves to protect each other is precisely what he has used to steal it all away.' Attempting to refill his glass and mostly missing, 'The wolves have won and the slyest of all was the one I loved most.'

Carlos finally stops, the shock of the news distilling into the terrible unfortunate reality it is. He notices Vince looking every bit beaten as he sits legs-crossed in the leather chair; his cheeks drawn and hair unusually unkempt, even his white suit that is always perfectly pressed is wrinkled and out of shape.

Checking his watch, 'Listen, I have to catch a plane to San Francisco this morning. Hopefully for the last time,' Carlos says with a warm smile. 'I'm only gone for a couple of days but when I'm back I'll help you sort this mess out, okay?'

Staring drowsily into the scotch glass resting on his thigh Vince doesn't respond.

'Hey,' Carlos says softly, 'there will be something we can do, Vince. Don't give up just yet.'

Looking up slowly with eyes wet and glassy Vince manages a weak smile.

* * *

'What a party, huh,' Julio whistles.

Under a cloudless blue sky the rooftop garden of the luxury *Fairmont Hotel* is lavishly styled with white linen cocktail tables, tuxedoed waiters carrying canapés, and a small mariachi band playing vigorously in the sun. Nicaraguan and FDN flags lap in a warm breeze, while blue and white sashes hang between tall palms with the words *Fuerza Democratica Nicaraguense* spelled out beneath them. This is by far the most extravagant fundraiser Carlos has been to in San Francisco with guests ranging from Mayor Dianne Feinstein, a swathe of FDN members from Miami, Central American press, and wealthy exiles parading their power.

'Business must be booming,' Carlos says flatly.

'Hey, come on. The day's only just getting started and already you're sour?'

Yawning, '*Perdon, hermano.* I didn't sleep well last night.'

'You didn't sleep well?' Julio says sarcastically. 'You, living the good life in San Diego and barely lifting a finger these days. I'm the one who just got out of the can don't forget.'

Smiling, 'You said it was a cake walk. You made connections, hit the gym, plus it gave you some time away from that crazy girlfriend of yours.'

Raising his eyebrows, 'I'm not gonna lie, that was the best part,' Julio says sipping his mojito. 'Of course, she was pissed that I was gone for three-months but man, you'd think showing her how the new distribution channels work meaning I'd have less to do with the coca than before would make her happy but oh no, not Lucile.'

'Some women just can't be made happy,' Carlos offers.

'Don't I know it.' After a moment, 'Have you spoken to Sofia?'

'No. Why would I?'

Shrugging, 'She still thinks you're going to come back to her.'

Frowning, 'Where'd you hear that?'

'Lucile.'

Shaking his head, 'I was done with Sofia a long time ago.' Then, looking around the rooftop garden, the fundraiser, which is really a front for so-called FDN members and drug traffickers to rub shoulders and boast about their efforts fighting for the cause, 'And I think I'm finally done with this city too, *hermano*.'

Choking on a cube of ice Julio's eyes go round.

Continuing, 'I am going to tell Norwin tonight that I'm out of the business, for good.'

Spitting the ice back into his glass, 'Geez Louise. How do you think he'll take it?'

Carlos shrugs his shoulders.

'Man, I don't know if now is such a good time. Ever since the new warehouses got raided by the DEA last month, Norwin is darker than ever. He's hot on my ass, you know, because I'm looking after them all.'

'But there wasn't any coca in any of them,' Carlos reflects.

'I know. But he's talking about there being a rat amongst the new guys,' Julio says miserably.

Raising an eyebrow, 'See, just another reason to get out, while I can.'

'So, what are you going to do?' Julio asks.

Giving his cousin a wry smile, 'Retire and wait for the day I can go back to our beloved Managua.'

Chuckling, 'What, you don't like it here in America?' Julio says. 'I like it, it's grown on me.'

Feigning surprise, 'You've come along way,' Carlos jokes.

'Yeah, well, it may be a long time before we see our beloved Managua, so I guess California is home until then.'

Looking at his drink, 'Home,' Carlos says distantly. 'When Samoza fell and we were forced to leave I feel like I've never found a home, Julio. Not here in San Francisco and not LA either. Now I find myself in San Diego,' he says with a shrug. 'A part of me was hoping this revolution in Nicaragua would have been over by now, that we could return—those that wanted to at least—and get back all that we lost. Our homes, our businesses, our lands.' Sighing, 'But there seems to be no end in sight. The Contras are barely a force, the FDN plays politics, the

CIA watching everything that goes on down there, and the coca,' Carlos trails off.

'Hey, the coca is the only thing keeping it all together. Without that we'd have nothing; us here in California and the Contras.'

Shaking his head, 'We have more money than we ever dreamed of and yet every week, every month we flirt with a danger that could take it all away.'

'There's no danger, while the Contras need our help,' Julio reminds him.

Nodding, 'And when the revolution is over, then what?'

'Who cares, *hermano*. You're right, we have made more money than we could ever have dreamed and who would have thought it? Us, fucking Nicaraguan immigrants making millions here. So what? We fucking deserve it; we deserve it on behalf of all the *campesinos* throughout Central and South America who break their backs and still have nothing compared to these greedy *Americanos*. Fuck 'em. For decades they have come and taken whatever they wanted from other countries, so who gives a shit that a handful of Latinos are finally getting something back. Not to mention the negroes too. They deserve to make something from this country more than us. You ask what will we do when the revolution is over? I say, what does it matter? Life always changes, the world moves on with or without us, *hermano. Si,* the revolution will be over but then there will be another one, or civil war somewhere, a President overthrown and a dictator put in his place. It never ends. You worry too much, man. When this is all over the *Americanos* aren't going to come for you and me, they're going to come for Ochoa and Escobar, for Juan Matta, Felix Gallardo, Lehder and Jung and all the other big players.'

Carlos thinks about what Julio is saying and concedes that there is truth in his words, but he can't ignore that there is a limit to what they are doing, a limit too few in this business seem to see.

'And how much money is enough then?'

Giving Carlos a tired look, 'Hey, man, if you want out then get out. I'm not gonna stop you and you better hope neither does Norwin, that's for sure. Me, I'm gonna keep making hay while the sun shines,' Julio says with frustration.

Looking at his young cousin with a renewed admiration, 'You know what?' Carlos says.

'What?'

'You're absolutely right, *hermano*. We make the road by walking on it,' he says holding up his drink with a warm smile.

Smirking, 'And eyes that see do not grow old,' Julio says chinking glasses with him.

A sudden commotion by the entrance makes both men turn as people hurry to greet newly arrived guests.

'Who is it you think?' asks Julio.

Shaking his head when he sees a tall Nicaraguan in a blue suit with fluffy greying hair, 'None other than Adolfo Calero himself.'

'The FDN big shot?'

'That's the one. Him, Aristides Sanchez, and Colonel Enrique Bermudez: the Iron Triangle.'

Julio whistles again, 'Lucky I wore my good suit.' Then, leaning forward, 'Is it true he's in with the CIA?'

Looking unimpressed, 'Isn't anyone involved with this revolution in with the CIA? Hell, I'm involved with the damn CIA.'

Laughing, 'Calero's on their payroll though, you're in their pocket.'

Shooting Julio a look, 'Don't remind me. There's another reason I want to get out. Mark my words, when all this is over, when the revolution is won or lost and the *Americanos* don't want all this coca coming in, you can bet your ass we're going to be in trouble.'

Slapping the table, 'Come on, again with the sour? For real, I haven't seen you in a month and this is how you're going to be all day?' Julio pleads.

Chuckling at his young cousin, 'Don't ever change, *hermano*.'

'Change? What am I gonna change for?' he says leaning back and clasping his hands behind his head. 'I got a good life. You might be tired of making the money but I'm not.'

Carlos sinks the rest of his rum before standing, 'I'll get us another round, eh.'

On his way to a bar setup beneath a large palm tree, Carlos feels a tap on his shoulder.

'Ah, well, if it isn't, *senor* Cabezas. It's good to see you, Carlos,' Popo Chamorro says agreeably with open arms.

'*Senor Chamorro, es bueno verte tambien.*'

'Allow me to introduce my associates from Miami, *senor* Octavio Cesar.'

'*Much gusto, senor,*' Carlos says shaking the squat man's hand.

Squinting and taking a chewed cigar from his mouth, 'Ah, yes, the man who took our coca connection from Los Angeles,' Cesar remarks.

Confused, 'And who was that?' asks Carlos.

'The negro. The one they call Freeway.'

Smiling, 'I'm afraid that was Danilo's doing.'

Raising a bushy eyebrow, 'Was it now?'

Nodding, 'Besides, it's all for the Contras anyway, right?'

Smirking and wedging the wet cigar into the corner of his mouth, 'Right,' the fat Nicaraguan says slowly.

'And,' Popo continues, 'this is Mr. Donald Barrios.'

Wearing a burgundy suit and silk mustard cravat, thick square-framed glasses with grey balding hair, Donald Barrios looks like an aging nightclub owner from the '70's. Extremely likeable and gregarious, he's a businessman of such varied involvements people struggle to tell what he actually owns and what he doesn't. More than this however, Donald Barrios is a close friend to Norwin Meneses and here he is standing with Popo Chamorro, the Miami FDN member Ferdinand Sanchez arranged for Carlos to divert a portion of Norwin's cocaine to. Of course, once he made the necessary arrangements with Troilo Ferdinand, Carlos had only infrequent involvement with the scheme, however, be that as it may, he is all too aware that skimming Norwin's coca all this time is a mighty cross Carlos hopes he'll never have to bear.

Swallowing, 'I have heard the name. It is a pleasure to finally meet you, Mr. Barrios,' Carlos says inclining his head.

'Oh no, the pleasure is all mine, Mr. Cabezas. I've heard very good things about you.'

Carlos feigns a smile.

'Tell me,' Popo Chamorro continues, 'how come you haven't come to Miami in so long? You're still taking care of things for Norwin aren't you or has Sebastian Gonzalez taken your job?' he says with a chuckle.

'Of course I am. It's just the situation here in California has changed,' he says with a reassuring shrug. 'These days I'm in San Diego looking after some other business.'

This is the best answer he can come up with, uncertain of how he really feels or what he really wants, and even more uncertain of expressing himself in front of such well-connected individuals.

Donald chuckles, 'You can't fool me, Mr. Cabezas.'

'And how's that, Mr. Barrios?'

'If you're getting tired of Norwin busting your ass then you should come see me in Miami. Lots of opportunities for a man of your talents.'

Although Donald and Norwin have a long history, Carlos is a little taken aback with how candidly the man from Miami is speaking about his boss. 'Thank you, Mr. Barrios. I'll keep it in mind.'

Leaning closer, 'No need to be apprehensive, Mr. Cabezas. You should know I've got an ear on just about anything that happens in Miami, especially with my Nicaraguan friends.' Then, giving Popo a look, 'So, don't worry, your secret is safe with me.'

Carlos doesn't respond.

Putting his arm over Carlos's shoulder, 'Few people understand Norwin like I do. Business is business after all and we need to look after our own interests too.'

'That we do,' Carlos says uneasily.

Popo nods. Then, discretely despite everyone present being in the coke trade, 'And what about down south, everything still under control?'

'You haven't missed a delivery yet, have you?' Carlos says raising his eyebrows. 'Don't worry, I'm still flying down there and making sure things run smoothly.'

'Good, good. Because there's a lot of people depending on that.'

Carlos smiles.

'Alrighty then,' Donald Barrios says patting Carlos on the shoulder, 'we'll see you tonight at the dinner?'

'That you will.'

With a sinking feeling in his stomach, Carlos walks back to the table.

'Where's the drinks?' Julio asks. Then, dropping his sunglasses down his nose, 'What happened to you? You look like you've seen a ghost.'

Shaking his head, 'I just bumped into Popo Chamorro and Donald Barrios.'

'And?'

'And Barrios knows about Norwin's coca for the FDN.'

'Oh ohh.'

Frowning, 'Then he offered for me to come work for him in Miami?' Carlos says strangely.

Whistling, 'You think Norwin would let you go work for Barrios?'

Carlos shoots him a look, 'You think Norwin likes losing pocket change?' Sighing and shaking his head, 'I'm not working for Barrios. And I'm not staying in San Francisco either.'

Later that night the fundraising soiree continues in the *Fairmont's* Tonga Room: a Polynesian-inspired tiki bar and restaurant of straw huts, cane furniture, flame-torches, and gawking wooden Moai surrounding an artificial lagoon complete with on-the-hour rainstorms and volcanic eruptions. Dimly lit paper lanterns ring the pool, while a young Tony Bennett impersonator with a three-piece band perform classics from a small floating bandstand. Cigar smoke hangs heavy in the air and waiters rush back and forth from the kitchen carrying silver dishes of dry-aged steak, Maine lobster, and New England clam chowder, while rum and champagne flow endlessly from the bar. Politicians, press, members of the FDN, traffickers and businessmen move about the restaurant like a game of adult musical chairs seizing opportunities to conveniently seat themselves next to just the person they were hoping to see. This is the time when deals are hatched, promises are made, and handshakes determine the fate of the unwitting and innocent. Nicaragua's future is not in the hands of its people but in the sweaty palms of rich exiles and drug smugglers.

With a wedge of pink rib-eye on the end of his fork, 'Did you know that in this hotel is where Tony Bennett first sang, *I left my heart in San Francisco?*' Julio says with a mouth full of charcoaled cow.

Looking up dubiously from his steamed Atlantic cod, 'Where do you come up with this stuff?' Carlos asks.

'What? I mean, everyone knows Tony Bennett but that song put him on the map, changed his whole career.'

'You have a soft spot for *Americanos* now?'

'What's that supposed to mean?'

'It wasn't so long ago you couldn't stand John Wayne and Clint Eastwood.'

Pointing his fork, 'Tony Bennett's Italian! And besides, they're actors, that's different. Movies are all about the make-believe, passing off what isn't true as true. Music, now that comes from the heart.'

'Is that right?'

'*¡Claro esta!* Music is the soul singing. It's life coming out in words, you know.'

'And what about him?' Carlos asks coyly.

Frowning, 'Who?'

'The kid pretending to be Tony Bennett, isn't he acting?'

'He—but the voice, it comes from, from within.'

Smirking, Carlos raises his eyebrows inviting Julio to continue making his case.

Dropping his fork loudly onto the plate, 'Why you gotta ruin everything, huh?' Sliding out of the booth, 'Always being too smart for your own good, *idiota.*'

Wiping his mouth with a napkin, 'Come on, I was only joking. Where are you going?'

Walking off, 'To take a piss,' Julio yells over his shoulder.

Looking around the restaurant at the people he knows and those he doesn't, Carlos reflects how life is such a thin reality, a veil resting atop layers of possibilities. What possibilities? The dozens taking place tonight, the moves being made, the offers, the negotiations, the conditions and compromises. Not everyone wins in life, in fact, most don't. We just strap ourselves in for a bumpy ride hoping for the best, the best being a series of attempts to do one thing before getting diverted or derailed onto something else; a juggling act trying to make something of yourself, while struggles and setbacks descend like raindrops in a storm that lasts however long you happen to live.

'*Hola, Carlos,*' Peña says appearing at the table.

Looking up and finishing his mouthful of fish, '*Hola, Peña.*'

Lighting a cigarette, '*Que tal tu noche?*'

Gesturing his knife and fork to the table of food, 'Couldn't be better,' Carlos says indifferently.

Peña nods before glancing around the restaurant, 'Norwin would like a word with you.'

'Now?'

'*Si*, now.'

Carlos stands and follows Peña through the Tonga Room weaving around tables, avoiding rushing waiters, and giving fast handshakes to people in the business. Peña stops for no one, stalking through the restaurant like a panther prowling the jungle: silent and smooth and with a menacing grace.

Sitting at a dimly lit corner-booth, Norwin Meneses sits tearing at chunks of white lobster tail with his bare hands. At the table are Alberto and Hernan, too enjoying the feast, with napkins tucked into their collars and garlic butter glistening in the corner of their mouths. There's a raucous of laughter as Peña and Carlos arrive.

'Ah, Carlos,' Norwin blurts, mouth full of white meat, 'where have you been all day? We should call you fucking international man of mystery you're never around.'

The men laugh again.

At least he's in good spirits, Carlos thinks. 'You wanted to see me?'

Pulling the napkin from his neck, 'I did,' Norwin says cleaning his fingers before scrunching the white linen into a ball and tossing it onto his plate. 'Leave us,' he states plainly to Hernan and Alberto who exchange an uneasy look before removing their napkins and sliding from the booth. Leaning against a bamboo post Peña stays behind, barely looking but always watching.

'Sit,' Norwin says gulping down a glass of rum and fixing his bushy black moustache. 'We need to talk about San Diego.'

Sliding in and clearing his throat, 'What's to say?' Carlos begins. 'There's no market so business—'

'No, no, not business,' Norwin says waving a dismissive hand. 'I mean you and that *puta,* Nancy.'

Carlos struggles to hide the shock that Norwin, who has never stepped foot in San Diego, knows about his relationship with Nancy Hoover. A relationship they have gone to great lengths to keep a secret.

'Come on, Carlos. You don't think I don't know about you and her?' Shaking his head disappointedly, 'What chance do you think you have with her anyway, how's a mayor going to look being with a coca trafficker, eh?'

'I-I—'

Smirking, Norwin continues, 'Don't worry, I know the power of the pussy but your problem isn't being in the business, it's that she belongs to Jerry and Jerry isn't someone you want to cross. Someone *I* don't want you to cross. I have invested a lot of money down there and I don't need you and your dick fucking it up.'

Frowning, 'How do you know about her?'

'Please, you insult me. Of course I know about her. I know about everything that goes on with my guys.'

Carlos thinks for a moment, recalling his earlier realization that this is going to be his last night in San Francisco and that would mean declaring it to Norwin. He could kill for a drink, something to wet his throat and ease what must come out. Instead, 'I'm done,' he says hoarsely.

'Done?'

Licking his lips, 'I want out. Out of the business, out of everything,' Carlos musters.

Norwin raises his bushy eyebrows before starting to chuckle, slow at first then slamming the table and laughing so hard small bits of lobster launch from his mouth.

'He wants out, Peña. He wants out,' Norwin says snorting and rubbing his eyes.

Carlos waits nervously; of all the reactions he was preparing for, Norwin almost in tears laughing wasn't what he expected.

'My dear, Carlos, do you remember what you were doing when I first met you? You were a drug runner for Jorge Morales flying marijuana into El Paso like a postman. You, an officer of the Nicaraguan National Guard. You should be thankful I brought you in.'

'I am,' Carlos says sincerely.

'Good. Because everything you have is because of me.' Then, staring at him long enough to make it uncomfortable, 'So you're out when I say you're out.'

A tense silence fills the space between the two men. Carlos dwarfing the scrawny Norwin in his ill-fitting beige suit and yet there is present an imbalance of power, scales tipping and not in the tall Nicaraguan's favor.

Licking his teeth clean, 'I want you to know that I know about the coca you are skimming for the Sanchez brothers,' Norwin says coldly with dark vacant eyes.

Holding his breath Carlos knows not to react, not yet. Norwin likes to talk, to make people sweat, make them cower in the wake of the uncertainty of how he'll respond.

Looking past the tall Nicaraguan, Norwin clicks his fingers and in an instant Carlos finds an arm gripped tight around his neck squeezing the air out of him. He latches onto the thick forearm and his knees bang against the underside of the table but there is nothing he can do; the grip is too tight. Hernan appears out of the darkness grabbing Carlos's wrists and pressing his hands palm down onto the table. Calmly reaching across the plates of food Norwin picks up a steak knife, wipes it clean with a napkin and stabs it into Carlos's hand, pinning it to the table. The tall Nicaraguan grimaces but there's no air in his lungs to make a sound. With his vision tunnelling, is this it? Carlos thinks. Here, in front of all these people, is this where Peña pulls out his gun and ends him?

'Carlos, listen to me,' Norwin says, breaking his suffocating delusion. 'When they let go, you leave the knife in, okay?'

His face turning red and eyes bloodshot, Carlos doesn't answer.

Hernan gives Carlos a repentant look, reluctant to put a good man he has known for many years in such discomfort.

'Hey, you hear me?' Norwin says clicking his fingers.

'*Si*, I hear you,' Carlos manages to squeak.

Watching him squirm a little longer, finally Norwin nods and Alberto and Hernan release their grip. Carlos heaves, sucking precious oxygen into his body before grinding his teeth as a fresh pang of pain radiates from his punctured and bleeding hand. Taking a few more deep breaths, he reminds himself that it's just a knife and this situation could be much, much worse.

'How could you be so stupid, Carlos? What am I to do now?' Norwin says with a shrug. 'You have been good to me, loyal up until this indiscretion but you know I don't believe in second chances. Second chances are for *mamónes*, suckers. If someone crosses me once, what's to stop him from crossing me again? Why give the *ladrón* another shot?' he says dispassionately before sinking the rest of his rum.

Carlos is stone cold as thoughts race through his head. How did he find out? How long has he known? Who ratted on him? Can he feel his fingers? Was it Popo? Ferdinand? Or maybe even Donald Barrios? Perhaps Aristides Sanchez mentioned in passing what he was doing not realizing that the mere whisper of his name would be like carving it into Norwin's flesh. More importantly, why isn't he dead already?

'Ferdinand and Troilo,' Carlos says through gritted teeth, 'they asked me to do it, to do it for Nicaragua.'

'I know, but do you really think I give a shit about the FDN? Do you really think the FDN gives a shit about the Contras? How long have the Sandinistas been in power now, five years? And nothing's happened.' Sighing, 'You think too much Carlos, care too much, that is your problem. You can't save Nicaragua, not even the FDN can.' Shaking his head disappointedly, 'You are no longer who you used to be, even I can see that and now the demands of the business have grown beyond you.'

Speaking between labored breaths, 'Things, things just panned out differently than I thought they would here in California. First the move to LA and then being sent to San Diego for so long and to do what?'

Norwin raises his eyebrows, 'Well, that was unintended. Julio filled your shoes here, Sebastian took over the Cartels, and Danilo and that Ricky boy move more coca in a week than anyone else does in a month. But what does that matter? We cannot prepare for when life changes in an instant, we can only stand by our actions and be judged for those alone, can we not?'

Carlos closes his eyes and nods.

Resting his elbow on the table with his chin in his hand, Norwin looks as though he's deciding which tie goes with which shirt rather than the cruelty of leaving Carlos's hand staked to the table.

'We have known each other a long time,' Norwin says sentimentally, while lighting a thick cigar. 'Almost five years we've been in California putting in the hard yards and without you maybe it wouldn't be what it is. We ploughed the dirt with our bare hands and at last the corn grows plentiful.'

'Indeed it does,' Carlos manages.

'And I want you to know that if it weren't for the missing coca going to the FDN you'd be dead.'

'I-I'm sorry,' Carlos offers.

'I know you are.' Then, puffing on his cigar, 'I suppose it is rather fortuitous then, you wanting out and me discovering you have been stealing from me.'

Chewing on that thought for a moment, Norwin reaches across and pulls the knife from Carlos's hand. Studying the blood on the blade with the cigar in the corner of his mouth, 'It would seem destiny is trying to speak to us, no?'

Clutching his hand and wincing, Carlos doesn't respond.

Taking the cigar from his mouth Norwin squints through a puff of smoke, 'You think running from who you are will make you someone else? That starting a new life will wash you of your sins? Life isn't that easy, Carlos. Most people ignore the bad so they only see the good in the world. Me? I want to see the bad in everyone to remind me that we're the same deep down. We're all dogs in the street willing to fight for our next meal. Even willing to kill if that's what it comes to.'

Shuffling out of the booth Norwin extends his arms, while Peña helps put on his beige jacket. Picking up a clean napkin and tossing it to Carlos, 'You have made a lot of money and I'm not going to stop you from going off and spending it.' Putting the cigar in his mouth and fixing his tie, 'But if your time is up then it is up,' he says plainly. 'I wish you well.'

Wrapping the white linen around his bleeding hand Carlos watches Norwin and Peña walk off. He sits quietly for a moment, bewildered at what feels like an escape from the jaws of death. No one crosses Norwin Meneses and lives to tell it. Then again, Norwin Meneses wouldn't have what he has if it weren't for Carlos, even the spiteful little man hinted as much.

He watches Norwin greet a table of FDN leaders, laughing and shaking hands with the men who are happy to accept his financial contributions regardless of the violence he invokes to make it happen. Then, seeing Adolfo Calero stand from the table and embrace Norwin before having their photo taken together, Carlos realizes—perhaps for the first time—that maybe the FDN won't ever take Nicaragua back.

Gingerly making his way back to their table, Carlos finds Julio sitting on his own finishing the rest of the rib-eye.

Seeing Carlos's hand wrapped in a bloodied napkin, 'What the hell happened to you?' Julio asks.

'Norwin,' Carlos says wincing, 'he found out about the coca for the Sanchez brothers.'

'Mamma Mia,' Julio whispers. 'I knew that wasn't a good idea,' he says regretfully.

Raising his eyebrows, 'The Sanchez brothers are very powerful Nicaraguans,' Carlos offers.

'Yeah, but it wasn't fair of them to put you in that position.'

Frowning, 'What position? To help get our country back?' Gulping down a rum, 'I'd do it again.'

After a moment, 'Did you tell Norwin you wanted out?' Julio asks.

Nodding, 'Seeing as I was stealing from him anyway, he was happy to see me go.'

'Just like that?'

Squeezing his wrist, 'Looks like it.' Then, after a thought a wry smile creases Carlos's lips.

Frowning, *'Qué pasa, hermano?'* Julio asks.

'I'm finally out.'

* * *

Arriving back in San Diego the next afternoon, Carlos climbs the stairs of his Ocean Beach apartment with his spirits lifted, finally set free from the drug world; a world appearing glamorous from the outside but in reality, fraught with violence and danger and illegality of devastating proportions. No more Norwin or Peña or Danilo, no more weekly flights in and out of Central America or meetings with FDN leaders and traffickers discussing how much coca or money is going to whom or where or when. No more nervously waiting for tons of cocaine to move across the hemisphere, or arranging drivers and dealers and business fronts. No more painstakingly laundering millions of dollars every month. No more risking his life for the FDN or Max Gomez, and no more wondering if today's the day the DEA kick in his door and put him in a cell for the rest of his life. He's done with it all and all it took was five years of hard work and a steak knife through his hand.

Now that there is nothing holding him back from starting a new life, he is free to choose how he spends his time and what to care about. Reaching his door, he'll call Nancy first and tell her that he's out of San Francisco for good, then he'll check on Vincent Miranda and see what help he can offer the poor man.

Entering his apartment and closing the door behind him, he switches on a wall light and notices a man in a grey suit sitting on the sofa.

Taking a step forward, 'Jerry?' Carlos says frowning.

'Mr. Cabezas,' Jerry says slowly inclining the drink in his hand.

Extending from the shadows of the kitchen, the barrel of a gun gently presses against the side of Carlos's head.

'*Hola*, Carlos,' a voice from the dark speaks.

Closing his eyes, '*Hola*, Peña,' the Nicaraguan says heavily.

Pressing the gun firmly into his temple, '*Vamos*,' Peña says urging Carlos to move into the apartment.

Slowly walking down the short hallway with legs that have gone suddenly weak, a pit opens in Carlos's stomach and he can feel the life draining out of him. Beating hard and heavy his heart aches inside his chest yet there is a coldness creeping through him, a numbing of his limbs.

Coming to the living area and seeing that a clear plastic sheet has been placed in the middle of the room and a dining chair at its center, Carlos hangs his head as a forlorn smirk creases his lips. Everyday thousands of people die and yet not one of those people stops to think, today is the day my journey ends. We never think it's our turn until it is and that incomprehensible confusion humiliates all thinking persons, we who grip so tightly the certainty of our world and yet there lies that final curtain that arrives in our darkest hour, where the reason for a God finally presents: to help guide us beyond the known into the unknown. And despite the otherwise enduring absence of omnipotence, we yearn for one final and fleeting balm to ease us into that long night.

'*Toma asiento,*' Peña says gesturing to the chair.

Carlos slowly sits down and cradles his hands in his lap, ignoring the presence of Jerry Dominelli.

'I thought Norwin wasn't going to kill me over the coca for the FDN?' Carlos says.

Dragging over a dining chair and facing it backwards, Peña straddles it resting his arms across its back and lighting a cigarette.

'Because it was for the revolution,' Carlos adds.

Taking the smoke from his mouth, '*Estoy bromeando?*' Peña says with a frown. 'Come on, Carlos, there's no revolution. The Contras are fighting a lost cause and the FDN is no different from any other political party holding out their hand for donations.' Taking a long drag, 'The only reason Norwin supported it was because of how much coca it got him into America. It's the reason half of the FDN is even what it is. And that's the reason Norwin is pissed,' he says pointing his cigarette at Carlos. 'You were giving his coca away not for some righteous cause but to simply fill the pockets of the Sanchez brothers, and Popo and Caesar in Miami, his fucking competitors of all people.'

Closing his eyes, Carlos grinds his molars.

'Besides,' Peña continues, 'he isn't killing you because you were giving away his coca. He's killing you because you let a rat into the house.'

Frowning, 'A rat?'

Reaching into an inside pocket of his jacket, Peña retrieves a clear zip-lock bag and tosses it at Carlos. Landing in his lap, he can see that inside of it is a tanned slender finger with a pink polished nail and a large emerald ring sitting just above the knuckle that it's been severed from.

'*Si*. That *puta* of yours, Sofia,' Peña continues. 'Norwin says she's the one responsible for all those raids.'

Scrunching his face with confusion, 'What? How? I haven't seen her in months.'

Drawing on his cigarette and raising his eyebrows, 'Perhaps that's why. She was getting back at you, no?' Peña suggests coyly. 'Not that it matters anymore.'

Racking his brain for what Sofia could know about the business, about warehouse locations, about deliveries and drivers, Carlos tries piecing together such fragments and whether it could be her or not. Then, remembering the last night he saw Sofia and how she warned him that she knew so much hairs begin to prick up on his skin but no, not even she is that stupid.

'Those warehouses, they were all pick-up spots run by new guys. It could have been any one of them,' Carlos suggests.

Shaking his head slowly, 'No, the warehouses hit were from separate divisions. No one that low knows about the locations of the other places. It had to be someone higher up, someone overseeing it all or,' taking a drag of his smoke, 'someone who was there with them, watching.'

Carlos frowns in disbelief. Then, remembering what Julio had told him yesterday at the fundraiser; how he'd shown Lucile the new network as way of making her see that he wouldn't be so close to the coca any more. Then recalling how emotional she got at the night club complaining that the cops came to Julio's house the night the shipping tanker got raided, and how worked up she was at the station where Julio was being held. Lucile, Carlos realizes, it's her; she's the rat.

'Now,' Peña continues, 'it would seem you have slowly been distancing yourself from San Francisco, from LA, from the business. And then you tell Norwin that you want out all of a sudden,' he says leaving his point unfinished and drawing on his cigarette with dark, unblinking eyes cutting through the smoke.

Carlos isn't the one that brought a rat into the house, but he knows that doesn't matter either. He's gone too far with Norwin, with drug trafficking, even with his past in the National Guard; choosing the wrong path time and time again.

Sighing, 'I would never betray Norwin like that,' the Nicaraguan says knowing it's the truth and yet it meaning nothing to Peña.

Nodding agreeably, 'But you'd steal his coca and give it away?'

'That, that was for the FDN, for Ferdinand and Troilo Sanchez.'

'So?'

'It was to help the Contras, damn it, to help Nicaragua!' Carlos says angrily, holding onto the hope that the FDN will save his homeland despite Norwin and even Danilo's indifference.

Unmoved, Peña drags on his cigarette.

Shaking his head, 'I gave more to the cause than Norwin ever did,' Carlos says spitefully.

Smirking, 'That's right, you gave what wasn't yours to give.'

Smugly, 'You seem to make a habit of that, don't you, Mr. Cabezas,' Jerry adds from the sofa. 'Taking what isn't yours.'

Carlos sniggers, 'She deserves better than a lying con artist, Mr. Dominelli.'

'Oh, like a cocaine dealer perhaps?' he says patronizingly before sipping his drink.

For the first time in Carlos's life that label hurts him. He came from a proud family, went to university before joining the military as an officer. He was valued and respected, loved by his family and friends. Generous and reliable, kind and caring, determined and hardworking. A measured lover of life, smart, thoughtful, accomplished at many things and despite all of that it is in these dying moments that the last thing he is remembered as is a lowly drug dealer.

'I had a feeling you were a man of poor judgement when you befriended that dirty fag, Vincent Miranda,' Jerry says patronizingly. 'That piece of trash.'

'He's a good man, better than most,' Carlos defends.

'You mean was,' Jerry says deliberately before sipping his scotch.

Frowning, 'What do you mean?'

'Oh, didn't you know? Vince hanged himself last night,' Jerry says casually.

The words score the part of Carlos that has any feeling left. A sad fate is one of God's cruelest jokes, he thinks.

'After he found out George had sold that house of his in Encino, well, there really wasn't much left to live for was there? Especially considering he had, what are they calling it, HIV or something,' Jerry says swirling the ice in his drink. 'No wonder George was leaving him. Vince was a dead man clinging to what he was going to lose anyway.'

'What is HIV?'

'Oh, you didn't know that either? It's some disease only faggots get.' Then, walking over from the sofa and standing next to Peña, 'In a town as small as San Diego how did you not think I wouldn't find out about you and Nancy?'

Smirking and shaking his head, 'Because I don't care about you, Mr. Dominelli. I may be a drug dealer but at least I do not hide that that is what I am. You on the other hand are all that is wrong in the world. You appear to be something you are not. You lie, you cheat, you steal, and you stab innocent people in the back, and you do it all in a fine suit with a handshake and a smile.'

Jerry stares at Carlos.

Continuing, 'You sit at the top of a house of cards and I cannot wait to see you come tumbling down.'

Choking back a laugh, 'See me? Oh, I doubt you'll be seeing anything other than the fish feeding on your dead body, Mr. Cabezas.'

There is truth to Jerry's unceremonious parting words that Carlos can't deny. This is his day and it has come at last and words fail him how sad he feels. A sadness for all the things he will never get to do and for all the things that brought him joy that the mere passing memory of are for reasons unclear to him made somehow more special. The sudden pang of how bittersweet life is as everything he has come to know and love will turn to dust momentarily.

The slight squeak of Peña slowly screwing a silencer onto the barrel of his gun draws the men's attention. No matter how familiar one is with death, there is in those remaining moments a strange static in the air, an inertia of time and space as though God is dog-earing the event, making note of a transgression that cannot be forgiven, a crime against the preciousness of life.

'Any last words, Carlos?' Peña asks slowly pointing the gun at him.

Closing his eyes, '*Casa,*' he says quietly. '*Finalmente.*'

Peña squeezes the trigger and the humid tropical air makes Carlos's chest and brow start to bead with sweat. Dreamily he watches tall palms rustling in a warm afternoon breeze as cubes of ice crack, melting in a glass of rum he can't remember pouring, while the black void, small and pointed, reaches out and grabs Carlos's life and scatters it pink and mist-like onto the plastic.

XXII
THE COLONEL

High above the Gulf of Mexico, a small jet crosses the blue sky en route to a secret Costa Rican location. Inside the luxurious eight-seater cabin, a tan leather seat squeaks under CIA Director Casey's shifting weight. His nose softly whistling with each frustrated breath as he reads an article from the *Times* about Nicaragua's recent election. Uncrossing then re-crossing his legs, his mouth silently mouths the journalist's words reporting the landslide Sandinista victory formally ushering in President Daniel Ortega and his Socialist government.

'Have you read this trash?' he says bending the paper down and peering at the Colonel over his clear-framed spectacles.

Staring out of a small oval window, 'Read what?' Oliver North responds without lifting his gaze.

'What Ortega said after winning the election. Here, listen to this, "*They say we're anti-democratic,*" that's us apparently, "*but we know what real democracy means. Democracy is literacy, democracy is land reform, democracy is free education and public health.*"

North gives Casey a blank look.

'Can you believe this?' Casey continues. 'Christ, these tinpot nations don't know up from down, do they? They want all the spoils of a developed world but have no clue as to how to achieve them. Here, just have it all for free, that'll solve everything. Don't they understand even basic economics. Develop decent goods and services and make people pay for them, and by making people pay for them, well, they're going to need a damn job aren't they, and working is how a man pulls himself up out of the mud. But if everything is free then that man is just going to stay in the sty, isn't he? And that man is no longer a man, he's a lazy pig waiting for his day to the slaughterhouse.'

'Who cares, it's the *Times*,' North says dismissively.

Frowning, 'Who cares?' Shaking the paper at him, 'this is what the American people are reading, Ollie.'

'And?'

'We can't have people believing the government should just give them handouts. They had their free education and it cost us billions. And what did it achieve? An entire generation spoiled by liberal ideas about taxing the wealthy, providing more social services and eradicating social inequality.'

'So, if the article is trash, then what's the problem?'

Narrowing his grey eyes, 'The problem is it's the truth and the truth is *not* what the American people need to hear. It's not what will get them out of bed in the morning and it's not how our great country operates. America is the greatest functioning democracy in the world and it is so precisely because inequality affords us to silence the voices of those whose only contribution is social and political dissent.'

Leaning into the aisle, North calls for the attendant; he can tell Casey is just getting started and only a stiff drink will dampen the ensuing vitriol.

'Yes, sir?' a blonde woman says in a fitted black jacket and skirt.

'A whiskey please?' the Colonel says.

'With soda, sir?'

'No, neat.'

Nodding, 'Anything for you, Director?'

'No, thank you,' Casey says gruffly, bothered by the interruption.

Clearing his throat, 'You were saying?' North says.

After a moment Casey continues, 'People think truth is a right, that they're somehow entitled to it, entitled to know how their freedoms and liberties are secured.' Scoffing, 'A ridiculous notion. No, the truth of what really goes on in this world will not liberate nor embolden people. Part of the duty of shaping a civilized and harmonious nation is precisely by denying the citizenry ugly truths that they cannot stomach. Just look at what we did in Vietnam with the Phoenix Program, MKULTRA, and you know the rest.'

'We lie to protect,' the Colonel says only half interested in the Director's lecture.

Looking long and hard, 'No, Colonel. We lie when we tell them nothing. We don't lie by telling them things that aren't true. You understand the difference, I hope? It's disinformation for their betterment. And we'll know our disinformation program has worked when everything the US public believes is what we've told them to believe. Until then the damn liberals and socialists of this country will always question authority, question the government, question the very mechanisms that put a roof over their head and food on their table. And this,' he says jabbing a wrinkled index finger into the newspaper in his lap, 'is the very breadcrumb that gives people reason to question and doubt the integrity of everything we're trying to do. That there is some better way of achieving civil order and obedience for some three-hundred-million people.'

Tossing the paper aside and looking out of the window, 'There are far too many people in this world who think they're smarter than they really are.' Raising his eyebrows, 'And that's the beauty of capitalism, Colonel. It creates jobs to keep people busy and a pecking order so they know their place, while Jesus keeps them in line.'

Returning with a glass tumbler of whiskey and a napkin, 'Here you are, sir,' the attendant says putting the drink on the wooden trim of North's armrest.

Taking a large gulp, the Colonel hopes Casey has finished.

'A landslide victory of all things,' the Director says distantly before turning to the Colonel with renewed frustration. 'And just how in the hell did this happen, Ollie? Didn't I tell you back in March to ramp things up? I thought you had this under control for chrissakes,' he says incredulously.

'I'm doing my best, sir,' North says through tight lips.

With his jowls starting to flare, 'Your best? Then how does this happen? Where were the propaganda protocols, the scare tactics, the kidnappings, sabotaging voting stations? How did, A, that many Nicaraguans get out and vote, and, B, why did so many vote for that Commie bastard Ortega? Do I have to spell out how we keep the black vote in America as low as we do?' Counting on his fingers, 'You reduce the number of voting stations in their neighborhoods, you make them hard to get to, you understaff them so people spend half their day lining up, and you don't open them on weekends. Simple. And just like that you cut off three-quarters of the African-American voice. If we didn't do it that way, can you just imagine whom we'd have in the Senate?'

North is fully aware the black voice poses a serious political threat but when you serve in war with them—African-Americans, that is—when you share food and shelter, when they save you from stepping on a VC mine, and when you're looking in their scared eyes and holding their guts in, while they bleed to death, well, you never quite look at the color of a man's skin the same again, and the CIA Director's clinical approach to subjugating them leaves the Colonel more than a little perturbed.

Now it's North's turn to count on his fingers, 'Pardon my frankness but need I remind you I have no funding, no official approval to be down here, we're training farmers and boys how to use a rifle, and we're relying on goddamn traffickers to get weapons and supplies in and out of the camps? So, yes, under those circumstances, I am doing my best.'

Casey removes his glasses and begins wiping them with a handkerchief, 'You're wrong about one of those things, Colonel,' he says calmly.

North crunches his molars.

'The CIA may not have official approval to be meddling in Nicaragua but the NSC sure as hell does. You can do whatever you want so long as the NSC determines it as being in the interest of national security.' Putting his glasses back on, 'Now, Colonel, in your mind does Nicaragua's fervent shift towards Socialism along with their anti-American rhetoric pose a potential threat to the United States and its people?'

Pursing he lips, 'Yes.'

'That's exactly right. And that's precisely what this meeting in Costa Rica is about.'

Sighing, 'To sit down with our agents and work out what to do next,' North says knowingly.

'Oh, no. That's not it at all, Colonel. I know exactly what we're going to do next, but I want you and all the senior field officers to sit down in a room together and see each other eyeball-to-eyeball.'

North furrows his brow expectantly.

Leaning forward Casey continues, 'I want every man to know each other, to see the faces of the agents he must trust so that in the event something goes wrong you'll all have each other's backs.'

Giving the Director a pensive look, 'You think the situation here could get any worse for us?'

'There's always a risk that our endeavors to support the Contras will be exposed, but giving weapons and clothes to freedom fighters is hardly something condemnable. That's just supporting a fair fight. No, my concern is poisoning farmland, torching schools, blowing up bridges and kidnapping people will land us in humanitarian hot water. And that's not to mention funding the whole shindig by selling weapons to the damn Iranians.'

Clearing his throat, 'Well, not all of the funding.'

'Oh, that's of little concern. If any of that business ever sees the light of day whom are people going to believe: the US Government or criminal drug traffickers? The very notion that we've gotten into bed with the likes of Jaun Matta, Milian Rodriguez, Norwin Meneses and God knows how many others, all foot soldiers for Escobar no less, is so preposterous the mere mention of such a proposition will be laughed at.'

The leather squeaks as the Director sits back in his chair and gazes out of the window, 'I know the CIA gets up to a lot of nasty business, but we do it because we have to. It's what keeps our country safe.' After a sigh, 'They say horrible atrocities are committed during war, and, well, a lot of horrible atrocities are committed outside of war too, people just don't know about it but they sure as hell like the smell of peace when they wake up in the morning.'

* * *

Touching down at the *Tobías Bolaños International Airport* just after eleven-am, a late morning humidity floods the small Learjet when the cabin door opens. Greeted by bright sunshine and blue sky, Oliver North and Bill Casey climb into an awaiting black Continental and make their way to a CIA safe house in the city-fringe district of Geroma, a short distance from the US Embassy. Heavily tinted bulletproof glass cuts off almost all sound coming in allowing their conversation to continue.

'I'm sorry I'm in such a foul mood, Colonel,' Casey says removing his glasses and pinching the bridge of his nose. 'You heard about Will Buckley going missing in Beirut last month?'

'I heard.'

Shaking his head, 'He's a good friend of mine and it pains me that I don't know where he is. And I know no amount of missiles we sell to Iran will get him released. Gosh, the mind wanders which of those God forsaken towelhead terrorist groups has him and the God-awful abuse he's being subjected to as we speak.' Then, speaking almost meditatively, 'I'd give anything to have him back, have him safe and sound on American soil.'

'I understand, sir,' North offers tentatively. 'I lost a lot of good men in 'Nam. I lot of good men I'd trade a hundred other lives to get back.'

Bill Casey gives a wry smile before putting his glasses back on and resuming a more stoic demeanor, 'Tell me some good news, Colonel?' he says.

'Well, Felix is doing a fine job out of Ilopango. Between him, General Bermudez, the camps along the Honduran border and John Hull's ranch to the south, we're able to move all the munitions, supplies, and,' clearing his throat, 'high value cargo in and out of the region at will. Felix has also recently acquired two more aviation companies to run resupply missions for the Contras.'

'Who are they?'

'*Vortex Air International* is run by Michael Palmer. And Pat Foley heads *Summit Aviation*. They're both Americans.'

'Very good,' Casey says noting them down in his diary. 'Are they on CIA payroll?'

'Yes.'

After adding that detail, 'That reminds me—here, take this,' the Director says reaching into his briefcase and handing the Colonel a black leather ledger. 'I want you to keep a private account of all the weapons and payments coming from Iran, Israel, everything that Richard and the *Enterprise* handles.'

Thumbing its pages, 'Okay.'

'There are a lot of stokers in the fire here and I don't want us losing track of what's happening. You, Colonel, need to know exactly what is coming in, from whom, how much, and where it's going. All of it.'

Hesitantly, 'Including the white stuff going through Ilopango?'

'Especially that. Our dependence on it will be temporary but I don't want scumbag traffickers thinking this whole Contra effort is a trip to Disneyland. It's a means to an end and a cost well worth the consequence but for God's sake keep track of it, you hear me, Colonel?'

'I understand.'

'If Bob McFarlane or Johnny Poindexter or Casp Weinberger pick up the phone and want to get up to speed on any delivery, any transaction or any foreign official who so much as had a coffee or wiped his ass on this, you need to be able to tell them whether they had cream, sugar, or corn for dinner. Am I making myself clear?'

'Crystal, sir,' North says crunching his molars.

'Good. Now, when's Richard arriving?'

'This afternoon.'

'All right. We think it'd be best to move a branch of the *Enterprise* directly into Honduras seeing as Ortega has won the election and this thing has at least a couple of more years on it.'

Frowning, 'We, sir?'

'Ted Shackley. Richard already knows about this but you two will need to flesh out the details, organize logistic channels, aid contracts, and so forth. Recruit some of the local military to help out.'

'But what about *R&M Equipment*? They're already distributing weapons for us out of Tegucigalpa.'

Closing his diary, 'Time to shut them down. I want this kept completely in-house. So far, the *Enterprise* is predominantly funded out of sales to Iran and Afghanistan. It's clean. Unfortunately, aside from the good work those

R&M boys provided the Contras early on they've also been dealing directly with traffickers and accepting drug money, and we can't have that.'

North raises his eyebrows, 'They've gotten greedy.'

'No, they've gotten sloppy.'

North shrugs indifferently, 'So, if the *Enterprise* moves into the region to wholesale weapons to the Contras, just how is the *Enterprise* going to get paid?'

'By the FDN, of course.'

'And the FDN get their money by and large from the traffickers.'

'And that's all the difference we need. So long as the FDN are paying the *Enterprise*, the *Enterprise* stays squeaky. Look, we're not here to impose some kind of moral or ethical compass. We are here to prevent Communism, Colonel.'

North knows all too well that during conflict lines are drawn in the sand and when the wind blows or opportunity suits, those lines are brushed away and new ones drawn, often somewhere else with little or no concern about who falls on which side, so long as the people with the stick get what they want, and America is always holding the stick.

'So, you've been in touch with Shackley?' North asks casually.

'Well, of course. Ted and I are old friends, Colonel. We're always in touch,' Casey finishes with a smirk.

Suddenly serious, 'How much does he know about what we're doing?'

Wedging a cigar into the corner of his mouth, 'Oh, I'd say about as much as you. Maybe more.'

North's molars crunch.

Pulling off *Boulevard Ernesto Rohrmoser*, the Continental weaves its way through a maze of streets as a dense city-fringe suburbia takes shape. Narrow two- and three-story houses squeeze beside each other varying in architectural design from colonial-era to art deco, while lush green parks and small paved plazas are dotted throughout the blocks.

Turning into an unsuspecting belowground garage next to a Laundromat and corner store, the three-story corner allotment is a drab collection of apartments and makes for an intentionally inconspicuous Costa Rican CIA safe-house.

The plain-clothed driver leads them through a warren of hallways and narrow stairwells with black wrought iron bannisters, broken tile steps, and peeling pastel mint wall paint. Reaching the top floor the driver punches in a code on a keypad and several locks on a heavy steel door can be heard retracting.

Walking down a dark hallway Director Casey suddenly stops, 'Oh, when's the hit on Pastora happening?'

'Three days from today.'

'Where?'

'At a secret press conference in La Penca, southern Nicaragua.'

'Very good,' Casey says sharply before sticking the cigar back into his mouth and resuming his march down the hallway.

Reaching the last door, muffled voices can be heard laughing and conversing jovially from inside. Without knocking, Director Casey grips the doorhandle and storms in, the Colonel following right behind, and the room full of plain-clothed agents immediately falls silent.

'Okay, you sonsabitches,' William Casey shouts, 'listen up and listen good because I'm only going to tell you once.'

Going to the door, Colonel North slams it shut ensuring the meeting is held in complete privacy.

Later that day, in a room plastered with maps, travel routes, inventory logs, a corkboard littered with photos of individuals and descriptions of their backgrounds, whereabouts, associations, covers or any other information pertinent to their role in the Contra effort, the Colonel stands by a window with a phone to his ear peering casually between blinds to the street below.

'Is that so?' North says with a curious raise of his eyebrows.

'Indeed, Colonel. But I'm afraid my resources are stretched as thin as it is.'

Then, walking past North's temporarily commandeered office is the very solution to his problem.

'Okay, Lazarus, I'll take care of it. Wire me the coordinates as soon as you can.'

'Thank you, Colonel. Your efforts are much appreciated.'

'Think nothing of it. I know you're under duress so anything I can do you just ask.'

'I will, sir.'

'Be in touch,' North finishes before hanging up the receiver.

Walking to the door, the Colonel pokes his head out into the hallway, 'Dewey!' he shouts. 'A moment of your time, if I may?'

Station Chief Duane Clarridge enters the messy office and dumps a pile of dossiers on the table before sitting heavily in a chair,' What is it, Colonel?' Then, motioning to the files, 'Bill's got me knee deep in Sandinista targets and the list is longer than what my wife wants for Christmas.'

Half leaning, half sitting on the corner of the table, 'I just got off of the phone with the man in Costa Rica and he's in a spot of trouble.'

'What sort of trouble?'

'Oh, the good kind. That bookkeeper of his has fifteen-hundred kilos of you know what sitting in Bolivia just waiting to get picked up.'

'So, what's the problem?'

'Fifteen-hundred kilos is quite the payload. No one in our current outfit can pick up that much weight at once. We're going to need a DC-4. Can you help?'

Clarridge moans before giving the Colonel a tired look.

'Come on, you're still the Station Chief, aren't you?' North pleads. 'Think of it as one last favor before you head over to the Middle East.'

'One last? I've been doing you nothing but favors this whole time, Ollie. Can't you get Mike from *Vortex Air*? He flies a DC-4.'

'I'm afraid not. He's on a State Department contract to drop aid into Nicaragua and it'll look suspect if he's seen flying as far south as Bolivia.'

Looking unimpressed, 'You know, Ollie, when I said you needed to be doing more down here, I did mean you, not me.'

'Yes, but this is your neck of the woods. We just need to get it from Bolivia to Ilopango,' North says enthusiastically.

Shaking his head, 'All right, where exactly is it?'

Smiling and hopping down from the table, 'In a valley called Chapare, a few clicks east of La Paz. Felix is wiring me the coordinates any minute now.'

Sliding over the black ledger he received from Director Casey, North scribbles in notes of this latest acquisition.

Leaning forward in his chair, 'What's that you've got there?' Clarridge asks.

Flipping it closed, 'Oh, just something to help me keep track of things,' North says with a wink.

Sighing, 'Well, I better skedaddle; got a lot of Commies that need killing,' Clarridge says casually as if he's seeing his accountant about making deductions on his income tax.

North nods cordially before turning back to the corkboard, a smug smile creasing his lips. It's all coming together, not without disruption of course, but he can feel the tide turning, the control being wrestled back in his favor and his grip on the reins tightening. He'll be damned if the Sandinistas stay in power; not on his watch.

With a gentle knock on the open door, 'Ollie, Ollie, Oxenfree,' Richard Secord says softly.

Standing with him is Albert Hakim, the Iranian arms dealer who holds a stake in the *Enterprise* along with Richard and Ted Shackley.

'Gentlemen,' North smiles.

Entering the office, 'It is good to see you, Mr. North,' Hakim says shaking the Colonel's hand.

Despite the humid tropical climate of Costa Rica, Albert Hakim is wearing a navy suit, pressed white shirt and burgundy tie. With black hair soft and neat, smelling of sweet rosewater cologne, and wearing a Turquoise stone the size of a quail egg set in a gold ring on his right hand, his presentation is as charming as his reputation. A polite man, kind and sincere, and a pleasant conversationalist who is as disarming as he is agreeable and for such reasons making him a wonderful negotiator, Albert Hakim could convince you to take the shirt off of your back, give it to someone in need and somehow find a way to get paid for it.

'Albert, I didn't realize you were here,' the Colonel remarks.

'You know me, I go where business calls, yes.'

'Of course,' North says with a wry smile. 'Please take a seat,' motioning to the chairs and taking a seat himself at the desk.

'So,' he continues, 'I understand the *Enterprise* is to open up shop in Honduras? Seems quite a bit of effort if this thing wraps up in the next year or two.'

Richard Secord smiles, 'Look, I like Bill Casey's enthusiasm but when you're on the ground you quickly realize these things often take longer than you hope. I mean, look at how long Vietnam played out not to mention the proxy wars that took place around it.'

'Besides,' Hakim adds, 'this is not such a terrible thing. The longer the Contras and the FDN need US assistance, the longer the *Enterprise* stays in business, yes.'

Oliver's molars grind, frustrated by the seemingly inseparable nature of war and those keen to profit from it. Is this what he has become, a man who wants to prolong conflicts in order to financially capitalize from them, he, a former soldier who fought tooth and bone to end the bloodshed of war and return home.

'Oh, don't be like that, Ollie,' Richard soothes, noticing the Colonel's displeasure. 'What does it matter to us if the Sandinistas fall next year or in ten years? You'll still need a job, you'll still have conflicts to fight, and you'll still be reliant on companies like the *Enterprise* to negotiate and deliver equipment and supplies.'

Frowning, 'I don't want this to last years, Richard. What's happening in the Middle East is of far more importance.'

'And what's happening in the Middle East won't be over any time soon either. You're focusing on the wrong things here, Ollie. Do you realize how successful Shackley and his Secret Team were in Laos? The man's a genius, pulling strings we can't even see. Christ, Vang Pao accrued more personal wealth than the King in the years we were there. Look, these things take time, and so they should. You don't want to come in and just pull the rug out from beneath Daniel Ortega now that he's been elected because Nicaraguans will feel cheated. Better to let the Sandinista Government discover how difficult leading a country is, while the FDN, with your help, can chip away and expose how detrimental and disastrous a socialist system really is. This isn't a war anymore, don't forget. It's at best a slow burning revolution in a country that's just recovering from a revolution,' Richard says matter-of-factly.

'And that's why we are here, Colonel, yes,' Hakim adds. 'Moving the *Enterprise* into Central America further secures your position and bolsters the supplies to the Contras ensuring they stay necessarily equipped to see-out this campaign.'

Looking at the corkboard and taking a moment to reflect on all of the work he has put into the Contras, the FDN, securing supply channels, camps, airstrips and all the other mechanisms to keep this effort grinding forward and realizes perhaps Richard is right. What matters is control. Who cares if the Sandinistas are in power so long as they don't succeed. And considering he, the NSC and a great deal of CIA personnel are across the Contra effort in a completely classified capacity, well, he can do whatever the hell he wants because this isn't war, this is subterfuge.

'We don't mean *R&M* any ill will,' Richard continues, 'but they're out of their league on this. There's plenty of people they can still do business with. The Argentines, Pinochet's Republican Army, heck, we'll give them the Salvadoran Air Force but so far as supporting the FDN, that can't be left up to a company openly dealing with drug traffickers,' he sniggers.

'Just so, why mix oil and water?' Hakim adds.

Frowning, 'What's that supposed to mean?' the Colonel asks.

'I have spoken just this morning with Menachem Meron in Washington and Defense Minister Moshe Arens in Israel, and they are holding one-hundred containers of weapons for us. That's thirty-million dollars' worth, Mr. North.'

'Well, hot damn. Why didn't you tell me?'

Smiling, 'We wanted to surprise you, Mr. North. Tell you in person.'

'You sneaky sonsabitches,' the Colonel says grinning before standing and walking to a large map of Central America. 'Well, if the Contra effort is indeed years in the making then let's batten down the hatches and put a ring of fire around Nicaragua. Where are you planning on putting your warehouse?' he inquires.

'The capital, Tegucigalpa,' Richard informs him.

Taking a red pin and pricking it into where the city is on the map, 'Good. I have camps here, here, here and here,' the Colonel says pressing red pins at each location. Then, taking green pins and pressing them into the board, 'And airstrips obviously here in Ilopango, but also here at Las Mangas getting supplies to General Bermudez, here at Danli, and then just south of the border at a private ranch.'

'Who owns it?' Richard asks curiously.

'An American by the name of John Hull. His hamlet is what has afforded us to create an entire southern front.' Then, adding three more red pins, 'Which has allowed us to setup camps here, here, and here.'

Turning to Richard Secord and Albert Hakim with a renewed sense of vigor, 'One-hundred containers you say? Then get it to Felix as soon as you can and I'll use our aid outfit to get it where it needs going.'

'See, good news,' Hakim says smiling.

'And I needed it. Feels like every time I take two steps forward, I take one step back.'

'That is a matter of perspective, Mr. North,' the Iranian man says warmly. 'On the contrary, each time you are forced to take one step back you find a way to take two steps forward.'

XXIII
BUMBLE BEE

'Fuck,' Amac Galil spits. Then, drawing on his cigarette, 'I thought you said this back road was meant to be unguarded?' he says bitterly.

'It-it was,' Peter Torbinson says nervously from the back seat.

Exhaling smoke through his nose, 'Yeah, well, it's not.'

Licking his dry lips, 'They, they must have increased security.'

Twisting around and giving the photojournalist a look, 'Oh, you think so?' the Iranian assassin says dryly.

Idling softly a hundred yards from the checkpoint, Felipe Vidal, Amac Galil, Roberto Gaguine and Peter Torbinson sit in one of John Hull's beat-up humanitarian vans that has been re-labelled with stickers of Costa Rican news station, *Telenoticias Canal 24*. It's a clear sunny afternoon and the jungle around them is thick and overgrown, making entry to the small southern town of La Penca impassable by any means other than through this checkpoint.

'Relax,' Felipe says flexing his hands on the worn steering wheel, 'we still have our media passes and we still have our story. Better to test them here with only two guards,' the Cuban says thoughtfully.

'Better to not test them at all,' Amac complains.

After a moment, 'All right, we better get going otherwise they will think something is fishy.' Looking into the rear-view mirror at Torbinson and Gaguine, 'Everybody be cool.' Then, noticing Amac loading the chamber of his

SIG-Sauer pistol before putting it back under his jacket, 'That means you too, man,' he says gently.

Pulling the van back onto the dirt road, Felipe drives slowly towards two rather bored looking military soldiers. However, with AK47s hanging from their shoulders and radios on their vests, it is crucial they avoid sounding an alarm.

As Felipe slows down one of the soldiers stands in front of the van, while the other approaches his window.

'*Hola, senores,*' Felipe says warmly.

Glancing at the side of the van, 'What are you doing here?' the soldier asks.

'We are here for the press conference.'

'Which press conference is that?'

'The one for Eden Pastora, of course.'

The soldier feigns surprise that they know of this media event, 'And you all are?'

Felipe, answering for everyone, 'I'm the driver, this here is the sound technician, and in the back is the photographer and the cameraman.'

The soldier nods to the other guard who begins walking around the vehicle, peering overtly through the dirty windows as he goes.

'May I see some ID?' the soldier at the driver's window asks.

'Of course,' Felipe says handing him his media pass.

Reaching the trunk of the van the soldier gives it a knock with his fist and Roberto Gaguine calmly gets out of the vehicle to assist his inquiry.

'Open,' the soldier demands.

Roberto obliges, lifting the trunk and revealing a few bags of camera equipment.

Motioning with his rifle, 'Show me inside.'

'Sure, sure,' the Argentine spy says unzipping the bags and revealing their contents.

Felipe watches them closely in the rear-view mirror, while Amac slowly moves his hand towards the inside of his jacket.

'Hey,' the guard at the window snaps, 'what are you doing?'

'Oh, my papers,' Amac says casually taking his ID from an inside pocket and reaching across to give it to the soldier.

Squinting, 'Hussein Tehzar.'

'That's me,' Amac states.

'Where are you from?'

'Persia.'

'Please be careful with that,' Roberto says loudly. 'Very expensive equipment, yes.'

The soldier is inspecting the video camera. First fidgeting with the lens before removing the battery pack and replacing it. Should he find the stick of C4 explosive hidden inside its tape compartment they would find themselves in more trouble than they'd like.

Pointing at the camera, 'See, *Sony*. Very good brand,' Roberto converses as he gently unlatches the safety buckle of the ten-inch hunting knife hanging from his hip, while Felipe watches in the rear-view mirror as the soldier's fingers move across the operating buttons before finding the white raised letters that read, EJECT, and presses it.

'Disculpe!' Felipe says turning to the soldier holding the camera. 'Did you hear the joke about the Cuban, the Iranian and the Argentine driving in a van?'

Seizing the opportunity, Roberto grips the handle of his knife and swings, plunging the blade hilt-deep into the chest of the soldier holding the camera, while almost simultaneously Amac pulls his pistol and fires a single shot into the chest of the guard standing at the driver's window.

Squinting one eye closed, 'It was no joke,' Felipe remarks calmly. Then, sticking a finger in his ear and wiggling it, 'Jesus, that was loud,' he adds seemingly unbothered that a gun went off inches from his face sending a bullet of death rocketing past him.

'Mr. Hansen, you cool back there?' Felipe asks.

Squatting next to the soldier, Roberto pulls his knife out of the body and cleans the blade on the dead man's sleeve, *'No problema aqui, amigo.'*

'Bueno,' Felipe says getting out of the van and looking around. 'All right, let's move the bodies over there, under the tree.'

Amac climbs out and helps drag the soldiers into the thick jungle floor, while Roberto breaks off broad leaves to help conceal the bodies.

Standing beside the van looking worried, 'Wo-won't someone realize the guards are missing?' Torbinson asks.

Smiling and patting him on the shoulder, 'This is Nicaragua, Peter,' Felipe says. 'People will think they got bored and left, or there was a shift change but no one came to take over their post.'

'What about their jeep?' Amac questions.

Thinking for a moment, 'There is a valley up ahead. Roberto, you drive it and follow us. When we find a good spot, we'll push it over the edge.'

'Just so,' the Argentine says agreeably jogging over and jumping in.

The van and the jeep continue along the dusty road without problem, stopping only to send the small military truck down the hillside to its leafy grave. An hour later they arrive at the town of La Penca buzzing with activity with cars, taxis, and vans with small satellite dishes on their roofs parked haphazardly, as well as no shortage of military trucks and soldiers wandering around in surprising number. Eden Pastora isn't some mild inconvenience or malign threat to what Colonel North, the FDN, and the Contras are trying to achieve in the region. No, Eden Pastora, also known as Commander Zero, is a military threat of tremendous reputation. During the revolution—the first one that is—Pastora lead the largest militia in Southern Nicaragua and were the first to call themselves the Sandinistas, however, after only a couple of years he had become disenchanted with Daniel Ortega and Tomas Borge's new government and formed his own revolutionary party in an effort to confront these pseudo-Sandinistas now taking up residence in Managua who were turning to a life of decadence; the very thing that drove them to revolution against Anastasio Somoza in the first place. A master of guerrilla warfare, Pastora is regarded as a hero to many highland Nicaraguans and commands hundreds if not thousands of his own Contra troops. Yet, here in lies Colonel North and the CIA's issue with Commander Zero: he cannot be controlled, he cannot be bought, and he cannot be persuaded. He revolted against Somoza, then he revolted against the newly established Sandinista Government, and no doubt he will revolt against the US backed Contras as he is determined to lead Nicaragua towards a future built by its people for its people and without the help or hindrance of foreign influence. He's dangerous, unwavering, and willing to die for a cause that he sees as more righteous and noble than what Ortega has distilled the revolutionary movement down to, and certainly more virtuous than partnering with the United States who always ensure their own agendas are realized, no matter the cost. And despite accepting early CIA support, Eden Pastora offers no assurances or certainties when receiving handouts but takes such support knowing it is because they see his worth, not because he is holding out his hand. That said, regardless of his importance to the broader Contra movement, he is nonetheless a liability, one that could undo years of groundwork Colonel North, the CIA and the FDN have laid to get to this point. And despite his hero status amongst the Contras and certainly the significance of the public image he adds, he is a venomous snake whose head must be severed. Of course, assassinating a beloved Contra idol who commands thousands of men with undying devotion for him could be seen as having a devastating impact on the morale and fortitude of the Contra cause, but when news spreads that it was Pastora's former Sandinista compatriots that orchestrated to have him killed, well, that will galvanize thousands of Contra sympathizers to take up arms against this indecent, immoral, and unpatriotic Government who would so pitifully murder one of their own heroes, and underscore just how shallow and despotic Ortega, Borge and the rest of the spoiled rats in Managua have become.

'Let's just hope there isn't anyone from *Telenoticias Canal 24* actually here,' Amac mumbles as Felipe parks the van at the end of a row of media vehicles and surveys the small-town swarming with journalists and Contra rebels.

'Get a load of this,' he says leaning over the steering wheel.

'Who would have thought so many people would be here,' Roberto Gaguine says with surprise.

'Is this bad?' Torbinson asks.

Lighting a cigarette, 'No, it's good,' Amac answers.

Turning to the photojournalist, 'The more people, the easier for us to blend in,' Felipe explains. 'If we lie low, we won't be noticed.'

'What's the plan then, *amigo?*' Gaguine asks.

Despite the number of cars and people jamming the dirt roads and open-air plaza, the mood appears calm. Small groups of journalists clump together smoking and talking, while the odd person can be seen napping in a reclined car seat or foldout chair.

Seeing a reporter walking past, Felipe quickly rolls down his window, *'Hola, muchacho. Cuando Eden Pastora esta llegando?'*

'A las ocho,' he replies without stopping.

Sighing, 'Pastora won't be here until eight o'clock. Looks like we have a few hours to kill, gentlemen,' Felipe says to the men. 'As for the plan: I'll accompany you, Mr. Hansen and you, Mr. Torbinson into the building where the press conference is to be held. Mr. Galil will wait here with the van. After you plant the camera, you are to complain that you forgot an audio cable and leave to go retrieve it. Mr. Torbinson and I will be waiting for you at the back of the room, then we'll walk outside where you will then trigger the bomb. During the panic, we will make our way back to the van and leave La Penca.'

Nodding enthusiastically, 'And what shall we do until then?' Torbinson asks.

Turning his jacket into a makeshift pillow and nestling into it, 'We wait,' Amac Galil mumbles.

'Just so,' Gaguine adds tilting his head back over the seat and closing his eyes.

Felipe gives Torbinson a gentle smile before resigning for the afternoon ahead of a crucial night.

As twilight descends on the town of La Penca, small cinderblock buildings and bamboo huts glow in dim warm light. The main *taberna* is full with journalists and there's a steady stream of customers at an empanada stand fastened to a timber wagon and a sedate looking donkey giving the occasional swoosh of his tail.

Walking back to the van with freshly baked empanadas, Felipe wakes the men.

'Buenos dias, senores,' he says climbing into the front seat. *'El tiempo de la comida,'* he says handing them each a warm parcel of food.

Lighting a cigarette, 'What time is it?' Amac asks hoarsely.

'Seven-thirty.'

Raising his eyebrows, 'Time to go to work,' the Iranian says slapping his cheeks.

Roberto Gaguine twists his neck in both directions, giving his bones a delightful crack, while Torbinson gingerly picks at the pastry in his hands.

As they begin eating, a buzz seems to go through the town when suddenly a convoy of military jeeps comes roaring through. Journalists frantically abandon the little restaurant, the plaza too, rushing to their cars and vans retrieving camera equipment and microphones and handheld recording devices.

'All right, gentlemen, party time,' Felipe says keenly.

Tossing their empanadas aside, Roberto Gaguine and Peter Torbinson climb out of the van and collect their camera equipment from the trunk. The Argentine inspects the C4 in the tape compartment, ensuring the blasting caps are secured properly.

Seeing Torbinson's face awash with trepidation, Gaguine puts a hand on his shoulder, 'Don't worry, *amigo*,' he says warmly. 'Many men die in war; they have to in order to know who is still willing to fight.'

The photojournalist's eyes fidget, 'It's not that, Mr. Hansen. Won't the explosion kill more than just Eden Pastora?'

Giving him an understanding look, 'It is better to not think about it. Come on, we have a job to do.'

Sliding across to the driver's seat and lighting a cigarette, 'Don't forget,' Amac mumbles to Felipe.

Tucking a pistol in the back of his waistband and pulling his shirt over to conceal it, 'I know, man,' the Cuban says with a wink.

Hurrying off, Felipe Vidal, Roberto Gaguine, and Peter Torbinson quickly join the band of journalists rushing towards a small building, blending in and looking no different to those around them eager to see the Nicaraguan hero. Contra rebels in military fatigues gather around the entrance watching closely the reporters and media personnel. Despite his calm demeanor, Felipe recognizes the danger in killing the soldiers on the back road earlier in the day and whether or not they will somehow be noticed. As they get to the entrance, the crowd bottlenecks as soldiers appear to be glancing at peoples' press passes. Seeing this, Felipe motions for Gaguine to place the camera on his shoulder to better hide his face, and although he speaks wonderful Spanish, he looks nothing like a cameraman from Costa Rica.

As they approach a soldier, Felipe holds out his media pass, '*Hola. Tres de nosotros,*' he says inclining to his compatriots.

A flurry of camera flashes brightens the room as Eden Pastora walks on stage, creating a big push of reporters trying to get in. The bottleneck squeezes and the soldiers give up checking press identification. Once inside, Felipe pulls Torbinson by the arm and finds an inconspicuous spot at the back of the room close to the door, while Gaguine pushes his way to the front where video cameras are being setup in front of a small table.

Standing in camouflaged army greens with a gun belt hanging loosely from his hip and a black beret tilted low over his dark eyes, Eden Pastora cuts an imposing figure. Tall with broad shoulders and a discerning gaze, there is a palpable sense of pride and focus about him. As is true of all heroes, his reputation precedes him, yet the mere sight of Eden Pastora conversing with his Lieutenants has an almost hypnotic effect, an absorbing desire to lay eyes on a man whom history will be determined to remember.

Despite the room full of journalists, reporters, and Contra rebels, people now appear to move freely in and out of the building, giving Felipe immediate comfort that the rest of the plan can proceed without hitch.

'Hey,' Felipe says softly to Torbinson, 'you going to take some photos or what?'

'Oh,' Torbinson says fumbling for the camera hanging from his neck before beginning to snap away.

'*Ay, maldición!*' Roberto Gaguine says to no one in particular. 'Where's that damn cable?' he adds rummaging through his camera bag.

Despite no one around him paying any attention to his predicament, he continues the charade patting the pockets of his vest and repeating the process of thoroughly searching his bag for the non-existent missing cable.

'*Disculpe, muchacho,*' the Argentine says to a man next to him testing the zoom of his camera, 'keep an eye on my equipment for me, eh? I need to grab a cable from my car.'

Mildly disturbed, '*Si, si, no problema,*' he says dismissively before returning to the inspection of his own camera.

'*Muchas gracias,*' Gaguine says getting up and walking away.

Making his way through the crowd he eyes Felipe at the back of the room before casually joining him.

'All good?' Felipe asks softly.

'A-OK, *amigo*,' the Argentine says retrieving a small detonator from his pocket. 'When do you wanna see fireworks?'

'Not yet. Wait until Pastora sits down.'

Nodding, 'Get a load of him, huh,' Gaguine says. 'Something mysterious about him, no. Like a panther,' he adds reflectively.

Felipe gives him a look.

'Just like Che Guevara. He was an Argentine, don't you know,' Gaguine continues. 'Most people think him Cuban because of the revolution but no, he was a *gaucho*,' he says making a fist.

'You are proud he was from Argentina?' Felipe, an exiled Cuban, questions.

'Of course, even our enemies can still be great men.'

Raising his eyebrows, 'Well, just like Che, Pastora also thinks too much of himself and soon worms will burrow in his skull.'

A burst of camera flashes lights up the room once again as Eden Pastora takes a seat in front of half a dozen microphones ready to address the media and all the people watching the live telecast across Central and South America.

'*Buena noches*, ladies and gentlemen,' Pastora begins in a smooth, deep voice. 'I'd first like to thank you all for making the effort to come to this rather inconvenient location, but when powerful people wish to see your head on the end of a noose, you must take such measures to ensure the voice you have within still has a mouth to speak it,' he says chuckling.

'Look, that's him!' Robert Owen exclaims.

In the third-floor living room of the suburban villa safe-house, Station Chief Phillip Holtz along with John Hull and Colonel North's aide are watching the live feed of Pastora's press conference. While Hull and Holtz are already half way through a bottle of scotch, the young NSC courier is nursing his first glass, struggling with the liquor as much as he is his nerves witnessing an assassination about take place.

With the sleeves of his button shirt rolled up and his tie loose around his neck, Holtz looks like a family man whose just finished a hard day's work rather than the overseer of hired hitmen about to neutralize a military threat. As for Hull, with a scotch in one hand, a chewed cigar smoldering in the other, and looking particularly comfortable in a brown leather armchair, the old man looks as excited as the day his daughter married Captain Luis Rivas and entered into the more drug friendly arm of the FDN.

'All right, all right, calm down there, sport,' Hull quiets. 'Don't wet your pants just yet, ain't nothing happened.'

In the dark room brightened only by a couple of brass table lamps and the glow of the television, all three men lean forward listening to Eden Pastora's speech and what will momentarily be his final words.

'I come here to southern Nicaragua not with an olive branch in my hand but a knife. Let it be known that President Ortega is a wolf in sheep's clothing and the people who voted for him are his blind flock following him down the very path Anastazio Samoza paved before him.'

'Hot diggidy,' Hull cheers. 'That there some fighting words. Maybe your boys shouldn't off him, looks like he's got a bone to pick with them Sandinistas.'

'Shh,' Owen complains.

'And I am sorry to say that the Contra fighters backed by the US are just as bad. They are traitors selling Nicaragua to the highest bidder and poisoning the well of our beloved country.'

Raising his glass, 'And that's why he is,' Holtz remarks.

'I come here tonight to make my position known. I am sending out a call to all true Nicaraguans, to raise arms, to fight the true fight, and to show the world you are not afraid. Our fathers and our brothers fought and died in the revolution so that the land would return to its rightful owners. Ortega fought but now he takes that land for himself. This is a call to anybody listening, that to fight alongside Eden Pastora is to fight alongside—'

A blinding light and loud explosion engulf the room before static fills the television set.

'Bang,' Holtz says quietly before gulping down his scotch.

Wedging his wet cigar into the corner of his mouth, '*Yeeha*,' Hull celebrates clapping his hands. 'That's what you get for crossing the red, white and blue, you sonuvabitch!'

With eyes wide, 'Is, is that it?' Owen asks anxiously.

Standing and walking over to the bottle of scotch and refilling his glass, 'That's it, Mr. Owen,' Holtz says calmly.

Staring at the fuzzy television, the young courier swallows nervously with a hollow gaze.

'Cheer up, son,' John Hull says relaxing back in his chair. 'Notch another one up for the good guys. That right there will put a smile on the dial of old, Ollie, that's for sure.'

Swirling the amber liquid in his glass, 'Now, to just make sure news spreads that the Sandinistas were responsible and that little mission will go a long way for us,' Holtz reflects.

Standing in the now-empty plaza, Felipe Vidal, Roberto Gaguine, and Peter Torbinson look back towards the small building where soldiers and reporters can still be seen coming and going.

'Ready, *amigo?*' Gaguine asks.

'Ready, Mr. Hansen,' Felipe says seriously.

Smirking and taking the detonator from his pocket, 'Time to get paid, *amigos*,' he says pressing the trigger.

A huge explosion rips through the building sending flames out of the doors and blowing the windows out of nearby dwellings. Peter Torbinson is the only one who jumps in fright, while Felipe and Roberto look on gauging the size of the blast and the likelihood that it has caused Pastora's death.

Within moments people start fleeing the burning building, the initial few screaming and running before the injured and bleeding stumble out in great numbers, searching for safety in the confusion and chaos. Military jeeps come screeching into the plaza and soldiers jump out to help those wounded and burning.

'Okay,' Felipe says, 'we better start running too.'

As they make their way through the small town, Gaguine leads them down an alley for extra cover.

Stopping suddenly, 'Let's go this way,' Felipe says.

When the men stop and turn, he puts a single bullet between the eyes of the photojournalist.

Looking at the now dead double agent, 'What happened?' Gaguine asks casually.

Shrugging, 'We couldn't trust him with the truth.'

The Argentine raises his eyebrows in agreement.

Running down another couple of streets, they turn a corner to see three soldiers standing by the van shouting at Amac Galil whose sitting in the driving seat with his hands raised.

'This can't be good,' Gaguine comments.

Running over and hoping to negotiate him out of whatever situation he has gotten himself in, Felipe interrupts, '*Senores, senores!* There was an explosion!'

When the soldiers turn and look at Felipe, Amac shoots the closest one in the side of the head, while Gaguine flings his knife at another, staking him in the throat. Drawing his gun, Felipe shoots two rounds into the chest of the third solider but not before he squirts a few rounds of his AK47 into the dirt.

Amac starts the van and Felipe jumps in the front seat, while Gaguine gets in the back. As they screech off two military jeeps tear around the plaza pursuing the source of the gunshots.

'Take the back road,' Felipe says calmly

Crunching the van into third gear, 'Where do you think I'm going,' Amac replies dryly.

The closest jeep sprays the back of the van with bullets, shattering the rear window and making them all hunch down.

'Mr. Hansen,' Felipe says.

'*Si, amigo?*'

'Under your seat is a machine gun. Be so kind as to return fire,' the Cuban says calmly.

Squatting down, Gaguine lifts the wide cushion to find an M16 machine gun lying atop a variety of other weapons and munitions. Grabbing it and kneeling on the seat he opens fire through the rear window, peppering the jeeps with a barrage of rounds.

Swerving the van onto the narrow dirt road, 'We can't outrun them, man,' Amac mumbles with restrained adrenaline.

'I know,' Felipe says opening the glove compartment and grabbing two grenades. Holding one in each hand he flicks the pull rings and begins counting.

'*Un, dos...*'

Glancing uneasily at him, 'What are you waiting for, man? Throw them,' Amac says impatiently.

Shaking his head, '*Tres, quattro,*' Felipe counts aloud, while Gaguine and the jeep continue exchanging gunfire.

Hanging out of the window and checking the distance of their assailants, '*Cinco,*' Felipe says tossing the grenades over the back of the van.

They bounce on the dirt road before detonating almost instantly beneath the first jeep causing it to explode in a ball of fire. With nowhere to go, the trailing jeep collides with the fiery wreck sending it cartwheeling into the jungle.

Whistling, 'Good job, *amigos,*' Gaguine says sitting down with a sigh and resting the M16 across his legs with the barrel still smoking.

Turning around and smiling, Felipe shoots the Argentine spy in the head, spraying the ceiling of the van in a burst of bright blood and bits of brain.

'And I'm afraid we couldn't trust you either, *amigo.*'

XXIV
FREEWAY RICKY

Sitting on a hard chair and resting his chin on his hand, Rick stares at the tubes coming out of Ollie and linking their way up to a quietly beeping machine. Heart rate, blood pressure, oxygen saturation, temperature; colored lines bouncing rhythmically as they monitor Ollie's weak vital signs.

Rick sat in the waiting room of the Martin Luther King Community Hospital for six-hours, while the doctors performed delicate spinal surgery. Afterwards, they told Rick it went well—all things considered, like a bullet shattering his third lumbar vertebra—but because he wasn't family, he wasn't allowed see him. Rick tried telling the hospital staff that since Ollie's momma was dead, he was the only family Ollie had, but rules were rules they said.

Rick has been visiting every day, staying for a few hours despite Ollie mostly sleeping the whole time. He's been heavily sedated to help reduce the swelling around his spine; the first few days after surgery the most crucial for healing, as well as determining the extent of Ollie's injury, which, from what the doctor told Rick yesterday, doesn't look good.

The beeping on the machine speeds up a little as Ollie blinks his eyes open.

'Hey, homie,' Rick says softly. 'How you feeling?'

Licking his dry lips, 'Feeling like shit,' Ollie says hoarsely.

'For real. You aiit? Can I get you something?'

'Just some water.'

On a side table is a jug of water and a plastic cup with a straw in it. Rick fills the cup before holding the straw up to Ollie's mouth and letting him take a few sips.

Taking a deep breath, 'That's better,' he says weakly.

After a moment, 'You spoken to the doctors today?' Rick asks.

'Yeah.'

'So, you know what's up then?' Rick asks hesitantly.

Ollie's eyes start to well, 'I ain't gonna walk again,' he says staring at his limp legs.

Shaking his head, 'I'm sorry, man.'

Shrugging, 'Could've been worse. Could've ended up dead like Moses and Lonzo.'

Twelve people were shot bad that night two weeks ago, two fatally, and a bunch of others sprayed with shotgun shells.

'Got some good news though,' Rick says.

'Oh, yeah?'

'You ain't gonna believe who put Chinese Dave up to do the hit.'

Ollie doesn't ask, just raises his eyebrows.

Pursing his lips, 'Montel and Ramone.'

The beeping on the machine spikes, 'You fucking kidding me? We done made those niggas!' Ollie says furiously. 'How you find that out?'

'The only cat we know that knew Chinese Dave was Buddy, so I called him up and after some convincing he told me that Dave ended up connecting with Montel and Ramone about a year ago. Then, once we hooked up with Danilo and became the number one coke dealer in LA, they got in his ear about us rising higher than we deserved.'

Frowning in disbelief, 'All while we were selling them cheap ass keys?'

'Uh huh. Now, Chinese Dave being the loose Lone Ranger motherfucker that he was apparently got it in his head that if he took us out, he'd become the *numero uno* Nicaraguan coke connect.'

'Why the hell didn't Buddy give us the heads up?' asks Ollie.

'That's what I said, but Buddy said Chinese Dave was always talking crazy talk. Ain't no way to tell what that nigga was really thinking.'

Ollie puts his hands over his face and sighs, 'Well, don't make no difference now, does it.'

After a moment, 'You can't right the past but you can still write the future,' Rick says knowingly.

Looking uncertain at him, 'You sure you wanna be doing this?' Ollie questions.

'I'm sure.'

Chewing his lip, 'You know, this is the number one thing we said we'd never get involved with, Rick. In fact, we did what we did just so we could stay out of any gang related situation.'

'What choice do I have, O? Shots have been fired and if we don't fire back then niggas gonna think they can step all over us now.'

'Yeah, but you take heat to Montel and Ramone then you cutting ties with the entire Bloods set. That's not only gonna effect business, it's gonna reignite turf wars and gang violence like we haven't seen in a long time,' Ollie finishes worriedly.

After a sigh, 'I know.'

'We ain't gangbangers, Rick. You dancing to a tune we never wanted to hear, man.'

Nodding, 'That's why I'm calling in Honcho for help.'

'Honcho? What's he got to do with this?' Ollie asks.

'We side ourselves with the Crips and we get protected for life.'

Frowning, 'Or targeted.'

'Not if we out of the game.'

After a moment, 'So, what's Honcho get out of starting a drug war?' Ollie questions.

Rick raises his eyebrows, 'First dibs and majority of the coke we get in.'

Taking a deep breath, Ollie chews his lip.

'Look,' Rick continues, 'Honcho is going to think he's winning the lottery by getting the lion's share to the Nicaraguan dope but in truth, he's exactly who we've been looking for to take over the business. Let him deal with block negotiations, stash houses, hustlers and dealers and cooking up and all that.

This is what we've been wanting. With Honcho taking over distribution we can finally sit back and be wholesalers, just like Danilo has been to us.'

'Too bad it came too late,' Ollie says despondently. 'It was all fun and games until somebody had to get shot.'

Rick doesn't say anything because he doesn't know what to say. Watching his best friend laying in hospital knowing his life will never be the same makes him feel guilty, guilty because he's grateful that someone other than himself got shot that night.

'I paid for their funerals, Moses and Lonzo,' Rick says breaking the awkward silence. 'Was a real nice ceremony, lots of flowers, matching caskets, you know. We all went back to Lonzo's house for the wake and you wouldn't believe it—the biggest, brightest rainbow opened up in the sky when we were in the backyard getting the barbeque going. Michelle told the girls it was daddy letting them know he was up in Heaven looking down at them, but then they started crying and I think that's when it hit home that Big L was really gone.'

Ollie is quiet.

Clearing his throat, 'I gave the families five-hundred-thousand each,' Rick says.

Looking down, 'Money don't bring people back, Rick. And millions ain't going to make my legs work again either.'

Looking down at his hands, 'I know.'

Sighing, 'You got a wife and baby girl now, so if you're gonna do this do it right.'

Nodding, 'I got you, homie.'

'I mean it, Rick. You clean this mess up good and plenty.'

Smiling his bucktooth grin, 'Hey, you know me, O. I ain't do nothing by halves. After what I got planned, the whole hood ain't never gonna fuck with us ever again.'

'Good.' Then, cracking a half smile, 'Maybe I'll have to put a Jacuzzi in the living room and sit my ass in it. Get one of these nurses to give me a sponge bath every day. What do you think?'

Chuckling, 'Sounds like a damn fine idea.'

That afternoon in Laguna Beach at the home of Ronald J. Lister and CEO of Pyramid International Security Consultants—a fancy name for a dubious weapons and surveillance equipment company—stands unshaven in a faded red velvet bathrobe drinking reheated two-day old percolator coffee, while rattling-off technical features of an array of premium military-grade tactical firearms that Rick and his men are rummaging through.

Lister's niche buyers are high-ranking officers and members of Central American political parties, small revolutionary forces, and well-paid mercenary squads who have the financial backing to furnish their weapon caches with the most advanced technology available. Have you ever wondered when watching the news and seeing a small skirmish take place in a developing country you can't find on a map and the footage shows a rocket propelled grenade obliterating a corner block or how such seemingly impoverished locals got their hands on C4 explosives with remote timer detonators? Well, Lister's how, which is not surprisingly why he also happens to be loosely affiliated with the FDN and the Contras, and why Danilo put Rick in touch with him.

Taking a loud sip of his stale Joe, 'Look, I'm not saying the weapons you boys can get your hands on are bad, but I am saying these are better. Much better.'

'Yeah, well, a gun is a gun ain't it?' one of Rick's men comments.

Giving a wry smile, 'Chew on this, if you will—?'

'Hermes,' he says giving Lister a sideways glance.

'Right, Hermes. Take that little incident two weeks ago that has got you all in this hot mess; three unhindered men shot at dozens of people at a distance of no more than thirty feet and only two fatalities.' Making an unimpressed face, 'That there is an equipment choice failure, albeit of rather fortunate proportions for you gentlemen. That said, I'd be hesitant to make the same mistake they did lest you want to go tit for tat.' Then, chuckling to himself, 'But who am I kidding, these weapons here aren't designed to go tit for tat, they're designed to eliminate.'

Fat Joe flicks a switch on a submachine gun sending a red laser beam across the room.

'Like that one you're holding, Joe,' Lister says inclining his mug of coffee. 'That there is a *Heckler & Koch* MP5K with optic mount.'

'What's this on the front?' Fat Joe asks.

Swallowing a gulp of coffee, 'A muzzle suppressor. Makes that puppy only as loud as someone clapping their hands, while firing thirteen rounds per second of high velocity ammunition.'

'Oh hell, I've seen one of these before,' Benzo says clocking the pump action of a shotgun.

'Yeah, when SWAT is kicking your damn door in,' Redmon jokes.

'Mmm, a *Franchi SPAS*,' Lister says with a smile. 'Italian made semi-automatic shotgun suitably nicknamed the Commando's Key. But the real kicker is loading it with those bad boys.'

Grabbing a box of shells and reading the side, 'Twelve-gauge hesh incendiary shells,' Redmon says slowly.

'What's incendiary?' Joe asks.

'Boom,' Lister says dramatically. 'Explode on impact.'

'Damn, we got better equipment than LAPD,' Benzo says impressed.

'How you get your hands on all this shit?' asks Redmon.

Leaning his elbow on a wood-laminate wall partitioning the kitchen and living room, 'I may or may not have connections with certain defense and intelligence agencies whom have a vested interest in private contractors selling top of the range weapons to groups they can't,' he says coyly. 'But you didn't hear that from me.'

Opening another box, 'Fuck, this nigga got grenades too,' Joe says excitedly.

Digging deeper, 'And night vision goggles,' Benzo finds.

'What they for?' Joe asks.

'For seeing in the night, dumbass.'

'I know that,' he says dryly. 'I mean, what are *we* gonna use them for?'

Pointing with his coffee mug, 'Ask, Mr. Freeway. He's the one who requested them.'

Looking pensively at his crew, Rick explains for the first time his strategy in detail, 'Homies, tonight we're going after Montel and Ramone, this you all know. What you don't know is, we're also hitting all their major blocks.'

Rick's men all exchange uncertain looks.

'That's a lot of heat, Rick,' Redmon says.

'And a lot of toes we be stepping on too,' Joe adds.

'And that's exactly the plan,' Rick says boldly. 'You gotta feel the fire to know it's hot. This is the first time anyone has taken a shot at us, and the first time we've ever had to shoot back. That's why I'm leaving no stone unturned.'

'But by the time we do one, even two hits, their whole crew are gonna know that we done started something and ready themselves for retaliation,' Joe comments.

Walking over to the table and picking up night vision goggles in one hand and a two-way radio in the other, 'That's what these are for,' Rick says. 'We're going to hit all their blocks at the exact same time.'

There's a general hush in the room.

'Think about it,' Rick continues. 'When the cops do a big time bust, they raid all the houses linked to the drug ring at the same time, don't they. So, that's what we're gonna do. Using these radios you're gonna stake out Montel and Ramone's main spots, then on my signal we're gonna light them all up at the same time.'

'Ain't that gonna start a drug war between the Bloods and the Crips?' Benzo asks curiously.

'Don't worry, I'll take care of that,' Rick assures. 'You guys just take care of putting niggas in your sights when I say so.'

Finishing a loud slurp of his stale coffee, 'Yeah, I'm going to pretend I didn't hear any of that,' Lister says casually.

In the dead of night, the wheels of Rick's plan are in motion. At various locations around Nickerson Gardens, cars quietly roll up to curb sides outside houses and apartment blocks belonging to Montel and Ramone. Wearing black ski-masks and bulletproof vests, guys lock and load magazines into submachine guns and incendiary shells into semi-automatic shotguns.

* * *

Sitting by himself on a small outdoor table under the buzzing red and white neon glow of *Hawkins House of Burgers*, Rick sinks his teeth into a juicy west coast slider, while reflecting on all of the things that have led to a moment he never saw coming: someone putting a gun to his head and almost pulling the trigger. It wasn't that Rick thought he was invincible; he had just never given anyone a reason to have beef with him. Everything he had done had been to avoid someone ever wanting to do that, figuring that by making coke cheap and selling it without favor it would keep everyone happy. And it worked too, at least for a while. Gang violence had dropped over the last few years as a wave of euphoria and drug money swept across South LA. He knew that by singlehandedly flooding the market with a premium commodity, not only would homies be getting rich one after the next, but there would be less and less reason to be in conflict with one another. Not that any of that matters anymore; all that matters now is getting square with Montel and Ramone, and letting the hood know not to fuck with the skinny, bucktoothed kid from Texas.

A young waitress wearing a stained and splattered white apron brings a basket of fresh onion rings to Rick's table.

'Here you go,' she says kindly. 'You want anything else? Because we about to turn off the fryers?'

'Nah, I'm good. I'll be out of your hair in a few minutes.'

'No bother. Take your time,' she says before going inside.

Pulling back the sleeve of his jacket, Rick checks his watch, 'Any minute now,' he says quietly to himself.

Staying low and in a line, Rick's men move like SWAT shuffling down alleyways, creeping up stairwells, or dropping over back fences. Three teams of heavily armed guys get into position, readying themselves to carry out a timed and coordinated attack.

Squatting behind an aboveground pool in the corner of a backyard, one hooded man pulls a radio from his vest pocket.

'Yo, this is Redmon. My team's in position,' he says quietly.

A moment later, behind the cover of trees and bushes out the front of *Imperial Courts Recreational Centre*, a voice replies.

'Yeah, this Hermes. We good to go too,' he crackles on the radio.

Then, three men squeezed in a fire exit stairwell of an apartment building, 'Fat Joe ready to drop the mic. Just say boo,' he says.

Putting an onion ring in his mouth, 'Good,' Rick replies into a two-way radio. 'Everybody sit tight until I say so.'

As he puts the radio into his jacket pocket, the bright lights of a Mercedes pulls up and parks. After a moment, Montel gets out but taking no notice of Rick sitting down eating, he glances around confused before looking quizzically at his pager.

Putting another onion ring in his mouth, 'You looking for someone?' Rick says casually.

'Rick?' Montel says startled. 'Shit nigga, I didn't even see you.' Then, frowning, 'What the fuck you doing in Nickersons?'

Pointing an onion ring to the sign above his head, '*Hawkins House*. Best burgers in LA, supposedly.'

Montel looks around suspiciously before walking towards Rick, checking his pager one more time.

'He'll be here any minute,' Rick says cryptically.

Narrowing his eyes, 'Who will?'

Tossing a deep-fried ring into his mouth, 'Your boy, Ramone.'

Glaring, 'And how the fuck would you know that?' asks Montel.

Before Rick can answer, the flood lights of a blue Chevrolet Blazer flash across their faces making both men turn.

Ramone gets out and walks over, 'Yo, M.' Then, seeing Rick, 'You didn't say Freeway was meeting us,' he adds curiously.

Turning to Rick, 'What the fuck is going on?' Montel demands.

Screeching around the corner, a black van with its side door open bounces onto the curb and out jumps three men with bulletproof vests and ski-masks brandishing shotguns.

'Hands up mothafuckers,' a big guy shouts in a deep gravelly voice.

Montel and Ramone both freeze, gripped by the sudden realization that they've been duped into coming here.

Rick takes out his radio, 'Green light, homies. Secure the spots.'

Stepping forward and motioning with his gun, 'Get in the van, right now!' Honcho yells.

In shock, Montel looks at Rick with his mouth agape, 'You serious? You fucking setting us up?' he says.

Standing from the table and dusting his hands, 'Get in the van, Montel,' Rick says coolly.

Shaking his head in disbelief, 'You're making a big mistake, Rick.'

Raising his eyebrows, 'No, I'm fixing one. Now, get in the fucking van.'

Within a few minutes they're back at Montel's house. Honcho and Chubb have tied the two dealers to dining chairs and dragged them into the living room.

'You got balls, Rick, I'll give you that,' Montel begins. 'But you starting something that don't need to be started. Now, before you go too far here, let me remind you that you in Nickerson Gardens. That's Bloods territory. Our crew are all around here and they be itching to come at you the second they find out what's going on.'

'All around, you say?' Rick says coyly. 'You mean like Charlie and Eddie over at Imperial Courts? Or Marquis on 115th Street? How about, Cliff and Floyd, they still on Croesus Avenue? I bet they are. In fact, I know they are,' Rick says with a wry look.

Ramone gives Montel a concerned look.

'We got you and your crew pinned down,' Rick adds.

'Bullshit. Even you ain't that stupid.'

Picking up the phone from a side table, Rick places it in Montel's lap, 'Go ahead, call your spots, see if I'm telling the truth.'

With his mouth suddenly dry, Montel picks up the receiver and dials a number.

'Hello?'

'Eddie, it's Montel.'

'What the fuck is going on? Crips' niggas up in here looking like Navy Seals and shit.'

Montel stares at Rick blankly.

'Yo, Montel. You there? What the fuck we meant to do?'

With a wry smile, 'You wanna call 115th Street?' Rick suggests.

Without taking the phone from his ear, Montel presses the hookswtich on the base and ends the call before dialing another number.

After a couple of rings someone picks up, 'It's Montel. You niggas cool?' he says trying to remain calm.

'Yo, MJ, we far from cool, nigga. These hooded motherfuckers done shot up the house, they killed Terry and Enzo, and now they got fucking machine guns pointed at my fucking face.'

Swallowing, Montel slowly hangs up the phone.

'Okay, I hear your warning loud and clear, Freeway, so what's up?'

'Warning?' Rick says choking back a laugh, 'You and Ramone are double-crossing mothafuckers. You killed two of my guys. You shot up a dozen homies and their women. You put my boy Ollie in a wheelchair for the rest of his life all while being in business together.' Shaking his head, 'This ain't no warning, Montel. This is the mothafucking end of the road for you two niggas.'

'Hold the fuck on; we didn't do any of that shit,' Montel states.

'Chinese Dave did,' Ramone pleads.

'Yeah, and you two put him up to it. That makes you accountable.'

Sniggering, 'Are you forgetting how tight we are with the Bloods, Freeway?' Montel reminds him. 'You do this and you're gonna have them on your ass till the end of your days, nigga.'

'Which won't be fucking long,' Ramone spits.

Then, twisting around, 'As for you, Honcho,' Montel continues, 'you done reignited some serious beef between the Bloods and the Crips, I hope you know.'

Tilting his head, 'Strong words for a pussy tied to a chair,' the big man says.

Rick gives them a wry smile, 'You know what's thicker than blood, Montel? Cash. And when you have enough of it you can buy anybody.'

Looking skeptical, 'You think you're gonna buy your way out of what you've done tonight?' Montel states.

Raising his eyebrows, 'I already have.'

Frowning, 'The fuck you mean?'

'Earlier today I went and saw Rufus and Arthur Hayes and told them exactly what I was doing,' Rick explains. 'Told them how you two earned payback, and that I got nothing against the Bloods or anybody else. That said, I know I'm about to fuck some shit up tonight, which is why I gave them a peace offering.'

Montel and Ramone exchange a nervous look.

'Thirty kilos of uncut dope,' Rick says plainly. 'That's a million dollars' worth to look past putting you two and your crew in the ground and forgetting all about your asses. And surprise surprise, they happily obliged.'

'No. No they didn't,' Ramone says desperately. 'They wouldn't have sold us out like that. Jesus, Mary.'

'Why wouldn't they?' Rick offers. 'They knew we were gonna have to come back at you regardless. The coke is just insurance so this doesn't go back and forth between me, them, or the Crips for that matter.'

Then, nodding to Chubb, the big man retrieves a small jug of petrol and begins pouring it around the living room.

Seeing this, Montel and Ramone start fighting against their bindings.

'Come on, Rick, please! It doesn't have to be like this!' Montel says, gripped by the fear and seriousness of the situation. 'Please, man, tell me how can we make this right?'

'You can't,' Rick says calmly.

Taking a lighter from his pocket, Chubb tosses it onto the sofa and with a loud whoosh half of the room goes up.

'No! Please!' Ramone yells bouncing in his chair.

Fighting against the ropes, 'You can't burn us alive!' Montel pleads with terror in his eyes.

Stepping in front of Rick, 'He ain't,' Honcho says before firing his shotgun point blank into Montel's chest, sending him toppling backwards.

'Oh no,' Ramone utters helplessly before Honcho unloads two twelve-gauge buckshots into his body.

Quickly making their way outside, Rick, Honcho, and Chubb take a moment to watch Montel's house catch fire.

Taking the radio from his pocket, 'Go ahead. Take em' out,' Rick crackles.

Pulling up his ski-mask, 'You know, Rick,' Honcho starts, 'Most niggas' bark is worse than their bite, but you, Freeway, you cut from a different kind of cloth, son.'

Rick smirks but then becomes serious. Watching the house quickly becoming engulfed in flames, the fire reflecting in his eyes, he understands this isn't a victory but a bridge being burned on a path he can't go back on. By his hand a dozen men are meeting their maker tonight and Rick can't help think about the domino effect of life. Some people call it God's plan but Rick has seen too much fucked up shit to know that's a stupid way of seeing things. People make choices and that puts them in certain positions, and other times it doesn't make a difference what decisions you make, the world is still going to fuck you no matter what. That ain't God's plan; that's the cookie crumbling.

1985

XXV

THE COLONEL

Through the panoramic views of the fifth-floor Presidential Suite of *The Savoy Hotel*, the night lights of London glint and glimmer across the River Thames from the Canary Wharf to as far as the House of Parliament and beyond. Sitting in an opulent living room filled with gaudy furniture, mahogany paneling, and brass chandeliers, Oliver North and Manuel Noriega have spent the evening discussing the delicate matter of international politics.

'So, what do you say, Colonel, do we have a deal?' the leader of Panama says measuredly.

Manuel Noriega's heavily pockmarked face remains expressionless beneath dark brooding eyes made bloodshot from the expensive whiskey they've slowly been drinking. With an unflinching yet sedate stare, it is difficult to read what the squat General is thinking; only hours spent in his presence lend to a fractional insight as to what might be going on inside that corrupt, opportunistic, calculated, and egotistical mind of his. Fortunately, Colonel North has developed a rather cordial bond with the dictator, which hasn't been particularly difficult to fertilize seeing as both the Director of the CIA and Vice President Bush have kept Manuel Noriega securely in their back pocket over the years, using Panama as a rather inexpensive strategic stronghold, as well as capitalizing on Noriega's litany of contacts to smuggle weapons, launder money and conceal secret US military activity in the region.

'Come now, Manuel, you know I can't just snap my fingers and give you what you want,' the Colonel replies.

Making a face, 'Oh, forgive me, I thought you were a big fish now. My mistake,' Noriega adds cynically.

Refusing the bait and smirking, 'America operates a little differently to the countries around where you're from, you know that.'

'Yes, yes,' rolling his eyes, 'so much red tape and checks and approvals,' the little General says dismissively.

'Look, there's a helluva lot I can say yes to but you're asking a lot.'

'And look at what you are getting in return, Colonel,' Noriega pleads. 'You use my military bases to train your troops, use my ports so your ships can come and go, while you spy on the Sandinistas, and you use my network to smuggle weapons and money into Nicaragua. Not to mention benefiting from my close relationship with the cartels, don't forget.'

'All right, all right,' North says uncomfortably.

'As far as I see it,' Noriega continues, 'I am not asking for much at all. A little favorable publicity to help restore my reputation within your Government.'

'And why the sudden concern with your image?'

'I know *senor* Poindexter is none too happy with my relationship with the cartels but for those of us in the jungles, we see coca as no different than you see oil in the east. You fight over it, you make deals, and you rob others so that you may have more for yourself. It is the same thing.'

Swirling and smelling his drink, 'Admiral Poindexter fully understands how valuable you are but he does have to answer to some very high up people as to why America should maintain positive relations with Panama. That's why the less you involve yourself with illicit matters, the easier it is for him to work with you, that's all.'

Sipping his whiskey, 'And that is why I am asking what I am asking. I know it is no secret who I do business with, Colonel, but nor is it a secret which countries benefit from such dealings. And I would say America sits right at the top of that list,' Noriega says raising his bushy eyebrows.

'And for that we are grateful, Manuel,' North says slowly. 'That's why you've been on the CIA payroll for as long as you have.'

'And for that I am grateful, *senor* North. And look, I am certainly happy to cut back, shall we call it, but I'm afraid a good friend of mine, Milian Rodriguez, has just been arrested in Florida by the FBI and no doubt I'll show up in his records in relation to those illicit matters.'

Oliver North is unmoved having no idea who Milian Rodriguez is or his relationship with Manuel Noriega.

'Which is why,' the General continues, 'when this news breaks to *senor* Poindexter I think it important for he and the rest of your friends in Washington to remember how generous I am with the US's presence inside Panama.'

Putting down his glass and inching forward, 'Look, I know you and George Doubleya are close, and I'm trying my best to extend his courtesy because, frankly, I like you, Manuel. You've got a pair of brass and I see a lot of me in you but Christ, a million dollars cash is quite the sum just to make you look good back home,' North finishes, pained by the request.

'Oh, but, Colonel, the million dollars isn't for me, the million dollars is for you.'

Confused, 'And how's that?'

'I want America to see Panama not just as an asset, but as an important ally.'

'Is that so?'

'Of course. That's why I'm going to wreak mayhem on the Sandinistas for you,' the General says with a straight face.

Raising his eyebrows, 'Well, you failed to mention that a minute ago.'

'Easier to ask for something and get it then ask for something and have to give something in return.'

'Play nice, Manuel.'

Smiling, 'I kid, I kid. I too like you, *senor* North, and that is why I am going to do this thing for you.'

Sitting back in the soft armchair considering the content of their conversation, 'Now, you've piqued my interest but getting Panama into hot water with Nicaragua would be in contravention of the express will of the United States Congress.'

'*Tsk, tsk*, Colonel. The United States is not asking Panama to do anything, official or otherwise. But I, Manuel Antonio Noriega Moreno, am doing you this favor, just as you will be doing me a favor in return.'

Oliver's molars crunch, 'And just what does wreak mayhem involve?'

Taking a gulp of his whiskey, 'I have men inside Managua.'

'Where?'

'The airport, an oil refinery, a power plant. I can get inside the government too and get rid of some important people. Obviously, not in the Interior Ministry but near enough to send them a message that Panama and America are brothers,' Noriega says making a fist. 'And the best part is you don't have to waste precious Contra lives to make it happen.'

The Colonel thinks long and hard about Noriega's proposition. Although Bill Casey and Vice President George Bush both have utilized the General's willingness to support the US's foreign political agenda, it has always been at arm's distance. Noriega's propensity and proclivity to benefit from drug trafficking is widely known, and having turned a blind eye to such activity in the past to now depending on a certain degree of safe passage for the betterment of the FDN, this goes yet another step further, and the closer the Colonel gets the less deniability he is afforded.

'All right, Manuel, let me see some plans, some assurances—'

Leaning over the side of his chair and retrieving a manila folder, Noriega tosses it onto the mahogany coffee table, 'Here you go. Locations, logistics, scale of disruption, it's all there.'

Surprised by his preparation, the Colonel scans the documents.

'There's also details in there for another airline company to help your resupply efforts and launder monies,' the General adds.

Looking up sharply, 'You mean, transfer financial aid.'

Noriega feigns a smirk, 'It is called DIACSA and my best pilot runs it. His name is Floyd Carlton and I've told him to make himself completely available to your needs. Get your man Felix to make contact.'

The Colonel nods before glancing over more of the files.

'One-million dollars and clean up my reputation, *senor* North, and I will roll Sandinista heads down the streets and burn buildings to the ground.'

Looking up and smiling, North begins scribbling on a piece of paper, 'Let me speak to my superiors and when I get the green light, expect a call from this man.'

Reading the bit of paper, '*Senor*, Roger Stone. Is he a good man?' Noriega asks.

'A good man he is not, but good at what he does, he is,' North says.

Tucking the note into his shirt pocket, 'That is good enough. Okay, Colonel. I'm afraid I must retire. I am still on Panama time and the weather in London is most disagreeable.'

'I understand completely, Manuel,' North says with a yawn. 'I'm off to Beirut in the morning and back to Washington the following day, but I tell you this whiskey is making me feel like not doing a damn thing,' he says admiring the drink in his hand.

As Noriega stands, he signals to the adjoining room where two women in rather revealing cocktail dresses emerge. Walking over, they each put a slender arm around the General's waist, while their catwalk model height puts their breasts almost at his eye-level.

'Don't work too hard, Colonel. One mustn't forget the finer things in life otherwise what would be the point in all this fighting,' he says raising his eyebrows.

* * *

Two days, six flights and three different time zones later, Oliver North swallows a couple of Aspirin with his morning coffee, while Admiral John Poindexter and deputy Secretary of State Elliott Abrams consider Manuel Noriega's offer to assist in the sabotage and destruction of Sandinista resources, in exchange for one-million dollars, of course.

'I wonder what he means about helping him clean up his act,' Poindexter mulls aloud. 'I mean, if he really is serious about repairing his reputation, he should be willing to do that for nearly nothing, the sonuvabitch. Especially seeing as Milian Rodriguez has goddamn records of his laundering millions for the Cali cartel. Speaking of which, why in the hell did Felix reach out to the goddamn bookkeeper for the cartels for money?' the Admiral asks furiously.

Clearing his throat, Clarridge replies from the back of the room, 'Felix was charged with the hard task of seeking out financial donations from mutually interested parties who saw the Sandinistas as much of a threat as we did. Sir.'

'Is that so?' Poindexter says unimpressed by the quality of the reasoning. 'And what about the goddamn NHAO contract for *Frigorificos de Punta Arenas* he was responsible for arranging, which, thanks to Milian's arrest, we now know was shuttling drugs back and forth through the Gulf to the tune of two-hundred thousand dollars a week?'

'An unfortunate slipup,' Clarridge says.

Narrowing his eyes, 'Our President has a public campaign against widespread drug use in our country and you call giving a fishing company a publicly funded aid contract so they can transport CIA chaperoned cocaine a slipup?' Then, turning to North, 'And now Noriega has his name written all over the same records and he wants us to make him look good? Jesus Christ, Colonel.'

'Look, my sense is that Manuel's offer is sincere and that he does indeed have the capabilities to execute what he says. That's what we should be focusing on here,' North says tactfully.

Shaking his head, 'A million dollars is an outrageous sum of money though, Colonel. If he wants us indebted to him so he can blackmail us down the track then I'm not interested.'

'I'll have Robert Owen look into it but I'm sure we can cover the cost through the *Enterprise*.'

Slightly taken aback, 'A million dollars, just like that?' Poindexter asks curiously.

North nods indifferently.

Frowning, 'You better be keeping the NSC above board, Ollie. I know this is a hot mess and once I take over Bob McFarlane's position as National Security Advisor in a few months you won't be getting any push back from me, but for Christ's sake don't get yourself in a compromising position with the uncompromising trash down there. We've got a good thing going with Iran and Israel. Plenty of weapons coming your way for the Contras and plenty of leverage to get hostages out of Lebanon. We don't want to screw that tenuous arrangement up by giving Noriega an inch more than he deserves.'

'I understand what you're saying Admiral but I don't think we have anything to worry about with Manuel. We've always known he played both sides, filling his pockets with payoffs from the cartels, while bolstering Panama's national interests by letting our defense organizations basically have free reign in his country. But he's shown time and time again we can trust him.'

Looking unconvinced, 'He's too cavalier with his illegal activities, Ollie. I don't like it.'

'And unfortunately illegal activities come part and parcel with any Latin American leader. We can't cut ties with them all and be left in the dark, especially if Manuel really has access inside Managua.'

Sighing, the Admiral raises his eyebrows for the moment in silent agreement.

Sensing Poindexter's concerns dissipating, North continues, 'His proposal seems sound to me and Dewey Clarridge believes we can make the appropriate arrangements for reasonable operational security and deniability.'

Turning to Elliott Abrams, 'And where does Shultz sit on this?' Poindexter asks.

Fixing his wireframe glasses, 'The Secretary of State feels that the Sandinistas are a cancer in our own landmass that must be cut out and that any negotiations would be a euphemism for capitulation if the shadow of power is not cast across the bargaining table,' Abrams says with well-rehearsed severity.

Sighing, the Admiral continues, 'Well, nobody gives a damn about negotiating with them, least of all me.' After a moment, 'All right. But we cannot, and I repeat cannot, be involved in any conspiracy or assassination. You and George and Bill may like Noriega but I sure as hell don't. And if I don't then you know it's going to be a tough sell to get him in God's good graces with the rest of the Administration.'

'I'll take care of that,' Elliott Abrams offers. 'I've bailed out Noriega a few times in the past, this shouldn't be a problem.'

'That so? And what about this apparent relationship between him and Milian Rodriguez?' Poindexter questions.

'It is what it is,' Abrams says indifferently. 'People will want sanctions imposed against him of which we'll agree to but only *after* the Sandinistas have been dealt with. I'll make it clear that Socialism is a far bigger threat than any of the problems we may have getting cozy with Panama. Besides, we don't know yet what will be made public from Milian's arrest and whatever does will simply be an issue of perception management.'

'See,' North says. 'Nothing to worry about.'

Pursing his lips, Poindexter seems to concede.

'And you'll get in touch with Roger Stone?' the Colonel asks Abrams.

'For the PR, you bet. We're continuing to leak stories to the papers about the Sandinistas involvement with the cartels, so we can suggest this is all a smear campaign against Noriega because of his close relationship with the United States. I mean, are people really going to believe we would ever be directly involved with traffickers anyway? The notion is palpably absurd,' Abrams says chuckling.

'Utterly ridiculous,' the Colonel adds before bottoming up his coffee.

'Well, then. Move ahead with Noriega's offer. Keep me in the loop but I trust your judgement, Ollie,' Poindexter says agreeably.

Smiling, 'I'll do that,' the Colonel says.

'If there's nothing else?'

'Oh, Bueso Rosa,' Clarridge blurts, reminding North of one more minor titbit to address.

'What about him?' Poindexter scrunches his face.

'Well,' North begins, 'as you know the Honduran General is hiding out in Chile avoiding an FBI extradition mandate for his role in organizing the attempted assassination of President Córdova of Ecuador.'

'And?'

'And he wants my help.'

'It's one thing after another with these Latin American countries, isn't it. Help with what exactly? He was caught on tape, several times might I add, orchestrating the murder of his Commander in Chief *and* arranging the sale of, what was it, ten-million dollars' worth of cocaine in Miami to make it happen. He's looking at twenty-years.'

'Which is precisely the problem,' North says reluctantly. 'Rosa has been a top shelf CIA asset for quite some time, as well as being mightily supportive of our FDN forces in Honduras.'

'So, what?'

'So, that makes him privy to a lot of sensitive information,' North says seriously. 'Elliott here knows General Rosa very well and can attest to his immeasurable importance in furthering our interests there.'

Taking the arm of his glasses out of his mouth, Abrams expands the Colonel's point, 'His training of Battalion 316 and taking care of God knows how many suspected leftist troublemakers alone played a major role in securing pro-American sentiment in Honduras.'

'Christ, we awarded him the Legion of Merit for it,' North adds.

'Staring down twenty-years may just make him break his long-standing silence about the resistance effort, as well as other more sensitive operations,' Clarridge admits.

'We really don't need him spilling the beans,' North adds. 'Not when we've finally got this Contra revolution up and moving.'

Sighing deeply, 'What are you asking, Colonel?' the Admiral asks pained by the situation.

'Clemency.'

'Out of the question.'

Looking at Clarridge and back to Poindexter, 'Imprisonment back in Honduras?' North tables.

Frowning, 'For international drug smuggling and corroboration to assassination? The FBI will never have it.'

'Leniency then. He's been a major supporter of US causes in Honduras, we at least owe him that.'

Poindexter makes a face.

'Sir, there are assets we can slam the door on and throw away the key, but Bueso isn't one of them,' Clarridge explains.

Giving his head a capitulating shake, 'All right, he's your man, Ollie, you do the work.'

'I'll speak to General Paul Gorman,' Abrams says making a note in his diary. 'He and Bueso worked closely for a number of years during his command in Latin America. He'll be a valuable collaborator for Bueso's defense.'

'Thank you, Elliot,' North says. 'I'll arrange a meeting with the Justice Department for next week and we can lobby the imperativeness of Bueso's early release.'

Standing, 'Just make sure we stay focused on what is important here, Colonel,' Poindexter says with a hint of concern with how bold North is becoming.

'Don't worry, Admiral. There's nothing more important to me than extinguishing the Sandinistas from Nicaragua,' the Colonel assures.

Shaking hands and escorting the two men from his office, Clarridge gives North an exhausting look.

'At least we got there in the end,' the Colonel says refilling his cup of coffee.

Taking a seat on the oak settee, 'Can their heads really be that deep in the sand?' Clarridge says painfully. 'I didn't realize Poindexter was so tight in the ass. If he's this worked up about Manuel, imagine if he knew how the cheques were really being cut down there. Christ, how does he think the FDN have even half of what they do?'

Taking a sip, 'With the Israeli's help, of course. And the *Enterprise*.'

Choking back a laugh, 'Guns and ammo don't feed and clothe nearly fifteen-thousand Contra fighters.'

Raising an eyebrow, 'We shouldn't complain,' North says respectfully. 'Johnny's a good man to work with, and far better than Bob McFarlane even though he's been happy to sell Khomeini everything including the kitchen sink if it means getting hostages out of Beirut and keeping a lid on Communism.'

Giving a casual shrug, 'Not that it matters much for me seeing as I'm finally out of Latin America.'

'It'll be a shame not working with you on the Contra effort, Dewey. Sure you can't stay?'

'You know me, there's nothing I like more than killing Commies but no, this whole Will Buckley kidnapping has the Agency deeply concerned, especially now what with all of his agents turning up dead or disappearing. Seems they've tortured the poor man into revealing his network over there, those Hezbollah sonsuvbitches.'

Crunching his molars, North sighs deeply knowing all too well the risks and sacrifices military and agency men make for their country; sacrifices the liberals all too easily forget despite benefiting daily from men like Buckley and the thousands of other nameless servicemen who paid for our freedom with their lives.

'Did Bill tell you about him calling Ted for help with Buckley?' Clarridge asks coyly.

'Shackley?' North says sharply. 'He's not even with the Agency anymore, what bargaining power does he have?'

'A lot, evidently. Bill had him fly into Hamburg last week to meet with Manouchehr Hashemi.'

Frowning, 'Head of the SAVAK secret police in Iran?'

'That's the one, along with none other than your old pal, Ghorbanifar.'

'Ghorbanifar! Jesus, almighty,' North says, dumbfounded.

'Oh, cool your jets, Ollie. You were using him to negotiate with the Iranians too, don't forget.'

'Please, that was in the early days and once Richard Secord and the *Enterprise* got up and running, we went cold on him.' Taking a sip of coffee, 'Ghorbanifar and Shackley, unbelievable,' North mumbles.

'Hey, don't get me wrong, I still think he's a stinking rat.'

'I thought the CIA issued him with a burn notice after we were done with him?' the Colonel asks.

'We did, but just because someone's a liar doesn't mean they don't also possess the truth.'

Smiling and shaking his head, 'You CIA kind are a different breed, aren't you. Well, what was the meeting about?'

'What else, getting more weapons into Iran to fight the Iraqis, and getting the Iranians to tell Hezbollah to stop kidnapping damn Americans because it's really starting to piss us off.'

'And how did it go?'

Shrugging, 'Couldn't tell you. That's a question for Bill and Ted.'

Everywhere and nowhere. North is always a little unnerved by Shackley's coming and going in affairs that effect national security; affairs the Ghost seemingly has a hand in yet with no liability or repercussion to the moves he makes.

'I don't blame Bill though,' Clarridge continues. 'Ever since Hezbollah bombed that military barracks in '83 and killed two-hundred-and-forty-one US military personnel, things have been going backwards. You were there yesterday; you saw what a shitshow it is.' Raising an eyebrow, 'I guess that's why the Director needs me over there. All hands-on deck.'

Finishing his coffee, 'All I know is these damn kidnappings are bad for morale,' North says bluntly. 'And trading weapons for hostages is only telling the terrorists to keep on doing it.'

'Well, trading weapons keeps your cover for how Contras are really being financed, don't forget.'

A gentle knock on the door interrupts them.

Peaking her head in, 'Sir, there's a wire from Lazarus,' Fawn Hall says.

Holding out his hand, 'Give it to me.'

The secretary hands the Colonel a slip of paper before exiting the office.

Squinting as he reads, 'Oh, for Christ's sake,' he says seething. 'I know we're relying on goddamn traffickers but you'd think they'd have a little respect for what's at stake down there.'

'What's the issue?' Clarridge asks.

'As you know, it would seem that Mario Calero is perhaps the biggest middleman in Central America, and those two outfits Felix recently incorporated—*Vortex Air* and *Summit Aviation*—are both part-owned by Mario.'

'And?'

Holding up the wire, 'And Felix seems to think he isn't exactly playing ball with our resupply flights.'

'How so?'

Tossing the slip of paper aside, 'By sneaking in more powder than they're telling us. That's not all. I received a wire from Bumblebee who's under the impression that Mario and Jorge Morales are old pals. And if that is the case then you can bet your bottom dollar that Morales's planes are compromised too.'

'These freeloading sonsuvbitches,' Clarridge says irritated. 'You'd think protecting their goddamn aircraft they'd have the decency to pay us our cut.'

After a moment, 'What do you think I should do?'

'Stick a firecracker up Mario's ass!' The Station Chief shouts. 'Make him realize who he's messing with.'

Sighing, 'This is all I need,' North says with frustration. 'Seems the Admiral is justified in his concern with Milian Rodriguez's arrest. I mean, *Frigorificos* was receiving NHAO aid contracts and so is *Vortex* and *Summit*. If the FBI start poking their noses around down there, affiliates of the FDN, and the Nicaraguan Humanitarian Aid Organization, we're going to need to stonewall them hard and fast.'

'Ollie, you're head of the goddamn NSC. You're one of the few people that, in the interest of national security, can tell the FBI to take a fucking hike,' Clarridge reminds the Colonel.

'I know but I'd prefer it not to get to that. We need these aviation outfits to keep ferrying supplies to the Contras like a heart needs blood. I don't want any one of them shut down let alone investigated.'

'So, what do you want?'

'What I want is to redirect any attention should it come. I need someone smart and someone I can trust to lead the NHAO. A shrewd negotiator but likeable, believable,' North says thoughtfully.

'Why didn't you say so, I've got just the man.'

'Who?'

'Robert Duemling. He's been in the State Department's foreign affairs since the '60's and worked in more countries than I can name.'

'What's he doing now?'

'He's in Egypt working with the Sinai peacekeeping force.'

'Peacekeeping? Doesn't quite sound like what I'm after.'

Smiling, 'Oh, no. Duemling is just the man you want. He's a lapdog on the outside but a pitbull behind closed doors.'

Raising his eyebrows, 'And he'll be all right working with Mario Calero and the rest of the NHAO's subsidiaries?'

Smirking, 'Cleaning up messes our defense organizations make is what Duemling does best. He won't just work with Calero, he'll tell that sonuvabitch how to better run his enterprise.'

'Is that so?'

'All jokes aside, Robert Duemling will keep the NHAO looking squeaky clean, while ramping up its productivity. I'll get on the phone to him today.'

'That's much appreciated, Dewey.'

The intercom on North's desk buzzes, *'Sir, Mr. Caffery is here to see you,'* Fawn crackles.

Walking over and pressing a button, 'Thank you, Fawn, send him in,' North says.

Tentatively entering Colonel North's office is Paul Caffery, head of DEA's narcotics desk here in Washington.

Waving him in, 'Come in, Paul, don't be shy,' North says warmly.

Clearing his throat, 'Good morning, Colonel,' Caffery says shaking hands.

'Paul Caffery, Duane Clarridge, CIA Latin America,' North introduces the two men. 'Coffee?'

'No thank you, sir.'

Nodding, 'Please take a seat,' North gestures to the settee. 'Now, I hear you guys ran quite a successful little sting operation with our man Barry Seal.'

'Your man? You mean ours,' Caffery corrects. 'You and the CIA cut him loose, don't forget.'

Smiling, 'Oh, let's not get caught up on syntax, now. Assets come and go as they're needed, isn't that right?' North suggests.

'Yes, well, I don't know what he was getting up to while flying resupply ops for the Contras but that man has a Rolodex full of contacts throughout Latin America,' Caffery begins. 'Pilots, mechanics, banks in the Caribbean, secret landing strips and refueling stations, loan sharks, weapon stashes, whorehouses, you name it. It's actually quite incredible. The man is a goldmine for intel.'

North and Clarridge exchange a quick glance.

'Fortunately, for you gentlemen,' Caffery continues, 'those contacts also involve fringe members of the Sandinista Government.'

'Hold on a second,' Clarridge interrupts. 'If the DEA is after the Medellin Cartel, why and how did Seal get a deal arranged in Nicaragua?'

'Seems in that Rolodex of his Seal had a very close associate of the Sandinista Interior Ministry by the name of Frederico Vaughn. Now, from the intel shared between our agencies we know for a fact President Ortega's cronies are receiving generous payoffs for allowing cocaine to be smuggled through Nicaragua, we just didn't know who was authorizing it or where it was taking place. That was until Seal showed up at our office. The Medellin Cartel only care about one thing, being the top dog in Colombia. Being the first cartel to expand into the newly reformed Nicaragua was an important foothold in delivering their cocaine into Mexico and the US faster, and so Seal promised Escobar and Ochoa VIP access.'

'Through this Frederico Vaughn?' Clarridge asks.

'That's right. Two birds, one stone. DEA get what we want, CIA get what you want, and Seal gets to fly the coop.'

'You have a file on Vaughn?' North inquires.

Handing North a dossier, 'Not a particularly deep one,' Caffery admits. 'As far as we can tell he's outside of official politics but maintains very close relations with several of the Sandinista cabinet. A businessman of sorts but with interests in supporting the rebuilding of Nicaragua. We have a stack of photos of him at dinners and events rubbing shoulders with Ortega, Borge, and a whole bunch of other political elites.'

Looking over the file, 'And how did the sting go down?' North asks.

'After a couple fly-in fly-out meetings with leaders of the Medellin Cartel and Frederico Vaughn, a deal was agreed on whereby Seal was to load three-thousand kilos of cocaine just outside of Managua destined for Miami. We fitted his C-123 cargo plane with two hidden cameras and a remote control concealed in his jacket pocket to snap photos of the whole thing.'

Opening a manila folder and pulling out large albeit grainy photographs, Caffery spreads them out on the coffee table for North and Clarridge to see.

Pointing, 'That's Seal and his co-pilot Emile Camp, that's Frederico Vaughn and two Nicaraguan Customs officials, and that's Pablo Escobar with his top lieutenant Gonzalo Gacha.'

'My, my, my, Agent Caffery. A job well done,' Clarridge compliments looking at the photos.

'So, what's the plan from here?' the Colonel inquires. 'You think you could arrange Seal to do a deal with Vaughn and Escobar outside of Nicaragua, arrest them both at the same time?'

'That's not—'

Interrupting, 'What about getting this Vaughn on camera buying weapons from Seal?' Then pointing at Caffery and raising his eyebrows, 'Soviet weapons?'

'Now, hang on a fast minute.'

'What?'

'This is a DEA operation and Seal is *our* undercover,' Caffery says firmly. 'We don't want another Kiki Camarena on our hands and we still haven't arrested Miguel Gallardo for it either. Kiki was one of our top agents and lost his life to blown cover. This meeting is a courtesy, that's it. Now, you may be above my pay bracket, gentlemen, but need I remind you my goal is to stop the international cocaine trade stemming from Colombia, not merely incite bad press about the Sandinista Government at the cost of informant lives or burning bridges that connect the DEA directly to Pablo Escobar.'

Visibly offended, 'And need I remind you who in the hell you're talking to?' Clarridge rebukes. 'We're not just above your pay bracket, we're above your clearance level, your jurisdiction, and your goddamn intelligence.'

'All right, all right, calm down,' North placates. 'Okay, Agent Caffery, what do you plan on doing with these photos then?'

Clearing his throat, 'They'll be added to the DEA's case against Escobar and the Medellin Cartel, and provide vital evidence in our ongoing investigation,' Caffery says matter-of-factly.

Clarridge turns away in a huff.

Laughing, 'Ongoing to what end?' North says cynically. 'Every man and his dog know who Escobar and the Medellin Cartel are. As far as I can see, there are far more useful things to be done with these photographs,' he implores.

'Like what, Colonel?'

'For starters, there's a very important House vote coming up on an appropriations bill to fund the Contras. If the public were to see that the new Nicaraguan Government has a hand in trafficking cocaine into the US, that would make people very concerned, so much so that a Yes vote would mean a lot of money to pump into Latin American operations, of which the DEA could benefit significantly from.'

Giving North a wry smile, 'I'm afraid the DEA isn't interested, Colonel. Like I said, I'm only here as a courtesy, not to muddy the waters between our agencies.' Standing and collecting his things, 'You can keep those photos but Seal is our informant now and the Medellin Cartel is our primary concern, not the political destabilization of Nicaragua.'

Crunching his molars, 'That's a shame to hear, Agent Caffery,' North says plainly. Then, standing and shaking his hand, 'I do appreciate the courtesy. Hopefully we can repay the favor soon enough.'

After Caffery leaves Clarridge begins re-examining the photographs, 'All right, Ollie, what are you really going to do with these?'

'What else, let the public know exactly what these Sandinista Commies are up to.'

'And the DEA's investigation into Escobar?'

'Screw the DEA. We've got bigger fish to fry than Pablo Escobar. Who cares about the Medellin Cartel or the Cali Cartel or Miguel Gallardo in Mexico, so long as the FDN and the Contras continue getting the support they need, that's all that matters. If Manuel Noriega can play both sides then damn well so can I.'

Raising his eyebrows agreeably, 'What about Seal?'

'What about him? He's exhausted his use anyhow.'

'Once these photos get shown to the public, Escobar will be all over Seal like stink on shit.'

Smirking, 'That's precisely the plan, Dewey.'

XXVI
FREEWAY RICKY

Across from an *El Pollo Loco* and a *99 Cents Only* store on the corner of Normandie Avenue and West Redondo Beach Boulevard, Rick stands in a parking lot rubbing his chin with a furrowed brow as he scrutinizes large blueprints laid out on a table. Wearing a grey suit one size too big, a white shirt with a multi-colored tie loosely done up, and a pair of red *Nike Air Jordan's*, Rick is visiting the jobsite of a motel he's building. It's eight-thirty-am on a mild April morning and the LA sky is bright blue, there's a gentle breeze making nearby palm fronds rub, and a medley of hammers and drills resounding behind him from the two-story timber and brick construction site.

Things have changed a lot in the last six months since Rick took out Montel and Ramone and handed over coke distribution to Honcho and the Grape Street Crips. Now, Rick makes a substantial residual income despite rarely ever coming into direct contact with cocaine anymore, allowing him to focus on building a legitimate business empire. So, ever since that fateful night that's all he has been working on.

'Hold up, hold up, where are these windows, Sal?' Rick asks pointing at the blueprint.

Putting his ham-like fists on the table and leaning over, 'They're the bedroom windows on the north wall,' the building manager says in a thick Calabria accent with a cigarette dangling from his lips.

'They're too small.'

'Whatayamean, small?' the stocky Italian man says gesturing his hand as though pinching something in his fingers.

'Small. As in tiny, like your brain, Sal. I told you already I need bigger windows, why I need to tell you again?'

Sal takes his cigarette from his mouth and gives a frustrated puff.

'Am I even looking at the latest plans?' Rick complains.

'Yeah, they're the latest plans. Why wouldn't they be the latest plans?'

'Then why am I still looking at these small ass windows?'

Pinching something again, 'Whataya need such big windows for? You know how expensive glass is?' Sal protests.

'Expensive? You ain't even paying for it,' Rick says exasperated.

'But I gotta organize new ones to be cut from the distributor, then they gotta be delivered, then my guys gotta redo the timber studs and plasterboard. That's time, Rick, a lot of time that I gotta pay my workers.'

Eyes bulging, 'Then pay them, ain't that what I'm paying you for?'

'Hey, what am I, an asshole? Get the fuck outta here with that.'

'You might not be an asshole but you don't know shit about the motel business.'

Turning away, 'This fucking *moulie*,' the manager says under his breath.

'Hey, don't give me none of that *moulie* shit, Sal. All you *eyetalians* walking around thinking your shit don't stink since *Rocky* came out.' Facing the building, 'Look, the building goes like this,' Rick says stretching his arms wide, 'which means all the bedroom windows are facing north. You follow me?'

'Yeah,' Sal says grudgingly.

'That's why I want big windows, so people can have a nice view of the city, see the planes flying over Downtown, you know what I'm saying.'

'Yeah, I hear what you're saying but it's a fucking motel, not the *Ritz*. Plus there's a *Lodge's* up the street anyway.'

'Ain't no one stay at *Lodge's* except hookers and hobos. Why do people come to LA, Sal? The beach, Disneyland, family. That's why I got a motel in Ocean Park for people who wanna see Santa Monica and Venice. I got one in Anaheim for people going to Disneyland. And this one here in Gardena because it's on the doorstep of South LA. And do you know why people stay at my motels, Sal? Because they that little bit flashy but still affordable.'

Sal raises his eyebrows and exhales loudly.

Continuing, 'I got phones next to beds, TV sets with Satellite movies, and fluffy ass towels. It's budget but with a few home comforts thrown in, you understand. And ain't nobody doing them like I'm doing them.'

Sal takes off his dirty white hard hat and scratches his thickly creased forehead.

After a moment, 'You hear something buzzing?' he says.

'Yeah, drills and hammers and shit,' Rick comments.

'No, something ringing, like a telephone,' Sal presses.

Rick frowns before realizing the sound is coming from his briefcase sitting at the end of the table. Flicking the gold latches and opening the case, inside is mostly empty except for two ten-grand stacks of cash, a 9mm pistol, and big *Motorola DynaTAC* cell phone.

Holding the grey brick against his ear, 'Yo, yo?'

'Hola, Ricky boy.'

'Danilo, that you?' Rick says surprised.

'Of course, who else would it be?'

'I dunno, the Tooth Fairy. What's up?'

'I need to speak to you.'

Giving Sal a look before turning away, 'Everything cool?' Rick says in a hushed voice.

Although Danilo and Rick have been in business for several years now, they only see each other a couple of times a month, sometimes less. They stay in regular contact, of course, but the need to catch up in person is infrequent as their coke business has, and is, running like clockwork.

'Si, of course. Circumstances have changed somewhat but this is a conversation we need to have face to face. Can you meet me?'

'Yeah, I'm around the corner in Gardena. You at your office?'

'Si.'

'Aiit, I be there in ten.'

'Bueno.'

Tossing the cell phone into his briefcase and clicking it closed, 'I gotta jet,' Rick says walking to his silver Corvette, 'but listen to me loud and clear, Sal. Big windows,' he says climbing in.

Mumbling through the cigarette in his lips, 'Yeah, yeah.'

Starting the car with a deep rumble, Rick presses the electric window down, 'Don't yeah, yeah me.'

'I said, yeah, whataya fucking want?'

Crunching into reverse, 'I want big fucking windows, Sal!' Rick shouts before pulling out of the lot and thundering down Normandie Avenue.

Arriving at Danilo's building, Rick walks down the glass-walled hallway passing office after office, each one bathed in morning sunlight and as empty as the last. Norwin Meneses owns the block but only the lower floors are leased to legitimate businesses, while the top floor is always kept vacant except for Danilo's sparse corner office.

Strolling like a college kid walking the halls of campus, Rick lopes along slurping on an ice-cold *Sprite* with an *In-N-Out* paper bag scrunched in his other hand.

Seeing Rick through the window, Danilo waves for him to come in.

Leaning back in his leather chair, 'Ah, *buenas dias*, Ricky boy,' the tubby Nicaraguan says with the drab view of Carson behind him.

Finishing a loud slurp of cold beverage, 'And a good morning it is,' Rick says with a big bucktooth grin.

Looking curiously at the takeaway bag, 'What's in there?'

Taking a seat in front of the desk, 'A cheeseburger. You hungry? I brought you one.'

'A cheeseburger for breakfast?' Danilo says curiously.

'Yeah, what's wrong with that?'

Bemused, 'It's nine-o'clock in the morning.'

Unwrapping the warm red-and-white-checked parcel with glee, 'Man, a cheeseburger tastes good any time of the day, especially an *In-N-Out*.'

'What makes this *In-N-Out* so special?'

'It's done right,' Rick says admiring the burger as though it's an uncut diamond. 'A soft warm bun, a little melted cheese, lettuce, tomato, and a juicy beef patty. It's quality you can taste,' he finishes with almost a twinkle in his eye.

'Is that so?'

Taking his first mouth-watering bite, 'Mmm hmm. Just like your coke too,' Rick mumbles.

'You are comparing this burger to coca?'

With thousand-island dressing coating the corner of his mouth, 'Absofuckinglutely. You have to understand *In-N-Out* are burger specialists. They focus on simplicity, doing one thing right and that's it.' Taking another ravenous bite and continuing, 'You know how many different kinds of burgers you can get at *In-N-Out*?'

'No.'

'Three. That's it. In forty years they've only ever sold three burgers.'

Impressed, Danilo raises his eyebrows.

'When you onto a good thing you don't change nothing. The coke you bringing in from the jungles and the recipe I use to make crack hasn't changed in five years and look how successful we been.'

Chuckling, 'Well, that I cannot argue with, but it does bring us to the reason why I have asked you here.'

'Oh yeah? You said everything was cool, right?' Rick asks seriously.

'*Si*, of course. Actually, better than all right, much better.'

Stuffing several fries into his mouth, 'How much better can we get?'

The muffled sound of a toilet flushing from an adjoining bathroom makes Rick stop chewing.

Entering Danilo's office from a side door is a scrawny Latino man in a brown silk shirt with soft thinning hair, a bushy moustache, and a thick cigar smoldering in his wet mouth who, clearly unbothered by first impressions, is still in the process of zipping up his fly.

'Ricky boy,' Danilo says, 'allow me to introduce, *senor* Norwin Meneses.'

Quickly wiping his fingers of grease and sesame seeds, Rick stands and shakes Norwin's hand.

'Good to meet you at last,' Rick says warmly. 'I ain't heard a lot about you, except that you the man, that is.'

Norwin smirks his fat lips and, taking a seat in the chair beside Rick, takes out a handkerchief and wipes his hand.

Grabbing the takeaway bag from the desk, 'Can I interest you in a cheeseburger, Mr. Meneses? They as good as they get,' Rick offers.

'*No gracias, senor Ricky*. My breakfast is *cohiba* and a black coffee.'

Leaning back and crossing his legs, Norwin seems to be inspecting this peculiar Freeway Ricky figure, solely responsible for selling thousands of kilos of cocaine.

Taking the cigar from his mouth, 'Tell him,' Norwin directs Danilo.

'Ricky boy,' Danilo begins, 'do you remember when I was telling you about the war going on in Nicaragua and how some of the profits from the coca go back to the Contras?'

'Yeah.'

'Well, what I didn't tell you is that the Contras are heavily supported by the US Government.'

'No shit.'

'Indeed. Of course, it is all very hush hush because they are not allowed to be doing this, which is why the coca is so important to them.'

'It is what is funding the whole thing,' Norwin adds.

'Well, I'll be,' Rick says. 'You talking about some deep undercover CIA shit, ain't ya?'

Waving his cigar casually in the air, 'The CIA, the NSC, the very top of this Government are dependent on the coca we are bringing into the country,' Norwin boasts.

'That's why,' Danilo continues, 'we have been able to import as much as we have over the years. Of course, it is not the CIA themselves who are flying in the coca, but they have airbases and aviation companies we use to move the powder through.'

'Crazy,' Rick says shaking his head. 'Just like that, huh?'

Danilo inclines his head, 'Just like that.'

'These companies are protected, you see,' Norwin says examining the tip of his smoking cigar. 'Covered by humanitarian aid contracts and such, so that Customs or the FBI are prevented from sticking their *puta* noses in.'

'That's right,' Danilo says. 'These private companies fly weapons and supplies from the US into Central America, and when they fly back, they bring the coca with them. And the *Americanos* helping the Contras really need the money because every month or so there is a new outfit added to the resupply effort despite the biggest traffickers in South America owning them,' he says with a chuckle.

Resting his half-eaten burger in his lap, 'I, for one, ain't surprised, what with all that heroin coming over during the Vietnam War and shit,' Rick says thoughtfully.

'Heroin?' asks Danilo.

'Yeah, the heroin scene in New York during the '70's. You don't know Frank Lucas?'

'Should we?'

'Man, what Lucas did with smack in New York is, is what I've done with coke here in LA,' Rick says laughing. 'And everyone knows that Frank was connected to some high up military guys running the show out of the Golden Triangle. Problem is, how in the hell you gonna prove that? Who people gonna believe, a millionaire drug dealer or the CIA? And yet, the fact that Frank was a millionaire drug dealer should be proof enough that that nigga was getting some serious help.'

Narrowing his eyes, 'There is an important difference between what we are doing and this Frank Lucas,' Norwin states.

'Oh yeah, what's that?'

'Our coca is for the Contras. The US Government want to see a free and democratic Nicaragua as much as we true patriots do, and they need all the support they can get.'

'Which is why with the resupply effort receiving such significant support and protection, we are able to move twice as much as coca as before,' Danilo explains.

'Three times,' Norwin mumbles chewing on his cigar.

'And, now that there is going to be even more coca coming in, we need you to push it even harder,' Danilo finishes enthusiastically.

'How much harder can I push it?' Rick says with a laugh. 'I'm already moving a hundred keys a week.'

Taking the chewed cigar from his mouth, 'In LA you are, but America is a very big place, *senor Ricky*,' Norwin reflects. 'Danilo has told me how you make the crack cocaine here and then send it to Denver and Kansas City, and you have a cousin in, where is it?' he says looking to the portly Nicaraguan.

'St Louis,' Danilo answers.

'*Si*, St Louis. You are only arranging for him to get ten-kilos a week. Why not make it fifty?'

A little taken aback, 'You talking about some big numbers, Mr. Meneses.'

Sitting back and smirking, 'How much was this Frank Lucas worth?'

'I dunno, about fifty-million I think,' Rick seems to recall hearing this figure thrown around.

Squinting, 'How would you like to be worth ten-times that?' Then, taking a puff of his cigar, 'Maybe twenty-times.'

Taking a deep breath, 'No offence, Mr. Meneses, but you caring an awful lot about making money when it sounds like you supposed to be caring about your country,' Rick says curiously.

'You got me,' Norwin replies sarcastically despite remaining inexpressive. Taking the chewed cigar from his mouth and crossing his legs, 'But you must remember, *senor Ricky*, war is all around us, and there are two types of people in this world. One, those who think peace will soon arrive despite burying their fathers and sons, and two, those who know this wheel never stops spinning and are smart enough to profit from it.'

What Rick has left out about Frank Lucas is that despite amassing over fifty-million dollars in drug revenues, he eventually got busted and was sentenced to seventy-years jail time; a fate Rick would rather avoid.

Seeing Rick's delay in jumping at the opportunity to get his hands on triple the amount of cocaine, 'You are still thinking about getting out of the business?' Danilo inquires.

Nodding, 'Yeah, that's the plan.'

'Out?' Norwin says in disbelief. 'Ricky, Ricky, Ricky, don't be a fool. So long as the war goes on this is a license to print money. You are in a position many dream of but only few ever get the chance to live.'

Thinking about his past, a wry smile creases Rick's lips, 'Check it. Five-years ago I had four-hundred dollars to my name. A year later I had a hundred-thousand. The year after that I made my first million. Now, I own—I dunno—forty, fifty houses, businesses, I'm building my third motel, and I got tens of millions stashed all over the city.'

Smiling, 'So what's the *problema?*' Norwin implores.

'Six-months ago a homie I knew put a gun to my head and was a hot second away from pulling the trigger.'

Norwin squints through the smoke of his *cohiba*.

'You right, Mr. Meneses, I got more than I could of ever of dreamed but just like a dream, it can all disappear in a flash,' Rick says clicking his fingers. 'I know they call you *El Rey del Drogas*. That makes you the king and up in San Fran that might mean you untouchable, but down here in South Central LA, I may have started the crack game but I definitely ain't gonna be the one to finish it. That ain't how it works in the hood. You get what you can get, while you can, then you get gone.' Then, after a moment, 'Seems I finally answered that million-dollar question, Danilo.'

Raising his eyebrows, the bookkeeper invites Rick to share his revelation.

'It's not just the coke game I'm getting out of but I'm getting out of the hood too. I don't wanna be stuck in a world where no matter how far I've come, it ain't far enough. I'm packing my bags with more cash than I can carry and I'm running for the exit.'

Speaking calmly, 'And where are you running too, Ricky boy?' Danilo asks. 'You have a wife and child now. Packing up and leaving everything behind is more difficult than you think, trust me.'

Rick is quiet having not thought about how to juggle life outside of the hood when the hood is all he has, not understanding that for him the two are inseparable.

Taking the cigar from his mouth, 'What is the street price of a kilo these days?' Norwin asks.

Chewing his lip, 'About forty-thousand.'

'Well, *senor Ricky*, how does twenty-thousand per kilo sound?'

'Damn,' Rick says, the word escaping like a whisper.

Putting the cigar back in his mouth, 'Every man has his limit to what he wants to do with himself, this I can understand, but let twenty-thousand a kilo for the next year or two make it easier for you to step back, while making twice as much as you have now.'

Pushing the point, 'You've worked too hard for too long to give up this opportunity, Ricky boy,' Danilo adds. 'Naturally, there is a time to call it quits, but that time is not yet.'

Pulling up to a huge cream two-story house in El Camino Village, Rick sits in the driveway thinking about the conversation he's just had with Danilo and Norwin Meneses. Looking up at his new home he bought because it was the most expensive property for sale at the time and figured that meant it must be the finest too, it boasts ten bedrooms, six bathrooms, and upstairs balconies overlooking a swimming pool; far bigger than he and Marilyn would ever need but then that's what you do when you've got millions of dollars falling out of your pockets, isn't it? Yet, despite living in a beautiful home in a nice neighborhood, El Camino Village is as far as he's made it out of the hood and it's less than fifteen-minutes from Willowbrook, Vermont Vista, and Avalon Gardens; the ghettos of South Central LA.

Shutting the door of the Corvette, Rick makes his way through a lavish interior of crystal chandeliers, plush beige carpets, mahogany timber inlays, pearl white tiled hallways, and rooms furnished with items Marilyn picked straight out of a catalogue. Rick might not have beach views like Buddy up in the Palisades, but his house is a whole lot bigger, that's for sure.

Standing in the kitchen he watches Marilyn sitting on the slate steps of the swimming pool bouncing their six-month old daughter, Felicia, in the shallow water.

Walking outside, 'Hey, my cuties,' Rick says loosening his tie.

'Oh, hey, baby.' Then, looking at Felicia, 'Can you say, hi, daddy? Can you say, hi?' Marilyn says slowly.

Squatting down, Rick gives Marilyn a wet kiss before gently kissing Felicia's forehead.

'How's daddy's little girl?' he asks splashing the water in front of her.

'She's good,' Marilyn answers. Then, talking to her baby slowly again, 'She drank all her bottle, didn't you?'

Taking a seat on a nearby deck chair, Rick sighs heavily.

'You okay baby?' Marilyn asks.

'Yeah, just thinking.'

Bouncing the baby in her lap, 'You always thinking. How's the motel looking?' she asks.

'It's looking aiit. Should be up and running in three or four months.'

'That's good.'

After a moment, 'I had to go see Danilo this morning.'

'Oh yeah, what did he want?'

Raising his eyebrows, 'To offer me a deal too good to be true.'

'Oh really. And?'

'And what?'

'Is it too good to be true?'

'Well, it's twenty-grand keys. That's half of the price they are on the street,' Rick says plainly.

'And what do you have to do for it?'

Chewing his lip, 'Nothing except make sure Honcho can handle the increase in volume, which he will, and go see my cousin Dennis again.'

'Why do you need to go see Dennis? I thought you said he was turning over okay money in St Louis?'

'He is but he's only doing ten kilos a week and he's about to be getting fifty.'

Giving a surprised look, 'Can he even sell that much coke?'

'Not in St Louis he can't, but fifty keys means he can tap into Cincinnati, Philly, maybe even New York finally,' Rick says with a spark of enthusiasm.

Thinking about Frank Lucas again, the success and fame he had from becoming the first black drug king pin, how he sat front row at boxing matches and road up to clubs in limousines, and wonders if it was all worth it in the end.

Giving a wry smile, 'Well, well, well, if it isn't mister, I want out of the drug game, sure looks like you're staying in,' Marilyn teases.

'Come on now, you know I still want out. Why I want to risk all of this?' Rick says spreading his arms wide. 'It's just hard to say no to money made easy because of the years of hard work I've put in.'

Marilyn giggles dubiously.

'Besides, I ain't got nothing to lose. Danilo sends the coke straight to Dennis anyway. I'll just have to go see him when the first shipment comes in to make sure he knows how to cook that much weight, then that'll be it.'

'Oh, that'll be it, huh?'

'Yeah,' Rick says standing, a little frustrated that Marilyn keeps laboring her point, that and what seems like the inescapability of getting out of the hood.

Smiling, 'You can say that all you want, baby, but as much as you try you can't leave the hood, and do you know why?' she says knowingly.

'Why?' Rick says annoyed.

'Because the hood is what has made you,' Marilyn says deliberately.

Putting his hands on his hips, he gives her a sour look.

Walking over to the edge of the pool Rick wonders if getting out is just a pipedream, a fantasy that'll never come true because a ghetto drug dealer isn't meant to exist anywhere outside of the ghetto. Besides, after he hooks Dennis up, he'll continue to pull further and further out of the drug game, and what he does now compared to the old days—driving around in cars full of cash or coke, cooking half-a-million dollars' worth of crack in tiny apartments, doing deals in Miami with badass Central American cats, to building a drug network making a million dollars a day in profits—barely makes him feel like a drug dealer at all. So, if this is as good and as far away from the hood as he can get, is that such a bad thing?

'I'm not trying to upset you, Rick. I'm just calling it how I see it. Anyway, you shouldn't be worried about leaving. Finally, everybody knows who Freeway Ricky is. You're the king of LA, baby. You dreamed big and it came true.'

Looking thoughtfully into a bright blue LA sky, the view over his landscaped backyard framed with tall slender palm trees, Rick thinks about how crazy his life has been and how far he's come; from living in a trailer in Arp, Texas, surviving off of food stamps, to him and his mom sleeping on his aunt's sofa before dropping out of high school and turning over his first eight-track with Ollie for four-hundred dollars.

'Yeah, the dream is free but the hustle is sold separately,' Rick says distantly as the seed of freedom he seemingly planted so long ago finally cracks. Then, closing his eyes and smiling his big bucktooth grin, Rick lets himself fall backwards—fully clothed—into the water.

* * *

Three weeks later, on the third story of the historic redbrick Lafayette Square Police Department building, a detective sitting at his messy desk punches in the number for the Los Angeles County Sheriff's Office. Flicking through a file with the phone wedged between his ear and shoulder, the detective holds up a mug shot of Rick's cousin, Dennis, and waits patiently for someone to pick up his call.

'This is Detective Samuels; how can I help?'

Sitting upright, 'Detective Samuels, was it? This is Detective Caruso from Lafayette PD in St Louis. I have some information regarding a narcotics ring that may be of use to you.'

'Out of St Louis? You're a little ways out of our jurisdiction, Detective Caruso.'

Smirking, 'Well, hear me out. There's a local dealer here that's been operating out of Tower Grove East, one of our more unsavory drug saturated districts, and he's really exploded on the scene in the last twelve months selling that crack cocaine shit. Now, we've been tapping his phones for the last couple of months and it seems a very interested member of his operation resides in South LA.'

'Go on.'

'Well, it would appear this fella from LA is responsible for coordinating the supply of cocaine here in St Louis. Now, for the past several months the volume they're trafficking has only been ten kilos of pure coke a week, but about a month ago this LA man contacted our suspect informing him that his supply was going to increase to *fifty* kilos.'

'Have you got a name for the LA contact?'

'At that point in time, no we didn't, hence why I haven't called you until now. Anyway, we finally get around to raiding this guy's properties a couple of days ago and it appears we just missed your man.'

'And how do you know that?'

'We timed our raids to coincide with the arrival of the fifty kilos. We were able to arrest our St Louis guy along with a handful of his men who were in the process of turning the cocaine into crack. Then, after conducting a thorough search of Dennis's home, lo and behold, there's a *Pan Am* plane ticket stub in the trash. Now, we have phone recordings detailing your LA man's arrival in St Louis, his organizing of the fifty kilos, and his attendance at Dennis's house along with the coke. All of that makes him an accessory to distribute a wholesale quantity of cocaine. That's a big time player.'

'It most certainly is. And the name on the ticket stub, Detective Caruso?'

'Ah yes,' he says holding up a clear zip lock evidence bag with the ticket inside. 'That would be a Richard Donnell Ross.'

There's a snigger of disbelief on the other end.

'Something funny, Detective Samuels.'

'That's got to be, Freeway Ricky.'

'So, you know him?'

'Only his moniker. We've been after him for years only we've never been able to get a beat on him. Not his whereabouts, his name, not even a fingerprint.'

Smiling, 'Well, Detective, you certainly have his fingerprints now.'

XXVII
THE MAN IN COSTA RICA

Sitting in an open-top jeep in the shade of a hangar, Felix checks his antique watch and purses his lips seeing that the second hand has stopped ticking. Waiting for the arrival of planes at Ilopango is the Agent's most provoking of activities. No one is ever on time and rarely do they tell the truth about where they have come from or what they are hauling.

Leaning back in the passenger seat with aviator sunglasses hiding his eyes, Raphael gives a loud yawn.

'You think Milian's arrest will be a big hit for FDN finances?' Felix wonders. 'He was responsible for a significant proportion of their support.'

Inhaling thoughtfully, 'That depends how deeply the FDN is involved with the cartels. Beyond what we know, that is,' Raphael says.

'And how deep do you think they are?'

Shrugging, 'How deep does a river run?'

Frowning, 'Must you talk in riddles, Chi Chi?'

Sitting up and taking his sunglasses off, 'Look, everybody lies to get what they want. Each week planes are flying in with weapons and money before going back to the United States filled with who knows what onboard.'

'We know with what,' Felix says resentfully.

'But not how much. Okay, so they've been smuggling extra here and there, but if Bumblebee is right then it is much more than we thought.'

Felix rubs the deep lines on his forehead.

'Why do you think the Colonel asked us to stick a firecracker up Mario Calero's ass,' Raphael reminds him. 'There are many people profiting handsomely from this little revolution, but I don't think the Contras are one of them.'

Shooting Raphael a look, 'The FDN is getting plenty of support.'

Raising his eyebrows, 'The Contras are not the FDN.'

'Why are you telling me this now?' Felix demands, irritated by the constant deceit he must endure.

Laughing, 'I'm only telling you what you already know but do not want to hear, my friend.'

Giving Raphael an unimpressed look, 'I guess we'll find out when Morales arrives.'

'I guess we will,' Raphael says indifferently before resting his arms behind his head and resuming a more relaxed position.

The stillness of the warm day along with the perpetual waiting Felix does at this God forsaken airstrip time has seemingly forgotten makes his mind slip into déjà vu. He's been here before, on the tarmac of the small Salvadoran airbase sweating in the humidity as he awaits the arrival of a plane carrying vital cargo. Cargo intended to aid in changing the landscape of this volatile part of the world and yet he has the inescapable feeling that their efforts are only further embedding the corruption and consequence of mixing governments with drug traffickers for the purpose of political change. Opportunistic exploitation and participation with the dark underbelly of the cocaine trade, no matter how brief, will surely have long-term repercussions, and Felix can't help but think about the numerous attempts over the years to overthrow Castro's Cuba and the more they failed the more unscrupulous their strategies became. Is he as desperate now as he was back then though? Has the Contra effort gone on long enough or failed in its effort to retake Nicaragua? Despite it taking five years to get to the point of having amassed nearly twenty-thousand rebel fighters, securing multiple military camps and fronts, mining harbors, torching lands, assassinations, and the continued smearing of the Sandinista Administration to the international community, there has yet to take place a single concentrated attack on Managua. The Contra effort has been a slow burn from the beginning but it has undeniably been building, gradually growing into a recognizable force. And perhaps Colonel North is owed commemoration for his tireless efforts to connect and coordinate a convoluted collection of moving parts that has gotten the FDN to where it is; that is, into a mobilized position of threat capable of advancing, one day soon, on the house of Sandinista. And perhaps that is what they have gotten wrong about Cuba all this time. Too many half-hearted attempts striking when the coal was at best burning red, if only they had a little more patience to see that it burns hottest when it is white, and so the lean years of the Contras have in actuality allowed the vast network the Colonel has built to generate steam and momentum, and that, while no one was paying attention, the FDN and the Contra effort has grown, and continues to grow, into the revolutionary wave it needs to be and become the tide to lift all Nicaraguan ships.

Sitting up and shielding his eyes from the mid-morning sun, 'Well, here they are now,' Raphael says.

Descending out of a blue sky like doves coming home to roost are two small white Cessnas with sunlight glimmering off of their spinning blades. Touching down with a squeak as rubber hits the tarmac, the light planes circle back pulling up in front of Felix's jeep. The engines are cut and the pilots disembark, while the silent spin of the propellers slow to a stop.

'*Hola, senores,*' Felix says getting out of the jeep. '*Buenas dias.*'

'*Buenas dias,*' Jorge Morales replies warmly.

Hooking his thumbs under his belt and pulling his pants up, 'Everything go smoothly I trust?'

'*Si. No problema,* Agent Gomez.'

'*Bueno.* And what about you, *senor* Aguado, how did the Northern Front look?'

The Nicaraguan with sagging eyes shrugs, 'As a military camp should. Men, guns, a little mariachi music.'

The pilots chuckle but neither Felix nor Raphael find humor in their situation. Checking his watch he gives the scratched glass a gentle tap to get it going but to no avail. Drawing their attention, a small rusted refueling truck rumbles out between two hangars making its way over. Breaks squealing as it pulls to a stop, two men in Salvadoran uniform jump out, unravel a long hose, and begin pumping gasoline into the planes.

Grabbing his clipboard from the hood of the jeep and checking it over, 'After you return to Texas, *senor* Morales, I need you to go to MacDill Air Force Base just outside of Tampa. There is a shipment of weapons waiting for you there.'

'*Destino?*'

'Hull's ranch.'

'*Muy bien.*'

'What about us?' Aguado asks.

Scanning the log sheet again, 'No, nothing for you today.'

The squat pilot frowns and spits.

Ignoring his displeasure, 'Did you see Commander Bermudez in Choluteca, *senor* Morales?'

'*Si*, he was there and happy to see more munitions.'

'And how goes the runway extension?'

'Almost complete, just waiting for the asphalt to set, and then you'll be landing all sorts of aircraft down there.'

'Good to hear,' Felix says before glancing at his watch again with restrained frustration.

'If you check that watch one more time your hand is likely to fall off, partner,' Gary Betzner says fixing his bushy mustache.

Smirking, 'It's an old watch and often stops working. It's a bad habit of mine to keep looking at it, I know.'

'Well, even a watch that ain't workin' still tells the time twice a day.'

'That may be so but Carlton and Caballero are late and time is a train that waits for no one.'

'Whoa, whoa. No need to get all fancy schmancy. I was only making an observation, *aymeego*.'

Frowning, 'Time is a luxury I don't have, Mr. Betzner,' Felix says dryly.

Turning his ear to the sky, 'Well, wait no more,' the pilot from Arkansas says predictively, 'because that there is a DC-4 if I've ever heard one.'

All the men look skyward and after a few silent seconds, the faint rumble of a Panamanian military cargo plane can be heard echoing down the mountainside and across Lake Ilopango. Its bulging grey fuselage and four-engine propellers blur into shape as it slowly drops out of the sky, seemingly defying physics with the marvel of aviation engineering.

With Floyd Carlton and Alfredo Caballero's momentary arrival, Felix is keen to discuss the illicit and delicate nature of DIACSA's recent inclusion into the Contra effort, and despite the significant dependence on this source of funding, Felix's discomfort is alleviated only by the brevity with which he confers on such matters. Making his situation worse, while this war he must stoke remains covert and receives no official funding, he is forced to play cat and mouse with the cartels and their pilots, and despite his best efforts he finds himself moving from mouse to cat and back again almost indiscriminately; power and control swinging like a pendulum immune to his influence, sometimes staying a week or a month in his favor, and sometimes not.

Dabbing a pen to his lips, 'How much weight are you taking, *senor* Morales?' Felix asks frankly.

Jorge turns to his co-pilot, 'Gary?'

'Four-hundred kilos on the nose, Agent Gomez.'

Noting it down, 'And I am curious, what is your plane doing here, *senor* Aguado?'

Surprised by the CIA officer's query, '*Nada,*' the Salvadoran pilot says casually lighting a cigarette. 'I go where he goes,' he says with a puff inclining Jorge Morales.

Nodding, 'I see. But you have no cargo to haul so why are you here having your plane refueled when you could have flown straight back to Texas?'

Blowing smoke and then picking at a tooth with his thumbnail, Marcos Aguado contemplates his next words, 'I'm afraid I cannot tell you that, Agent Gomez,' he says finally.

'*Disculpe?*'

Taking another drag of his smoke, 'You heard me.'

Incensed by the pilot's disrespect, 'Best you remember who you are talking to, *senor* Aguado,' Raphael demands. 'The CIA can close doors faster than you can fly that plane of yours.'

Raising his bushy eyebrows, 'You could, but you won't. You need us too badly.'

'Marcos,' Jorge says firmly.

'Is that a fact?' Raphael returns.

'*Si*, it is,' Aguado continues unbothered by the sudden intensity of the conversation. 'Without us, the Contras have no weapons and the FDN no monies.'

Raphael moves to strike the pilot but Felix restrains him with a gentle touch on his arm, 'And without the CIA you would be sitting in a cell in Miami,' the CIA man says calmly. 'Don't forget who is also doing whom a favor. So, I will ask again, what is your plane doing here?'

The Salvadoran pilot doesn't offer an answer, instead drawing on his cigarette long and slow.

'Perhaps, gentlemen,' Raphael glares, 'you should pretend like we already know.'

After a moment Jorge Morales clears his throat, 'He is also ferrying powder back to the US, Agent Gomez,' he says hesitantly.

Nodding, 'How much?' Felix asks.

Morales gives Betzner a look, 'Three-hundred and twenty-kilos,' he says reluctantly.

Shaking his head and whistling, 'See, everybody lies,' Raphael muses, his frustrations momentarily elevated by having their concerns affirmed at last.

'*Senor* Gomez,' Morales continues, 'you have to understand we are just the pilots. As you have your Colonel in Washington, we have our bosses too. And they call the shots.'

'The CIA is your boss or did you forget that,' Raphael spits.

Smiling sympathetically, 'I wish it were that simple, *senor* Quintero.'

'It is that simple,' Raphael frowns. 'There is one goal here, to fund the FDN so the Contras can take back Nicaragua.'

'No, that is your goal, *senores*. The cartels' goal is to hold power and make money. The Contras, the Sandinistas, Nicaragua; they mean nothing to them.'

Felix counters, 'And yet without the Contras, the Sandinistas, and Nicaragua none of you would be here and the cartels would be moving half of what they do.'

Marcos Aguado sniggers.

'Something funny, *sabelotodo*?' Raphael demands.

'Half?' Aguado chuckles again before his tone becomes serious, 'For the cartels to move half of what they do, you would have to know how much they're moving in the first place, which you do not. *No tienes idea*. You are playing with fire, only it burns dark and you cannot see its flames. You are CIA, yes? Then you have rules to obey. The cartels, they have no rules. We may have papers that say our planes are flying for you and the FDN but you are right, *senor* Gomez, without the Contras and the Sandinistas we wouldn't be here, but the coca from the jungles would still find its way into pretty little America, and the cartels would still be making hundreds of millions of dollars.'

'So, what are you saying, we should be thankful you are taking advantage of us, of our protection?' Raphael asks.

Jorge replies, attempting to diffuse the situation, 'No, not at all, *senor* Quintero. What Marcos is saying is you are dancing with the Devil and upset because you do not like his tune.'

'What I am saying is,' Aguado states, 'the cartels do as they please and that should not surprise you.'

Raphael shakes his head disappointedly but can't argue against the pilot's logic that the cartels operate as independently as they do indecently, and who's to stop them when they are often more powerful and more wealthy than the very countries they operate from?

Fortunately for Morales, the uncomfortable stalemate is broken by the sound of Carlton and Caballero's cargo plane touching down and lumbering loudly across the tarmac.

'*Hola, amigos!*' Floyd Carlton yells out of a small cockpit window. 'What a beautiful fucking day, eh.'

Leaving the engines running they have to shout to be heard.

'Maxy Gomez, this is a surprise. I didn't think you were going to be here.'

Felix feigns a smile, '*Hola, senor* Carlton. You are late.'

Glancing skyward, 'What do you mean, the sun is still shining, Maxy. Come on, you know what *senor* Hull is like, he can talk the hide off a cow.'

Shaking his head, 'What cargo have you brought with you?'

'What else, the white stuff for them and the green stuff for you.'

'And how much white stuff?'

'However much they put on,' Carlton says laughing. 'The old girl can carry four tons, Maxy, anything not within a whisker of that I don't bother asking. I'm just the delivery guy, you know.'

'I understand. And how much cash?'

'That I know. Seven-hundred and fifty-thousand minus fifty for Manuel.'

'Fifty?' Felix frowns. 'The use of DIACSA is meant to be a favor.'

'It is a favor, that doesn't mean it's free, you know,' the pilot says chuckling.

The rear doors of the cargo plane open and Alfredo Caballero begins throwing duffle bags down onto the tarmac.

'The black ones are for them, the yellow ones for you,' Alfredo shouts.

Nodding, 'And where are you going from here, *senor* Carlton?' Felix asks.

'Tegucigalpa. Big weapons shipment from the *Enterprise*.'

'*Bueno*. I'm on my way there shortly also.'

'You want a lift, Maxy?'

'*No gracias, senor* Carlton. I'm afraid my arrival requires me to be less conspicuous.'

'Oh, no doubt,' the pilot says laughing.

The cargo door slams shut and Floyd Carlton toggles switches on the instrument panel readying the plane for take-off.

'Anything else, Maxy?' he shouts out of the window.

Looking at the duffle bags piled on the ground, 'No, I suppose that is all, *senor*. Safe travels.'

Giving Felix a casual salute, Carlton throttles up the engines and taxis back onto the runway.

'All right, load the planes. Chi Chi, you help them,' Felix says to the remaining pilots as he watches Carlton slowly lumber off.

As the men begin loading duffle bags of cocaine onto the Cessnas, Jorge and Felix share a private conversation.

'I apologize for my pilot's behavior, *senor* Gomez,' Jorge begins.

'No need, *senor* Morales.'

After a sigh, 'I appreciate that such arrangements are not ideal but I am afraid my hands are tied as much as yours are.'

Felix nods.

'On the bright side,' Morales continues, 'the Contras are well stocked and the FDN is getting more financial support than ever before. Does it really matter the cartels are getting away with a little extra on the side?'

Felix takes a deep breath considering the breadth of the cocaine trafficking taking place, 'Perhaps not. Perhaps it is a cost the CIA must bear in order to achieve our goals,' he says sullenly.

Morales smiles compassionately.

'Or perhaps,' Felix says seriously, 'it shows the Escobars and Gallardos and Caleros of the world that they take more than they should.'

A little taken back by the Agent's sudden turn, 'But is there really anything we can do?'

'You? Of course not. As you say, you are but a pilot, a pawn in the plans of those who wield power. Me on the other hand, well, there is much I can do.'

'Not without putting all of this in jeopardy, no?' Morales says uneasily.

Thinking, 'You do not tame a wild horse by feeding it, *senor* Morales. You use a whip and you strike it again and again until it does what you want.'

Whistling through his fingers, 'Last bag on and ready to go!' Raphael shouts.

Walking back, the pilots are closing the hatches and readying the planes for departure, but Felix isn't finished with Jorge.

'*Senor* Morales, please stay a minute, there is something I wish to show you.'

'Of course.' Then, turning to his pilots Marcos and Geraldo, '*nos vemos en Texas, muchachos.*'

'Fly safe, gentlemen,' Felix says without expression.

Geraldo thanks the CIA man, while Marcos Aguado flicks his cigarette away before climbing into the aircraft.

Standing beside Felix's jeep all four men watch the white Cessna taxi onto the small runway before its engines throttle high for take-off. As it begins its sprint along the tarmac Felix leans close to Raphael.

Whispering, 'Light the firecracker, Chi Chi.'

Pulling a small receiver from his vest pocket, Raphael flicks a switch and as the Cessna leans back to take flight an explosion rips it apart. The body of the plane blasting skyward and fragmenting into a thousand fiery pieces, while the nose and cockpit roll off of the runway in a flaming mess.

'Holy Hell!' Betzner yells.

'*¡Ay, Dios mio!*' Morales gasps. 'Help, ge-get help,' he stammers staring at the burning wreck. Then, turning to Felix and watching he and Raphael calmly climb into the jeep, Jorge's face changes from shock to bewilderment.

'It appears the CIA, too, can do as it pleases,' Felix remarks coldly.

Shaking his head, 'You, you did this?' Morales says in disbelief. 'My-my pilots. Do you know how much coca that was?'

Stuffing a pink piece of chewing gum into his mouth, 'Three-hundred and twenty-kilos,' Raphael says. 'On the nose,' he adds winking at Gary Betzner.

Starting the jeep, 'You let Mario Calero know the next time he flies powder through Ilopango we better know about it. All of it,' Felix says sternly.

'Don't forget who is in control here,' Raphael reminds.

Leaving Jorge Morales and Gary Betzner speechless, Felix wheels his jeep around and drives off, the pendulum swinging once again and the man in Costa Rica finding himself quite the cat on this fine morning.

* * *

Three hours later, Felix and Raphael pull up to a French-inspired bistro in downtown Tegucigalpa. Making their way through the fancy establishment of tall arched windows, brass fixtures, and white cane furniture, Felix can see the Sanchez brothers, Horacio Pereira and another man he doesn't recognize in a private room overlooking a gardened courtyard. Glasses of wine and rum litter the large round table, while the men devour large T-bone steaks and lobsters.

Casually entering the room, Felix forgoes any pleasantries and instead offers a cold and unwelcoming silence.

Almost choking on a morsel of meat in surprise, 'My, my, this is unexpected,' Ferdinand says. 'What brings you to Teguz, Agent Gomez?'

'More importantly, how did you know we were here?' Troilo says chuckling despite being rather concerned just how the CIA agent knew of their whereabouts.

Standing at the table and eyeing the men, 'I am on my way to see Commander Bermudez and thought I would pop by,' Felix says offhandedly.

Frowning, 'Commander Bermudez is in Choluteca to the south, no? Not quite on the way,' Ferdinand reflects.

Shifting in his chair, 'In fact, quite out of the way,' Troilo finishes.

'Yes, well, recent circumstances have led me to reassess certain FDN arrangements.'

'Recent circumstances?'

'Chiefly, the arrest of Milian Rodriguez and subsequent closure of his operations that were responsible for supporting the Contras, including the highly dependable *Frigorificos de Punta Arenas*.'

Rinsing his mouth with a large gulp of white wine, 'When one door closes another opens, as they say,' Ferdinand replies. 'And in our case, several of them,' he says chuckling.

Squinting, 'How do you mean?' Felix inquires.

Wiping the corners of his mouth with a white napkin, 'Don't get me wrong, *Frigorificos* was a serviceable outfit but small time considering how significantly things have increased over the last year.'

'Is that so?' Felix says raising his eyebrows. 'I was under the impression the Contras were still surviving off of rather paltry supplies, or so Commander Bermudez tells it.'

'Commander Bermudez,' Troilo scoffs.

'You get him two trucks and he asks, why not four?' Ferdinand continues. 'You get him five-hundred machine guns and he says, why not a thousand? You get him a helicopter and he complains it came from the Cali Cartel. He is a difficult man to please.'

Inclining his head, 'Some might say he knows what is required to win a war,' Felix offers.

'Regardless,' Troilo says, 'both Aristides and Adolfo Calero have secured many financial benefactors, Bumblebee is all over the cash and weapons coming through the *Enterprise* from the Middle East, and the powder from the cartels travels north without hitch thanks to you and that Colonel in Washington. Things could hardly be going better for the FDN.'

'Now adding DIACSA into the mix,' Horacio whistles. 'Having someone like Floyd Carlton on our side will counter any losses from Milian's arrest, so there is no need to worry.'

'Floyd Carlton, you know of him?' Felix asks.

Choking back a laugh, 'Everybody knows who Floyd Carlton is,' says the man in a beige linen suit who has up until now remained quiet.

'And who are you?' Felix asks, offended by his uninvited participation into the conversation.

'*Quien soy?* I'm Sebastian Gonzalez, from San Francisco,' he says smiling and offering his hand.

Ignoring the gesture, Felix looks at Ferdinand for a better explanation.

'He is Norwin's new man here to oversee things.'

'Where is *senor* Cabezas?' Felix says seriously.

'Carlos? He's gone, man,' Gonzalez says casually.

'Gone?'

Shrugging, 'Yeah, retired.'

Frowning, 'Retired?'

Ferdinand looks at Felix indifferently.

'Since when?'

'*Senor* Gomez,' Gonzalez begins nonchalantly, 'this may come as a surprise but drug trafficking does not offer long-term employment stability.'

'It is the fortune of fools,' Ferdinand adds thoughtfully.

'Kings one day and food for crows the next,' Troilo says raising his glass.

Is that the sound of the pendulum already swinging back, Felix wonders?

'Don't worry, I'm now your man between here and California and you should know Norwin is more eager than ever to make sure the FDN get all the support they need.'

'Is that so?'

'Oh, yeah,' Gonzalez boasts. 'Whatever you want, whatever you need, you just ask,' he says with a wink.

Felix is suddenly reminded of both the bravado and self-serving nature of those who move the cocaine; eager on one hand to appease the gatekeepers safeguarding the commodity, while on the other hand cutting every corner imaginable in order to boost their profits.

Glaring at the men, 'And yet, here you all are spending up money that would go far if only it reached the FDN.'

Frowning, 'What makes you think FDN money paid for all of this?' Ferdinand rebukes.

'Well, I don't imagine such lavishness has been afforded any other way.'

'To be fair, *senor* Gomez,' Troilo counters, 'the revolution has gone on for many more years than anyone thought it would. You must remember, we are also businessmen and supporting the FDN is no longer our sole agenda.'

Checking his watch and seeing the second-hand ticking rhythmically, 'You're not businessmen, you're traffickers,' Felix says distantly.

'I'm sorry?' Ferdinand says. 'What was that you said?'

Rubbing his wrinkled forehead before continuing with sudden vigor, 'You know, I'm getting pretty sick and tired of traffickers and pilots and so-called members of the FDN taking advantage of the Contra effort.' After a sigh, 'Do you know how long I've been in this shithole? Four years. Four years trying to squeeze blood from a stone, or perhaps more accurately, a penny from a prince. And for all my hard work, for all my efforts I get people like you thinking this is an opportunity to make yourselves rich.'

Giving his brother Troilo a confused look, 'Hey, Max, you might wanna reconsider how you're talking to us,' Ferdinand says plainly.

'We're on the same side, don't forget,' Horacio adds.

Raising his eyebrows, 'The same side? And which side is that, *senor* Pereira, because I don't recall the last time the fighters in the jungles had lobster and white wine for lunch.'

'Who do you think you're talking to?' Ferdinand reproaches. 'Do we look like drug pilots to you? Like petty criminals trying to jump a charge? We're not CIA property you can push around.'

Narrowing his eyes, 'But on the contrary, that is exactly what you are,' Felix says spitefully. 'You are the dead space between the FDN and the cartels. You're paper pushers but instead of paper you push cocaine around, moving it from one place to another making sure people, too many people including yourselves, get a share in the spoils. It is needless to say that the CIA has been as generous as we have purely for the sake of toppling the Sandinistas, and that is the sole agenda. So, if you think this,' gesturing to the table of fine food and alcohol, 'is going to continue, you've got another thing coming.'

With a sour look on his face, 'I hope you're not threatening us, *senor* Gomez,' Ferdinand says unimpressed by the Agent's unexpected lecturing.

'Oh no, please do not misconstrue these words coming from my mouth as idle threats, *senores*.' Then, kicking over the table, Felix pulls his handgun and holds it an inch from Sebastian Gonzalez's forehead, while Raphael draws both of his revolvers and points them at the Sanchez brothers.

'Gentlemen,' Felix continues, 'I was slitting Communist throats with shaving blades when you were still sucking your mother's bosom. The fact that I'm CIA should scare you but I clearly see it fails to do so. But, the fact that I'm CIA running a black operation that allows me to do anything I want should make you feel like shitting your pants every time you see me. Am I threatening you? No, not yet. But rest assured checking your car every morning for a bomb or questioning if your meal is laced with arsenic or wondering if the next time you take a piss are you going to have the misfortune of drowning in the toilet bowl doesn't particularly sound like fun, so perhaps pushing me to the point of threatening your lives in order for you to simply cooperate is not the best approach moving forward.'

'Does he normally talk like this?' Gonzalez mutters lighting a cigarette. Then, exhaling a long draft of smoke, 'Norwin will not be impressed by this rudeness, I can tell you that,' Gonzalez says unbothered by Felix's threats.

Scoffing, 'I may think twice about putting my gun to Escobar's head but you, *senor* Gonzalez, are a fucking grey spot to me and Norwin Meneses is gum stuck to the side of my shoe. As for you two, if I catch wind that you are pocketing money that should be going to the Contras, being Aristides cousin won't help you and I'd be very careful the next time I sit on the can.'

Ferdinand clenches his jaw, 'You are playing with fire, *senor* Gomez.'

Smirking, 'You know, that is the second time today someone has told me that.'

Inhaling on his cigarette, 'Has anyone else told you today you shouldn't go around sticking your gun in peoples' faces too?' Gonzalez whines smugly.

Looking down at this new face he does not know or care for, who represents the interchangeable façade of the cocaine trade's frontline, men who come and go without the weight of their misgivings on their shoulders, whose only job is to facilitate the gained power and financial success of those who pull the strings above them, reaping the rewards and shrugging the consequences of their actions and who have no cause or purpose but to indulge in the fleeting glory of being in the drug trade. Well, I am the fucking CIA, Felix thinks to himself before squeezing the trigger and putting two bullets in Gonzalez's chest.

The restaurant behind them erupts with screams as people madly flee the building, while Troilo, Ferdinand, and Horacio quietly watch blood seep through Gonzalez's beige suit before his body slides off of the chair with a thud.

'Crow food,' Raphael mumbles quietly.

Sighing, 'Don't forget sleeping with the cartels doesn't give you the same protection as being one,' Felix states plainly. 'I hope I have made myself clear?'

The three men exchange shocked glances but all remain quiet having never seen or heard Agent Gomez behave with such force or intimidation.

After a moment, *'Bueno,'* Felix says with a wry smirk. 'I shall take your silence as submission to what I am telling you. By the end of the year our goal is to have forty-thousand armed Contra fighters. That means food, clothing, supplies, guns and munitions, jeeps and trucks and boats and money, gentlemen. Money raised by the FDN is going to pay for all of it, do you hear me?'

With eyes wide and unblinking, '*Si*, we hear you, Agent Gomez,' Ferdinand says slowly.

Holstering his gun, 'See, now we are on the same side,' Felix says cynically, and for the time being the man from Costa Rica relishes the fact that the pendulum is yet to start its return journey.

***

Arriving in the late afternoon, the sky filled with soft undulating clouds and the sun a quivering ball of fire on the horizon, Felix and Raphael climb out of the jeep stiff and tired after a bumpy two-hour drive from Tegucigalpa. Here at the largest Contra camp on the Honduran border, would-be soldiers vary from unblemished boys as young as fourteen or fifteen to wiry and weathered men in their sixties, all gathering in small groups smoking or drinking or playing cards. Scores of khaki green two-man tents plot the grassy field without order, while dozens of small crackling fires brew pots of *la menta* tea or roast plucked waterfowl readying for supper; the scene serenaded by a gentle melancholic mariachi song singing softly from a lonesome *vihuela* somewhere off in the distance.

Beyond the tents, timber guard towers on stilts dot the perimeter, while tucked beneath the dark canopy of the jungle flatbed trucks and military jeeps line up in front of several cinder block buildings.

Walking over and poking their heads inside, soldiers are convening over a table of maps, while another sitting at a desk notices them.

'*Puedo ayudarte?*' the soldiers ask.

'*Buenas tardes, senor.*' Felix says warmly. '*Donde está, Commandante Bermudez?*'

'*Quién eres tú?*'

'*Agente Gomez y Quintero, CIA.*'

Nodding, '*El Commandante esta afuera.*'

'Outside?' Felix questions.

'*Si*, walking through the camp. *Un momento*,' the solider says picking up a radio.

After a brief and barely audible conversation, '*Bueno*. He is in D camp. Go out, turn left and walk fifty paces, then turn right at the well. Okay?'

'*Si, muchas gracias, senor.*'

As they leave, 'What's he doing walking through the camp?' Raphael wonders.

'I could not tell you, Chi Chi,' replies Felix.

Following dirt tire tracks vehicles have embedded in the grass, Felix and Raphael take further note of the Contra camp as they go. Beyond the rows of trucks free of rust and dent and jeeps with heavy mounted machine guns, a large canvas mess tent flapping in a warm breeze and teaming with soldiers helping themselves to steamed rice, black beans, and fried plantains, and the rows of green camping tents so new they still have fold creases on them, there is a peculiarity Felix can't quite put his finger on. Further along a seasoned captain is standing at a timber wagon demonstrating to a group of boys how to disassemble a rifle, while the bellowing laughter of a portly man in a stained white singlet catches their attention; having just won a card game he rocks back on a small wooden crate breaking it, sending the other players into a roar of merriment. Crossing their path, two shabbily dressed men arm-in-arm with bloodshot eyes singing terribly out of key stumble as a pair of bicycles bounce past ridden by teenagers with cigarettes dangling from their lips and passengers poised uncomfortably on rear racks. One of them smiles at Felix; his face revealing a jovial innocence devoid of the nightmare that awaits him. The distant mariachi music fades and is replaced by the scratchy sound of a boombox trying to pick up FM reception but only able to intermittently find the station. After brief argument, the boombox goes quiet, a cassette tape is inserted, and *Under Pressure* by *Queen* begins playing to the jeer of nearby soldiers. Sitting quietly on a timber slatted chair at the entrance to his tent and seemingly immune to the disorder around him, a man's eyes skip as he reads from the tattered pages of *Fiesta: The Sun Also Rises*, while escaping from the neighboring tent are the unmistakable fumes of marijuana smoke and copies of *Hustler* being tossed out of the tent flap with each passing laugh.

'They are more peasants and farmers than soldiers, no?' Raphael remarks.

'And everything else in between it seems,' Felix reflects. 'It seems the Commander is gathering any man he can.'

As they approach a stone-walled water well, a sharp whistle comes from a few rows into the camp. Dressed in military fatigues and cap, the squat Commander waves for them to come over.

'*Buenas tardes, Commandante,*' Felix greets.

Taking a small chewed cigar from his mouth, '*Buenas tardes, senores.* What brings you here?' Bermudez asks.

Looking around, 'Just here to see how you are faring, Commander,' Felix says considerately. 'How the Contras are faring.'

Sucking air through his teeth and raising his eyebrows, 'The Contras are clothed, fed, have a tent to sleep in and a gun by their head. What more can a soldier ask for?' Replacing the wet cigar Bermudez begins walking, inclining Felix and Raphael to follow, 'But you could have asked me that over the phone, no?'

Smirking, '*Si*, I could have but I prefer to see things with my own eyes.' Felix says. 'I am curious, Commander Bermudez, I would have thought you'd be with your captains and lieutenants discussing strategies and attack plans, not out here?'

Taking a puff, 'I too like to see things with my own eyes, Agent Gomez. I like to see the men I am sending off to fight. Looking into their eyes tells me what they are capable of.' Stopping at an old man lying in a ruined uniform in front of a smoldering fire with a bottle of rum under his arm, 'And what they are not.'

Frowning, 'They are your soldiers now, can't you tell them not to get drunk?' Raphael asks with an ounce more judgement in his voice than he intended.

'How old is he, *senor* Quintero? Sixty, sixty-five? The man probably lost his family and his farm in the revolution and now he is destitute, why else would he be here? Who am I to tell him how to deal with his demons.'

'Should I be concerned with the quality of soldiers you have at your disposal?' Felix inquires.

Puffing on the wet cigar, 'This is D camp, *senor* Gomez. The men here are the most recent to join the Contras and most are not ready for battle. The ones that will make it may be drunks today but are fighters tomorrow and soldiers the day after.'

'And the ones that don't make it?' Raphael wonders.

Sucking air through his teeth, 'They die.' Sticking the glowing cigar in his mouth, the Commander begins walking, 'But we all do one day so what does it matter?'

A crafty man, thoughtful and discerning and deserving of his rank, Commander Bermudez is a master tactician, his mind shifting chess pieces and his words playing games, and yet he speaks an uncomfortable truth, often telling you things that your eyes do not want to see.

Looking around and surveying the camp once again, Felix appraises its condition, suddenly and unexpectedly torn as to the true state of things brought to his attention not just by being here but by Bermudez's unnerving comments that succeed only in disarming one from a previous position of confidence. Now, the man in Costa Rica desperately tries convincing himself that it has all been worth it, that the Contra effort, regardless of how slow to develop, will succeed no matter how long it takes for money to be given or weapons to arrive or peasants to become soldiers.

Felix clears his throat, 'Well, aside from the anticipated and ongoing struggle to build Contra numbers, you certainly appear to be getting plenty of aid, no?'

Shrugging and speaking through his smoking cigar, 'Equipment, food, supplies, money, *si*, it all arrives steadily,' Bermudez says off-handedly.

'Is it not enough?' Felix asks, immediately regretting framing his words as a question.

'Enough for what? That is the question. Thanks to you, Colonel North, the FDN, slowly we grow the Contra numbers, yes, but to what end?'

Frowning, 'To revolt against the Sandinista Government, of course.'

'And yet in five years the Contra effort has not changed anything in Nicaragua, has it.'

And there it is, Bermudez's trap sprung and Felix standing with his foot in a noose he knows was there, 'You sound disappointed, Commander. As though we have achieved nothing in all this time.'

Removing his cap and wiping the sweat from his brow with a sleeve, 'I told you almost two years ago this is not the war that needs to be fought. Until Adolfo can do a better job lobbying to the *Americanos* how dire is our situation then I am afraid this is what I am to work with.'

Shaking his head, 'What more can I do?' Felix asks, frustrated that despite all he has done it is somehow in this moment being revealed as not enough.

'Perhaps there is nothing more you can,' Bermudez says with a raise of an eyebrow.

'Yet you complain you do not have enough to fight the true fight.'

'What can I say, this is Central America, nothing works as it should despite our best intentions. We do what we can but our world is corrupt one, and dreams fade like the setting sun.'

Frowning, 'Enough games,' Felix says irritably. 'What are you saying, Commander?'

Removing his cigar and spitting in the dirt, Bermudez looks around thoughtfully before replying, 'Adolfo lives the good life in America but does little here. Big shots get old and become too comfortable with their position, and when that happens, they have no fight left in them, not realizing history is a wheel going round and round. Once upon a time they were on the bottom so they fought hard but now they find themselves on top and they like the view, so maybe they'll stay there until they die.' Looking into the twilight sky considerately, 'Revolution is for the young willing to fight for their future, but if you are not willing to die then there will be no fight at all.'

Felix thinks about Troilo and Ferdinand Sanchez and Horacio Pereira, and how eager they were to aid the FDN in the beginning, but as time has gone on their effort has shifted and their cause has become one of individual and opportunistic gain disregarding of who loses out. And therein lies the difference between he and them: Felix Rodriguez, CIA Agent, whose profit in this revolution is not financial or even personal. He is merely an actor, an instrument of political charge and faceless representative of the US Government employed to carryout broader intentions that go beyond names and accolades yet assisting no less in shaping the landscape of the western world. And this is not what Felix came to Choluteca for, to be told of the futility of the Contra effort. It is a too vital a cause to be disregarded and too much effort made by him, the Colonel, the CIA, the NSC, even the American people through their faith in the government who have invested too much for this to fail. The spread of Communism must be stopped and if the United States cannot quietly snuff it from Nicaragua, of all places, how can they stop it elsewhere? Felix is operating with near impunity, cooperating with drug traffickers and murderers, with Iran and Israel, bribing peasants and farmers and drunkards to hold a gun and shout *¡Gratis Nicaragua!* all to keep America not just safe but strong, the irrefutable super power of the world, such is it stake and held in balance by, by this ramshackle of an outfit where soldiers have exchanged a pitchfork for an M16 but cannot find where the trigger is.

'There is an old poem we say here,' Bermudez reflects. 'Who sang it first no one knows but it goes like this:

> *There was a young girl of Nicaragua*
> *Who smiled as she rode on a jaguar.*
> *They returned from their ride*
> *With the young girl inside*
> *And the smile on the face of the jaguar.'*

After a moment, 'Do you understand its meaning, *senor* Gomez?' the Commander asks.

Frowning, Felix doesn't offer an answer.

'It means, no matter who you are, the jungle always wins.' Sucking air through his teeth and sighing, 'If I don't help take back Nicaragua in this lifetime, someone after me will and so history will eventually repeat. Perhaps not today or tomorrow, but the wheel is always turning, and the people on top too often forgetting that one-day they will be on the bottom.'

Pursing his lips, 'My only job is to bring Nicaragua to a revolution and bring democracy back,' Felix offers.

Shaking his head, 'You *Americanos* always thinking peace will come at the end of war, but war doesn't end any more than the rain does. The best we can do is help keep each other dry when it really starts to pour, and not let ourselves drown in a world of shallow dreams.'

Sighing, 'More riddles. What am I to do? I cannot stop,' Felix appeals.

Hinting a smile for the first time in five years, 'I know. You are like me, Agent Gomez, but you do not realize your efforts may be in vain. In us burns the need to keep going, to do what we must to right the course of destiny. Sadly, however, sometimes destiny differs from what we want her to be, no matter how hard we try to woo her.'

And just like that, Felix can feel the favor of the pendulum slipping, swinging back not after a week or a month like he hoped, but this time after only one day.

1986

XXVIII
A PRESIDENTS PITCH

Sitting at the Resolute desk, its dark oak timbers polished to a sheen, the President appears stoic and steadfast patiently awaiting his cue to call upon the American people to hear his plight and his concerns. Staring down the barrel of the camera, his face holding a calm poignancy, this one time Hollywood actor must stir within the nation's citizenry a deep emotional understanding of the peril and threat facing the American people.

Flanked by star spangled banners and photos of Nancy, President Reagan invokes the familiar father figure not just of a proud American family but as the father of the nation of which he must protect at all cost.

'Excuse me, Mr. President,' a man standing next to the video camera says. 'You're live in three, two—' he says mouthing silently *one* and pointing to the Commander in Chief.

Clearing his throat, 'My fellow Americans, I must speak to you tonight about a mounting danger in Central America that threatens the security of the United States. This danger will not go away; it will grow worse, much worse, if we fail to take action now. I'm speaking of Nicaragua, a Soviet ally on the American mainland only two hours' flying time from our own borders. With over a billion dollars in Soviet-bloc aid, the Communist government of Nicaragua has launched a campaign to subvert and topple its democratic neighbors. Using Nicaragua as a base, the Soviets and Cubans can become the dominant power in the crucial corridor between North and South America. Established there, they will be in a position to threaten the Panama Canal, interdict our vital Caribbean sea-lanes, and, ultimately, move against Mexico. Should that happen, desperate Latin peoples by the millions would begin fleeing north into the cities of the southern United States or to wherever some hope of freedom remained.

'The United States Congress has before it a proposal to help stop this threat. The legislation is an aid package of one-hundred million dollars for the more than twenty-thousand freedom fighters struggling to bring democracy to their country and eliminate this Communist menace at its source. But this one-hundred million dollars is not an additional hundred-million. We're not asking for a single dime in new money. We are asking only to be permitted to switch a small part of our present defense budget to the defense of our own southern frontier.

'Gathered in Nicaragua already are thousands of Cuban military advisers, contingents of Soviets and East Germans, and all the elements of international terror. Why are they there? Because as Colonel Gadhafi has publicly exulted, Nicaragua means a great thing. It means fighting America near its borders, fighting America at its doorstep.

'For our own security, the United States must deny the Soviet Union a beachhead in North America. But let me make one thing plain; I'm not talking about American troops. They are not needed; they have not been requested. The democratic resistance fighting in Nicaragua is only asking America for the supplies and support to save their own country from Communism. The question the Congress of the United States will now answer is a simple one: will we give the Nicaraguan democratic resistance the means to recapture their betrayed revolution, or will we turn our backs and ignore the malignancy in Managua until it spreads and becomes a mortal threat to the entire New World? Will we permit the Soviet Union to put a second Cuba, a second Libya, right on the doorstep of the United States?'

Holding up a map, 'This map represents much of the Western Hemisphere. Now, let me show you the countries in Central America where weapons supplied by Nicaraguan Communists have been found: Honduras, Costa Rica, El Salvador, Guatemala. Radicals from Panama to the south have been trained in Nicaragua, but the Sandinista revolutionary reach extends well beyond their immediate neighbors. In South America and the Caribbean, the Nicaraguan Communists have provided support in the form of military training, safe haven, communications, false documents, safe transit, and, sometimes, weapons to radicals from the following countries: Colombia, Ecuador, Brazil, Chile, Argentina, Uruguay, and the Dominican Republic. Even that is not all, for there was an old Communist slogan that the Sandinistas have made clear they honor. The road to victory goes through Mexico.

'If maps, statistics, and facts aren't persuasive enough, we have the words of the Sandinistas and Soviets themselves. One of the highest level Sandinista leaders was asked by an American magazine whether their Communist revolution will, and I quote, be exported to El Salvador, then Guatemala, then Honduras, and then Mexico. He responded, that is one historical prophecy of Ronald Reagan that is absolutely true.

'So we're clear on the intentions of the Sandinistas and those who back them. Let us be equally clear about the nature of their regime. To begin with, the Sandinistas have revoked the civil liberties of the Nicaraguan people, depriving them of any legal right to speak, to publish, to assemble, or to worship freely. Independent newspapers have been shut down. There is no longer any independent labor movement in Nicaragua nor any right to strike.

'I could go on about this nightmare; the black lists, the secret prisons, the Sandinista-directed mob violence. But as if all this brutality at home were not enough, the Sandinistas are transforming their nation into a safe house, a command post for international terror. The Sandinistas not only sponsor terror in El Salvador, Costa Rica, Guatemala, and Honduras, terror that led last summer to the murder of four US marines in a café in San Salvador, they provide a sanctuary for terror. Italy has charged Nicaragua with harboring their worst terrorists, the Red Brigades.

'The Sandinistas have even involved themselves in the international drug trade. I know every American parent concerned about the drug problem will be outraged to learn that top Nicaraguan Government officials are deeply involved in drug trafficking.' Then, holding up several grainy photographs, 'This picture secretly taken at a military airfield outside Managua, shows Federico Vaughn, a top aide to one of the nine commandants who rule Nicaragua, loading an aircraft with illegal narcotics, bound for the United States. No, there seems to be no crime to which the Sandinistas will not stoop; this is an outlaw regime.

'If we return for a moment to our map, it becomes clear why having this regime in Central America imperils our vital security interests. Through this crucial part of the Western Hemisphere passes almost half our foreign trade, more than half our imports of crude oil, and a significant portion of the military supplies we would have to send to the NATO alliance in the event of a crisis. These are the chokepoints where the sea-lanes could be closed. Central America is strategic to our Western alliance, a fact always understood by foreign enemies. In World War II only a few German U-boats, operating from bases four-thousand miles away in Germany and occupied Europe, inflicted crippling losses on US shipping right off our southern coast. Today, Warsaw Pact engineers are building a deep-water port on Nicaragua's Caribbean coast, similar to the naval base in Cuba for Soviet-built submarines. They are also constructing, outside Managua, the largest military airfield in Central America; similar to those in Cuba, from which Russian Bear Bombers patrol the US east coast from Maine to Florida.

'How did this menace to the peace and security of our Latin neighbors, and ultimately ourselves, suddenly emerge? Let me give you a brief history. In 1979 the people of Nicaragua rose up and overthrew a corrupt dictatorship. At first the revolutionary leaders promised free elections and respect for human rights. But among them was an organization called the Sandinistas. Theirs was a Communist organization, and their support of the revolutionary goals was sheer deceit. Quickly and ruthlessly, they took complete control.

'Two months after the revolution, the Sandinista leadership met in secret and, in what came to be known as the 72-hour Document, described themselves as the vanguard of a revolution that would sweep Central America, Latin America, and finally, the world. Their true enemy, they declared: the United States. Rather than make this document public, they followed the advice of Fidel Castro, who told them to put on a façade of democracy. While Castro viewed the democratic elements in Nicaragua with contempt, he urged his Nicaraguan friends to keep some of them in their coalition, in minor posts, as window dressing to deceive the West. And that way, Castro said, you can have your revolution and the Americans will pay for it. And we did pay for it. More aid flowed to Nicaragua from the United States in the first eighteen months under the Sandinistas than from any other country. Only when the mask fell, and the face of totalitarianism became visible to the world, did the aid stop.

'You see, when the Sandinistas betrayed the revolution, many who had fought the old Somoza dictatorship literally took to the hills and, like the French Resistance that fought the Nazis, began fighting the Soviet-bloc Communists and their Nicaraguan collaborators. These few have now been joined by thousands. With their blood and courage, the freedom fighters of Nicaragua have pinned down the Sandinista army and bought the people of Central America precious time. We Americans owe them a debt of gratitude. In helping to thwart the Sandinistas and their Soviet mentors, the resistance has contributed directly to the security of the United States.

'Since its inception in 1982 the democratic resistance has grown dramatically in strength. Today it numbers more than twenty-thousand volunteers, and more come every day. But now the freedom fighters' supplies are running short, and they are virtually defenseless against the helicopter gunships Moscow has sent to Managua. Now comes the crucial test for the Congress of the United States. Will they provide the assistance the freedom fighters need to deal with Russian tanks and gunships, or will they abandon the democratic resistance to its Communist enemy?

'In answering that question, I hope Congress will reflect deeply upon what it is the resistance is fighting against in Nicaragua. Ask yourselves: what in the world are Soviets, East Germans, Bulgarians, North Koreans, Cubans, and terrorists from the PLO and the Red Brigades doing in our hemisphere, camped on our own doorstep? Is that for peace? Why have the Soviets invested six-hundred million dollars to build Nicaragua into an armed force almost the size of Mexico's, a country fifteen-times as large and twenty-five times as populous. Is that for peace? Why did Nicaragua's dictator, Daniel Ortega, go to the Communist Party Congress in Havana and endorse Castro's call for the worldwide triumph of communism? Was that for peace?

'Clearly, the Soviet Union and the Warsaw Pact have grasped the great stakes involved, the strategic importance of Nicaragua. The Soviets have made their decision—to support the Communists. Fidel Castro has made his decision; to support the Communists. Arafat, Gadhafi, and the Ayatollah Khomeini have made their decision; to support the Communists. Now we must make our decision. With Congress' help, we can prevent an outcome deeply injurious to the national security of the United States. If we fail, there will be no evading responsibility; history will hold us accountable. This is not some narrow partisan issue; it is a national security issue, an issue on which we must act not as Republicans, not as Democrats, but as Americans.

'You know, recently one of our most distinguished Americans, Clare Boothe Luce, had this to say about the coming vote; in considering this crisis, Mrs. Luce said, my mind goes back to a similar moment in our history, back to the first years after Cuba had fallen to Fidel. One day during those years, I had lunch at the White House with a man I had known since he was a boy, John F. Kennedy. Mr. President, I said, no matter how exalted or great a man may be, history will have time to give him no more than one sentence. George Washington, he founded our country. Abraham Lincoln, he freed the slaves and preserved the Union. Winston Churchill, he saved Europe. And what, Clare, John Kennedy said, do you believe my sentence will be? Mr. President, she answered, your sentence will be that you stopped the Communists, or that you did not.

'Well, tragically, John Kennedy never had the chance to decide which that would be. Now leaders of our own time must do so. My fellow Americans, you know where I stand. The Soviets and the Sandinistas must not be permitted to crush freedom in Central America and threaten our own security on our own doorstep. Now the Congress must decide where it stands. Mrs. Luce ended by saying, only this is certain. Through all time to come, this, the ninety-nineth Congress of the United States, will be remembered as that body of men and women that either stopped the Communists before it was too late, or did not.

'So, tonight I ask you to do what you've done so often in the past. Get in touch with your Representative and Senators and urge them to vote yes; tell them to help the freedom fighters. Help us prevent a Communist takeover of Central America.

'I have only three years left to serve my country; three years to carry out the responsibilities you entrusted to me; three years to work for peace. Could there be any greater tragedy than for us to sit back and permit this cancer to spread, leaving my successor to face far more agonizing decisions in the years ahead? The freedom fighters seek a political solution. They are willing to lay down their arms and negotiate to restore the original goals of the revolution, a democracy in which the people of Nicaragua choose their own government. That is our goal also, but it can only come about if the democratic resistance is able to bring pressure to bear on those who have seized power.

'We still have time to do what must be done so history will say of us; we had the vision, the courage, and good sense to come together and act—Republicans and Democrats—when the price was not high and the risks were not great. We left America safe, we left America secure, we left America free; still a beacon of hope to mankind, still a light unto the nations.

'Thank you, and God bless you.'

(Transcript of President Reagan's public address on March 16, 1986)

It worked, too. During fiscal year 1985 to 1986, the Boland Amendment enacted its most restrictive funding measures in regards to defense organizations attempting to destabilize foreign governments and read, *No funds available to the CIA, the Department of Defense, or any other agency or entity of the United States involved in intelligence activities may be obligated or expended for the purpose of which have the effect of supporting, directly or indirectly, military or paramilitary operations in Nicaragua by any nation, group, organization, movement, or individual.*

Despite this, the Boland Amendment will expire on October 17, 1986, and thanks to President Reagan's rousing and emphatic speech the House will vote Yes to diverting funds necessary to defeating the Sandinista scourge festering in Nicaragua and the portion of the CIA budget allocated for the Contras will go from zero to one-hundred million dollars overnight. Until this funding goes through however, the CIA and NSC will continue circumventing Congressional approval by illegally trading arms with Iran through Israel, all of which will be overseen by retired Major General Richard Secord and the *Enterprise*. In the meantime, the year 1985 leading into 1986 will mark the peak of Norwin Meneses and Danilo Blandon's cocaine importation, made possible only by CIA and NSC intervention and protection whose single goal is to keep the FDN and Contra rebels together, body and soul. During this time the DEA will see repeated investigations squashed, set back, or jeopardized so much so that the amount of cocaine flooding out of Colombia by the Medellin Cartel alone will reach ten-billion dollars a year in sales, prompting Forbes magazine to put Pablo Escobar and Jorge Ochoa on its list of the world's richest men.

All this during a time when President Reagan's domestic war on drugs where men were sitting in jail, victims of his Administration's three-strike rule and serving out decade-long sentences for selling breadcrumbs worth of cocaine, cocaine that was available in breathtaking abundance for reasons unknown to them except its widespread availability and the fact that in neighborhoods of entrenched social poverty and marginalization, it enabled people to turn one-dollar into two, and for many that was far better than waiting for jobs they were destined to never get.

XXIX
FALL FROM GRACE

Appearing out of the sky like pigeons swooping in for breadcrumbs, Cessnas now come and go with astonishing frequency at Ilopango, dropping-off and picking up high value cargo with as much regularity as the US postal service. Having never looked so busy, the airbase is populated not only with small delivery aircraft but now it is common to see large cargo planes like bulging DC-4s or huge C-123s parked awaiting refueling or having their holds loaded with crates of weapons. Far from being the once sporadically used and secret CIA location, the last eighteen-months have given rise to an organized transport and shipping outfit of staggering routine as dozens of known and not-so-known pilots serving a variety of agendas for a variety of employers—all of which falling under the broad FDN umbrella, of course—pursue renewed careers in the drug smuggling game.

One such outfit and familiar face being that of Terry Reed who you may remember from a few years ago when Colonel North promoted him from weapons and cocaine running to training Contra pilots at an airbase just outside of Mena, Arkansas. Having gotten in early and shown a steady reliance to handle clandestine NSC operations, Reed has more recently found himself in charge of a weapons factory now requiring him to pop his head into Ilopango every other week.

Standing beside Reed watching Salvadoran soldiers push the last crate of weapons on board is Luis Posada; another Cuban exile who, after the Bay of Pigs Invasion, had been trained in anti-Castro terrorism by the CIA where over the next several years, while simultaneously working as a secret agent in Central America, became involved with cocaine trafficking and money laundering, eventually earning a burn notice from the Agency. The silver lining of this dismissal allowing Posada to climb the ranks of Venezuelan Intelligence and forming the *Coordination of United Revolutionary Organizations*: an anti-Castro terrorist group that proceeded to commit dozens of kidnappings, assassinations, and bombings over the next several years, but most notably the downing of Cubana Flight 455 on October 6, 1976. Travelling from Barbados via Trinidad to Havana, two C-4 time-bombs were detonated shortly after take-off, killing all seventy-three people on board, including all twenty-five members of the 1975 Cuban national fencing team. An investigation ensued and for his role, Posada found himself in a Venezuelan jail before escaping and heading to Chile expecting to be welcomed with open arms by Augusto Pinochet for his role in killing Orlando Letelier, a Chilean politician and critic of Pinochet's. However, Posada was handed back to Venezuelan authorities where he awaited trial for eight long years before escaping once more, this time smartly calling up his old Bay of Pigs pal, Felix Rodriguez. Now going by the alias Ramon Medina, this sly snake in the grass is Ilopango's chief of logistics, responsible for arranging safe houses for pilots, drug payments with cash flown in from Miami or the Bahamas, and overseeing the final and crucial stage of weapons being transported to the Contra frontlines.

Handing Reed a map, 'Six crates ready for camp twenty-three located here,' Medina says pointing to a red mark. 'Then back here for four more crates going to camp seven. Okay?'

'Got it,' Reed says.

'Bueno.'

Walking back towards the hangars with the map tucked under his arm, a voice calls out from behind a DC-4 starting its engines.

'Reed! Terry Reed, that you?' the voice shouts.

Ducking beneath the wing with a smile full of tobacco-rotten teeth is a man he knew was only a matter of time before he'd see.

'Pat Foley, you old dog,' Reed says warmly.

'Well, I'll be damned,' Foley says cheerfully. 'Don't tell me they got you in this hot mess too?'

Smiling and shaking hands, 'Fortunately, not quite as knee deep as you,' Reed jokes, referring to Foley and *Summit Aviation's* long history of smuggling cocaine, with or without CIA consent.

'That so?' Foley says with a chuckle. 'So, what brings you here?'

Pointing over Pat's shoulder, '*Southern Air Transport*, that's me.'

'Sounds about as obscure as it should. What are you moving?'

Clearing his throat, 'Trans-shipping items in support of foreign politics,' he says deliberately.

Laughing, 'Yeah, and what are you *really* moving?'

Shrugging, 'Same as *Summit Aviation*. Weapons, field supplies, medicines, and what not.'

Squinting one eye, 'Powder too?'

'I was but not anymore. They've got me set up with a weapons factory called *MachineryInternational* in Vera Cruz, Mexico. There's another one in San Jose, Costa Rica but HQ is in Tegucigalpa. They call the whole thing the *Enterprise* and it's run by some retired Air Force General. So, I suppose what I'm hauling is all above board.'

Smirking, 'I'm not sure anything we're doing is above board,' Foley says digging his thumb and forefinger into a pouch of *Work Horse* chewing tobacco and wedging a ball of leaves into the corner of his mouth.

Raising his eyebrows, the comment reminds Reed of the dangers of working for the CIA and what happened to Barry Seal, his old co-pilot from their *Air America* days.

'You heard about Seal?'

Wiping his fingers on his pant leg, 'Yeah, everyone's heard about that poor sonuvabitch. He was a buddy of yours, wasn't he?'

'Something like that.'

Spitting, 'And ain't that the pickle we're in,' Foley says with defeated frustration. 'On the one hand we're basically working for the damn CIA but on the other we're moving cargo for the cartels, well, some of us at least. I'm making two trips a day, four days a week, and that's just *Summit*. Add to that DIACSA, *Vortex Air*, and who knows how many of those sky maggots and aerosplats coming and going,' he says gesturing to a Cessna touching down behind them. 'Now you with, what's it, *Southern Air Transport*. Man, the CIA is working us harder than the cartels ever did and we can't say boo about it less we end up like Barry, bullet ridden in Baton Rouge.'

Sighing, 'Yeah, certainly is a funny old situation we're in, that's for sure.'

'So, you in the air today?'

'Me? No, just here to see my pilots off. They've been flying a DC-4 but this is their first run with that C-123 I just purchased.'

'Oh yeah, who's your pilots?'

Nodding towards a group of men playing cards in the shade of a hangar, 'Bill Cooper and Wallace Sawyer.'

'Bullseye Bill and Dirty Wallace? Why didn't they say so?'

'Oh, you know how Ilopango goes, everyone here is tight-lipped about who they're flying for and what they're flying with.'

'Ain't that the truth.'

Sitting around a small foldout table, cigarette smoke hanging in the humid and breathless air, pilots and crewmen of planes that have briefly stopped at Ilopango pass the time playing Five Card Draw, while drinking American-branded beers that have lost their chill to tropical oppression. Faces are mostly familiar around here but when they aren't they come vouched by someone worth their salt; the transportation of cargo through Central America bringing with it a certain caliber of individual, often measured by their time flying for the cartels and the quality of the stories they can regale.

With a stack of creased dollar bills in front of him, Michael Palmer of *Vortex Air*, is perhaps the most well-known pilot flying resupply missions for the Contras. With a mop of sweaty brown hair and disarming sociability, his perpetually relaxed demeanor is a likely condition of the stunning protection he receives from the CIA. For instance, only last month did he make an emergency landing on San Andreas Island after loading up on too much marijuana—seven-hundred pounds of weed being closer to a thousand-pounds when it hasn't fully dried—when the Colombian police detained the plane and discovered that Palmer along with his co-pilot had criminal records. Complaining that he was in fact on a top secret US Government mission and demanding to be released, the police called the State Department who called the CIA who called the Colombian police back and lo and behold, after pushing two-hundred pounds of sweet Mary Jane right onto the tarmac, Palmer promptly took off without reprimand, while giving the authorities a single-fingered salute.

Sitting to his right is Frank Darnold, an old solo Cessna cowboy who mainly delivers cash dropped off at the secret Salvadoran airbase and taking it to Contra camps, mansions owned by members of the FDN such as the Sanchez brothers and Popo Chamarro in Miami, or to banks in the Bahamas for safe keeping. With a bushy moustache and sideburns, and sweat beading his forehead below a damp Confederate flag bandana, Darnold possesses a harmless mumbling self-commentary, almost like having one of those Christian sermon radio channels on in the car but set so low it's barely audible; a result of clocking up two-decades of flying time alone in the cockpit. You could say he's part of the furniture at Ilopango but Darnold is more like the gruff, old resident dog lazily roaming his jungle backyard just waiting to keel over and die without anyone so much as noticing.

Across from Mike Palmer are the newer additions to Ilopango but no less experienced navigating their way around the Gulf: Bill Cooper and Wallace Sawyer. A couple of *Air America* veterans out of Laos and Thailand that Reed has always maintained close ties with, often employing them whenever he scored jobs bigger than he could handle himself. Of course, none have been more lucrative than this NHAO contract to ferry weapons into Nicaragua on behalf of the CIA. For the past three months Cooper and Sawyer have been flying a DC-4 out of Mexico and for the most part landing directly into Contra camps with only the occasional need to swing through Ilopango for refueling.

However, with Felix Rodriguez pursuing the Contra effort with increased gusto, the recently acquired C-123 can deliver more supplies requiring it to be loaded up here. Unlike a DC-4 that can land on smaller runways, the C-123 drops its cargo from the sky, which is where the rather handsome man sitting to Sawyer's left enters the picture. Never caught without a soft pack of *Camels* in his top pocket and one ready to go behind his ear, Eugene Hasenfus is a stocky, rugged man befitting of his occupation as a cargo pusher. With forearms adorned in marine-inspired tattoos and blonde hair shaved to an army brat buzz cut, his crow-eyed gaze and steely grey eyes make him a dead ringer for Clint Eastwood circa *The Good, The Bad, and The Ugly*, if only he were eight-inches taller.

They say still waters run deep, and as a man of few words and slow, deliberate movement it would be easy to think that such a cool and calm exterior hides a more discerning and calculated mind. Far from it, Hasenfus prefers nothing more than the comfort of a bottle of bourbon, the company of his pit bull named Apple Sauce, and the view across Lake Michigan from his log cabin in Marinette, Wisconsin. He's a simple man of simple pleasures, deriving most of his knowledge of current affairs from a *Hustler* magazine often found rolled up in his back pocket.

The last man seated at the table is Leigh Ritch, Palmer's co-pilot and Robin to his Batman. A politely spoken Texan native with thick blonde locks, he met Palmer in jail just outside of Guadalajara, Mexico about five years ago. Ritch was caught at an airstrip stealing a Cessna after losing his to the local cartel three nights prior in a tequila-inspired bet on a rigged *lucha libre* wrestling match. Meanwhile, Palmer had been arrested for drunk and disorderly behavior at a brothel after not paying, claiming that the business transaction was for an allotted amount of time, not when he merely blew his top. Anyhow, Ritch and Palmer got to talking and the two realized they had a lot in common, namely that they were both drug pilots, and the rest was history, as they say.

Clumsily shuffling the cards with gnarled and smoke stained fingers, 'Bill, you're in for a dollar, and Mike you're in for two,' Darnold mutters around a dangling cigarette.

Throwing two wrinkled one-dollar bills into the center of the table and continuing his story, 'So, I'm looking at the five-hundred pounds of weed thinking, my Cessna Buck-Fifty has a load limit of four-hundred and eighty-pounds, what am I gonna do, right. And you fellas gotta remember, I got Miguel fucking Gallardo, the guy who is now the biggest drug kingpin in Mexico, looking at me like I don't know what in the Hell I'm doing. Anyway, he's sees that I'm sweating and says, Well, why did you bring such a small fucking plane? And I says back, Why have you got so much goddamn weed? He looks at me like I'm the saloon drunk and says, This is just what was left over. Now, not only do I gotta think quick here but I need to look smart too, so I turn to my co-pilot and ask him how much he weighs. He says about hundred-and-forty pounds. I say, Well, hotdog, enjoy your holiday in Guatemala and left him there without so much as a peso in his pocket.'

All the men erupt with laughter.

Taking a sip of his lukewarm *Miller Lite*, 'Yeah, that was my first drug flight through the Gulf almost fourteen-years ago now,' Palmer says reminiscently.

Raising a tinned *Loan Star*, 'And here's to another fourteen, Mr. Palmer,' Ritch toasts.

Tilting his bottle, 'Why, thank you, Mr. Ritch.'

'Let's go, Frank, deal these cards,' Bill Cooper moans, squinting across the tarmac. 'I think our plane's almost loaded.'

Tossing the cards one-by-one across the table, 'All right, don't get your knickers in a knot, they're a coming,' he mumbles with his smoke more ash than cigarette.

'Speaking of, how's it feel riding Barry Seal's last bucket?' Palmer asks casually.

Twisting over the back of his chair, 'That's Seal's C-123?' Sawyer wonders.

'Was, of course. He originally purchased it from the CIA, did his thing for a few years before selling it back to them after they cut him loose.'

'That so?' Cooper says thoughtfully behind his cards.

'Funny how everything in this business seems to come full circle,' Ritch muses.

'Yeah, or everything comes back to bite you in the ass,' mumbles Eugene Hasenfus using a folded dollar bill to floss something out between his teeth.

The men all chuckle.

'Seal's plane you say, that there's some bad luck,' Darnold says dully.

'The Hell's wrong with you, Frank?' Palmer reproaches. 'You know better than to say something like that right before a flight.'

Undeterred, Frank Darnold continues tactlessly, 'Don't matter what I say, fact is, that there is the last plane Seal flew for them CIA boys before they had him gunned down.'

'They didn't gun him down,' Ritch says frowning at his cards. 'Escobar's henchmen did for getting the drug lord and his men on camera.'

'Yeah, but the CIA let Escobar know that Seal had done it,' Darnold counters.

'And where to find him,' Eugene Hasenfus adds, struggling to determine if his Wayne Gretzky's make a strong hand or not.

'That's right,' Darnold contends. 'And you can bet your bottom dollar old Gomez here had something to do with it.'

'Gomez?' Cooper says confused.

'Max Gomez, the CIA guy who runs this show,' the old cowboy says like it's common knowledge.

Leaning back in his chair, 'Don't you mean Felix Rodrigo?' asks Cooper.

Scrunching up his wrinkled face, 'Can't say I've heard of a Felix Rodrigo.'

'Well, either of those names is better than I've ever gotten,' Hasenfus complains. 'I only know him as, the man in Costa Rica.'

Throwing six dollar bills into the middle of the table, 'That's because you're a cargo kicker, Gene,' Palmer says slyly.

Leaning on his elbow, 'And what's that supposed to mean?'

Smirking, 'Come on now, you know there's a pecking order.' Raising a flattened hand, 'Throttle jockeys, then sparkies, then junk pushers,' his arm getting lower with each job title.

Giving him a dry look, Eugene Hasenfus blows a long draft of smoke at him in reply.

'Wait on, how can he be the man from Costa Rica if we ain't even *in* Costa Rica?' Darnold questions.

Putting his cards down, 'You sure we're talking about the same fella?' Cooper asks.

'Mexican guy with a genteel look about him only you don't wanna piss on his boots,' Ritch joins the discussion.

'I thought he was Cuban,' Darnold says, ash falling from his cigarette.

Reorganizing his cards, 'Oh, you definitely do not want to get his whiskers in a knot if the stories I've heard can be believed,' Palmer says stoking alarm in the men.

'Like what?' asks Sawyer.

'Oh, like blowing up planes with pilots on board.'

'And their cocaine,' Ritch adds.

'*Geezouchrist,*' murmurs Sawyer.

'Wait,' Cooper says frowning, 'this the guy always tapping that watch of his?'

'That's the one,' Palmer nods.

'What's the deal with that ticker anyway?' Sawyer wonders. 'If it can't tell the time then what's it telling him?'

'I heard it was, Che's?' Palmer says.

'Whose?' Hasenfus asks.

'Che Guevara.'

'The Cuban revolutionary the CIA executed?' Sawyer says, his mouth agape.

Bill Cooper whistles.

'Not the CIA, but Gomez,' Darnold objects.

'You mean Rodrigo,' Sawyer corrects.

'Same thing.'

'When did Guevara die, again?' Cooper asks.

'Late '60's I think,' Sawyer hazards a guess.

'*Sheesh*, twenty years ago and he still wears the watch?'

'A watch that doesn't work, mind you,' Darnold reminds.

'Maybe that's the point,' Palmer says.

'What is?' asks Sawyer.

'Maybe he's not wearing it so it can tell him the time, maybe he's wearing it as a reminder.'

'A reminder for what?' Hasenfus asks with confusion.

'Don't know. Maybe that the things we do go beyond time, last forever. That kinda thing,' Palmer says with an air of casual mystery.

All the men are quiet.

Arriving at the card table, 'You boys are normally worse than a sewing circle,' Foley remarks. 'What's a matter, pussy got your tongues?'

Giving a wry smile, 'We were just talking about old Mr. Costa Rica Felix Max Gomez Rodrigo, here,' Palmer says.

'Rodri-*guez*,' Reed corrects.

'What's that now?'

'Max Gomez and Felix Rodriguez, he's one and the same.'

'Well, I'll be,' Darnold says snuffing out his cigarette into a dish overflowing with butts.

'You know what these CIA guys are like,' Foley adds, 'a different name and a different handshake for every goddamn person they meet.' Then, spitting a glob of brown saliva, 'Terry Reed, let me introduce Mike Palmer and Leigh Ritch of *Vortex Air*, and aerosplat extraordinaire, Frank Darnold.'

'Hey, Terry,' Cooper says, 'did you know that plane of yours was Seal's last ride?'

A little surprised, 'Is it now?' Reed queries.

'Sure was,' Palmer informs. 'Let me guess, that CIA contractor, Harold Doan, sold that C-123 to you?'

'Now, how would you know that?' Reed says with a curious smile.

'Because Doan picks up just about every craft on the airways down here. The CIA bankroll him so if there's a plane that needs to be got, he goes and gets it, no fuss no muss. And he deals planes faster than Frank deals cards.'

The men chuckle, while Darnold mutters something indiscernible.

'Interest you in a *Miller*, Mr. Reed?' Palmer says pulling a beer from a small blue cooler by his feet.

'Thanks but maybe next time,' Reed says warmly.

'That our flight path?' Bill Cooper asks, seeing a map tucked under his arm.

'Sure is.' Handing it to Cooper, 'You boys have a good flight and I'll see you back in Vera Cruz.'

After forty-minutes of routine flight time, the C-123 piloted by Bill Cooper, Wallace Sawyer, and cargo kicker, Eugene Hasenfus starts its descent in preparation for their first of three airdrops today. With the Contras having recently pushed across the border, it has become vital to keep the camps well supplied so they can continue menacing the sparse Sandinista military that are struggling to keep tabs on the rebel forces' guerrilla movements.

After two passes of where their drop point should be, Cooper angles the pitch of the plane to drop altitude and get a better look.

'Ain't we getting a little low?' Sawyer says.

'I know, but how else in the Hell are we gonna find this drop point?' Cooper says searching the thick jungle to his left. 'That damn Bermudez is always moving his camps about down here.'

Looking out to his right, 'I didn't think he'd made it this far south,' Sawyer says thoughtfully.

Frowning, 'Ah heck, lemme see if the kicker can see anything.'

Leaning over a crate of weapons with the green quilted blanket blurring by below, Eugene Hasenfus is casually smoking a cigarette, while perusing the pages of a *Hustler* magazine with unperturbed placidity despite the roar of the C-123's twin engines filling the cargo hold through the open tail door. Having been the cargo kicker on a thousand flights for the CIA's *Air America* operation in Laos, these Contra runs are as easy as delivering the morning paper in comparison and the impending short free-fall out of the back so unlikely he doesn't bother wearing a chute anymore.

'Hey, Gene,' Cooper crackles into the kicker's headphones, *'you seen our drop zone wiz past back there?'*

Taking the cigarette from his lips and lowering the mouthpiece, 'I ain't been looking,' he says tilting his head to get a better view of the page he's on.

'Well, put down that damn nudie magazine and have a look would ya, otherwise we're gonna be running circles up here.'

With almost dramatic bothersome, Hasenfus folds the *Hustler* closed and begins walking towards the rear of the plane, keeping a hand on each crate as he goes. Coming into greater view as the air whips at his clothes is the spectacular lush jungles of northern Nicaragua: a breathtaking patchwork of undulating green dotted here and there by crystal blue lakes or grey rock faces where mountains have eroded to vertical cliffs, and when the clouds depart and the sun shines unabated, the canopy brightens suddenly like hot water blanching florets and somehow encouraging greater vibrancy in the rainforest than there was but a moment before.

Flicking his cigarette into the air, Hasenfus casually stands on the hinge of the open tail door searching for the Contra camp below.

Back in the cockpit, 'Hey, I'm spotting something shiny on our two-o'clock,' Sawyer says uneasily.

'Check the map again, that may be us,' Cooper directs.

Grabbing a creased map and holding a compass against crudely drawn lines, Wallace Sawyer squints trying to determine their location. Then, looking back out of the window his eyes go wide seeing the silent but unmistakable flash of cannon fire.

'Oh, no,' he says, the words escaping like a whisper.

Ba-boom, ba-boom, ba-boom, ba-boom.

The deep thud of an S-60 anti-aircraft gun rounds off sending shockwaves through the trees around it and birdlife fleeing en masse. Piercing the plane's underbelly and shattering the cockpit windows, brass foot-long shells rip through the nose of the plane like knifing holes in Swiss cheese.

'Christ in Hell!' Cooper yells pulling up and away as shattered glass peppers his face like infuriated confetti with a score to settle.

The instrument panel sparks violently with orange and red lights flashing and alarms blearing throughout the craft. The sudden bank sending Hasenfus cartwheeling across a crate and landing on the other side of the cargo train with the wind knocked out of him.

Bleeding from dozens of cuts, 'Mayday! Mayday! We're taking flak!' Cooper yells into the radio. 'I repeat, we are taking enemy fire!'

Turning to his co-pilot, Cooper grimaces seeing that a shell has torn Sawyer in half from hip to shoulder.

Ba-boom, ba-boom, ba-boom, ba-boom, ba-boom.

A second barrage of shells takes out the right engine in a fiery explosion, forcing the plane out of its climb and immediately into a starboard leaning final phase of gravity's rainbow.

Pulling hard on the controls and almost blind with blood in his eyes, Cooper's arms are at breaking point, 'We're going down! I repeat—we're going down!' Then shouting over his shoulder, 'Gene, if you're back there, evac now cos' we're not gonna make it!' His voice full of restrained terror as a pilot's worst fear comes to fruition.

Holding onto a rail in the fuselage, Hasenfus's feet momentarily lift off the ground as the plane suddenly dips in altitude, while the view of the jungle below disappears and is replaced with an empty blue sky. Then, gravity returning like the bottoming-out of a roller-coaster loop and the g-force pulling low and hard in his gut, Hasenfus looks dejectedly up at the parachute packs hanging behind the cockpit, realizing the impossibility of reaching one, strapping it on, and jumping from the plane in time. With the howling wind yanking at him in what feels like an appeal to accept the obviousness of his fate, the veteran kicker notices the cargo release lever and immediately recognizes his only way off of this doomed aircraft is to ride one of these crates and hope to Jesus Almighty for a sprinkling of divine intervention.

Fighting the accelerating descent of this now thirteen-ton metal weight hurtling towards its impending jungle grave, Hasenfus reaches for the handle and yanks on it, releasing the cargo train carrying everything from guns to landmines to medicine. One by one the crates roll along their track and begin dropping out of the rear of the craft with their chutes deploying like the cosmic hoods of box jellyfish; the thin blue atmosphere their surrogate ocean.

Leaping onto a crate with a passing hope it's not filled with Claymore, Eugene Hasenfus hunkers down against his wooden ride and grips the chute straps with white-knuckled intensity. Feeling eerily similar to Major Kong in *Dr Strangelove*—minus the willing exuberance—Hasenfus is jettisoned from the C-123 and as his parachute opens so begins his breathtaking fall from grace, while descending with him is what will later become the fateful proof of America's covert and corrupt cooperation in the Contra revolution.

With its wing engulfed in flames and leaving a trail of black smoke suspended in the air, Hasenfus watches from his windy vantage the thick jungle swallow the plane whole before belching a ball of fire in gratitude for the offering. After a passing thought for Bill Cooper and Wallace Sawyer, and with a thousand-feet to go until he perhaps meets his maker, Eugene's focus returns to his pressing predicament.

Kneeling on the crate with the wind assaulting him, Hasenfus hastily recalls that low-velocity cargo drops at a speed of twenty-eight feet per second, and a skydiver at landing has a drop speed of twenty-five feet—a negligible difference, one would hope—however, two major concerns spring to mind. The first and perhaps most crucial, is he riding low-velocity cargo? Higher-velocity cargo falls at over seventy feet per second, and if that's the case than he may as well be Major Kong at this point because that's an impact that'll shoot his asshole out of his nose and pop his head off like a champagne cork along the way. His second concern is that if he is in fact fortunate enough to be riding low-velocity cargo, a crate of weapons drops straight down like a ship dropping anchor whereas a skydiver glides into a smooth landing. And no matter how you slice it, that's going to hurt.

Five-hundred feet to go. Can he jump off? Then what? No, that's stupid. The jungle floor is rushing at him. Maybe he is riding high-velocity cargo after all. And maybe he is sitting on four-hundred pounds of Claymore mines and when he hits the turf, he's going to go *kaboom!* anyway. Is that how Claymore works?

'Come on, Jesus,' Hasenfus muses, surprised by his own calm.

Three-hundred feet now and a pair of lime Pacific parakeets fly effortlessly by, ignorant of his ensuing dilemma.

'Cheeky bastards,' the cargo kicker mutters.

Peering over the side of his ride, Hasenfus is hit by a sudden rush of nerves. Trees and branches and even the jungle floor itself are now clear and distinct, while the closeness of the canopy puts the speed of his decent into sharper and suddenly more concerning context.

They say fortune favors the brave, and we sure do a fine job of remembering those who take hold of their situation by the scruff and make something from nothing, forging legend and heroic standards humanity can later live by, saying, this is the testicular fortitude man is made of if he is willing to dig so deep inside himself. Muhammad Ali, Neil Armstrong, Douglas MacArthur, Larry Flint. Truth be told, however, this is often an overstatement for throughout history nameless graves score earth's mantle paying tribute to the untold number of poor idiots whose odds were clearly stacked against them despite how courageous, or stupid, their intent. But fortune also favors the foolhardy and desperate through fate's mercurial mistress, Lady Luck, and by such chance, Eugene Hasenfus just so happens to have that tasseled and buxom figure tattooed onto his forearm.

At one-hundred feet his point of impact at last becomes evident. Aiming, or rather falling, smack bang in what will be in any moment the middle of a wide umbrella-like canopy belonging to a giant ceiba tree whose long and slender branches reach out like Mother Nature's primordial embrace. Unlike the movies where an ejected pilot is caught safely by his chute snagging on a tree branch, the crate Hasenfus is riding weighs four-hundred pounds and they penetrate the tree like a cannon ball.

The chute snags but tears instantly, snapping two straps and toppling the crate end over. Suddenly airborne, Hasenfus tumbles through some lighter growth before slamming gut-first into a branch, breaking ribs and what feels like bursting his spleen, before crashing his way down the eighty-foot tree from branch to branch like a marble in a pinball machine. Hitting the ground with a bone-breaking thud, he lies unconscious for a period of time unknown to him, blood leaking from a number of places and pooling in the dirt beneath him.

Later, dazed and confused and slipping in and out of consciousness, Hasenfus barely registers the blurry figures standing over him. Wincing when one of them pokes him with the end of a rifle, he knows he's broken bones, several of them. As for his rescuers, they're military, of that he can tell. And Spanish speaking too. Though the important question remains: are they Contras or Sandinistas? He'll soon find out. There is one thing he is certain of though and that is he is alive. A mythical wreckage rider who will live to tell the tale. Wait till the boys here about this one, Hasenfus muses through cracked and bloody teeth before going blank again.

XXX

THE BLONDE GHOST

Shards of daylight fall across an oak dining table from between cream velvet vertical blinds obscuring the view of an indiscernible downtown Latin city. A crystal blue bay twinkles in the distance framed by tall colorless buildings, while a lush green strip of parklands hugs the coastline before disappearing into what appears to be a cobble-stoned district owing to the city's historic past.

Sitting in the dark with a phone to his ear, the Blonde Ghost rubs his temple pensively, while spread before him are newspapers from a variety of Latin American countries—*The Buenos Aires Herald, Havana Sun, The Rio Times,* and Nicaragua's *La Prensa*—all reporting the apparently irrefutable proof that the United States and the CIA have been supporting the Contra revolution.

It's been three days since the fateful downing of *Southern Air Transport's* C-123 and the resulting capture of Eugene Hasenfus who, up until the contents of these articles, had been detained by the Sandinista Government with neither private government wire or public statement as to his condition or what he was doing on board an aircraft flying over northern Nicaragua.

Of course, Felix knew within an hour that the plane had gone down, and by that evening received intel that Hasenfus had indeed survived and been captured; an outcome worse than his untimely death if only he had obligingly perished. What Felix, and by extension Colonel North, Director Casey, Admiral Poindexter, Richard Secord, and the Blonde Ghost didn't know was firstly, and most crucially, what cargo had survived the crash, and secondly, how much Hasenfus could divulge about the secret involvement of the CIA supporting the Contras. And, according to these front-page articles, quite a lot had both survived and been divulged.

Poor Eugene Hasenfus who, despite being a surprisingly decorated air freight crewmen of admirable loyalty and patriotism, will inevitably fall victim to the unsurmountable US Defense Force's unwavering deniability, and in such process of speaking his truth will he be met with stonewall after stonewall discrediting his character, reputation, and above all his clear misunderstanding of what missions he was carrying out and for whom, because that is how the Administration and its agencies not only protects itself but protects the American people.

But one man's word against the might of the United States' most revered and covert organization isn't worth the air it'll take him to say it, and yet say it he will until he realizes the betrayal his country will show him isn't half as bad as the emotional and financial ruin he'll experience for staying true to that word and, perhaps most tragically as to its rarity in life, the truth will not set him free but bury him.

As for what physical evidence managed to survive the fiery wreck, well that has put the aforementioned gentlemen in some rather hot water.

Sighing, 'I really don't know what you're asking me, Ollie,' the Ghost says flatly. 'You know there's nothing I can do to help you now.'

'Can't we stop it?'

'Stop what?'

'The press from running it?' the Colonel says desperately. *'Or, or say that it's just Sandinista lies?'*

Leaning forward in his chair as if to make his point clearer, 'Ollie, do you know what they have? They have a crashed plane registered to *Southern Air Transport*, a shell company might I remind you, receiving a NHAO contract that you authorized to deliver non-congressionally approved weapons to support a foreign revolution. They also have in their possession crates of those weapons belonging to *Machinery International*, another CIA run outfit, but most crucially, they have a little black book that somehow survived that crash where written inside are CIA codenames, secret airstrip locations, offshore bank account numbers, and of all things phone numbers belonging to offices in Washington for Christ's sakes. So, no, Ollie, there is no stopping it.'

The Colonel crunches his molars, *'But they're your goddamn weapons, Ted! Weapons the Enterprise purchased and packaged.'*

'And because of you that's now a problem that Richard and I are going to have to solve. But unlike you, we have layers of protection. Do you remember when I told you at the start of all of this about insuring yourself, Ollie?'

Silence.

'I said, however many layers you think you need to put between you and the illegality of what you're doing, you'll need more. Now, not only have you failed to do that but you've been recklessly cavalier over the last year signing checks your position can't cash.'

'Is that so? And yet you've happily benefited from the significant increase in weapons contracts I've pushed through the region, profiteering to no end from my reckless cavaliering.'

'Tsk, tsk, Ollie. This isn't a race. Wars and revolutions are as certain as rain in November. No matter how hard you try to stop them they'll come around again and again whether you like it or not.'

'You told me to push hard, to bypass Congress, to get dirty,' the words coming out like fire.

'That doesn't mean to get stupid, Ollie. But I can see we're well past that.' Switching the receiver to his other ear, 'The goal here was long-term control, not short-term victory. And to that end you have displayed a complete disregard for patience, for planning, and most importantly for protecting yourself and those around you.'

'Well, who gives a rat's ass now, Ted. I need to know what to do to get me out of this shit.'

Almost smirking, 'Don't you get it? There's an investigation and your name is at the top of the list, Colonel. There is no, getting out.'

'Then I'll squash it like I did all the others. I'm the goddamn head of the NSC and this is a matter of national security,' North says trying to convince himself as much as Shackley.

'This isn't the FBI or the DEA looking into a crooked agent, Ollie. This is the Attorney General of the United States investigating whether you have abused Constitutional and Congressional powers. And I'll let you in on a little secret, you have.'

Seething, *'So, what are you saying, Ted?'*

'Look, your only path forward is to deny and misdirect anything to do with supplying the Contras, with the *Enterprise*, the FDN, the airstrips, Hulls ranch, even with our friend Felix. No one will believe traffickers over Administration officials, rest assure. However, you will need to put accountability and blame somewhere in order to absorb the full focus and unlawfulness of what you've been doing. Now, I have already spoken to certain people, people above you, and they are all in agreement that the sale of weapons to Iran for the primary purpose of freeing hostages in Lebanon is all we're going to admit to and all we need to admit to. Everything else never happened.'

'Is that it?' North says furiously. *'That's all you can do for me? This was all your goddamn idea.'*

Shaking his head, 'No one in the Administration is untouchable. Not you, not Director Casey, not even Ron. If you want to be untouched then you need to be outside of the House.'

'Like you?'

'Like a ghost.'

'Jesus,' North says hopelessly. *'Can't you pull some strings?'*

Leaning back and crossing his legs, 'I can pull strings, Ollie, but I'm afraid by the looks of it, you're a dead weight.'

'What's that supposed to mean?'

Shackley doesn't respond.

'What have you heard, Ted?'

Checking his watch, 'Time's up, Ollie. They're coming.'

'Who's coming?'

'A couple of investigators working for Attorney General Meese.'

'What do they want?'

'To search your office, of course.'

There go those molars, grinding enamel so hard Shackley can hear the crunch.

'And I bet you're sitting in that room of yours surrounded by cabinets full of evidence to put you away.'

Jesus,' North whispers.

Shackley can just picture North's face with stun and stupidity written all over it as he looks around his office, crippled by the shock of the sudden collapse of this house of cards the Colonel built for himself, upheld by drug smugglers and fraudsters, and brokering deals with crooked foreign governments and corrupt presidents.

Not that any of this matters to Shackley. He's made his money, lots of it too. And the Ghost is right; what fundamentally drives war or revolution is found deep inside man, something primal, visceral, and by draping uniform and rank over top of it we try to turn it into something righteous, even patriotic, but there is no peace waiting at the end, only one man's desire for power and control over another and so inevitably the storm clouds return and history repeats. The pot of gold at the end of the rainbow belonging to people like Shackley and Secord and Hakim who profit off of gum-boots and umbrellas.

'Ted?' North says after a lingering silence. *'Ted?'* the Colonel says again.

Ignoring the Colonel's persistent and almost juvenile pleas, the Ghost takes the phone from his ear and gently hangs it up, closing the first of many doors on the Contra revolution.

XXXI

THE COLONEL

'Ted?'

There's no response on the other end.

'Ted?' the Colonel repeats with bated breath.

'Goddamn you!' North yells as cold despair turns to boiling rage.

Slamming the phone onto its base he grabs it with both hands and throws it across the room.

With a throbbing vein gorging in the middle of his forehead, the Colonel pulls everything off of the desk in a fit—brass lamp, white marble bust of MacArthur, photo frames, antique cigar box—before slumping down breathless with his back against the desk's side and an incredulous fury igniting inside of him, staggered by the sudden and unjust insinuation that he has done anything other than put the United States and its objectives first and to pursue such endeavors at all costs. His heart is thumping at the preposterous and offensive suggestion that he has somehow jeopardized the Contra effort by recruiting assets absolutely necessary to build and support a military force capable of not only defending Nicaragua from Communism but the entire region too, an accusation he will not tolerate nor accept.

'I didn't do anything wrong,' the Colonel mumbles to himself. 'I did what I was told, what I was supposed to do. People, they don't understand what we have to do to keep this country safe, to keep it from falling apart. The truth is the problem. They can't handle the truth, that's why we do what we do, hide it from them for their own damn good.'

Then, looking up at a cream filing cabinet in the corner of the room, Shackley's words ping inside him.

Rushing over to it and opening the top drawer, North pulls out a manila folder. Flicking through its pages he immediately realizes how bad it looks now that the situation has turned. Throwing the folder onto the floor, he grabs another dossier, furiously scans its pages before tossing it down with the other. This goes on until the first drawer has been emptied and the documents—ranging from private wires, action plans, Contra movements, weapons contracts, briefings, records of agents, agents' assets, agents' assets' assets—lay scattered on the carpet.

Beneath his desk is a small paper shredder, which North drags over to the pile of documents in the middle of the room and begins pushing papers through.

'Come on, come on,' he says irritated by the painstaking slowness with which the shredder is eating the pages.

Rushing to the door and sticking his head out, 'Fawn, get in here!' North yells to his secretary before going back to the filing cabinet and resuming his frantic scrutiny of now what can only be described as incriminating material.

Appearing at the door, 'Is everything all right, sir?' Fawn asks with concern.

'Close the door. And lock it,' North says sharply.

Confused and flustered she shuts the door behind her, 'What's going on, sir? I heard you shouting.'

'Forget that. Quickly, start shredding those papers.'

Hesitantly, Fawn Hall kneels on the ground next to piles of strewn documents and folders. Holding a dossier in each hand, 'What, you want me to shred all of this?'

North is pulling out folder after folder, quickly scanning their contents before throwing them down at his secretary.

'Yes, yes, all of that!'

'But-but why? What's going on, sir?' she appeals, confused by the erratic nature never before seen in the Colonel.

'They're coming,' North says distractedly.

Tentatively starting to push documents through the shredder, 'Who's coming, sir?'

'Them—Meese's investigators.'

'Attorney General Meese?' Fawn says with alarm. 'Why are they coming here?'

Rushing to another filing cabinet, 'Don't worry about that, just shred those damn files.'

After a moment, 'Is, is destroying these documents illegal, sir?' the secretary asks worriedly.

A sudden knock on the door makes them both turn and freeze.

Muffled voices on the other side can be heard before knocking again.

'Colonel North are you in there? This is Agent Castle and Agent James from the Attorney General's office.'

Motioning for Fawn to shush, North waits to see if perhaps they'll leave.

Knocking again, *'Sir, I advise you to open this door.'*

Crunching his molars, 'I'm busy!' North shouts before gesturing for Fawn to keep shredding documents.

'Colonel North, we have direct orders from Attorney General Meese to enter your office and take into our immediate possession documents pertaining to the Nicaraguan Contras,' a voice yells.

'Why? So you can put American soldiers and agents' lives at risk?'

'That isn't for us to decide, Colonel.'

North completely removes a bottom filing cabinet drawer and empties it right into his secretary's lap, 'I don't know anything about that C-123 that got shot down!' he shouts trying to buy time.

'Again, Colonel, that is none of our business. Now, will you please open this door!'

Kneeling down, North begins stuffing the already loaded shredded with more documents causing the machine to groan with the pressure.

The banging on the door, this time with greater urgency, makes the secretary gasp.

With his forehead beading with sweat, 'Don't worry, Fawn. They're here for me. You won't be in any trouble, I promise you,' North tries to calm.

Then, remembering the black leather ledger North stowed in a secret drawer of the walnut table, he rushes over and retrieves it.

Pausing and staring at it momentarily, he realizes this item alone is perhaps the single most incriminating piece of evidence against him, against the NSC, even the CIA and it, above all else, needs to be destroyed.

Looking at the paper shredder desperately, there's no way it can chew through a leather diary, while tearing out handfuls of pages will take more time than he has.

'Colonel North! Open this door now!'

Pulling Fawn to her feet, 'Here,' he says frantically.

'What?'

'Take it!' North says with eyes that are white and unblinking.

'What? Where?' his secretary stammers nervously.

'Anywhere!' he says sternly, stuffing the ledger into the waistline of her skirt before roughly buttoning-up her jacket to conceal it. 'Don't tell me where. If I don't know then I can't lie.'

'But, sir, what if I—'

'We're coming in, Colonel!' the voice cuts her off.

The banging is replaced with the unmistakable sound of someone kicking in the door, and with each hit the hinges heave in their timber grooves.

'Quickly, stand over by the door and don't say anything,' North directs his secretary. 'Just slip out when they're talking to me.'

'I—I,' Fawn stutters.

'Listen,' he says grabbing her by the shoulders, 'you haven't anything to worry about. You don't know what's in any of this stuff. You were just following my instruction to shred these documents, that's it.'

Another kick and the door is about to come in.

'All right, quickly now, stand over there,' he says shoving her aside before vigorously running his fingers through his hair and straightening his shirt to neaten his messy and flustered appearance.

Crack! The lock on the door finally gives way, splintering as it violently swings open, hanging barely by its now busted hinges.

Storming in frustrated by the Colonel's belligerent reluctance to cooperate, Agent Castle looks like an angry parent ready to scold a child for putting *Crayola* all over the walls. However, seeing a mound of documents and folders piled around a shredder still painfully chewing its way through a wad of pages, the Agent's intent quickly shifts to one of questioning.

Putting his hands on his hips, 'What do you think you're doing?' Agent Castle says astonished by the clear attempt to conceal responsibility.

'Protecting our goddamn country, you pencil neck weasel,' North spits.

Noticing Fawn Hall standing frozen in the corner of the room with her arms wrapped nervously around her, 'Who are you?' asks Castle.

'She's my secretary,' North answers.

Squinting, 'Get out.'

North swallows as Fawn hurries out of the room, knowing that's at least one bullet he's dodged.

Squatting by the shredder, Agent James eyes the documents attempting to be destroyed, 'So, the reports from the Sandinista Government about that C-123 are true then, Colonel?' he says glancing up.

'That depends. Are you going to believe Communist liars or the people trying to lead this country?'

Raising his eyebrows, 'Well, it would appear you are destroying evidence. Sir,' James states plainly.

To question Colonel North's loyalty to his country would be a grave mistake. He understands more than most not only what is at stake but also what must be done. It's far too easy for people at home—be they contrarians, anti-war protestors, or peace-loving lefties—to truly grasp the harsh realities of political and military maneuvering to keep this country at the top of the food chain. North's fundamental flaw, however, is his inability to distinguish between his own interests and the requirements of the law. Yes, he is a staunch defendant of American values yet he simultaneously shows a willingness to controvert them.

'This, this isn't destroying evidence,' North defends spitefully. 'It's keeping people safe. Safe while doing a job ninety-nine percent of the population can't or wouldn't do, that's what this is.'

'That may be so, Colonel,' Castle says, 'but there are rules to abide by, and if we don't adhere to those rules than we are no better as a country than the authoritarian and fascist regimes we are trying to defend ourselves against.'

Narrowing his eyes, 'How dare you imply I am doing anything but putting the democratic freedoms of the American people first,' North asserts.

Frowning, 'And yet the manner in which you are so recklessly trying to defend those freedoms are in fundamental conflict with democracy itself. You are a servant of the people, Colonel, not a freewheeling judge, jury, and executioner of foreign policy.'

'That's easy for you to say when you don't know what's happening on the frontline of battle, how ill-equipped the soldiers we are supporting are.'

'And by frontline, you mean the foreign territories where US intervention has not been authorized? And soldiers *you* are arming without Congressional approval.'

Crunching his molars, 'Allegedly,' North says through gritted teeth.

Shaking his head, 'You're some piece of work, Colonel.'

Standing behind the Agent are two office assistants holding empty cardboard boxes. Agent Castle tells them to begin collecting the files, including what is inside the shredder.

'You're making a big mistake,' North threatens mildly. 'Have you spoken to Director Casey? He'll have your ass for breakfast over this.'

Peering up from the documents in his hands, Agent James glances hesitantly from North to Castle, 'He doesn't know,' he says quietly.

Frowning, 'Don't know what?' North asks.

Clearing his throat, 'Director Casey was rushed to hospital earlier today,' Castle says delicately.

'What, what do you mean?' the Colonel says shocked by the news.

'They think it's a stroke,' the Agent offers. 'I'm afraid I don't know any more than that.'

The ground sways beneath the Colonel's feet. Director Casey isn't only North's trusted superior whose judgement and guidance through this mess would be invaluable, but he's also a friend and mentor, a man the Colonel has looked up to for the better part of a decade, and whose unwavering and unforgiving approach to foreign affairs is as subtle as a hammer you don't see coming.

Staggering to the cream-cushioned cherry-oak settee, the Colonel slumps down, his mind foggy and the voices in the room suddenly muffled and distant.

Rubbing his temples, 'The Ghost,' North mumbles. 'This is all his fault.'

Furrowing his brow, 'What did you say, Colonel?' Castle inquires taking a step closer.

North looks up at him blankly, not realizing he spoke aloud.

'Are you suggesting Theodore Shackley had something to do with all of this?' the Agent questions.

North purses his lips and crunches his molars, his bottled rage returning and yet the target of his fury is a phantom with voice but no physical body to share the weight of failure and consequence.

Chuckling with disbelief, 'Preposterous,' Castle says dismissively.

Everywhere and nowhere.

After a few minutes, the Agents and their office assistants finish rummaging through what's left inside the filing cabinets and drawers of Colonel North's office and leave the room looking ransacked as though burgled. Agent Castle says something but his words are empty and soundless.

Blinking and coming-to, Director Casey, North thinks to himself.

Walking to where the phone is lying on the floor, the Colonel turns it upright and places the receiver back onto its slot.

It starts ringing immediately.

'Hello,' North says hoarsely.

'It's me, Clarridge. I've been trying to reach you for the last hour, where have you been?'

Crunching his molars, 'Busy.'

'Have you heard about Bill?'

'Only a moment ago.'

'Well, it's bad.'

'How bad?'

'He's non-responsive.'

Frowning, 'What does that mean?'

'It means he can't talk, Ollie. His brain's bleeding out and there ain't no one behind the wheel.'

'Jesus,' North whispers.

'So?'

'So, what?'

'Between Southern Air's plane going down and Bill's emergency, you need to have that phone attached to your hip.'

'Oh. I, I had Messe's men here?' North says distantly.

'Whose?'

'Attorney General Meese, he sent some investigators around just now.'

'Christ. What did they want?'

Looking around the messy room, 'Evidence.'

'Those goddamn backstabbing sonsuvbitches. What'd they take?'

'A lot.'

After a quiet few moments, *'What are you going to do?'*

Sighing, 'Trust in the Lord and get a good lawyer, I suppose,' the Colonel says blankly.

XXXII
THE MAN IN COSTA RICA

Holding the phone against his ear with a dour look on his face, Felix stares solemnly out of his office window. Gently pulling down on a dusty venetian blind to get a better view of the airstrip, he watches a small Cessna take flight into a cloudless blue sky, military trucks zigzag around the runway carrying supplies to awaiting cargo planes, and in the shade of a hangar men still playing cards despite the downing of *Southern Air's* C-123 four days ago.

'I understand, Colonel,' Felix says softly before slowly putting the receiver on its base with a heavy click.

'What did he say?' Raphael asks eagerly sitting next to Ilopango's head of logistics, Luis Posada, who looks rather indifferent about the repercussions regarding recent events.

Standing in front of a wall adorned with inventory papers, flight logs, supply-chain maps for sea and air, and colored pushpins anchoring black and white photos of key Contra figures, Felix puts his hands on his hips and sighs.

'He says our time here is over.'

Waiting, 'That's it?' asks Raphael in disbelief.

Sitting heavily in his chair, '*Si*, that's it,' Felix says looking dejectedly over a messy desk stacked with documents and folders.

Standing abruptly, 'I told you North was going to fuck this up,' Raphael fumes. 'After all this time we finally get this close and now he wants to pull the pin!'

Raising his eyebrows, 'So much of this operation was illegal, Chi Chi, there is nothing we can do,' Felix replies unemotionally.

'But we are here, in Central America, with all the pieces in place to keep going,' Raphael implores. Then, going to the window and raising the blinds, 'Look out there. Planes and pilots ready and waiting to deliver guns and supplies to thousands of Contra fighters. For them it is not over,' he beseeches.

Raising his eyebrows, 'And all of those planes and pilots and weapons are here because of the NSC and CIA. We have no choice but to pack up. We were never meant to be here in the first place,' Felix says defeated.

'*¡Maldita sea!*' Raphael spits clinching his fist. 'Five years, Felix. Five years of hard work and now the fruits of our labor gone, just like that. The Sandinistas stand defiant and Cuba—'

'Will always be Cuba,' Felix interrupts delicately.

Seething, 'No. We can go on,' Raphael points to Posada. 'The factories, the airstrips, the FDN, the coca. They're all still there and there is still the personnel to continue the cause.'

Felix pinches the bridge of his nose, 'There will be an investigation, probes sent to look into every nook and cranny of this campaign.' Cradling his hands in his lap, 'The only thing for us to do is ensure all evidence of our involvement here disappears.'

Shaking his head, 'Unbelievable,' his aide says turning away and looking out of the window.

'Full deniability, Chi Chi. That is what we have sown into every pocket of what we have done down here, and it is the one thing that allows us to pick up the fight again one day.'

'One day? *Mierda,*' Raphael says dismissively.

Smiling sadly, 'You are forgetting I am an Agency man. Gone are my days of working for assassination squads, for Brigade 2506, for the Ghost. Though it has felt like it at times, I am not a rogue mercenary. I have superiors to answer to, and they themselves accountable to the American people.'

Turning around, 'Why cushion them? Why must they be kept in the dark about what really goes on in this world? America, God's country,' Raphael says satirically, 'the great democracy built upon lies and domestic propaganda.'

Frowning, 'Calm down, Chi Chi.'

Pointing his finger, 'No. If the America people hadn't been led down a path of deception about how it has become the great nation it is then perhaps the struggle to stamp out Communism wouldn't be made so difficult for us.'

'What's that they say?' Posada offers. 'When you forget how the pig is killed you like the taste of pork better.'

'What's that supposed to mean?' asks Raphael.

'It means most people don't really want to know the truth. They just want to be reassured that what they already believe is true. And for *Americanos*, what they don't know can't hurt them, and the *Americano* Government likes to keep it that way. Isn't that right, Felix?'

Leaning back in his chair, 'The inner workings of global politics is not for the layperson, Luis. The benefit of keeping people uninformed to facts beyond their reckoning often outweighs the benefit of trying to make them understand that which they cannot comprehend,' Felix contends despite being in no mood to discuss politics.

'And yet here you are,' Posada continues, 'five years into a covert campaign to prevent Communism spreading in Latin America, which one would think the American people would eagerly support, but alas such knowledge is kept from them and now that they peak behind the curtain, you run and hide for fear of the consequences that may paint the country in bad light.'

Pursing his lips and thinking, 'I do not believe any citizenry would fully appreciate or understand the lengths their leaders and agencies must go to preserve such freedoms and liberties, especially as one has in the United States,' Felix says plainly. 'Freedom comes at a cost.'

'And it appears the price is ignorance,' Posada says smugly.

Sitting upright, 'What is wrong with you two?' Felix snaps. 'You don't think these circumstances pain me no less? I too wanted our efforts in Nicaragua to lead to a move on our beloved Cuba. Success against the Sandinistas would demonstrate the value and necessity of giving Communism no place to thrive, justifying a renewed crusade against Castro. And now what?' he says eyes wide and unblinking. 'You are right, Luis. We must run off with our tail between our legs. You think I don't see that?' he adds furiously.

The men are quiet.

After a moment, 'What about Operation 40?' Posada questions.

'What about it?' Felix asks.

'Forty men is all it took to attack numerous Cuban interests abroad, not to mention put in motion the Bay of Pigs Invasion.' Raising his eyebrows, 'Maybe you have been with the Agency so long and forgotten what the few are still capable of achieving.'

Shaking his head, 'Operation 40 is dead, so I do not follow what you are suggesting, Luis?'

'It isn't dead, it's in hiatus. Start it back up again?'

'How?' Felix says annoyed by Posada's vague pitch.

'The CIA needs all evidence of its involvement with the Contras destroyed, yes? Well, there is a helluva lot of money stashed in dozens of Salvadoran safe houses. Financing who's left of the 40 is much easier than supporting thousands of soldiers, no?'

Quintero gives Felix an inspired look.

'Who is left?' Felix inquires, dubious at the idea as much as that there are original members still capable of carrying out secret and coordinated attacks.

'Me, Guillermo Novo, Gaspar Jiménez, Villo Gonzalez, Eugenio Martinez.' Shrugging, 'That's more than enough.'

Scoffing, 'Gonzalez and Martinez were both involved with Watergate.'

'And both pardoned by Reagan, so what?'

'They're tainted. The CIA can never involve itself with these men again,' Felix explains.

Posada leans forward, 'I'm not talking about the CIA, I'm talking about you, Felix. We owe our lives to Cuba, to our comrades killed or captured and who remain prisoners on their own Mother Land. We owe it to Orlando Bosch who sits in a jail cell, rotting away.'

Frowning, 'Bosch went too far,' Felix says thoughtfully.

'No. It is we who did not go far enough.'

Resting back in his chair and looking to the cracked and peeling ceiling, 'There is a fine line between terrorism and violent protest, Luis. Orlando Bosch undermined the righteousness of his endeavors by killing too many innocent people. Far too many.'

'Is that what the *Americanos* have taught you?' Posada jabs.

Felix doesn't respond.

Laughing bitterly, 'You have indeed been with the Agency too long, old friend.' Then, his tone becoming serious, 'It is unjust to apply the moral law of conscience to us Cuban liberators because the *Americano* conscience is not the same as the *Cubano* conscience. The *Americanos* have not lived through what we have lived through, they have not lost what we have lost. It is too easy to call me or Orlando or Gaspar a terrorist simply because we fought against tyranny and oppression to a bloodier end, that our desire to pursue justice for Cuba runs deeper than it does in others, then it does in you. And what makes matters worse, the CIA actively support and finance people like us until such time, in their eyes, they see that our cause is no longer necessary to them or that our actions have gone too far, not realizing we have no alternative but to fight or die, and they turn on us, denounce us, deny their complicities in order to uphold *their* moral law when it suits them. Well, what about us, Felix? How are we meant to sleep at night knowing our fight is not over, that what stands in our way is the moral standard of some other country that does not know what it is to be us?'

Felix is quiet, his eyes moving from Posada to Raphael and back again before looking at the piles of paperwork on his desk as he considers the undeniable weight of his comrade's words.

Sensing the effectiveness of his persuasion, Posada continues, 'There is money and explosives stored throughout El Salvador that only we know where, enough for us to spend the next decade taking aim at Castro and his men that tout the treachery of Cuba and the continued oppression of its people,' he says with measured passion. 'The louder a war gets the quicker it is over. The Contra revolution was kept quiet and look how little it achieved for all the years it simmered away. Now, Cuba must wait again?' Shaking his head, 'Pretending the US wasn't involved was the *Americanos* biggest mistake here.'

Sighing deeply, 'Perhaps. But these are dangerous times, Luis. The Cold War is as perilous now as it was during Kennedy's presidency. It would be imprudent for the US and its agencies to not act with a certain degree of caution as well as subterfuge, lest we invite international sanction onto ourselves and play right into to Russia's criticism of American foreign affairs.'

Smirking, 'History is full of conspiracies, Felix, and yet possesses truths far stranger than fiction can ever imagine. People tell stories with no regard or distinction for fact. And how can they not? They see things happen with their very own eyes that their Government says never took place, and so the blanks are filled with all manner of conjecture, most of it wrong and yet some of it right.'

Frowning, 'What are you saying, Luis?'

'What I am saying is, the world will know but a fraction of what really took place in Nicaragua, and tales about who was here and what they did will pale compared to the truth. But before the CIA departs, scatter the breadcrumbs of your fare so that others may keep the fight going. And rest assure there will be no harm in doing so for people will say you did when you didn't, and didn't even if you do.'

Looking at Raphael, 'Why must everyone talk to me in riddles?' Felix says dubiously.

Laughing, 'Look at it this way, the safe houses need to be turned over anyway, at least doing this ensures Castro and his followers remain targets in our sights, and at worst I have at least protected *senor* Reagan from impeachment.'

* * *

Leaning on the hood of his jeep parked in front of a plaster-flaked apartment building adorned with a huge sun-faded *Coca-Cola* billboard, Felix and Raphael wait patiently. The sun beats down in a cloudless Salvadoran sky, while church bells ringing softly in the distance remind the CIA Agent to check his antique watch. Tapping the glass face gently, Felix sighs.

Coming out of a doorway with a duffle bag in each hand, Luis Posada adds them to the full trunk of an idling light-blue Range Rover. Slamming the door shut and banging on the window, the four-wheel drive pulls off of the curb and disappears into the midday traffic.

Walking over to Felix, 'Okay, that's it, the last safe house emptied.'

Taking a small notebook from his shirt pocket, 'How much money was there?' Felix asks.

Lighting a cigarette, 'Two-fifty,' Posada mumbles.

Scribbling it down and adding up the numbers, 'Brings the total to two-and-a-half million,' he says with a raise of his eyebrows. 'Any files?'

Turning back to the doorway, two men exit the building holding boxes of paperwork and folders, 'That's it there,' Posada gestures.

Watching as the men put the boxes into the back of a burgundy station wagon, Felix is filled with an inexpressible emptiness. Of course, all campaigns and missions come to a close, but often there is a knowable end—a target eliminated, a coup toppled, the success or failure of a propaganda initiative swaying an election—but the cessation of the US's involvement with the FDN and the Contras has come suddenly and without expectation. Years of painstaking work and strategy ruined by the singular crash of a plane; one of thousands that has crisscrossed the region and yet one going down is all it took to end the Contra revolution. Sure, the FDN will continue to fight for there still thrives an array of Nicaraguan exiles of immense stature and political power, and who still have close ties with the cocaine trade, but it has taken the CIA and NSC the better half of a decade to make the Contras what they are today, and without this US support the Contra cause will likely sink like a flooding ship.

'*Bueno*. Make sure it's all destroyed, Luis,' Felix says flatly.

Taking the cigarette from his mouth, 'Hey, cheer up, Felix. Okay, so the Sandinistas will remain in power for a few more years but they will not go unassailed, and now neither will Castro, thanks to you.'

Felix looks unimpressed, struggling to see any real silver lining and especially not with putting rogue assassination squads back into business.

Putting his foot on the bumper and resting his arms on his knee, 'As much as you feel that your actions may go against that conscience of yours, this is as good for Cuba as it is for America.'

'And how's that?' Felix asks with a frown.

Blowing smoke, 'The other side wins only when you stop fighting, Felix. Look, these safe houses had to be turned over anyway and as much as you feel torn about who profits and who suffers as a consequence, remember that there are many people other than *Americanos* in this world fighting for their own justice.'

Felix nods, appreciating the complex tapestry of the modern world and how there is no escaping the ongoing difficulties societies face as bloody histories seep into the bed sheets of new days, the past as present now as it will be in the future and with it the furious fight of those who've been left out in the cold demanding to be given back what was once theirs. And yet who decides which path is the right one? How can there exist a moral law of conscience, while there exists moral indifference and apathy? Is justice an elusive dream, just like peace at the end of war?

Posada extends his hand, *'Es hora de despedirse, viejo amigo.'*

Gripping his hand tightly, Felix is filled with a rush of sentimentality; a longing to join the resistance and one day free Cuba as he had when he was younger, and yet the gratitude that he doesn't have to for America is his home now.

'Para Cuba,' Felix says warmly before watching Posada flick his cigarette into the street, climb into an awaiting car and drive off.

Resting his elbow on the door the CIA man looks around thoughtfully.

'Are you getting in?' Raphael asks from the passenger seat.

Thinking for a moment, 'There's an old saying, Chi Chi, that my father used to tell me. A society grows great when old men plant trees whose shade they know they shall never sit in. But I fear we are fast living in a world where man lives only for himself. Worse, for himself at the cost of his children.'

Taking a deep breath and exhaling loudly, 'A hard truth that cannot be denied,' Raphael agrees.

'Do you remember what Bermudez said in the camp that night about there being no end to war?' Felix asks.

Squinting, 'I think so.'

'I was just thinking, maybe he is right only he has it the wrong way around. Perhaps we are already living in a world of shallow dreams precisely because we think we can stop the rain from falling despite standing beneath its very downpour.'

'Now who's talking in riddles,' Raphael jokes.

Felix smiles wryly but is gripped by the sudden blooming of this revelation and continues, 'Bermudez also said, history is a wheel turning, but maybe the wheel needs to be broken to stop it from repeating. All this time we have been trying to make the wheel spin as though if we keep going, keep fighting we will end up somewhere better than where we are now, but all the time ignoring that to make the wheel turn it costs—'

'*Disculpe, senor Americano, tienes un dollar, por favor?*' a little boy says tugging on Felix's shirt.

Giving the boy a quizzical look, 'How did you know I am an American?' Felix asks.

Scratching at a scab on his elbow, 'The way you are standing.'

Raising his eyebrows and smiling, 'And how is it that I am standing in such a way?'

'This is Salvador, *senor*. People who stand on the street doing nothing are either poor or *turista*. And you do not look poor.'

Raphael chuckles from inside the car, 'Seems Luis is right. You have been with the Agency too long, even a *niño* can spot you.'

Shaking his head gladly, 'You know, I have something better than a dollar for you.'

The little boy's eyes swell with delight.

'Here, take this watch,' Felix says unfastening the leather band. 'I'm afraid it doesn't work very well but it is quite old and quite valuable.'

'*Ay, caramba*' the boy whispers taking it in his small dirty hand.

'It belonged to Che Guevara. Do you know who that is?'

'*No, senor.*'

'Well, remember his name and remember that this watch once belonged to him.'

Turning it over and inspecting it, 'Is he a great man?'

Reflecting on the conversation he was having before the boy interrupted them, Felix fumbles for an answer.

'I'm not sure,' he says hesitantly. 'Maybe he was, but he is dead now.'

'Oh.'

Getting on one knee, Felix helps clasp the watch around the little boy's bony wrist, 'Take good care of it, okay?'

'*Si, senor. Gracias.*'

After the boy walks off, 'You are not sure if Che was a great man or not?' Raphael says looking accusingly at Felix over the top of his sunglasses.

Raising his eyebrows, 'Time will remember him, but not us. Is there not greatness in that?' Felix considers.

Narrowing his eyes, 'He was a Communist who would see the free world shackled and on its knees, Felix,' Raphael says in disbelief.

'And how goes our world, eh? Maybe Guevara was trying to break that wheel.'

Raphael gives him a pensive look.

Hoping into the jeep, 'Come on, let's go have a beer,' Felix says warmly. 'It may be a long time until we see each other again, Chi Chi.'

1987

XXXIII
A PRESIDENTS PLEA

Taking a few sips of water, the President sits at the Resolute desk preparing himself to deliver yet another public address relating to the Iran-Contra scandal. This time however, his words will attempt to cushion his involvement in the affair now that the explosive Kerry Hearings have finally concluded.

'Here we go, Mr. President,' a man standing next to the video camera says. 'You're live in three, two—' he says mouthing silently *one* and pointing to the Commander in Chief.

'My fellow Americans, I've said on several occasions that I wouldn't comment about the recent congressional hearings on the Iran-Contra matter until the hearings were over. Well, that time has come, so tonight I want to talk about some of the lessons we've learned. But rest assured, that's not my sole subject this evening. I also want to talk about the future and getting on with things, because the people's business is waiting.

'These past nine months have been confusing and painful ones for the country. I know you have doubts in your own minds about what happened in this whole episode. What I hope is not in doubt, however, is my commitment to the investigations themselves. So far, we've had four investigations—by the Justice Department, the Tower board, the Independent Counsel, and the Congress. I requested three of those investigations, and I endorsed and cooperated fully with the fourth—the congressional hearings—supplying over two-hundred-and-fifty-thousand pages of White House documents, including parts of my own private diaries.

'Once I realized I hadn't been fully informed, I sought to find the answers. Some of the answers I don't like. As the Tower board reported, and as I said last March, our original initiative rapidly got all tangled up in the sale of arms, and the sale of arms got tangled up with hostages. Secretary Shultz and Secretary Weinberger both predicted that the American people would immediately assume this whole plan was an arms-for-hostages deal and nothing more. Well, unfortunately, their predictions were right. As I said to you in March, I let my preoccupation with the hostages intrude into areas where it didn't belong. The image—the reality—of Americans in chains, deprived of their freedom and families so far from home, burdened my thoughts. And this was a mistake.

'My fellow Americans, I've thought long and often about how to explain to you what I intended to accomplish, but I respect you too much to make excuses. The fact of the matter is that there's nothing I can say that will make the situation right. I was stubborn in my pursuit of a policy that went astray.

'The other major issue of the hearings, of course, was the diversion of funds to the Nicaraguan Contras. Colonel North and Admiral Poindexter believed they were doing what I would have wanted done: keeping the democratic resistance alive in Nicaragua. I believed then and I believe now in preventing the Soviets from establishing a beachhead in Central America. Since I have been so closely associated with the cause of the Contras, the big question during the hearings was whether I knew of the diversion. I was aware the resistance was receiving funds directly from third countries and from private efforts, and I endorsed those endeavors wholeheartedly; but—let me put this in capital letters—I did not know about the diversion of funds. Indeed, I didn't know there were excess funds.

'Yet the buck does not stop with Admiral Poindexter, as he stated in his testimony; it stops with me. I am the one who is ultimately accountable to the American people. The admiral testified that he wanted to protect me; yet no President should ever be protected from the truth. No operation is so secret that it must be kept from the Commander in Chief. I had the right, the obligation, to make my own decision. I heard someone the other day ask why I wasn't outraged. Well, at times, I've been mad as a hornet. Anyone would be; just look at the damage that's been done and the time that's been lost. But I've always found that the best therapy for outrage and anger is action.

'I've tried to take steps so that what we've been through can't happen again, either in this administration or future ones. But I remember very well what the Tower board said last February when it issued this report. It said the failure was more in people than in process. We can build in every precaution known to the world. We can design that best system ever devised by man. But in the end, people are going to have to run it. And we will never be free of human hopes, weaknesses, and enthusiasms.

'Let me tell you what I've done to change both the system and the people who operate it. First of all, I've brought in a new and knowledgeable team. I have a new National Security Adviser, a new Director of the CIA, a new Chief of Staff here at the White House. And I've told them that I must be informed and informed fully. In addition, I adopted the Tower board's model of how the NSC process and staff should work, and I prohibited any operational role by the NSC staff in covert activities.

'The report I ordered reviewing our nation's covert operations has been completed. There were no surprises. Some operations were continued, and some were eliminated because they'd outlived their usefulness. I am also adopting new, tighter procedures on consulting with and notifying the Congress on future covert action findings. We will still pursue covert operations when appropriate, but each operation must be legal, and it must meet a specific policy objective.

'The problem goes deeper, however, than policies and personnel. Probably the biggest lesson we can draw from the hearings is that the executive and legislative branches of government need to regain trust in each other. We've seen the results of that mistrust in the form of lies, leaks, divisions, and mistakes. We need to find a way to cooperate while realizing foreign policy can't be run by committee. And I believe there's now the growing sense that we can accomplish more by cooperating. And in the end, this may be the eventual blessing in disguise to come out of the Iran-contra mess.

'And there's another area that will occupy my time and my heart: the cause of democracy. There are Americans still burning for freedom; Central Americans, the people of Nicaragua. Over the last ten years, democrats have been emerging all over the world. In Central and South America alone, ten countries have been added to the ranks. The question is: will Nicaragua ever be added to this honor roll? As you know, I am totally committed to the democratic resistance—the freedom fighters—and their pursuit of democracy in Nicaragua. Recently there's been important progress on the diplomatic front, both here in Washington and in the region itself.

'My administration and the leadership of Congress have put forth a bipartisan initiative proposing concrete steps that can bring an end to the conflict there. Our key point was that the Communist regime in Nicaragua should do what it formally pledged to do in 1979: respect the Nicaraguan people's basic rights of free speech, free press, free elections, and religious liberty. Instead, those who govern in Nicaragua chose to turn their country over to the Soviet Union to be a base for Communist expansion on the American mainland.

'The need for democracy in Nicaragua was also emphasized in the agreement signed by the five Central American presidents in Guatemala last Friday. We welcome this development and pledge our support to democracy and those fighting for freedom. We have always been willing to talk; we have never been willing to abandon those who are fighting for democracy and freedom. I'm especially pleased that in the United States diplomatic initiative, we once again have the beginnings, however uncertain, of a bipartisan foreign policy. The recent hearings emphasized the need for such bipartisanship, and I hope this cautious start will grow and blossom.

'These are among the goals for the remainder of my term as President. I believe they're the kinds of goals that will advance the security and prosperity and future of our people. I urge the Congress to be as thorough and energetic in pursuing these ends as it was in pursuing the recent investigation.

'My fellow Americans, I have a year and a half before I have to clean out this desk. I'm not about to let the dust and cobwebs settle on the furniture in this office or on me. I have things I intend to do, and with your help, we can do them.

'Good night, and God bless you.'

(Transcript of President Reagan's public address on August 12, 1987)

EPILOGUE

Flying low over South Central at twilight, a police helicopter zooms above hundreds of houses evenly gridlocked across indistinguishable streets—all with hundreds in their names—glowing in the night behind barred windows and locked doors.

His forehead beading with sweet, a man wrinkles his brow as his eyes look to the ceiling, nervously following the muffled sound of the helicopter before the faint wails of a baby crying pulls his attention.

'Yo, Theresa,' he says standing over a kitchen stove, 'I think I hear the baby.'

On a nearby yellow laminate kitchen table, a drawn looking woman drops her spoon into a warm bowl of macaroni and cheese and closes her eyes.

'Baby,' the man repeats distractedly, 'the baby's crying.'

Pushing herself up from the table, 'I know. I heard you the first time, Marcus,' she says tiredly.

Walking barefoot down a carpeted hallway with her oversized and threadbare tee shirt hanging loosely off of one shoulder, she passes through a dimly lit living room hazing with smoke where three men are slouched on matching beige corduroy sofas watching television. Spread across a glass coffee table is a half a pound of weed, cigars, rolling papers, two 9mm handguns, and a set of silver picture frames of a family posing with big smiles.

'Look, there he is,' one man says. 'Turn it up. Let's see what the President's got to say for himself.'

'My fellow Americans, I've said on several occasions that I wouldn't comment about the recent congressional hearings on the Iran-Contra matter until the hearings were over. Well, that time has come, so tonight I want to talk about some of the lessons we've learned.'

Paying no mind to the men, Theresa quietly makes her way through the house to a small dark room at the back. Leaning over the crib and picking up a six-month old baby, she begins swaying in a vain attempt to resettle her.

After a sigh, 'You already awake, my sweet?' the woman says softly, cuddling the infant. 'Maybe you hungry?'

Pulling the collar of her shirt down and exposing a swollen breast, she offers the baby milk. After several frustrating efforts, she gives up.

Stroking the baby girl's soft afro, 'You just wanna come out and see what's going on, don't you, Ivy?' she says soothingly. 'Okay, let's go see what all the fuss is about then.'

Back down a hallway of peeled paint and chipped skirtings, Theresa returns to the living room and gently jiggles baby Ivy in the corner, while watching the end of President Reagan's public address.

'Since I have been so closely associated with the cause of the Contras, the big question during the hearings was whether I knew of the diversion. I was aware the resistance was receiving funds directly from third countries and from private efforts, and I endorsed those endeavors wholeheartedly; but—let me put this in capital letters—I did not know about the diversion of funds. Indeed, I didn't know there were excess funds. Yet the buck does not stop with Admiral Poindexter, as he stated in his testimony; it stops with me.'

(Transcript of President Reagan's public address on August 12, 1987)

'Look at this. That Colonel North and them high up CIA folk got themselves in some real shit now, getting busted and dragging the President into their mess.'

'Whatayou mean dragging him in? You best believe the President knew everything that was going on,' another man says.

'You think so?'

'Nigga, I know so. Why you think he being slyer than Wile E. Coyote. Check it, Reagan went on TV last December and said he didn't know *anything* about weapons for hostages. Then he goes on TV in—what was it, March—and says it was time for him to come clean. Okay, so he admits that he *did know* about selling those weapons for hostages but somehow didn't know that the money for them was being sent to Nicaragua? Yeah, right. Then, we have those piss ass Kerry hearings where North and Poindexter say they were helping the Contras like it was Christmas and they both admitted to shredding documents that had Reagan's signatures on them? Come on, man. If that ain't a God damn cover up then I don't know what is.'

The man raises his eyebrows in reluctant agreement.

'And he's gonna get away with it too.'

'Oh, yeah?'

'Shit yeah, why you think they call him the Teflon President? Ain't nothing stick to this mothafucker.'

'Why was they sending all that money to Nicaragua?'

'To stop the Russians or something. And it was all for nothing because ain't Nicaragua gonna be anything but what them Nicaraguans want it to be.'

'You say, Niggaraguans?' another man says, eyes bloodshot from all of the weed they've been smoking.

'I said, *Ni-car-wahguns*, and you need to get your damn ears checked. Besides, everybody knows that the weapons and money and all that American aid was just a front to let coke come in and out of them jungles.'

'Why they need to do that for?'

'Because the coke money was making ten times what all that Government aid and weapons was making. They needed that drug money more than anything.'

'For real?'

'That's why that skinny pencil neck guy tried to commit suicide last year when this whole thing blew up.'

Squinting, 'Who?'

'Don't you watch the news? McFarlane, I think his name was. He was Reagan's security advisor or something. Yep, when that plane went down, he knew he did wrong and ate all them pills. And the CIA boss, that fat one, Casey, he dead too. Lucky for that North mothafucker he had a stroke or some shit and couldn't say what really went down. That's why the Colonel just sat there and denied all he wanted.'

'True?'

'You know it. That weapons for hostages bullshit wasn't even the half it. Reagan just using that as an excuse and a distraction about what they was really up to. Make no mistake, the Government used all that dope money to pay for whatever they was trying to down there in Central America. Hell, that's how Freeway Ricky made his millions. He was the one selling the CIA coke for the Nicaraguans.'

'Shiiit, he almost made it out too.'

'The Hell he did.'

'The Hell he didn't. Had those motels and shit. Rumor has it he owned over a hundred houses across South Central.'

'And he ain't sleeping in none of them. That nigga got life.'

'A nigga from the street can stray wherever he likes but he'll always belong to the hood, that's all I know.'

'Yeah, and the hood belongs to the damn prison system ever since that war on drugs three-strikes law bullshit this Reagan mothafucker brought in. How a nigga getting caught selling a couple grams of crack is getting put away for the same time that Freeway is for moving thousands of kilos of coke is fucking beyond me.'

'Ain't it all gonna stop soon enough though—the coke from Nicaragua, I mean—now that Freeway's in jail?'

Sniggering, 'Freeway Ricky might be gone but you best believe the crack is here to stay. Coke is still gonna make its way into the country whether there's a war on drugs or the CIA got their fingers in some scandalous shit or not. Okay, maybe—and I do mean maybe—the dope that the CIA were hauling will probably stop, for now, but that Escobar mothafucker just got put on the list of Forbes magazine for the world's richest men. Believe that.'

'Man, imagine being one of the world's richest men from selling cocaine.'

'Yeah, and you ain't gonna be a billionaire from selling dope unless governments are getting their cut to let it in their countries, that's for sure.'

'Shit be crazy.'

'The fucking CIA. More like the Cocaine Importation Agency.'

They all laugh.

After a moment, 'Maybe these CIA folk gonna finally get a taste of what San Quentin or Rikers Island feels like.'

'Yeah right. You can be CIA, DEA, or damn street cops, so long as you white and wearing a uniform, you can have blood on your hands and say you didn't do nothing and they still ain't gonna put you away.'

'That's right. The fucking CIA, Reagan and his whole damn Administration are corrupt as fuck.'

'But I seen those trials with John Kerry, those Reagan boys gonna get the book thrown at them, he said.'

'Oh, you think so? Well, I'll believe that when I see it because I saw the same trials and all I heard was them say, we's were doing it for our country and I can't say that, and I can't say this because of national security and shit. Them niggas ain't getting in any trouble, you watch. Mr. Teflon here and his buddy Bush ain't gonna let their men take no fall, believe that.'

Picking up a joint and lighting its tip.

'Don't smoke that,' Theresa complains. 'I got the baby right here.'

Frowning, 'Well, get your ass up outta here then,' the man mumbles through lips wrapped tight around the end of a neatly rolled spliff.

'Don't forget this is my house,' she says bitterly.

Glaring at her, 'And don't you forget who pays the fucking rent.'

Rolling her eyes, Theresa walks into the kitchen holding the baby on her hip.

Standing over two steaming pots on the stove, Marcus is deep in concentration stirring the gooey off-white mixture with a fork, lifting it out and letting it droop back down, testing the consistency.

Peering into the bubbly goo Theresa squints her eyes against the fumes, while the baby tugs at her shirt.

'Smells nasty,' she says making a face. 'How's it looking?'

'Almost there, baby,' Marcus says slowly. 'Actually, grab me a tray of ice cubes, I think it's done.'

Amongst mixing bowls, orange cartons of baking soda, and plastic measuring spoons, Theresa sits the baby on the messy laminate bench top.

'Here, play with this, baby,' Theresa says handing the infant an empty *Arm & Hammer* baking soda box to play with before fetching the ice from the freezer.

Handing Marcus the tray, 'You think you can get more out of it this time?' she says.

'I hope so.'

'Whatchyou mean, you hope so? We got bills to pay, Marcus.'

'Well, stop smoking what the fuck we meant to be selling,' he snaps back.

'Don't give me that. They in there saying how Freeway Ricky owns a hundred houses from selling ready rock and you can't even make a thousand-dollars.'

Dropping cubes of ice into the pots one at a time, 'Yeah, because every nigga is cooking crack nowadays thinking just that: he gonna be the next Freeway. May as well be selling fucking water.'

Shaking her head and looking towards the living room, 'If it wasn't for those Crips niggas in there taking half our goddamn profits,' Theresa says resentfully.

'I know, but without them Crips niggas in there we wouldn't have any coke to cook in the first place. Besides, what else we gonna do? Ain't no job paying three-seventy-five an hour gonna put food on the table.'

'Yeah, well, take a little more off this time; those niggas in there ain't gonna notice a little bit missing,' Theresa says.

'Aiit, I'll try,' Marcus says quietly.

Picking up the baby in one arm, Theresa grabs her cold bowl of macaroni and cheese from the kitchen table and disappears down a dark hallway, leaving Marcus to finish converting one-pound of coke into three-pounds of crack. Time passes, the crack is cooked, money is made, and lives are rocked; and so the cycle repeats all across South Central LA. Little changes for those making money and those who aren't. Society blooms for those who are lucky, while the decay and degradation continues for others living at the whim of those calling the shots.

Pulling her by the hand, Ivy leads her mother out of a hallway and into the living room where daylight fights its way through drawn curtains and the morning news emits from a television that seemingly never gets turned off.

With dark circles under her eyes and a small mound growing in her belly, Theresa collapses onto the sofa, ignoring her little girl's pleas to play; instead, reaching past an ashtray overflowing with cigarette butts for a discolored glass pipe and lighter. Leaning back and deaf to Ivy's moving mouth, Theresa heats the remnants of crack rocks sitting in the small bowl, closing her eyes and inhaling the metallic smoke through dry cracked lips.

Without expression, Theresa's bloodshot eyes begin to well before a single tear rolls down her cheek.

'Got to your room, baby girl,' she says softly.

'But mamma—'

'I said go.'

Staring blankly at the television, the morning news prattles without Theresa taking in a word.

'With the invasion of Panama over,' the newsreader says, *'General Manuel Noriega has surrendered and is awaiting extradition to Miami where he will face charges of drug trafficking, racketeering, and money laundering in what some are suggesting will be the trial of the decade. And staying in Central America, disgraced Air Force General, Richard Secord, who was indicted last year for conspiring with former NSC Deputy Director, Colonel Oliver North, Admiral John Poindexter and businessman Albert Hakim of defrauding the US Government of money and services, has had the Grand Jury charge Secord with nine additional felonies as a result of his false testimony before Congress during the Iran-Contra Kerry Hearings.'*

There's a clamor of pots and pans coming from the kitchen followed by quiet yet frustrated swearing.

'Theresa,' Marcus calls out, slamming cupboards and drawers. 'Where's the eight-track from last night?'

With the hit already prickling her skin, she takes a deep breath ignoring the question.

Sticking his head through the doorway, 'Yo! Where's the fucking eight-track we had?'

Wiping the wet streak from her face, 'We smoked it,' Theresa says flatly.

'The whole thing?'

Shrugging, 'I guess so.'

Storming into the room, 'The whole fucking thing?' Marcus says in disbelief. 'You smoked a whole goddamn eight-track?'

'It wasn't just me, Marcus! You had a hit, Justine had a hit, your fucking boy Lamar was here having a ripe old time. Don't blame this shit just on me!'

'I can't believe this shit,' Marcus says rushing back into the kitchen.

Then, a loud banging on the front door, *'Yo, it's Darryl mothafucker! Open this fucking door.'*

Holding a pair of saucepans, Marcus freezes, while Theresa begins laughing. *Bang, bang, bang!*

'Where's my money, Marcus?' the voice yells from behind the door. *'You're fucking due, nigga!'*

Playing quietly in her room with a tattered *Cabbage Patch* kid—the one with a tiara in her brown hair—and a purple *My Little Pony* with its pink mane all but cut off, Ivy stares at the closed door, frightened by the shouting coming from the other end of the house.

The voices get louder and begin yelling over top of one another until a series of loud gunshots silences the house. After a moment, a drawer opens followed by a cupboard before the front door opens and closes.

Clutching the doll in her hand, Ivy slowly gets to her feet, opens the door and walks carefully down the hallway.

Entering the living room, she can see her mommy lying face-up on the sofa, quiet and still.

'Mamma,' Ivy says.

Rubbing her nose with the back of her hand, the little girl walks over and chews her lip at the blood soaking through the front of Theresa's thin robe.

'Mamma,' she says again looking into eyes that are glassy and unseeing.

With her doll held tightly under one arm, Ivy walks around the sofa and stands in the doorway to the kitchen where her daddy is lying. Blood smears the bench top and cupboard, and now pools brightly beneath him.

Returning to the living room, Ivy stands looking at her mommy's hollow gaze before putting her doll next to her lifeless head. Then, slumping down with her back to the sofa, Ivy gently pulls her mommy's dangling arm across her chest and hugs it.

Behind her, the television still prattles softly:

'After almost a decade of fighting, the Contra revolution in Nicaragua has finally come to an end with the United Nicaragua Opposition party, led by Violetta Chamorro, claiming fifty-five percent of the vote over the former Sandinista leadership of Daniel Ortega. It is a historic moment for Nicaragua, as Chamorro becomes the first female President in the country's history.

The ousting of the Sandinista regime is a feat many said would not have been possible without the Bush Administration providing forty-nine million dollars of so-called non-lethal aid to Nicaraguan Contras—a group former President Reagan once referred to as the moral equivalent of our founding fathers—despite critics reporting that the funding enabled eight-thousand Contra troops to be redeployed into Nicaragua where they carried out a violent campaign of intimidation, political assassinations, and distributed thousands of propaganda leaflets.

The UNO victory closes a bloody chapter for Nicaragua, ending its political tug-of-war between dictatorship and Communism that has gripped the country for much of the twentieth-century. And, for the United States, perhaps the embarrassing wounds of the Iran-Contra scandal can at last be healed knowing there is no more damage to come for the American people or its image as a consequence of participating in yet another foreign conflict we ought not have.'

FALL GUYS, SCAPEGOATS AND PARDONS

Despite Daniel Ortega overwhelmingly winning the 1984 Presidential election, the long years of war with the Contras had decimated Nicaragua's economy to the point of collapse. Not only did widespread poverty ensue, but faith in the Sandinista Government waned in the years that followed, while the high hopes and promises of reform faded into the twilight.

In August 1989, the month that campaigning began for the up-coming 1990 elections, then President George W. Bush funneled $49.75 million of so-called non-lethal aid to the remaining Contras, as well as an additional $9 million to the *Unión Nacional Opositora* (National Opposition Union: UNO); today's equivalent of $2 billion of intervention by a foreign power, and proportionately five times the amount President Bush had spent on his own election campaign.

This financial donation enabled the Contras to immediately re-deploy 8,000 troops back into Nicaragua and effectively become the armed wing of the UNO, carrying out a violent campaign of intimidation and coercion that saw no fewer than 50 Sandinista political candidates assassinated.

Ruined by a decade of violent conflict, Nicaragua suffered 50,000 casualties (military and civilian) and $12 billion in damages during this time. With a population of only 3.5 million people and an annual GDP of $2 billion; this was the equivalent to the United States suffering 5 million casualties and a loss of $25 trillion to the economy.

The unsanctioned and covert support of the Contras demonstrated how desperately the Reagan Administration wanted to prevent Socialism spreading in Latin America, and uphold the guise of United States power and influence over its allies and enemies, both near and far. And when half a century of political ideology is on the bartering table, it is no surprise the lengths members of US agencies went to, as well as the relationships they fostered, in order to keep America strong, safe and supreme during the height of the Cold War.

Arm & Hammer is a work of fiction based on a litany of factual events, declassified documents, criminal evidence, court testimonies, published articles, and biographies of individuals who played a role in the Iran-Contra scandal. Acknowledgement of key sources of material include: *Whiteout* by Alexander Cockburn & Jeffrey St. Clair (1998), *Washington's War on Nicaragua* by Holly Sklar (1988), *The Jaguar Smile* by Salman Rushdie (1987), *Freeway Rick Ross: the Untold Autobiography* by Rick Ross with Cathy Scott (2014), an untold number of articles published by the *Washington Post, the New York Times, the Los Angeles Times*, and many others, and special acknowledgment to the *Dark Alliance* series published in the *San Jose Mercury News* (1996) written by Pulitzer Prize-winning journalist Gary Webb responsible for investigating, exposing, and providing incontrovertible evidence of the United States' Government protection of, and collusion with, international cocaine traffickers in their efforts to support the Nicaraguan Revolution. Gary Webb's career as a journalist would thereafter suffer relentless ridicule and scrutiny for the remaining years of his life. He died in 2004 as a result of two gunshot wounds to his head. His death was ruled a suicide.

Below are the factual (as much as research allows and verified where possible) backgrounds, accounts, and events related to some of the characters in *Arm & Hammer*.

NORWIN MENESES

Despite coming from a family intimately linked with the Somoza dictatorship (one brother was the Chief of Police, and two others were Generals in the National Guard), Norwin Meneses was a criminal known by the FBI as far back as 1978 for trafficking kilos of cocaine from his ranch in Costa Rica to Tampa and New Orleans prior to being granted political refugee status in the United States.

In 1981, at the recommendation of Donald Barrios of Miami, Meneses met Danilo Blandon at Los Angeles International Airport where they flew to Honduras and were informed about the official forging of the FDN. At this meeting, leaders of the FDN had instructed them to return to the US and begin selling cocaine where the profits would cycle back to the Contras.

By the mid '80's, Meneses was such a key financial contributor to the Contra effort that he often entertained Contra leaders, hosted fundraising dinners, and most infamously even had his photo taken with Adolfo Calero.

Ironically, in 1989 Meneses was retrospectively indicted for conspiracy to sell 1 kilo of cocaine back in 1984; the peak period of his cocaine trafficking. However, with the Contra effort over and so too the CIA protection that Meneses and his network was seeing, he left San Francisco for his ranch in Costa Rica where no attempt was ever made to secure his arrest or appeal to the Costa Rican Government to extradite him.

A year later, Meneses was arrested in Nicaragua trying to transport 750 kilos of cocaine. His link to the Bogota cocaine cartel in Colombia, Enrique Miranda, testified that from 1981 to 1985 Meneses transported his cocaine through the services of Marcos Aguado; a senior Salvadoran Air Force contract pilot for the US humanitarian aid flights going through Ilopango airbase. According to Miranda's testimony, Aguado flew Salvadoran planes to Colombia to pick up cocaine shipments and delivered them to US Air Force bases in Texas.

On the basis of Miranda's testimony and accompanying evidence, Meneses was sentenced by the Nicaraguan Courts to 30 years in prison.

DANILO BLANDON

After returning from Honduras with Norwin Meneses, Danilo Blandon setup dozens of business fronts to launder drug money through. According to Blandon's reading of Meneses's account books, Meneses had sold 900 kilos of cocaine in 1981. Despite this, as a cocaine wholesaler in LA Blandon got off to a slow start. Business remained stagnant until two years later (1983) when he made contact with Rick Ross, surging their numbers to around 5,000 kilos a year.

Through the first half of the 1980's, Blandon—the prime wholesaler of cocaine in Los Angeles—was not raided or inconvenienced in any way by any authorities. His importation of cocaine out of Latin America went unbridled until the Boland Amendment was lifted in October 1986, whereby he coincidently found himself issued with warrants by the FBI, IRS, and Los Angeles County Sheriff's Office. The warrants included an affidavit charging that Blandon was "in charge of a sophisticated cocaine smuggling and distribution organization operating in southern California. The moneys gained from the sales of cocaine are transported to Florida and laundered through... a chain of banks. From [here] the moneys are filtered to the Contra rebels to buy arms in the war in Nicaragua."[1]

Police raided twelve of Blandon's warehouses where no drugs were found. The local authorities were convinced that he had received a tip-off about the impending raids and cleaned up. Blandon fled to Miami where he was unable to successfully rebuild his business empire.

Returning to LA in 1991, the DEA arrested Blandon and his wife for cocaine trafficking. During his trial, assistant US District Attorney, J. O'Neale described Blandon as the "biggest Nicaraguan cocaine dealer," and the US Probation Office recommended a sentence of life in prison and a $4 million fine. However, because of his cooperation and financial support to the Contras, Blandon was sentence to only 4 years in prison. Clearly influenced by a higher authority, O'Neale filed a motion in 1993 with the Court stating that Danilo had agreed to become an informant for the Department of Justice and the DEA. In exchange for his cooperation, O'Neale requested that Blandon's sentence be reduced to time served and that he be released without parole or fine. The Court approved the request and Blandon was freed from prison in September 1994 having served only 28 months.

Danilo Blandon is the only person in US history to be granted a Green Card despite government knowledge of him being a wholesale trafficker of narcotics.

CARLOS CABEZAS & JULIO ZAVALA

A lawyer and accountant in Nicaragua, Carlos had served as a pilot in Somoza's National Guard before being exiled after the revolution. Both he and Julio were key traffickers for Norwin Meneses's cocaine ring in San Francisco, as well as leading figures in the anti-Sandinista movement in California.

In February 1983, the famous Frogman case in San Francisco involved Meneses's men getting caught by the FBI swimming to shore with 400 pounds of cocaine from a Colombian freighter. Carlos and Julio were two of the men arrested. Testifying that the cocaine-smuggling operation was to fund the Nicaraguan Contras, Carlos further explained that he had met a CIA agent in Costa Rica by the name of Gomez who was there as an overseer, ensuring drug profits were going to the revolution.

The FBI seized $36,000 in cash from Julio's bedside table, which investigators considered to be drug profits. Claiming that the money was intended for the Contras to purchase weapons, Julio's attorney submitted letters to the Court from two Contra leaders attesting that this was true. Although the money was returned, Carlos and Julio both served time in prison, while Meneses—the San Francisco drug kingpin for whom Carlos and Julio were working for—was never indicted, arrested or investigated in relation to the Frogman case.

Witnesses testified before the Kerry Committee in 1988 that Meneses had been tipped-off about the arrests "by his sources in US law enforcement."

RICK ROSS AKA FREEWAY RICKY

Born in Arp, Texas, Rick Ross moved to LA with his mother where they slept on sofas and lived off of food stamps. Showing promise as a tennis player in high school, Ross was forced to drop out when teachers discovered he'd never learned to read or write. He attended Trade Technical College but had to quit after being arrested for selling stolen car parts. Continuing in a career of petty crime, it wasn't long until Ross was introduced to cocaine by his college teacher, Mr. Fisher.

With Ross selling cheap cocaine to the Bloods and the Crips—and his demand for the drug sky-rocketing—Fisher soon put Ross in contact with his source, a Nicaraguan by the name of Henry Corrales working for Blandon and Meneses.

Ross's connection to the gangs and ghettos of South LA solved the distribution problems that had previously beleaguered the Nicaraguan cocaine ring in California. Eventually, Henry introduced Ross to Blandon, allowing the two biggest cocaine figures to flood LA with high quality cocaine.

Now scoring directly from Blandon, Ross was buying over 100 kilos of cocaine per week and selling as much as $3 million worth of crack a day. During this time, Blandon was also sourcing Ross with a steady stream of high-grade weapons and surveillance equipment supplied by former Laguna Beach police detective and security firm CEO with links to the CIA in El Salvador, Ronald J. Lister.

During the height of his drug dealing (1982 to 1989), prosecutors estimated that Ross bought and resold several metric tons of cocaine with a gross revenue to be more than $900 million; equivalent to $2.7 billion today.

Amassing millions of dollars' worth of real estate in LA, including dozens of houses, apartment blocks, and motels, Ross lived part-time in Cincinnati, Ohio. Still trafficking cocaine, Ross would purchase the drugs in Los Angeles and have his people transport it to several major cities across the country.

In 1989, one of those couriers was busted at the Cincinnati bus depot where the cocaine was linked to Ross and he was subsequently arrested on charges of trafficking cocaine and sentenced to 10 years in prison. Four years into this sentence, a new warrant for his arrest was issued because of an interception of a 1988 telephone call where Ross had organized to supply his cousin with several kilos of cocaine. Pleading no contest to conspiracy to possess cocaine, Ross served a short sentence to run concurrently with his federal time in Ohio.

During his incarceration, an FBI anti-corruption case had been opened in LA against a narcotics task force for corruption, of which, Ross was asked to give crucial testimony against the officers. For his cooperation, Ross's 10-year prison sentence was cut in half and he was released in September 1994.

Out of jail and still in possession of a lucrative real estate investment portfolio in LA, Ross was eager to leave the cocaine business behind. That was until six months later, Blandon—now a DEA informant—contacted Ross and, complaining of drug debts to the cartels, asked if Ross would purchase 100 kilos of cocaine. Committed to a life that no longer relied on drug trafficking, Ross reluctantly offered to find a buyer for Blandon instead. Acting as a middleman for the transaction, the deal was in fact a DEA sting operation and resulted in the arrest of Ross and several other LA drug dealers.

In November 1996, Ross was convicted of his third felony strike and sentenced to life in prison with no parole. However, realizing that his previous two convictions were technically part of the same trafficking conspiracy, Ross was able to appeal his life sentence and have it overturned. Re-sentenced to 20 years jail time, Ross was paroled in 2009. He now resides in LA, however, his entire fortune was seized, stolen or lost during his time in prison.

VINCENT MIRANDA

Raised in Palo Alto and of Portuguese descent, as a youth Vince Miranda had theatrical ambitions and hoped to become a dancer and singer. While in high school he worked as a soda jerk, busboy and waiter, and by his 21st birthday had saved enough money to buy 21 acres of land in his hometown of Los Banos.

In 1961 at the age of 28, Miranda purchased his first theatre in Huntington Park to boost business at his neighboring restaurant. His opening double-feature of *Cat on a Hot Tin Roof* and *The World of Suzie Wong* brought in only $70 on a Saturday night. A closeted homosexual and purveyor of pornography, Miranda quickly replaced those movies with adult films, which subsequently propelled him onto a lewd and lucrative career path.

Miranda was a delightful and sweet man who, in spite of his gentle and softly spoken character, was ruthlessly ambitious when it came to business. Slowly acquiring dozens of commercial properties and leases of run-down theatres and flophouse hotels, Miranda and his lover, George Tate, single-handedly shaped the Gaslamp District of San Diego for much of the '70s and '80s.

Their company, Walnut Properties, was served with dozens of civil lawsuits as the city routinely tried to condemn Miranda's theatres or file eminent domain proceedings against him, eager to rid Downtown of big screen smut and nudity.

Dying of cancer in 1985, Miranda owned 50 theatres and hotels across California; including co-ownership of the notorious and hugely successful Pussycat Theatres. George Tate and his young paramour Jonathan Cota inherited the entirety of Walnut's holdings.

JERRY DOMINELLI

Appearing in San Diego in 1979 as a high-flying financial investor, Jerry Dominelli paraded a lavish lifestyle centered around race cars and art that swept the city's close-knit elite community off of their feet. He presented a sophisticated Ponzi scheme of international investment companies, and in four short years Dominelli was able to swindle the people of San Diego out of $80 million.

A fixture of the San Diego social scene, Dominelli wooed many high profile individuals; none more so than the Mayor of the city, Roger Hedgecock, radio talk-show host, George Mitrovich, newspaper publisher, Larry Remer, and former Mayor of Del Mar and romantic lover, Nancy Hoover.

By 1984, Dominelli's fraudulent investments began to unravel as investors filed a federal lawsuit to force him into involuntary bankruptcy. Dominelli's indictment resulted in Hedgecock being charged with conspiracy to conceal $360,000 in illegal campaign contributions, forcing him to resign. Nancy also went to prison for 30 months for her role in a scheme that saw Remer receive $350,000 in donations to increase his newspaper platform and indorse Hedgecock's 1983 mayoral race.

In 1985, Dominelli was sentenced to 20 years in jail, during which time he suffered a severe stroke before being paroled back in Chicago after serving

10 years for what was an elaborate financial scam that shook San Diego to its economic and civic foundations.

FELIX RODRIGUEZ AKA MAX GOMEZ

Fleeing Cuba in 1959 following the revolution, Felix Rodriguez joined a group of exiles who received CIA military training in guerrilla warfare with the goal of infiltrating and seizing control of the newly established Cuban Government. Codenamed Operation 40 for it consisting of forty members, the group was authorized by President Eisenhower and presided over by Vice President Nixon and essentially functioned as an assassination squad.

However, Fidel Castro's grip on Cuba was more pervasive than the CIA assumed and within a year Operation 40 was officially disbanded into what would become Brigade 2506. Unofficially, the founding members remained active for at least another decade before certain individuals (Orlando Bosch for example) continued anti-Castro careers in espionage and terrorism.

In 1960, the CIA trained members of Brigade 2506 in Guatemala (including Rodriguez), began preparing them for the infamous failed Bay of Pigs Invasion. Of the 1,334 men who travelled to Cuba, an estimated 114 drowned or were killed in action, while 1,183 were captured, tried and imprisoned.

The CIA continued to train Rodriguez as an operative and in 1967 recruited him to lead a team to capture Che Guevara who was attempting to overthrow the US-backed government in Bolivia and replace it with a Communist party. Posing as a Bolivian soldier, Rodriguez caught Guevara, interrogated him, and authorized his execution. To this day, Felix still possesses Guevara's Rolex wristwatch and tobacco pipe, which he took as a trophy.

Becoming a US citizen in 1969, Rodriguez enlisted in the army and flew over 300 helicopter missions and was shot down five times. In 1971, Rodriguez trained CIA-sponsored units that worked for Ted Shackley's notorious Phoenix Program: a program focused on identifying and eliminating members of the Viet Cong via infiltration, capture, torture, counter-terrorism, interrogation, and assassination.

From 1982 to 1986, Rodriguez was the head CIA officer at Ilopango air base in El Salvador. There, he oversaw the vast network of the Contra supply effort, and appears in dozens of CIA assets and traffickers sworn testimonies as to being fully aware of the type of activities, personnel, and cargo moving through the location.

According to Milian Rodriguez—the money manager for the Medellin Cartel—Felix approached his old anti-Castro comrade in 1982 and requested a financial contribution of $10 million to be delivered on a per needs basis to support the Contras in exchange for protecting the cartel's drug lanes into the United States.

When Milian was arrested in 1985, the FBI seized financial documents including his 1982 expenditures, which listed a section titled "CIA" and recorded $3.69 million in payouts. One notable outfit Milian used to funnel cocaine to Miami and money to the Contras was frozen shrimp company *Frigorificos de Punta Arenas*, which also coincidently received a State Department contract to provide humanitarian aid to the FDN.

The true depth and detail of Felix Rodriguez's collusion with known criminals and drug traffickers is left to speculation (beyond what we know from sworn testimony), however, the fact that he was stationed at Ilopango for over half a decade during such time that there exists overwhelming evidence specifying Colonel Oliver North's explicit involvement with cocaine, and requests to transport drugs and money through Central America by various means, can only suggest it was indeed a great deal. Rodriguez was never questioned regarding his role as overseer of Ilopango air base in El Salvador.

MILIAN RODRIGUEZ

As the major money manager for the Medellin Cartel, Milian used a variety of shell companies to transport cash and cocaine throughout Central America. During the Iran-Contra hearings, Milian told Senator John Kerry that he had a liaison within the US Intelligence Agency [Felix Rodriguez] who was running the resupply effort and was fully aware that the funds came from drug profits.

The subcommittee never pursued these statements despite Milian's personal records corroborating his testimony that he had direct dealings with CIA.

Notable shell companies include the aforementioned *Frigorificos de Punta Arenas* and SETCO, which was owned by Juan Matta Ballesteros: a notorious drug smuggler whose airline had been flagged by DEA and US Customs for its history trafficking drugs since the '70s. SETCO received one of the first supply contracts to haul weapons to the Contras.

After Milian was arrested by the FBI in 1985 and sentenced to 43 years in jail for his role in laundering $11 billion in drug profits, he said, "If you have people like me in place its marvelous. The Agency, quite rightly so, has things they have to do which they can never admit to an oversight committee. The only way they can fund these things is through drug money or other illicit funds that they can get their hands on."[2]

JORGE MORALES & GARY BETZNER

Colombian-born resident of Miami and convicted drug trafficker, Jorge Morales was convicted of cocaine smuggling and sentenced to 16 years in prison in 1984 when the Justice Department offered to suspend his indictment under the condition he would contribute $1 million a year to the Contras and use his fleet of small aircraft based in Opa-Loka, Florida, to deliver weapons and supplies.

Invited to a meeting by Octavio Cesar (a CIA asset) and Popo Chamorro, they informed Morales that they had been cleared by the CIA to organize his planes to deliver guns and cash to the Contras. Morales explained to the Kerry committee investigators how for the next two years he gave at least $3 million in drug money to the Contras. His story is backed up by Gary Betzner's 1987 testimony to Congress in which the former Navy pilot explained how he made several flights in 1984 from Fort Lauderdale to airstrips in Costa Rica—including John Hull's ranch—and how none of the flights required any of the normal paperwork associated with an international flight.

Betzner went on to testify that after he had delivered weapons and explosives to these airstrips, duffle bags and wooden crates of cocaine were then loaded for the return trip and that he wasn't concerned about being caught because Morales had told him that the flights were "covered."

During Betzner's Congressional testimony, he identified two other pilots who flew weapons and drugs flights for Jorge Morales: that of Geraldo Duran and Marcos Aguado. Robert Owen would later testify during the Iran-Contra hearings that he advised Colonel North of his belief that Aguado and Duran were involved in drug smuggling.

JOHN FLOYD HULL

In 1983, Robert Owen introduced John Hull to Colonel North where shortly after his Costa Rican ranch was used to supply the Contras. During the Iran-Contra investigations, Hull admitted to receiving $10,000 a month from the NSC for his ongoing cooperation with the Contra effort.

Robert Owen began having regular meetings with Hull from 1984, one of which included CIA Station Chief Philip P. Holtz and several pilots at a CIA safe-house in San Jose, Costa Rica. A decades-old conspiracy also places Iranian assassin Amac Galil and ex-Cuban Felipe Vidal at some of these meetings where a plot to kill Eden Pastora was explored. It is furthered rumored that Hull, Owen and Holtz were together on the night of Pastora's attempted assassination, despite Hull telling a PBS reporter during an interview that, "I'm not an assassin, but if I had my way, Senators like Kerry and Kennedy would be lined up against a wall and shot tomorrow at sunrise."[3]

TERRY REED & EUGENE HASENFUS

Recruited by Colonel North in 1983, Terry Reed—formerly with Air America flying out of Thailand during the Vietnam War—was overseeing a base near Mena, Arkansas training Contras in resupply missions, night landings, precision airdrops and so on.

In 1986, Felix Rodriguez put Reed in charge of a weapons warehouse called Machinery International in Guadalajara, Mexico; another front company for the CIA-backed Contra effort. Purchasing a C-123 cargo plane that was formally owned by fellow drug pilot, Barry Seal, Reed employed the services of his friend William Cooper to begin flying resupply missions.

During one of these routine supply drops, former Marine and veteran cargo kicker for the United States Army, Eugene Hasenfus was on board the C-123 cargo plane when it was shot down over Nicaragua on October 5, 1986. Pilots William Cooper and Wallace Sawyer were both killed in the crash, and although Hasenfus was able to parachute down safely, he was captured by Sandinista forces, tried, and sentenced to 30 years in prison.

In addition to the downed aircraft providing incontrovertible proof that the US Government were participating in a covert and illegal operation to supply the Contras, a notebook had also survived the wreckage connecting the plane to an operation based in Ilopango, as well as phone numbers and direct lines to George Bush and CIA offices. The downing of the C-123 cargo plane uncovered and internationally publicized the Iran-Contra scandal for the first time, and was the catalyst that ended not only the Contra revolution but resulted in some of them most senior Administration and Defense officials being indicted and charged with a raft of felonies.

DIACSA, HONDU-CARIBE & VORTEX AIR

Although DIACSA gained a State Department contract to deliver supplies to the Contras in 1985, two of its principals, Alfredo Caballero and Floyd Carlton, had been indicted on charges of smuggling 900 pounds of cocaine into the US, as well as laundering $2.6 million in drug profits.

Caballero was a close friend of Mario Calero, while Carlton was General Manuel Noriega's favorite drug pilot. According to Noriega's personal aide, Carlton was making numerous flights shipping cocaine for the Cali Cartel in 1985 and 1986, the very period that he was also flying Contra resupply missions.

As for the aforementioned drug smuggling airline turn Contra resupply outfit SETCO, one of its partners was American pilot, Frank Moss. After flying more than a dozen supply missions for Juan Matta Ballesteros, Moss set up his own company called Hondu-Caribe in 1985 to ferry weapons from Honduran warehouse, R&M Equipment. Notes in Colonel North's notebook describe a conversation he had with Major General Richard Secord (Director of STTGI aka the Enterprise) in which they believed that $14 million worth of weapons had been paid with drug money.

One of Moss's DC-4 cargo planes was previously known to the DEA as a drug plane, while another was spotted dumping its cargo into the waters off of the west coast of Florida. When the plane landed at Port Charlotte airport, the Customs Service impounded it and agents discovered an address book containing phone numbers of Contra leaders, as well as for Robert Owen. It was also later revealed that Mario Calero held partial ownership of Hondu-Caribe.

Another interesting outfit that also received a State Department aid contract was Vortex Air, which Robert Owen suspected (and expressed to Colonel North) as being involved with drug trafficking. Vortex Air was run by Michael Palmer who the DEA believed to be one of the largest marijuana smugglers in the US at the time, as well as being a company that Mario Calero had an undisclosed involvement with.

LIUTENANT COLONEL OLIVER NORTH

A decorated veteran of war, Oliver North was assigned the position Deputy Director of Political-Military affairs for the National Security Council (NSC) in 1981. That same year, North assisted US Air Force Major Richard Secord, who was commanding high-level international covert operations, win Congressional approval for an $8.5 billion sale of AWACS to Saudi Arabia.

Secord's extensive network in the Middle East, along with his experience negotiating weapons sales and rumored involvement with EATSCO—run by ex-CIA arms dealer Edwin Wilson who would be sentenced to 52 years in prison—presented North with a clandestine framework to arm and support the newly formed Contra forces in Nicaragua.

However, EATSCO was investigated by the FBI in 1982 and found guilty of defrauding the Pentagon of millions of dollars. Although Secord denied any involvement, he was suspended during the investigation and despite reinstatement, he retired from the United States Air Force in 1983. No longer working for the Government allowed Secord and Iranian arms dealer, Albert

Hakim, to establish the Stanford Technology Trading Group International (aka the Enterprise)—a shell company consisting of a complex web of business entities to facilitate the sales of arms to Iran, as well as numerous lucrative side dealings assigned to it by Colonel North for the purpose of funneling profits and weapons to the Contras.

When Congress capped Contra funding the following year to $24 million, roughly a quarter of what the Reagan Administration deemed necessary, it drove North and National Security Advisor Robert McFarlane to acquire financial aid from alternative sources—this, as we know, was the selling of weapons to Iran, through Secord's Enterprise, under the guise of freeing American hostages in Lebanon, but also undeniably included the allowance, to varying degrees of accountability—of cocaine to enter the United States.

Aside from the sworn testimony of dozens of individuals involved either directly or indirectly with the CIA, their assets, the front corporations set up, and Defense Agency payrolls corroborating North and his agents' involvement, there also exists physical evidence. For example, notes of North's on July 9, 1984 describe a conversation to CIA Agent Duane Clarridge in which North "wanted an aircraft to go to Bolivia to pick up paste [cocaine]," and another entry on the same day stating, "Wanted aircraft to pick up 1,500 kilos."[4] There are also numerous memos Robert Owen wrote to North expressing concerns that several of the Contra leaders put forward by the FDN's Adolfo Calero were "involved with drug running," like Contra leader Sebastian Gonzalez who was a known associate of Norwin Meneses, or Owen's speculation that another leader, Jose Robelo's "potential involvement with drug running and the sale of goods provided by the USG [US Government]."

American historians Byrne and Kornbluh describe how Admiral John Poindexter approved much power to North "...who made the most of the situation, often deciding important matters on his own, striking outlandish deals with the Iranians, and acting in the name of the president on issues that were far beyond his competence. All of these activities continued to take place within the framework of the President's broad authorization. Until the press reported on the existence of the operation, nobody in the administration questioned the authority of Poindexter's and North's team to implement the President's decisions."[5]

Colonel North's brazen attempt to conceal and destroy evidence of his activities in Central America unquestionably imply an explicit knowledge and culpability that drug smuggling was intimately involved with the Contra effort. North's secretary, Fawn Hall, testified before Congress that she altered and shredded a large number of documents at his request, so much so that the machine jammed, while also smuggling documents out of North's office in her boots and inside her clothes. Unrepentant of his obstruction of justice, North proudly confessed to shredding documents, including the private ledger that CIA Director William Casey had told the Colonel to keep for the purpose of tracking the precise flow of money to the Contras.

Senator John Kerry's committee who investigated the Iran-Contra scandal concluded that both the CIA and those assigned to the campaign by North knew that drug traffickers had exploited "the clandestine infrastructures established to support the war and that Contras were receiving assistance derived from drug trafficking." Later, Kerry reflected that, "There is no question in my mind that people connected with the CIA were involved in drug trafficking, while in support of the Contras.[6] We had direct evidence that somewhere between $10 million and $15 million was going to the Contras. And I am quite sure that this was just the tip of the iceberg. The Contras were desperate for money. So, in a sense they took a bridge loan from anyone available and the drug lords were available."

In 1988 Major Richard Secord was indicted for conspiring with Colonel North, Admiral Poindexter and Albert Hakim to defraud the US Government of money and services, and for theft of government property. After the trials were over, in April 1989 the Grand Jury charged Secord with 9 additional felonies due to giving false testimony before Congress. He was sentenced to 2 years' probation after pleading guilty to one count of lying in a plea agreement.

Summoned to testify before publicly televised Congressional committee hearings formed to investigate the Iran-Contra scandal, North admitted to misleading Congress, shredding government documents at Director Casey's suggestion, and also testified that Robert McFarlane had requested he alter official records to delete references that they had assisted the Contras.

Colonel North was indicted in 1988 on 16 felony counts. After four months of trial he was convicted of three charges: accepting an illegal gratuity, aiding and abetting in the obstruction of a Congressional inquiry, and ordering the destruction of documents through his secretary, Fawn Hall. North was sentenced to a three-year suspended prison term, two years' probation, $150,000 fine, and 1,200 hours of community service. However, in 1990 North's convictions were overturned on appeal, citing that his Fifth Amendment rights were violated as witnesses in his trial may have been impermissibly affected by his Congressional testimony during the Iran-Contra hearings of which he received limited immunity for.

THE ADMINISTRATION

William Casey, Director of CIA — Although Casey was strongly suspected of being involved with Iran-Contra scandal, one day before he was scheduled to testify before Congress about is knowledge of the affair, he suffered two seizures and was hospitalized. Three days later, Casey underwent surgery for a brain tumor and died less than 24 hours after Richard Secord testified that Casey fully supported the illegal aiding of the Contras.

An Independent Counsel report submitted in 1993 indicated evidence of Casey's involvement stating, "Here is evidence that Casey, working with two national security advisers to President Reagan during the period 1984 through 1986—Robert C. McFarlane and Vice Admiral John M. Poindexter—approved having these operations conducted out of the National Security Council staff with Lt. Col. Oliver L. North as the action officer, assisted by retired Air Force Maj. Gen. Richard V. Secord. And although Casey tried to insulate himself and the CIA from any illegal activities relating to the two secret operations... there is evidence that he was involved in at least some of those activities and may have attempted to keep them concealed from Congress."[7]

Robert McFarlane, National Security Adviser (1983-1985) — Embarrassed by his role in the Iran-Contra scandal and feeling betrayed by his former colleagues, McFarlane attempted suicide with an overdose of valium tablets just two hours before he was due to provide testimony. McFarlane was later convicted of withholding evidence, but after a plea bargain was sentenced only to two years of probation.

Caspar Weinberger, Secretary of Defense — After his resignation, legal proceedings against Weinberger were pursued by Independent Counsel and in 1992 was indicted on 5 felony charges related to the Iran-Contra scandal, including lying to Congress and obstructing Government investigations.

Elliott Abrams, Assistant Secretary of State — In his 1986 Congressional hearings testimony, Abrams repeatedly and categorically denied that the US Government was involved in arming the Contras. After multiple felony counts were brought against Abrams in 1991, he admitted knowing that Colonel North was "encouraging, coordinating and directing the activities of the Contra resupply operation, and that North was in contact with the private citizens who were behind the lethal resupply fights."[8] Abrams was convicted of withholding evidence, but after a plea bargain was sentenced only to two years of probation.

Alan Fiers, Chief of CIA's Central American Task Force — Succeeding Duane Clarridge in 1984, Fiers went into Central America with the primary mission of supporting the Contras. In this capacity, Fiers became aware of Colonel North's efforts to circumvent Congressional limitations on aiding the Contras. A staunch supporter of Adolfo Calero and Enrique Bermudez, Fiers participated in concealing North's activities from Congressional investigators. He was convicted of withholding evidence and sentenced to one-year probation.

John Poindexter, National Security Adviser (1985-1986) — After succeeding McFarlane, Poindexter continued to oversee the transfer of weapons to Iran and North's activities with the Contras. Communicating through a private NSC computer channel, Poindexter and North sent each other secret messages that were unable to be intercepted by other NSC staff members. However, once investigations into the Iran-Contra scandal began, agents were able to recover some of these messages, which were later used to try Poindexter and North. Forced to resign in 1986, Poindexter was convicted in 1990 of 5 counts of conspiracy, obstruction of justice, perjury, defrauding the Government, and the alteration and destruction of evidence. These convictions were overturned on appeal in 1991 for the same reason the court had overturned North's, that witness testimony may have been influenced by his Congressional testimony during the Iran-Contra hearings of which he received limited immunity for.

Duane Clarridge, Senior CIA Agent — From the outset of becoming Head of CIA's Latin American operations in 1981, Clarridge had two main objectives; "One, take the war to Nicaragua, and two, start killing Cubans."[9] Instrumental in recruiting and organizing Contra forces, Clarridge admitted to the House Intelligence Committee staff in 1984 that civilians, nurses, doctors and judges were being routinely murdered by the Contras but claimed they were not assassinations, rather just normal "killing" and that "after all, this is war."

Despite being in regular contact with Colonel North throughout his tenure in Central America, and even appearing in North's notes where the Colonel expressed the need for an "aircraft to go to Bolivia to pick up paste [cocaine]," Clarridge denied any involvement with the illegal diversion of funds to the Contras. He was indicted in 1991 on 7 counts of perjury and false statements.

Robert Owen, NSC Liaison to the Contras — Acting as a go-between for Colonel North and the Contra leadership, Owen engaged directly with the likes of Adolfo Calero, Felix Rodriguez, John Hull, and many of the Contra pilots flying through Ilopango.

During his Congressional testimony for which he received limited immunity, Owen recited poetry for Colonel North whom he had been barred from communicating with during the hearings. Intoning before television cameras, "Ollie, your enemies are more clever and treacherous, we have so very little to give you in return. We want you to know that in our hearts and our prayers you are with us daily, not only in elegant churches, but on crude altars in the jungle,"[10] Owen said. The young courier went on to say that the Contras were in part sustained by "the knowledge that on this troubled earth there still walk men like Ollie North."

Throughout his time in Central America, Owen repeatedly expressed his concerns to North that many of those involved with the Contra effort were deeply involved with the drug business. Congressional representative, Louis Stokes, remarked that Owen's acceptance of immunity implied a sense of security that neither his nor North's actions were illegal.

Although the Iran-Contra scandal underwent four investigations, the extent of collusion with drug traffickers was never investigated or probed despite the incontrovertible evidence and testimony placing NSC and CIA staff in direct contact with drug smugglers, the State Department aid contracts and protection for front companies transporting cocaine, and the clear financial support the FDN were receiving from the drug trade.

By the time the investigations, charges, and trials were complete, and in the waning hours of his Presidency, on Christmas Eve, 1992, President George H. W. Bush pardoned all of the aforementioned US Government and Administration staff of all charges.

[1] Cockburn & St. Clair, *Whiteout*, pp. 15

[2] Cockburn & St. Clair, *Whiteout*, pp. 308

[3] Quote from a 1987 *PBS* interview when Senator John Kerry began investigations into Hull's activities

[4] Cockburn & St. Clair, *Whiteout*, pp. 35

[5] Kornbluh & Byrne, *The Iran-Contra Scandal: The Declassified History*, pp. 217

[6] Suro & Pincus, *The CIA and Crack: Evidence is Lacking of Alleged Plot*, cited in The Washington Post (1996)

[7] Walsh, Lawrence E., *Investigations and Cases: Officers of the CIA, Vol I: Final Report of the Independent Counsel for Iran/Contra Matters*, 1993

[8] Walsh, Lawrence E., *Investigations and Cases: Officers of the CIA, Vol I: Final Report of the Independent Counsel for Iran/Contra Matters*, 1993

[9] Cockburn & St. Clair, *Whiteout*, pp. 8

[10] Excerpt from a poem read as a closing statement by Robert W. Owen during the 1987 Kerry Committee Hearings